Praise for "Fashionably Dead"

Uproariously witty, deliciously provocative, and just plain fun! No one delivers side-splitting humor and mouth-watering sensuality like Robyn Peterman.

This is entertainment at its absolute finest!

by Darynda Jones,
NY Times Bestselling Author of the *Charley Davidson Series*

Dedication

This book is dedicated to authors Donna McDonald and JM Madden. Both of you believed in me when all I had was a pile of rejection letters and a huge dream. You are tremendously talented, generous and kind. I would not be where I am today without you. You beautiful ladies are my anchor and I am so lucky you're mine.

Acknowledgements

Writing may be solitary, but putting a book out is not. I am blessed to have so many amazing people in my life. *Fashionably Dead* has been a labor of love and I love all the people who helped me make this dream come true.

Mary Yakovets, your editing makes me look like a better writer than I really am. You are brilliant and you saved me from making an unforgivably gross mistake in my manuscript! LOL! Donna McDonald, your patience with my disastrous lack of computer skill and your mind-boggling editing astound me. You are my hero.

My beta readers, Kim Bloomfield, Kris Calvert, Jessica Hughes, James Kall, Jowanna Kestner, JM Madden, Christi Main-Ehrlich, Donna McDonald and Candace Sword are the best and I adore each and every one of you.

Rebecca Poole, my cover is beautiful. It's like you crawled inside my warped brain saw exactly what I wanted! Thank you. You are so very talented.

My Pimpettes are amazing! You make me giggle and you delight me. Thank you for your support. It means the world.

James Kall, thank you for the series name. You have made me pee in my pants since we were eighteen and I expect you'll be doing the same till we're eighty!

Kris Calvert, you taught me how to cut and paste and you are one hell of a blurb writer. You rock!

My critique partner, JM Madden, you are brilliant and hilarious. Without you I would have written myself off a cliff!

And my girl crush, Darynda Jones...your beautiful cover quote humbled me and made me cry. You are a wonderful friend and I think I'll keep you!

Last but not least, I want to thank my family. Hot Hubby, you put all my heroes to shame and I have the best kids in the world. None of this would be fun without you guys. Love you.

Prologue

I drew hard on the cigarette and narrowed my eyes at the landscape before me. Graves, tombstones, crypts...she didn't belong here. Hell, I didn't belong here. My eyes were dry. I'd cried so much there was nothing left. I exhaled and watched as the blue grey smoke wafted out over the plastic flowers decorating the headstones.

Five minutes. I just needed five minutes and then I could go back...

"That's really gross," Gemma said, as she rounded the corner of the mausoleum I was hiding behind and scared the hell out of me. She fanned the smoke away and eyed me. "She wanted you to quit, maybe now would be a good time."

"Agreed. It's totally gross and disgusting and I'm going to quit, regardless of the fact that other than you, Marlboro Lights are my best friend...but today is definitely not the day," I sighed and took another long drag.

"That's pathetic," she chuckled.

"Correct. Do you have perfume and gum?"

"Yep." She dug through her purse and handed me a delicate bottle.

"I can't use this. It's the expensive French shit."

"Go for it," she grinned. "You're gonna need it. You smell like an ashtray and your mother is inside scaring people to death."

"Son of a..." I moaned and quickly spritzed myself. "I thought she left. She didn't want to come in the first place."

"Could have fooled me," Gemma said sarcastically, handing over a piece of gum and shoving me from my hiding place.

"Come on," I muttered, as my bossy best friend pushed me back to my beloved grandmother's funeral.

***

The hall was filled with people. Foldout tables lined the walls and groaned under the weight of casseroles, cakes and cookies. Men and women, most of whom I knew, milled around and ate while they gossiped. Southern funerals were a time to socialize and eat. A lot.

As I made my way through the crowd and accepted condolences, I got an earful of information I could have happily lived without. I learned that Donna Madden was cheating on her husband Greg, Candy Pucker had gained thirty pounds from eating Girl Scout cookies and had shoved her fat ass into a heinous sequined gown, *for the funeral no less*, and Sam Boomaster, the Mayor, was now a homosexual. Hell, I just wanted to leave, but I had to find my mother before she did something awful.

"I loved her." Charlie stopped me in my tracks and grabbed my hand in his old gnarled one.

His toupee was angled to the left and his black socks and sandals peeked out from his high-water plaid pants. He was beautiful.

"Me too," I smiled.

"You know I tried to court her back in the day, but she only had eyes for your Grandpa." He smoothed his sweater vest and laid a wet one on my cheek...and if I'm not mistaken, *and I'm not*, he grabbed my ass.

"Charlie, if you touch my butt again, I'll remove your hand." I grinned and adjusted his toupee. He was a regular in the art class I taught at the senior center and his wandering hands were infamous.

"Can't blame a guy for trying. You have a nice ass there, Astrid! You look like one of them there supermodels! Gonna make some lucky man very happy one day," he explained seriously.

"With my ass?"

"Well now, your bosom is nothing to scoff at either and your legs..." he started.

"Charlie, I'm gonna cut you off before you wax poetic about things that will get you arrested for indecency."

"Good thinking, girlie!" he laughed. "If you ever want to hear stories about your Nana from when we were young, I'd be happy to share."

"Thanks, Charlie, I'd like that."

I gave him a squeeze, holding his hands firmly to his sides and made my way back into the fray.

As I scanned the crowd for my mother, my stomach clenched. After everything I had to put up with today, the evil approaching was just too much. Martha and Jane, the ancient matriarchs of the town and the nastiest gossips that ever lived were headed straight for me. Fuck.

"I suppose you'll get an inheritance," Jane snapped as she looked me up and down. "You'll run through it like water."

"Your Nana, God bless her, was blind as a bat when it came to you," Martha added caustically. "I mean, my God, what are you? Thirty and unmarried? It's just downright disrespectable."

"I'm twenty-nine, happily single and getting it on a regular basis," I said, enjoying the way their thin lips hung open in an impressive O.

"Well, I've never," Jane gasped.

"Clearly. You should try it sometime. I understand Mr. Smith is so vision impaired, you might have a shot there."

Their appalled shrieks were music to my ears and I quickly made my escape. Nana would have been a bit disappointed with my behavior, but she was gone.

Time to find the reason I came back in here for...I smelled her before I saw her. A waft of Chanel perfume made the lead ball in my stomach grow heavier. I took a deep breath, straightened my very vintage Prada sheath that I paid too much for, plastered a smile on my face, said a quick prayer and went in to the battle.

"Mother, is everything alright?"

She stood there mutely and stared. She was dressed to the nines. She didn't belong here...in this town, in this state, in my life.

"I'm sorry, are you speaking to me?" she asked. Shit, she was perfect...on the outside. Gorgeous and put together to a degree I didn't even aspire to. On the inside she was a snake.

"Um, yes. I asked you if..." I stammered.

"I heard you," she countered smoothly. "If you can't bother to comply with my wishes, I can't be bothered to answer you."

"Right," I muttered and wished the floor would open and swallow me. "I'm sorry, I meant Petra. Petra, is everything alright?"

"No, everything is not alright," she hissed. "I have a plane to catch and I have no more time or patience to make chit chat with backward rednecks. It was wrong of you to ask me to be here."

8

"Your mother died," I said flatly. "This is her funeral and these people are here to pay their respects."

"Oh for God's sake, she was old and lived well past her time."

I was speechless. Rare for me, but if anyone was capable of shocking me to silence, it was my mother.

"So, like I said, I have a plane to catch. I'll be back next week." She eyed me critically, grimacing at what she saw. "You need some lipstick. You're lucky you got blessed with good genes because you certainly don't do anything to help."

With that loving little nugget, she turned on her stiletto heel and left. I glanced around to see if we'd been overheard and was mortified to see we had clearly been the center of attention.

"Jesus, she's mean," Gemma said, pulling me away from prying eyes and big ears.

"Do I look awful?" I whispered, feeling the heat crawl up my neck as the mourners looked on with pity. Not for my loss, but for my parentage.

"You're beautiful," Gemma said. "Inside and out."

"I need to smoke," I mumbled. "Can we leave yet?"

Gemma checked her watch. "Yep, we're out of here."

"I don't want to go home yet," I said, looking around for Bobby Joe Gimble, the funeral director. Where in the hell was he and did I need to tip him? Shit, I had no clue what funeral etiquette was. "Do I have to...?"

"Already took care of everything," Gemma told me. "Let's go."

"Where to?" I asked. Damn, I was grateful she was mine.

"Hattie's."

"Thank you, Jesus."

***

Hattie's sold one thing and one thing only. Ice cream. Homemade, full of fat, heart attack inducing ice cream. It was probably my favorite place in the world.

"I'll have a triple black raspberry chip in a cone cup," I said as I eyed all the flavors. I didn't know why I even looked at them. I was totally loyal to my black raspberry chip. My ice cream couldn't talk back to me, break up with me or make me feel bad. Of course, my love could extend the size of my ass, but I wasn't even remotely concerned about that today. Besides, I planned a very long run for later. I needed to clear my head and be alone.

"Sorry about your loss, Sugar," Hattie said and I nodded. Her big fleshy arms wobbled as she scooped out my treat. "Do you want sprinkles and whipped cream on that, Baby?"

"Um..." I glanced over at Gemma who grinned and gave me a thumbs up. "Yes, yes I do."

"Me too," Gemma added, "but I want mint chip, please."

"You got it, Sugar Buns," Hattie said and handed me a monstrous amount of ice cream. "It's on me today, Astrid. I feel just terrible I couldn't be at the funeral."

"That's okay, Hattie. You and Nana were such good friends. I want your memories to be of that."

"Thank you for that, Darlin'. Ever since my Earl died from siphoning gasoline, I haven't been able to set foot near that goddamn funeral parlor."

I swallowed hard. Her late ex-husband Earl had siphoned gasoline since he was ten. His family owned the local gas station and apparently, as legend had it, he enjoyed the taste. But on the fateful day in question, he'd been smoking a cigar while he did it...and blew himself to kingdom come. It was U-G-L-Y. Earl was spread all over town. Literally. He and Hattie had been divorced for years and hated each other. It was no secret he had fornicated with over half the older women in town, but when he died like that, he became a saint in her eyes.

I bit down on the inside of my cheek. Hard. Although it was beyond inappropriate, whenever anyone talked about Earl, I laughed.

"Astrid totally understands." Gemma gave Hattie a quick hug and pushed me away from the counter before I said or did something unforgivable.

"Thanks," I whispered. "That would have been bad."

"Yep," Gemma grinned and shoveled a huge spoon of ice cream in her mouth.

"Where in the hell do you put that?" I marveled at her appetite. "You're tiny."

"You're a fine one to talk, Miss I Have the World's Fastest Metabolism."

"That's the only good thing I inherited from the witch who spawned me," I said and dug in to my drug of choice. I winced in pain as my frozen ice cream ass-extender went straight to the middle of my forehead.

"Are you okay?" Gemma asked.

I took a deep breath and pinched the bridge of my nose. God, I hated brain freezes. "No, not right now, but I've decided to change some stuff. Nana would want me to."

My best friend watched me silently over her ice cream.

"I'm going to stop smoking, get a real career, work out every day, date someone who has a job and not a parole officer, get married, have two point five kids and prove that I was adopted."

"That's a pretty tall order. How are you gonna make all that happen?" she asked, handing me a napkin. "Wipe your mouth."

"Thanks," I muttered. "I have no fucking idea, but I will succeed...or die trying."

"Good luck with that."

"Um, thanks. Do you mind if we leave here so I can chain smoke 'til I throw up so it will be easier to quit?"

"Is that the method you're going to use?" Gemma asked, scooping up our unfinished ice cream and tossing it.

"I know it seems a little unorthodox, but I read it worked for Jennifer Aniston."

"Really?"

"No, but it sounded good," I said, dragging her out of Hattie's.

"God, Astrid," Gemma groaned. "Whatever you need to do I'm here for you, but you have to quit. I don't want you to die. Ever."

"Everybody dies," I said quietly, reminded that the woman I loved most had died only a week ago. "But I've got too fucking much to do to die any time soon."

Chapter 1

Three months later...

"There are ten thousand ways to express yourself creatively," I huffed, yanking on my running shoes. "My God, there's acting, painting, sewing, belly dancing, cooking...Shit, scrapbooking is creative." I shoved my arms into my high school sweatshirt that had seen better days.

"You're not actually wearing that," Gemma said, helping herself to my doughnut.

"Yep, I actually am." I grabbed my breakfast out of her hand and shoved it in my mouth. "And by the way, I've decided to be a movie star."

"But you can't act," my best friend reminded me.

"That's completely beside the point," I explained, taking the sweatshirt off. I hated it when Gemma was right. "Half the people in Hollywood can't act."

"Don't you think it might be wise to choose a career that you actually have the skills to do?"

"Nope, I told you I'm making changes. Big ones."

I bent over and tied my running shoes. Maybe if I just ran forever, I would stop hurting. Maybe if I found something meaningful, I could figure out who in the hell I was.

Gemma picked up my soda and took a huge swig. "You're an artist and a damn good one. You should do something with that."

"Yeah, maybe," I said, admiring my reflection in the microwave. Holy hell, my hair was sticking up all over my head. "Why didn't you tell me my hair exploded?"

"Because it's funny," Gemma laughed.

"I'll never make it in show business if people see my hair like this," I muttered and tried to smooth it down.

"Astrid, you will never make it in show business no matter what your hair looks like. You may be pretty, but you can't act your way out of a hole and you suck as a liar," Gemma informed me as she flopped down on my couch and grabbed the remote.

"Your confidence in me is overwhelming." I picked out a baseball cap and shoved it over my out of control curls. "If the movie star thing doesn't work out, I might open a restaurant."

"Did you become mentally challenged during the night at some point?" she asked as she channel surfed faster than any guy I ever dated.

"Gimme that thing." I yanked the remote away from her. "What in the hell are you trying to find?"

"*Jersey Shore.*"

"For real?" I laughed.

"For real for real," she grinned.

"Don't you have a home?" I asked.

"Yep. I just like yours better."

I threw the remote back at her and grabbed my purse. If I was going to be a famous actress, or at the very least a chef, I needed to get started. But before I could focus on my new career, I had business to take care of. Very important business...

"Where are you going?" Gemma yawned. "It's 8:00 on a Sunday morning."

"I'm going running," I said, staring at the ceiling.

"Oh my God," Gemma grinned, calling me out on my lie. "Astrid, since when do you run with your purse?"

"Okay fine," I snapped. "I'm going to run a few errands and say goodbye forever to one of my best friends today."

Gemma gaped at me. Her mouth hung open like she'd had an overdose of Novocain at the dentist. "So today is the day? You really going to end it?"

"I don't really have a choice, since there's so much damn money riding on it."

"Oh my God," she squealed and punched me in the arm. "I'm so proud of you."

"Don't be proud yet," I muttered, praying I'd be successful with my breakup plans.

"You didn't have to take the bet," Gemma said.

"Yes, I did," I said and shook my head with disgust. "Nothing else has worked. Voodoo has to."

"Voodoo?"

"Yep."

13

"Good luck with that."

"Thanks," I said as I slapped on some lip gloss. "I'm gonna need it."

"Yes, you are," Gemma grinned. "Yes, you are."

***

It was hot and I was sweaty and I wondered for the umpteenth time if I was losing my mind. I needed to stop making bets that were impossible to win. Maybe I could be a social smoker or I could just hide it from everyone. I could carry perfume and gum and lotion and drive to the next town when I needed a nicotine fix.

"Excuse me, are you here to be hypnotized?" a feminine voice purred.

I glanced up from my spot on the filthy sidewalk and there stood the most beautiful woman I'd ever seen. I quickly stubbed out my cigarette, turned my head away in embarrassment and blew my smoke out. Reason number three hundred and forty-six to quit...impersonating a low class loser.

She looked foreign—Slavic or Russian. Huge violet-blue eyes, full lips, high cheekbones set in a perfect heart-shaped face, framed by tons of honey-gold blonde hair. Absolutely ridiculous. I felt a little inadequate. Not only was the face perfect, but the body was to die for. Long legs, pert boobies, ass-o-rific back side and about six feet tall. I was tall at 5 feet 9 inches, but she was *tall*.

"Well, I was," I explained, straightening up and trying to look less like a crumpled homeless mess from my seat on the sidewalk, "but they must have moved." I pointed to a rusted-out doorway.

"Oh no," the gorgeous Amazon giggled. Seriously, did she just giggle? "That's not the door. It's right over here." She grabbed my hand, her grip was firm and cool, and guided me to the correct door. A zap of electricity shot up my arm when she touched me. I tried to nonchalantly disengage my hand from hers, but she held mine fast. "Here we go." She escorted me into the lobby of a very attractive office.

"I don't know how I missed this," I muttered as she briskly led me to a very nice exam room. She released my hand. Did that zap really just happen? Maybe I was already in nicotine withdrawal.

"Please have a seat." The blue eyed bombshell indicated a very soft and cozy looking pale green recliner.

"I'm sorry, are you the hypnotist?" I asked as I sat. Something didn't feel quite right. What was a gorgeous, Amazon

14

Russian-looking chick doing in Mossy Creek, Kentucky? This was a tiny town, surely I would have seen her before.

"Yes, yes I am," she replied, sitting on a stool next to my comfy chair with an official-looking clipboard in her hand. "So you're here because...?"

"Because...um, I want to stop smoking," I told her and then quickly added, "Oh, and I don't want to gain any weight." If you don't ask for the impossible, there's no way you'll ever get it.

Miss Universe very slowly and somewhat clinically looked me over from head to toe. "Your weight looks perfect. You are a very beautiful young woman. Are you happy with your body right now?"

"Yes," I replied slowly. Was she hitting on me? I didn't think so, but...

"That's good," she smiled. "I can guarantee that you will never gain weight again after you're hypnotized."

"Really?" I gasped. My God, that was incredible. Smoke free and at a weight I liked. This was the best day ever.

"Really," she laughed. "Now let's get started."

"Wait, don't I need to fill out a bunch of forms and pay and sign my life away in case you accidentally kill me or something?"

Blondie laughed so hard I thought she might choke. "No, no," she assured me and quickly pulled herself together. "My receptionist is at lunch...we'll take care of it afterwards. Besides, I've never killed anyone by accident."

"Oookay." She was a little weird, but I supposed people with her occupation would be. She did guarantee me I would be smoke free and skinny. That did not suck. Wait...I needed to think this through. I was feeling unsettled and wary. She was odd, made me uncomfortable and had electric hands. On the flip side, she was very pretty, had a really nice office and promised no weight gain. Damn.

Would common sense or vanity prevail? And the winner is...vanity. By a landslide.

She leaned into me, her green eyes intense. I could have sworn her eyes were purple-y bluish. I was getting so tired. I prayed I wouldn't drool when I was out.

"Astrid, you need to clear your mind and look into my eyes," Miss Russia whispered.

"How do you know my name?" I mumbled. "I didn't tell you my name." Alarm bells went off in my brain. My pea-brain that never should have thought it was a good idea to get hypnotized at a strip mall on the bad side of town. You'd think a business called 'House of Hypnotism' might have tipped me off.

Crap. These were not the decisions a smart and responsible, if not somewhat directionless, twenty-nine year old woman should make. I should have listened to my gut and gone with common sense.

The room started spinning. It felt like a carnival from hell. Blondie's mouth was so strange. There was something very unattractive going on with her mouth. It got kind of blurry, but it looked like...wait...maybe she was British. They all have bad teeth.

"I fink ooo shud stooop," I said, mangling the English language. I tried again. "Oow do ooo know my name?" When did I put marbles in my mouth? Who in the hell dimmed the lights and cranked the air conditioner?

"Oh Astrid, not only do I know your name," she smiled, her green eyes blazing, "I know everything about you, dear."

Chapter 2

I opened my eyes and immediately shut them. What in the hell time was it? What in the hell day was it? I snuggled deeper into my warm and cozy comforter and tried to go back to sleep. Why couldn't I go back to sleep? Something was wrong...very wrong. I just had no idea what it was.

Ignoring the panic that was bubbling to the surface, I leaned over the side of my bed and grabbed my purse. It was Prada. I loved Prada. I proudly considered myself a Prada whore, *albeit one who couldn't afford it*.

Everything seemed to be in there...wallet, phone, makeup, gum, under-used day planner. Nothing important was missing. I was being paranoid. Everything was fine.

I eyed my beloved out of season Prada sandals lying on my bedroom floor. Shoes always made me feel better. Only in New York or Los Angeles would anyone know my adored footwear was four seasons ago. Certainly not in Istillwearmyhairinamullet, Kentucky. I got them on sale. I paid six hundred dollars that I didn't have for them, but that was a deal considering they were worth a solid twelve hundred.

I pressed my fingers to the bridge of my nose and tried to figure out what day of the week it was. Good God, I had no clue. I suppose exhaustion had finally caught up with me, but I couldn't for the life of me remember what I had done to be so tired. I vaguely remembered driving home from somewhere. I glanced again at my awesome shoes, but even my beautiful sandals couldn't erase the sense of dread in the pit of my stomach.

"Focus on something positive," I muttered as I wracked my

brain and snuggled deeper into my covers.

Shoes. Think about shoes...not the irrational suffocating fear that was making me itch. Bargains! That was it, I'd think about bargains. I loved getting a good bargain almost as much as I loved Prada. Unfortunately, I also had a huge love for cigarettes, and I needed to love one now. Right now. I rummaged through my purse and searched for a pack. Bingo! I found my own personal brand of heroin and lit up.

WTF? It wouldn't light because I couldn't inhale. Why couldn't I inhale? Was I sick? I felt my head; definitely no fever. My forehead felt like ice.

Okay, if at first you don't succeed...blah blah blah. I tried again. I couldn't inhale. Not only could I not inhale, I also couldn't exhale. Which would lead me to surmise I wasn't breathing. The panic I was avoiding had arrived.

"Fuck shit fuck fuck, this is a side effect. That's right, a side effect. A side effect of what?" I demanded to no one in particular since I was alone in my room. I knew it was something. It was on the tip of my brain...side effect...side effect of not smoking. Side effect of not smoking? What the hell does that even mean? For God's sake, why can't I figure this out? I have an I.Q. of 150, not that I put it to very good use.

"Wait," I hissed. "It's a side effect of the hypnotism."

God, that was bizarre, but that had to be it. I made that stupid bet with Gemma and got hypnotized to stop smoking by that big blonde Amazon at the House of Hypnotism. That's what I drove home from. I wasn't crazy. The Amazon must have forgotten to inform me that I wouldn't be able to breathe for awhile afterwards. That's what you get when you don't read the fine print. Did I even pay her? I'm sure I'll start breathing any second now. I'm so glad I figured this out. I feel better. For a minute there I thought I was dead.

I glanced out of my bedroom window at the full moon.

"Full moon? Oh my God, have I been in bed all day?"

I threw the covers off and stood quickly, still trying to figure out what day it was. The room spun violently and a wave of dizziness knocked me right back down on my ass. Little snippets of my dreams raced through my mind as I waited for the vertigo to pass.

God, that was a freaky dream. Oprah and Vampyres and yummy, creamy chocolate blood... you couldn't make that stuff up.

The room quit spinning and I stood up slowly, firmly grasping one of the posts of my beautiful four poster bed. I reached up high above my head, arched back and popped my sternum. Slightly gross, but it felt great. I ran my hands through my hair, rubbed the sleep out of my eyes and bit through my bottom lip. Mmm...crunchberries. I licked the tasty blood from my mouth.

I wondered what time it was. If it wasn't too late, I could get a run in and then I could...*bite through my bottom lip?? Crunchberries? What the fu...?*

In my frazzled mental state, I heard a noise in the hallway outside my bedroom. I immediately dropped to a defensive squat on the floor. Way back in high school they told us, if you hear an intruder, get low...or was that for a fire? Shit, that was get low for a fire...what in the hell do I do for a burglar?

Good God, I was in my bra and panties. The blue granny panties with the unfortunate hole in the crotch. Not a good look for fending off burglars. Not a good look ever. On my never ending list of things to do I needed to add *throw out all panties over seven years old.*

I remained low, just in case. I duck walked over to my closet and grabbed one of my many old cheerleading trophies out of a cardboard box so I could kill my intruder. It was plastic, but it was pointy. I'd been meaning to give them to my eight year old neighbor. Thank God I was a procrastinator. Wait a minute...As I death-gripped my trophy I was overwhelmed with the scent of rain and orchids and Pop Tarts and cotton candy.

What the hell?

It wasn't a dream. She was here? And apparently from the smell of it, she had a guest. I'd just cannibalized my own lip, my blood tasted like crunchberries, I could smell people in my house, I couldn't breathe, my skin felt icy, and I think I might be...

"Astrid, are you awake?" Gemma called from right outside my door interrupting my ridiculous train of thought.

Oh thank you, Jesus. "Yes." Was that my voice? It sounded deeper and raspier. And sexier?

"Get out here," Gemma yelled. "Get dressed and change that underwear...it's nasty."

"Gemma, I have to tell you something weird, but you have to believe me and you can't get mad," I said through my closed door, ignoring the insultingly accurate underwear comment.

"I think I already know," she said from the other side.

"It's not about my haircut."

"You got your hair cut without me?" Gemma was appalled.

Shit, I thought she knew about my hair. What did she know then? *Good God, what in the hell was wrong with my bra? The girls were spilling out of it. Were they bigger? Did my bra shrink?* "Gem, um...I swear I meant to tell you about my hair. It was spur of the moment. Mr. Bruce dragged me into the salon and the next thing I knew, he set my baseball cap on fire, cut my hair into long layers and put in some kick ass highlights."

"Fine, Astrid." Her voice got tinny and high. "Just don't be surprised if I go get a perm without you."

"You wouldn't."

"I might," she threatened.

"Gem," I begged, "with me or without me, Do. Not. Get. A Perm. That's so 1980s."

"You're right," Gemma sighed, "I'd get a lobotomy before I'd get a perm. What do you need to tell me?"

I gathered myself. I realized I was about to sound like an idiot, but when had that ever stopped me? I closed my eyes and let her rip. "Um...after my haircut, I got hypnotized by a big blonde Amazon gal to stop smoking, and now I can't breathe. I think it must be a side effect, but it's freaking me out." Gemma was silent on the other side of my bedroom door.

"You can't breathe?"

"No." I couldn't tell if she believed me.

"Are you sure?"

"I think I would know if I couldn't breathe," I shouted.

"Do I owe you a thousand bucks?"

"I'm not sure yet."

At least I was honest. The entire reason I'd gotten hypnotized was because I'd bet Gemma a thousand dollars I could quit smoking. I knew she thought it was a no-brainer bet due to the sorry fact that this was my ninth attempt to quit in the last three months. Nicotine gum, cold turkey, weaning off and all those self-help books weren't doing it for me. I needed outside assistance. Short of having my lips sewn shut, I hadn't been successful at quitting. Hypnotism was a last resort because having my lips sewn shut was simply not an option.

"Where did you get hypnotized?" she quizzed.

"House of Hypnotism over by the Chinese restaurant that serves cat."

Gemma was speechless. I was getting more nervous with each passing second. "Do you have a pulse?" she asked.

"I'm sorry, what did you just ask me?"

"I said," Gemma yelled through the door, "do you have a pulse?"

"What kind of a stupid question is that? Of course I have a..." I checked for my pulse, then I checked again, then I checked again and then I checked one more time. "Um...no," I whispered.

"You sure?"

"Positive."

"What's your skin temp?"

"Really cold," I told her.

What in the hell was wrong with her? She was awfully calm about the whole thing. She was silent for what felt like an eternity. These questions were right up Gemma's alley. She loved all things weird, especially anything astrological or supernatural. I could tell she was thinking because she was humming *'Billie Jean'*. Gemma, besides being a Prada whore who like me couldn't afford it, knew the lyrics to every Michael Jackson song ever recorded. She wore black for an entire year after he died. "I think I know what's going on." She began to hum *'Thriller'*.

"What's wrong with me?" I shrieked.

"Come out here, Astrid."

"Wait Gemma...am I dead?"

"Kinda," she said with excitement. The same kind of excitement she exuded when she tried to convince me of Bigfoot's existence. "Just get dressed and get out here."

I quickly whipped on some overpriced jeans that made my butt look asstastic and put on the first shirt my fingers touched. I pulled on some hot pink sequined Converse and made my way out to my living room. That took about ten and a half steps because my house was the size of a postage stamp.

Gemma was standing by the window bouncing like a ball, so excited she was about to burst...and the Queen of Daytime Talk was sprawled on my couch reading my diary. Wait...what?

"Holy Jesus," I gasped. "You're Opr..."

"Don't say it," my idol cut me off, throwing my diary aside as if I wouldn't notice she'd been reading my most private and embarrassing thoughts. "I'm not her, never fuckin' have been, never fuckin' will be. If you call me that, I'll leave. Trust me, that would be very fuckin' bad for you."

"Oookay, you have quite a vocabulary." I smiled, wondering if Gemma thought this was as screwy as I did. She did seem a little freaked, but not nearly enough to merit the fact Oprah was here. "If you're not Opr...I mean that woman who you look exactly like, then you are...?"

I peeked around my tiny living room and looked for cameras. This had to be for a show segment. Right? Gemma must be in on the whole thing with Oprah.

Was she going to redecorate my crappy house or give me a car or tell me something wonderful about my birth mother?

That was impossible. My birth mother was actually the woman who, for lack of a better word, raised me and there wasn't much wonderful about her. My Nana, may she rest in peace, was wonderful. Her daughter, my mother...not so much. Hopefully, Oprah was here to redecorate.

"You're a Vampyre and I'm your fuckin' Guardian Angel," I'm-Not-Oprah grunted.

Gemma squealed and clapped her hands like a two year old at Christmas. Apparently they'd become great friends already, possibly bonding over Bigfoot. The dizziness now combined with total paranoia overtook me as my knees buckled and I dropped to the ground like a sack of potatoes.

"Wow...so not what I was expecting to hear." My stomach was queasy. This was starting to make me tingle, and not in a good way. I'm-Not-Oprah had to go. "Well, golly gee, look at the time; I suppose you have a train to catch...to Crazytown," I informed her in a bizarre cheerleader voice that I had no control over. "So you'd better get going." *Vampyre my ass. I'm-Not-Oprah is cuckoo loco crazy.* I crawled over to my front door and opened it with shaking hands and body, letting Oprah know she had to leave.

I'm-Not Oprah had the gall to laugh, and I don't mean just a little giggle. I mean a huge gut-busting, knee-slapping guffaw. *God, I need a cigarette.* Oh but wait...*I DON'T SMOKE ANYMORE BECAUSE I CAN'T BREATHE.* I was completely screwed. There had to be a logical answer to this clusterfuck. I just needed to think it through.

Ignoring the unexplainable situation in my home, I curled into a ball by my front door and went back through what I could remember. First, I'd gotten my hair cut and colored because it looked like hell. Then I chain-smoked half a pack of cigarettes getting my nerve up to get hypnotized to quit. After almost vomiting from the sheer amount of nicotine in my system, I got hypnotized to stop smoking. Good thinking on my part. Next, the ridiculously attractive Amazon woman who hypnotized me was successful because I will never smoke again. Good thinking on her part.

However, it was also beginning to look like I would never breathe again. So technically I was dead. The lack of pulse and air intake could attest to this, but clearly I wasn't dead because I was curled up on the floor thinking somewhat coherently and Oprah was in my house...What in the hell was I talking about? None of this was possible. I was dreaming. That had to be it. I was dreaming. I pinched myself. Hard.

"Ouch...shit." Not dreaming.

I slowly stood up, determined to kick Her Oprahness out of my house. My whole body began to tremble as I locked eyes with the insane talk show host sitting on my couch. I couldn't believe I was standing here looking at Oprah, who says she's not, who's telling me I'm a Vampyre, which don't exist, and she's a Guardian Angel, which again...don't exist. Besides, if they did, they certainly wouldn't have a mouth like hers.

"Oh my God," I moaned as another bizarre wave of dizziness came over me. The room grew darker and smaller. I'm-Not-Oprah and Gemma started to get blurry and a burning began in my gut. Flames ripped through my stomach and violently shot into my arms, my legs, my neck and head. My insides were shredding. I was thirsty...so very thirsty. God, it hurt so much. I floated above myself as my body crumpled to the floor. The buzzing in my head was deafening. I tried to take a deep breath, but that went nowhere fast.

"I'm dying," I groaned.

Crapballs, did I have good underwear on? No! I still had on light blue grannies with a not on purpose hole in the crotch. Oh my God, I'm dying with bad underpants on. My mother will have a fit. I can hear her now, *"Well, with underpants like that, it's no wonder Astrid couldn't get a man. She kept buying all that Prada, but she should have invested in a couple of pairs of decent panties."* This was not good.

The blazing inferno inside me consumed my whole body. It was excruciating. I wasn't sure how much more I could take. I vaguely saw Oprah coming for me.

"Kill me please," I begged. She laughed and scooped me up like a rag doll and shoved my face to her neck. God, she smelled good. "Argrah," I gurgled.

"Just shut the fuck up and drink," I'm-Not-Oprah growled.

It was delicious, like rich dark chocolate, so smooth, so warm, so yummy. What was this? The pain slowly subsided and I realized I was curled up in I'm-Not-Oprah's lap with my teeth embedded in her neck. She was rocking me like a baby.

I removed what I'm fairly sure were my fangs from Oprah's neck. "What am I doing?" I calmly asked.

She looked down at me and smiled. Holy cow she looked like Oprah. "Drinking."

"Drinking what?" I inquired politely.

"O negative," she replied.

"O negative what?" I screeched, jerking to an upright position on her very ample lap.

"O negative Angel blood, dumbass," she bellowed. She stood up and dumped me on the floor as she walked over to retrieve my diary.

"Oh my God, you're not joking." I was horrified.

"No, I certifuckingly am not."

Chapter 3

Gemma and I'm-Not-Oprah sat on either side of me on the floor. Gemma held my hand and Oprah just stared.

"Soooo, Gemma, I suppose you've met Opr...I mean, well you know, I mean..." I was dying here. "What I'm trying to say is, you've met...dear God, help me out."

"Pam," they said in unison.

"Pam? Your name is Pam?"

"What's wrong with Pam?" Oprah, *aka Pam*, asked, her eyes narrowing dangerously.

"Nothing," I shot back quickly. That eyeball thing did not look good. "It's just I never expected an Angel to be named Pam."

"What the hell kind of name were you expecting? Tinkerbell?"

"Well, no," I replied. "She's a Fairy. Maybe something like Luna or Sky."

"Holy shit, would you like to be named something like that?" Pam yelled.

I shook my head. God, she was loud.

"You know what I like about you?" she continued.

"No." I feared her answer the same way I feared the IRS, credit card bills and Bryant Gumbel.

"I like that you have the word 'ass' in your name. It opens up so many possibilities."

"That's fantastic. Why are you here again?" I snapped

"I am here," Pam spoke very slowly, as if I were mentally challenged, "to guide your sorry blood suckin', Prada wearin' ass, through the ups and downs of the Vampyre world."

25

"Well, Mary Sunshine, there's no such thing as Vampyres and..." I started.

"Pam," she interrupted.

"Oookay, *Pam*. I will repeat my earlier sentiment. I'm not a Vampyre, so tell me whatever it is you think you need to tell me and you can go back to Pretend Angel Land."

"Ooooh noooo, Asshead. It don't work like that. I'm here to stay." Pam slapped her knee and hooted like a redneck watching a smack down on WWE.

"Astrid, it's actually really cool," Gemma, my very not dead human friend, tried to convince me over Pam's ruckus. "Pam's been telling me there's this whole Vamp hierarchy thing; Dominions, Havens and...and..."

"Congregants," Pam supplied, calming herself down.

"Right, Congregants and Houses." Gemma kept going. "There's a King, and Warrior Princes, and Princesses."

"Back. Up." I practically spit. "There's a Vampyre King?" I laughed, not believing a word.

"I would suggest you get that out of your system right now, Assface," my Guardian Angel said. "Cause pretty soon a bunch of Vamps are gonna come 'round, and laughing at your King is punishable by death."

"You're joking," I said with a huge grin on my face. I looked at Pam. I looked at Gemma. Pam. Gemma. Pam. Gemma. Nobody was smiling...except me. "You're not joking."

I was no longer smiling. Were they serious or certifiable? Maybe I was crazy. It was difficult to deny that I just drank blood from Oprah's, *I mean*, Pam's neck. And I liked it. Maybe Bigfoot did exist.

Gemma grabbed my hands and forced my focus to her, "Astrid, it's not that bad. A slew of Vampyre girls are going to start arriving soon with gift baskets and invites to parties so you can join their Houses!"

The word gift basket calmed my impending breakdown. "What do you mean, like sorority rush for dead people?" I put my finger in my mouth and felt around for my fangs. I considered this for a moment. Gemma knew I loved free stuff. I was kind of a free sample whore. It was clear from the smug look on her face that she thought she had me at *gift basket*. She couldn't have been more wrong.

"I don't want to be a Vampyre," I yelled, realizing that maybe they weren't yanking my chain. "I want to chain-smoke an entire pack of Marlboro Lights and throw up! I do not want to join some Kappa Alpha Dead House and become BFFs with bloodsucking freaks that smell like the old lady bathroom at the country club." I was on a roll. "That's right...skanky, Gothy Draculas with blood breath, weird bun heads and super long fingernails that curl over at the edges because they should have been trimmed three years ago. And there's no such thing as Vampyres!"

You could have cut the silence with a knife. Gemma looked dazed and Pam...well, Pam just looked confused. Gemma finally roused herself from the visual stupor that my tirade induced. "Dude, that was gross."

"I'm not really following the country club part," Pam stated.

"Don't try," Gemma told her. "I'm getting a Diet Coke, you want anything?"

"Mountain Dew or Budweiser," Pam said.

"I'm on it." Gemma left the room.

"What about me?" I whined. "Don't I get to have anything?"

"You already got to have Pam," Gemma tossed back from my kitchen, laughing like she made a good one.

I sat down on the couch and pouted. What had I done to deserve this? Of course nobody but me would do something to get healthy and end up kind of dead.

"Oh for shit's sake, you're not going to look like some skanky, Goth wannabe bloodsucker. What did the Vamp who changed you look like?" Pam projected as if she were speaking to a crowd of three hundred without a microphone.

The sheer volume of her question rendered me speechless for a moment.

"She looked like a Russian supermodel. Wait!" I shouted at Pam. "Do I look different to you?"

"How the hell should I know? I just met you, dumbass," she replied.

"Right. Gemma?" I yelled.

"Behind you," Gemma said, startling me. She handed Pam her beer. *Angels drink beer?*

"Gem, do I look different to you?" I asked.

"Well, you were being such a baby that I wasn't going to tell you, but...You. Are. So. Hot," she screeched. "If I didn't like dangly parts so much, I'd consider switching teams!"

I ran to my bathroom. Holy crap, I was fast. I looked in the mirror and I saw...nothing. Wait a minute...where in the hell was I? Gemma slipped into the bathroom behind me. She showed up in the mirror, but I was M.I.A.

"Dude," Gemma gasped, "you have no reflection."

We stood in silence absorbing this news. I tried several

different angles in case there was a trick to it, but no go. It was strange...my clothes were invisible, too. Anything I touched ceased to have a reflection.

"Okay, fine," Gemma said, rubbing my back, "maybe this is the price you have to pay for being so drop dead gorgeous. Oh hell, I didn't mean the dead part...I just meant..."

"It's okay," I said morosely. "Apparently, I am dead." My eyes filled with tears. I pressed my fingers to the bridge of my nose, trying to ward off the panic attack that was hurtling towards earth at frightening speeds. I was headed for a massive freakout.

Gemma grabbed me. "Let me describe you," she said soothingly.

"Okay," I blubbered, wiping my tears. "Oh my God, my eyes are bleeding!" I shouted.

"Shut the hell up," Pam yelled from down the hall. "All Vamps cry blood, cum blood, drink blood. Blood, blood, blood...it's all about blood with you dead people."

"That's disgusting," I said. I looked at Gemma, my eyes wide, "I wonder if I have any other bodily functions?"

"What do you mean?"

"You know, like do I still need to buy toilet paper and tampons?" I answered.

"NOPE," Pam yelled from way down the hall.

"Wow, she's got really good hearing," Gemma grinned. "Do you want to know what you look like?"

"Um...yes."

She stared at me for about a minute and tilted her head to the side. It was a very long minute. She was making me nervous.

"You're beautiful," she said simply. "I mean, you were beautiful before, but it got kicked up a bunch of notches. You're the kind of gorgeous where it's hard to stop looking at you. Your skin," she touched my face, "is paler, but it's perfect. It glows...it's ethereal. Your hair is a darker, richer brown and really shiny. Your lips," she examined my face, "have that I've-just-been-majorly-kissed swollen look. You still have that beauty mark high on your left cheekbone. Your eyes are that really cool amber gold color, but they sparkle now. And if I'm not mistaken, your eyelashes are longer, like they weren't long enough already."

I knew I was being vain, but I glanced toward the mirror again wondering if I just had to warm up or something...Nothing. Shit.

She circled me. "I gotta say, your body's jammin'. Rock hard abs. Legs are still long. Your boobs are definitely bigger and your butt's higher. Overall you're beyond hot." She smiled and squeezed my hands. "What do you feel like?"

Well, that explained my girls trying to escape from my bra. "I feel really strong and fast," I said. "I can hear really well and I can smell things."

"Do I smell?" Gemma did a quick pit check.

"You smell good, like rain and orchids."

"Ooooh, cool." She was delighted. "What does Pam smell like?"

"Pop Tarts and cotton candy. Gem," I paused, "do I have an aura anymore?" One of Gemma's hobbies was reading auras. She could read people before they opened their mouths. She had a gift for it.

"No."

"Is that okay?" I whispered.

"I think so." She hugged me. She felt warm and comfortable.

"Does Pam have one?" I asked.

"Yeah," Gemma answered reverently, "it's a pearly white with shots of purple and pink in it. It's the most beautiful aura I've ever seen. It's truly angelic."

"Do you mean to tell me that foul mouthed Oprah doppelganger really is my Guardian Angel?"

"Yep," Gemma giggled.

"Somebody up there must really hate me," I moaned.

"Yep."

Chapter 4

It was my first full day of being dead and it sucked.

I wavered between total freakout and dead calm mode...it just depended on the minute. Right now I was calm. I dutifully sat on the couch, pen and notebook in hand. I was wearing my favorite worn-in red tag Levis, a totally cool vintage Tony the Tiger T-shirt and some killer Prada flats. Being dead had a few advantages. I filled out my jeans and my T-shirts like a Playboy centerfold. The girls were amazing. I was a full C cup and they stood at attention even without a bra, which was a good thing considering none of my bras fit anymore. Of course I was also dead, couldn't breathe and had no idea if my hair was alright because I had no fucking reflection. On the flip side, my vision and hearing had also sharpened to the point I felt bionic. Not to mention my sense of smell. I'd almost passed out when I walked by my garbage can earlier. Why in the hell could I smell things if I couldn't breathe?

Sitting here with Pam felt a little like high school, getting lectured and taking notes, but this was different. This was a class I had no desire to take.

"What did I just say, Asswipe?" Pam asked me.

"Um...something about how to bite mortals to drink their blood."

"Go on," Pam replied, putting several Piggly Wiggly grocery bags on the coffee table in front of her.

"Well, after that I'm not sure 'cause I got so gacked I tuned you out."

"Oh for fuck's sake, you're gonna end up killing somebody," Pam said, slapping her big meaty Oprah hand to her forehead.

"No, I won't," I told her. "I'll just keep drinking from you."

"You can't," she yelled. She really had volume issues. "You have to drink from mortals. If you only drink from immortals, like me, you'll get too strong too fast and you'll be a danger to yourself and everyone else."

Pam, being the cruel, hateful, thoughtless Angel that she was, reached into the Piggly Wiggly bag and pulled out my favorite snack in the whole world. She dug into the bag of tortilla chips and double dipped into the extra hot salsa with gusto. This was evil, considering food now tasted like sawdust to me and I couldn't swallow it anyway. The only thing I could consume was blood. Apparently as I got older I would be able to ingest other liquids. According to my Vampyre Manual, fine bourbon laced with blood is quite the *in* thing for Vamps of a certain age. I watched Pam crunch and secretly hoped she'd choke, not that it would kill her. She was an Angel—an immortal, gonna live forever Angel with a foul mouth and an attitude problem.

"Shouldn't another Vampyre be teaching me this crap?" I snarkily asked.

"Well, considering you don't know any other bloodsucking losers, and we can't find the idiot who thought changing you was a good idea, you're shit out of luck," she replied, spitting teeny tiny pieces of tortilla chips the entire time she spoke.

Speaking of the idiot who changed me, we'd already gone looking for her. For the twentieth time Pam made me go through everything that took place between me and the big blonde Amazon.

Exactly two day ago, I sat on the dirty sidewalk bemoaning my lack of willpower and wondering if I was on crack thinking it was a good idea to get hypnotized to stop smoking. It only got worse from there. The big blonde Amazon took me into her office and killed me. The End.

And then apparently I drove home and slept for thirty-six hours straight.

Pam kept digging for more details, but I had none. That's when she insisted we visit the murder scene, hoping to jog my pathetic-ass memory. Her words, not mine. The ride over and back to the strip mall had certainly been a fun-filled hour and a half.

Gemma, Pam and I went after sundown. Pam wasn't quite sure how I would do in sunlight. To no one's great surprise the door wasn't there. There was no evidence whatsoever. This confused me and made me nervous. Something wasn't right.

Pam wanted some Chinese takeout, but we forbade her. No one was going to eat cat in my car.

The real highlight of the car trip though was Pam's backseat driving. After having threatened to pull over and put her out of the car eight times, I'd finally had it. I pulled over and turned around, ready to punch her in her big ol' Oprah mouth and she disappeared. That's right, she started glowing and just disappeared.

"Jesus Christ," I said, freaking out. "Where in the hell did she go?"

"No clue," Gemma said, looking under her seat.

"Do you think she bailed and went back to Heaven?"

"No," Gemma replied thoughtfully. "I think she's actually having fun down here."

Turns out, Pam had teleported back to my house. She said I drove like a blind person on crack and she couldn't take it. She napped for about four hours after that. Just so happens, teleporting really wears a gal out. All in all...just another weird day in my brand new weird fucked up life.

"All right, back to work," Pam said with a mouthful of chips. "Tell me the history, or whatever your sorry ass can remember."

"Give me a little credit here," I snapped as I wracked my brain, desperately trying to remember the bizarro History of the Vampyre. Shit. "There are, um, ten Dominions," I began, "each run by a Warrior Prince or Warrior Princess."

"What else?" Pam asked.

"Ease up," I told her. "The Dominions are territories. Basically they divided up the whole world into ten sections and the King gave a section to each of his ten children. Wait, I thought he had eleven children."

"He did—one died."

"Oh, okay," I said wearily, praying this would be over soon. "Name the Dominions," Pam said.

I stretched my arms up over my head, yawned and brought them back down about face level. I began to massage my hands, left palm facing me. "Okay," I said, "let me see...there's North America, South America, Africa, Australia, Antarctica, Europe, and Asia is divided into four Dominions since it's so large and diverse."

"Give me your hand," Pam said.

"No."

"Give. Me. Your. Hand."

I gave her my hand and she slapped me upside the head. I was busted. Thank God I was a Vampyre or else she would have given me a concussion instead of just a headache.

"You're cheating!" she shouted.

"I can't remember all this junk," I said shamefully and looked down at my palm where I'd written all the answers to the questions I knew she'd ask.

"Damn it to hell," Pam bellowed. "This is not high school. This information could mean the difference between life and death for you."

"I'm already dead," I snapped.

"Yeah, but you could be deader—like for real dead. How would you like that, little missy?" Pam demanded.

"Not much," I admitted morosely.

"Did you even read the manual? Do you have any idea what can kill you?"

"I think so," I whispered. I started to ease my way out of the room. I knew Pam was coming for me again, and she had a mean right hook.

"Don't," Pam said quietly. A quiet Pam was a scary Pam.

I flopped down on the couch, ready to get ripped a good one. I was an A student in high school and college. For some reason, I couldn't absorb this stuff. Maybe it's not that I couldn't, it's that I wouldn't. I didn't want to be a Vampyre. Vampyres were freaks of nature. Vampyres didn't even exist. I did not want an expletive-spewing Angel to be my main food source.

I wanted to eat chips and salsa and smoke and see my reflection. I wanted to go out in broad daylight and not have to wear a shitload of sunscreen, long sleeves, long pants, a hat and huge sunglasses. I wanted to have kids someday, but that was no longer an option, what with no functioning internal organs.

I did not want to have to worry about being staked through the heart with silver or being decapitated. Let's not forget about burning to death...wouldn't want to leave that little nugget out. Those are the three real ways to kill a Vampyre. What about holy water, crosses, sunlight, and garlic? All bullshit...they'd just make a Vampyre laugh or piss them off. All Hollywood fairytales, although there was some truth to the sunlight myth. While it wouldn't kill a Vamp, it could burn their skin quite badly. Who wants to look like a bloody piece of meat even for a short while?

I never really needed or wanted to know where every major artery in a human was so I wouldn't nick it with my razor sharp fangs, inadvertently killing same said human.

Mostly I really did not want my mother to find out. I was sure in her mind this would definitely be an insurmountable hurdle to my having a big career like hers. Like that was ever going to happen. I didn't want a big career like hers. I had absolutely no idea what I really wanted other than good friends, great sex and some Prada that was in season. At almost thirty, I worked as an art teacher at the senior citizens' center and had just received a crazy large inheritance from my Nana. I would have preferred to have my Nana instead of her money, but that wasn't the way the world worked.

Ask anybody who knew me...I was a good person. I was fun, but not extremely motivated unless it involved high fashion, art, or my friends. I'd recently heard my neighbor describe me as very smart, tall, single, financially irresponsible, quite pretty, boyfriend-less and kind. Great. I knew people in town were taking bets on how long it would take me to run through my inheritance money. Hell, they probably had good cause considering the amount I dropped on new clothes recently. The thing I was best at was shopping, but no one was lining up to pay me to do that...Holy shit, I was totally depressing myself.

"What would your Nana say?" Pam asked.

That stopped me. My eyes flashed and I could feel my fangs descend. "How dare you bring my Nana into this."

She had no right to...My body jerked and I had a strange deja vu. I looked at Pam for a very long moment. I stared into her Angel eyes, searching for something...that I found. My body relaxed and I started to feel lightheaded as I moved towards her. My fangs rescinded. I felt calm and centered.

"She'd say 'Buck up, Princess, it could be worse'," I told her quietly. I paused, my eyes never leaving Pam's for a second. "She sent you to me."

Pam said nothing. She just smiled. I reached for her and gently took her face in my hands. I touched my forehead to hers and let my bloody tears flow freely.

"Did she want you to tell me anything?" I asked hopefully.

"She loves you and she always will." Pam caught me as I collapsed and she rocked me like a baby until I cried myself out.

"I still don't want to be a Vampyre, but I can learn now," I whispered.

"I know you can, honey," she said. "I know you can."

Chapter 5

She was going to die if I didn't help her. The voice inside the tomb was not weak or sickly. It was strong and melodic and very insistent.

"Astrid, you have to help me," she begged.

"How do you know my name?" I asked, thrown by the familiarity.

"Because you are part of me," she replied. "Push the stone, Astrid. Help me, please. You're the only one."

"Why does it have to be me? I'm not strong enough," I insisted. Then I started to cry. I should get help. Big men or the police or a crowbar.

"You are strong enough," she said simply. "There's not much time left."

In that moment I knew she was right. I was strong enough. She was going to die if I didn't get her out. Now.

I walked slowly toward the tomb, my hands outstretched. I could feel the tingling in my fingertips. It quickly spread down my arms, through my chest and into my legs. My heart was pounding inside me, my stomach felt twisted and it was hard to breathe. The wind picked up and blew my hair wildly around my head. I was inches away.

"Push, Astrid," she gasped.

I awoke with a jerk. God, that dream seemed more real every time I had it, and I'd been having it since I was four years old. As I snuggled down deeper under my covers and tried to go back to sleep, I noticed movement on my ceiling. What the fu...? This Vamp vision was insane. The tiny cracks in my ceiling looked like faces, little mini faces with little teeny hands. Some looked angry, some sad, but most of them were laughing and pointing at me. I looked around my room to see if anyone else was here. Nope. I was definitely the object of their ridicule.

"What in the hell are you guys?" I stared harder and they started to morph into hideous itsy-bitsy monsters. They were fabulously gross, kind of like the Edvard Munch painting, *The Scream*. They were undulating and mocking me. Well, no surprise there...I was still in bed at 6:30 PM.

Sleeping during the day seemed to be working for me. I felt a little bit like a lazy sloth, but I had more energy and felt stronger at night. More importantly than adjusting to my new schedule, I had successfully avoided my mother for a week. She thought I had the flu and pink eye. She hated sick people, so there was very little chance of a surprise visit.

Truth be told, I was scared to be around my mother, or any mortals, except for Gemma. I was terrified I was going to kill someone by accident and that would suck, although Pam said as long as I fed regularly, I'd never have to kill anybody. Ever. The first hunger was the worst and no others would even compare. Thank God.

I guess I had always imagined Vampyres to be bloodsucking killers. It turns out we're only bloodsuckers. The killing is optional. So naturally I still hadn't fed from a mortal yet. I'd been feeding from Pam, but that was going to change. Too much Angel blood was going to make me a Super Vamp, and according to Pam, that was fucked up.

Along with being my main food source, Pam was trying to help me get the Green Eye thing down, also known as 'trancing'. I preferred just Green Eye. If I looked at a human, focused my power and willed my eyes to go green, I could get inside their head and make suggestions. For example; *"Hi, I'm going to bite your neck, drink about a pint of your blood...you'll really enjoy it. You won't remember a thing and you should never wear orange again. It makes your skin look like hell, bless your heart."*

"Look at me," I said to the little undulating things on my ceiling. They halted their gyrating and stared at me. I willed my eyes to go green and tried to communicate with them. Nothing. Clearly I'd lost my mind when I died. "So much for you guys being human," I muttered, rolling out of bed.

There are certain things that make your eyes go green automatically. Being extremely hungry, angry, excited or horny turns you green real quick. I tried to Green Eye Gemma a couple of times, but we both laughed so hard I gave up. Gemma graciously offered to let me feed from her, but I wanted to be sure I definitely knew all the human artery information before I bit into my best friend's wrist.

That was how most Vampyres fed. At the wrist. The neck

was too sexual. However with Pam, it wasn't sexual at all. Embarrassingly enough, it felt kind of like nursing with her. She held me like a baby. I bit her neck and felt love and comfort. I supposed you should just get it where you could find it.

Vamps could drink from each other, but that was a commitment most were not willing to make. If two Vampyres drank from one another, they were mated for life. Physically, mentally, emotionally, and sexually committed to each other for eternity. They must continue to drink from each other regularly.

To me that sounded like hell. I had commitment issues. It wasn't that I was a slut, but I couldn't imagine having sex with the same person for a thousand years or more. Not that I'd had a ton of sex with a ton of people, nor did I plan to. However, the flip side suggests that the blood exchange between Vampyres creates the most mind blowing, intensely orgasmic sex imaginable. That gave me pause, but not enough to be stuck with the same person forever.

"You guys are gross," I told the dirty dancing tiny monsters on my ceiling. I was amazed they were still there. I thought they were an optical illusion. They were so ugly they were cute, but the dirty dancing...that was not something I needed to see first thing in the morn...no, evening...wait...well, ever.

***

What in the hell was Pam doing? On my couch sat two of the most bizarre-looking Vampyres. I was pretty sure they were Vampyres. Wait...fangs. They were definitely Vamps. Pam was running around the room making gagging noises and huge raspberries. Which, by the way, sounded so much like the real thing, I had to check to make sure she was using her mouth.

Vampyre number one, who I dubbed Muffy, was dressed from head to toe in hot pink and lime green madras, a la bad country club circa 1980. Vamp number two looked like her name should be...Elvira. She had black hair, black fingernails, black lipstick, black eyes, black clothes...blah blah blah. She looked as Goth as they come, and seriously depressed. They both had their eyes trained on me and only me. That was when I realized they couldn't see Pam. This was confirmed when my three hundred pound Guardian Angel sat on top of Muffy, and Muffy didn't move or utter a sound.

Not only could I see Pam, but I could touch her and hold her and drink blood from her. God, this was strange.

Muffy, the prepster, plastered a huge pageant smile on her face and squeaked, "Hi! I'm Muffy from the Aurora House." *Oh my God, I got her name right?* "You must be Astrid!"

It was all I could do not to slap my hands over my ears. Pam had no such qualms. As Muffy spoke, her voice got higher and higher. I was sure she was sending signals to all the stray dogs in the surrounding counties. I kind of wanted her out of my house, but she had a really big gift basket. "Did you two just break into my house?" In all the movies Vampyres had to be invited in.

"Oh no," she squeaked, "the door was wide open and there was a note that said 'Welcome'. I suppose I should have called first," she shrieked. "I didn't realize you were having Paris Hilton over."

Confused, I looked over at the tiny, skinny, overly made-up Goth girl sitting on my sofa and said, "I'm sorry, your name is...?"

"Paris Hilton," the tiny Goth girl whispered in a childlike voice.

"Holy fuck! This is awesome," Pam screamed, throwing her big ol' Oprah hands in the air and falling off the couch in hysterics. I so didn't need her here right now. She'd clearly been the one to leave the note and my door open. We were going to have a little chat later. Even though they couldn't see or hear her, I could, and she was this close to making me laugh 'til I peed. She could barely control herself. If she wasn't immortal, I'd be concerned she was having a heart attack.

"Oookay," I gasped, trying to hold myself together. "Purely out of curiosity, is that the name you were born with?"

"Yes," Paris said, "and there is no relation...unfortunately. I'm from the Lucern House," she continued, completely ignoring the fact that Muffy was starting to hiss at her in bizarre little high-pitched squeaks that were making me grind my teeth. "We would love to have you join us, Astrid. Pledge The Dead!" Paris whispered as loud as she could and pumped both super skinny fists in the air.

I sat down and bit the inside of my cheek really hard, trying not to dissolve into hysterics. Pam, that traitor, was still rolling all over the floor, barely able to breathe after Paris' last outburst.

Not to be outdone Muffy shrieked, "Join the Aurora House and have a bloody good time!" She rolled her hands like a cheerleader, threw them up in the air and screamed in decibels not meant for the human ear, "Pun intended!"

Muffy was jumping up and down like a Mexican jumping bean. Paris was pumping her skinny arms and shaking her head like she was having an epileptic fit. And Pam...well, Pam was useless.

Did I have to join a House? Why couldn't I just be an

independent? There was no way in hell I belonged with either of these people. Were these my only two choices? Shit, shit, shit.

Just as I was about to ask everyone to leave so I could "think about it", hoping they'd leave those big juicy gift baskets, Paris *accidentally* punched Muffy in the head and all hell broke loose. Fangs descended and furniture got kicked out of the way. Muffy hissed like a wild animal in heat, picked up Paris Hilton and threw her out of my window. What the fu...? Glass flew everywhere. I screamed and hid under the couch that had gotten shoved up against my TV.

I heard a grotesque grunt, and a very bloody, teeny tiny Gothy Paris Hilton came flying back through my shredded window...the same window from which she had just been ejected. How in the hell did she do that? Paris expertly took Muffy down in a chokehold. She slammed Muffy's head into the floor so hard so many times that I knew for sure Muffy was for real dead. The sound of skull making contact with hard wood was just wrong on every level. Muffy was a goner.

But no, how wrong I was...

Bloody Muffy let loose a scream so high pitched that the glass on my TV shattered. She grabbed Paris Hilton's teeny tiny titties and twisted for all she was worth. Paris Hilton screamed and head-butted Muffy.

These Vampyres were crazy and they were destroying my house. My house. My cute little postage stamp house that was almost paid off. It wasn't much, but it was mine and this was not working for me. That preppy-assed screaming Muffy busted my window and my TV, and Paris Hilton had just dismantled my coffee table with a karate chop and was beating Muffy over the head with it. I wasn't sure how much more Muffy's head could take. This shit had to stop.

"Enough!" I shouted at the top of my lungs as my fangs descended.

"Get up," I said through clenched teeth, "and get the hell out of my house."

Both Paris Hilton and Muffy got to their feet slowly, looking around at my destroyed living room with shame.

"I am so sorry..." Muffy squeaked.

"Shut up," I growled, my eyes flashing. She did.

"Our Houses will pay for the damage," Paris Hilton informed me as if this were a regular occurrence.

"Damn right they will," I said. "Both of you need to leave and never ever come back."

They went to retrieve their gift baskets.

"Oh no, you don't," I snapped. "After that little display,

those baskets are mine."

"Of course," Paris Hilton said in her baby voice. "Well, if you change your mind, here's my card."

Muffy quickly pulled out her own card and tried to hand it to me. My glare stopped both of them in their tracks. If I'd learned anything from my mother, it was how to scare the hell out of someone with a glance. It worked.

"If you don't put those cards back in your pockets," I calmly informed them, "I will shove them so far up your asses you will have to pull them out of your mouth. Do you understand me?"

They put their cards back and exited quickly. Where in the hell had Pam gone? Why couldn't they see her? This Vampyre thing was appealing less and less to me and I was fairly sure there was no way out. Furthermore, their gift baskets sucked. Muffy's was loaded with day-glow colored madras clothing, Topsiders, Lacoste and a Minnie Ripperton CD.

Paris Hilton's was loaded with black crap that was barely in style during the 1980s, although there was a pair of Converse black high tops. Paris Hilton - 1, Muffy - 0.

I walked out to make sure that Muffy and Paris were gone, and there on my porch swing sat one of the prettiest Vampyres I'd seen yet. Her skin was as black as night. She had high cheek bones, full lips and sparkling black eyes. Her hair was wild and curly. Her body was long and lean. She was stunning.

"Who are you?" I asked suspiciously. I didn't have time for anymore crazy.

"Your new best friend," she laughed. Her laugh sounded like bells. She stood up with the predatory grace of a panther, and walked over to me. Now that was what I was talking about. This girl was what I expected a Vampyre to look like.

"I'm Venus...I'm from the Cressida House. We are Vampyre defense specialists. We're also Prada whores," she smiled and winked. "We would love for you to join us, Astrid."

Venus handed me the new Prada hobo bag filled with really good sunscreen, a totally rockin' pair of Prada platforms in my size, Chanel sunglasses, a couple of bags of O negative *for emergencies* and a brand new iPhone. If I could still breathe I would have been hyperventilating. I hesitated for a moment, realizing how materialistic I must seem, but quickly dismissed it. I mean, Oh. My. God. The new hobo! It wasn't even on sale to the general public yet.

"Hell yes," I said, grabbing my new Vampyre buddy and planting a big wet one on her cheek. Things were looking up. Gemma would freak when she saw the bag.

"Why don't you come back to the Cressida House with me for the rest of the night and tomorrow? We've got a lot to cover. Don't worry about your living room. The Lucern and Aurora Houses will repair the damage Muffy and Paris caused." She chuckled and held out her hand. I grabbed it and looked around for Pam. She stood in the doorway watching me.

I turned to Venus. "I just need to tell my...um...roommate where I'm going."

"Do you need to go in and find her?" she asked.

"No, I..." I whipped back around. Had Pam left? No, she was still there.

My Guardian Angel smiled her approval and nodded her head. None of them could see her. Why couldn't other Vampyres see her? I turned back to Venus who was waiting for my answer.

"No, she'll be cool," I said, following Venus down my driveway to her car.

I glanced back one last time at Pam, who had turned around, bent over, whipped her pants down and mooned me. I laughed and shook my head in wonder and disgust.

"What?" Venus asked.

"Oh, nothing," I said, "life's just changing really fast."

My new pretty Vampyre buddy considered me for a moment, smiled, and squeezed my hand. "It's all good my friend. It's all good."

Chapter 6

Holy hell, this was not what I expected. The Cressida House, which happened to be the most beautiful mansion I'd ever seen, was huge and overwhelming. I pressed my arms to my sides, afraid to touch anything. Everything in the place looked priceless.

"So this is it," Venus grinned. "What do you think?"

"Um...*wow*," I mumbled.

Venus laughed and led me through the foyer that was at least ten times the size of my house.

The home was grand yet tasteful. Dark, heavy woods gave it a masculine feel, but the huge crystal chandeliers and exquisite floral arrangements in stunning etched glass bowls kept it from being too manly. The grand staircase in the foyer would have been breathtaking, *if I'd had any breath to take*. All the rugs were Persian and I'm sure cost more than my college education. The curtains were thick and brocade and fell like water from windows that had to be at least fifteen feet high.

Of course, this was nothing compared to all the real Picassos, Rembrandts, Degas, Monets and all the other original paintings that covered the walls. I felt like someone had made a mistake inviting me to belong to such a beautiful place. I stayed close to Venus. My new Vampyre senses made me very aware we were not alone.

"The estate also houses a gym, a fight training center, movie theaters, a bowling alley and all sorts of other cool things," Venus explained as we made our way toward some very large and intricately carved doors. I considered turning around and making a run for it, but Venus took my arm and guided me on.

42

"The property is approximately one hundred acres and we have stables where some very famous race horses are maintained."

These Vamps were loaded. Apparently, living for centuries paid off.

"The third and fourth floors of the main house have bedroom suites for those of us who live on the compound like me," she continued. "The entire fifth floor is exclusively for the use of our Warrior Prince of the North American Dominion. He loves Kentucky and spends a good deal of time here," Venus said proudly. "Come on, you ready to meet everyone?"

"No," I whispered.

"Don't be silly," she said as she opened the huge doors. "They'll love you."

I gasped as she revealed a massive ballroom filled with the most gorgeous dead people I'd ever seen in my life.

"Hello, my brothers and sisters," Venus announced grandly. "This is Astrid. She will be joining our House."

All conversation stopped and every eye in the ballroom turned to me expectantly. I wanted to die. *Whoops, already dead.* "Um...hi. Nice to meet everyone. I...you know...died a couple of days ago and I...um, think you have a really nice house and..."

"Why don't I introduce you around?" Venus thankfully cut off my mortifying intro and proceeded to walk me around the room.

I spent the entire evening in the grand ballroom meeting more Vampyres than I ever knew existed. Both male and female Vampyres belonged to the House. Some of them lived there, some of them didn't. They were all very attractive and very nice in an uncomfortably dangerous sort of way. I was an immediate hit, due to Venus sharing the "shove it up your ass and pull it out of your mouth" story. Vamps seemed to enjoy things with a hint of violence attached. My horrifying opening speech seemed to be forgotten. Thank God.

"Venus," I whispered, "everyone is so beautiful. What happened with Muffy and Paris Hilton?"

"Oh," Venus shook her head, "that's a bad story."

"How bad?"

"Quite bad," a stunning Asian female Vampyre informed me. "Back in the 1920s a band of Vampyres thought it would be amusing to *change* a circus freak show."

"Suffice it to say it wasn't funny at all. It was horrific and cruel. Most of them didn't make it," Venus explained. "They were given no choice and were treated brutally."

"Oh my God, did they catch the Vampyres who did it?"

"Oh yes," the stunning and increasingly scary Asian Vamp

said. "They were tried and eventually put to a death as brutal as the ones they caused."

Her excited smile creeped me out. I moved closer to Venus.

"Our Warrior Prince will not tolerate atrocities," a pale, but beautiful male Vampyre said.

I noticed many bowed heads. It was like the Warrior Prince was some kind of god-King. Weird. This whole monarchy thing seemed a little outdated to me, but I stayed quiet. He was due to visit the Cressida House soon, and as a new Vampyre, I would be granted an audience with him. Whatever.

Some of the freak-Vamps, which was their term, not mine, still worked in fringe carnivals, but most like Muffy and Paris Hilton had tried to blend in with society...some with more success than others. They had their own Houses—Lucern and Aurora. They had been invited to join the Cressida House, but decided to form their own instead. Neither Lucern nor Aurora had recruited a new member in over fifty years. No surprise there.

"Really they're harmless, except for the massive property damage they cause everywhere they go," a lovely dark-haired Vamp explained.

"How many are there?" I asked. Why did I find this so morbidly fascinating?

"At last count there were thirty-eight or forty freak-Vamps, depending with whom you are speaking," a sexy Vamp with a Spanish accent informed me.

"Oookay," I laughed, "Can't Vampyres count?"

"No, no, dear child," a blonde Vampyre named Crispin that looked half my age chimed in, "it's rumored that the Siamese twins separated themselves, and being immortal, they each just grew back another twin."

What the fu...? I tried not to let my jaw drop on that one, but trust me, it was difficult. Even a couple of the seasoned Vamps looked like they had a tough time with it.

"I do find it interesting that you were changed without consent," Crispin added, sipping on his blood-laced cocktail and making me uncomfortable with his scrutiny.

"Give her time," Venus cut in quickly, moving me away from Crispin.

"We're a secret. You can only share this with people you would trust your life with," Venus said, leading me out of the ballroom.

"What happens if I slip up?" I asked, already knowing the answer.

"Revealing the existence of Vampyres is punishable by

permanent death."

Alrighty then.

"There is one other thing you need to know," Venus said. "There are Rogue Vampyres in the area draining and killing mortals. We do not tolerate this kind of behavior."

Well, that was certainly good to know. Apparently there was no reason to kill a mortal to eat. Ever. This Rogue issue seemed to happen every fifty years or so and was *of course* punishable by death. Not my idea of wholesome Vampyre fun. I was to report anything unusual.

What in the hell did that even mean? Everything in my life was beyond unusual now. I realized when I'd left I hadn't told them about Pam. Something had held me back from sharing every corner of my life with them. Maybe next time.

***

My house was too clean. Something was wrong. What in the hell was that smell? Pine Sol, bleach, and stanky vanilla room deodorizer? Good God, what did she do? I was only gone one night.

"Pam, where are you?" I called.

"In here, sweetness," she called back. Sweetness? I am so screwed...she either killed someone and buried them in the backyard, or she blew my entire savings online betting.

"Pam, I'm getting a little queasy here," I said, rounding the corner to my destroyed den. "You usually swear at me within twelve seconds of my arrival."

"Fine, Assbag, get in here. We've got company."

Please help me God, could it get any worse? Yes...yes it could. Was Paris Hilton back?

Pam was alone. Thank you, Jesus. She was sprawled out on my semi-broken couch. Clearly the Vampyre fix-it crew hadn't shown up yet. She was reading my email. I supposed she'd finished my diary.

"Did you have a lovely field trip, jackass?" she asked, closing my laptop and patting the couch beside her. I plopped down and curled up next to her.

"Yeah, nice butt by the way," I said, referring to her moon and Pam cackled. "I joined the Cressida House. They seemed fairly normal for Vampyres, and I made a new friend named Venus. Where did you go last night?" I asked her accusingly, "I thought you were my Guardian Angel."

"I am and I was here," she replied in a serious tone that I had never heard. I looked at her for a moment and decided to let it drop. I also decided that this was not the time to explore why

45

none of the Vamps could see her.

"Where's the company?" I asked.

"It's in your bedroom," Pam smirked.

"What do you mean by *it* and why in God's name is *it* in my bedroom?" I shouted. Shit, Pam's love of volume seemed to be rubbing off on me.

"*It* has been sent here to teach you how to fight. Apparently the higher ups," she gestured to the heavens, "saw you hiding behind the couch last night. We have come to the conclusion that you are a wimpy, pansy-ass Vampyre and you need to learn how to defend yourself. Not run behind furniture like a damn coward."

"Are you sure you're an Angel?" I asked, still totally amazed that this disgusting, profane, Oprah look-alike named Pam was even remotely celestial.

"Damn straight, Assbuckle."

"That's lovely," I continued, "so my fighting coach is in my bedroom?"

"Yes."

"Is it a male Angel or a female Angel?" I asked.

"It ain't no Angel, baby. It's a male *Fairy!*" Pam announced.

"He's gay?"

"No! He's not gay," Pam yelled. "He's a Fairy...you know, as in 'I've got wings, and I'm really sexy, and I'm magic, and I'm hung like a horse'...you know." She looked at me expectantly.

"No, no, actually I don't know." I was getting seriously confused and quite honestly a little alarmed by the 'hung like a horse' part.

Pam continued again as if English was my second language. "Well anyway, I don't think he's gay. I suppose he could be. He doesn't seem gay. I'm sure he was scoping my boobs and I'm pretty sure he would love to get down on my..."

"Nooo. No, no, no, no!" I screamed. "Stop! Don't want to hear it." I flapped my hands against my ears to block her out just in case she was still talking. Her mouth wasn't moving. I slowly took my hands away, ready to start beating my head again if necessary. "Is he sleeping?" I asked, my hands still poised mid-air.

"For shit's sake, I don't know. Go look and see." She picked up my cell phone, began scrolling through my texts and dismissed me with her middle finger.

I marched down the hall ready to face whatever was in there, threw open my bedroom door and gasped. Not quite as ready as I thought...There on my celery green down comforter surrounded by my hunter green and cream pillows lay a one hundred percent buck ass naked Arnold Schwarzenegger.

"Hello, my liebchen," he joyfully bellowed with the full on Austrian-German accent.

"Hi," I said and tried to avert my gaze from Arnold's abundant privates. "I'm Astrid, and you are...?"

"The Kevin, your Fairy Fighting Friend," he shouted with gusto. What was it with all these loud immortals that looked like celebrities?

"Of course you are," I muttered as he leapt off my bed and came at me with both arms extended with all regions south a-swinging in the breeze with a vengeance. I quickly sidestepped the lovin' headed my way, which caused The Kevin to bash into my doorframe.

"Ahhhhhhh!" The Kevin moaned, grabbing his nose. "You are quick, my little strudel princess," he yelled with pride. "You will be a good fighter! I think you broke my nose."

"God, I'm so sorry," I yelped. "Why don't you sit down?" I grabbed a wad of tissue and pressed them to the fountain of blood gushing from The Kevin's nose.

"And smart, too!" The Kevin mumbled as I seated him back on my comforter that I now really needed to wash. It was a good thing I wasn't hungry. The Kevin's blood smelled delicious, like hot buttery caramel corn and baked cinnamon apples. That would have been seriously awkward, not to mention uncouth, had I gotten busy and licked his face clean.

"The Kevin..." I started.

"You can call me The Kev—all my friends do."

"Oookay, The Kev, it's nice to meet you. I'm sorry I broke your nose...and you're going to have to cover yourself," I added quickly.

"What do you mean, O Beautiful One?" The Kev asked.

I took a deep breath. Did he really not know? "Your privates, The Kev. You have to keep your privates covered."

"Because they make you want me?" The Kev smiled seductively with a huge wad of tissue hanging out of his nose.

"Nooo..." He was definitely not gay. Why wasn't I attracted to him? He was gorgeous and naked and in my bedroom. Was there something wrong with me? I needed to be diplomatic without crushing The Kev. "You have very...um, nice privates, but you're more like a brother to me." I smiled and tilted my head to the side giving The Kev my most sincere and sweet sisterly look. Was he going to buy that shit?

The Kev considered this for a moment and seemed satisfied. He grinned and said, "By my privates, do you mean my buttocks and my rod?"

God help me. "Yes," I tried to smile, despite the fact he'd called his penis a rod. "That's exactly what I mean."

"No problem, my little Krumecaca." he said.

"Krumecaca?"

"It's a cookie," The Kev enlightened me.

"Of course it is."

***

Life with The Kev and Pam was dysfunctional at its best, and insane at its worst. The Kev loved me and Pam. Pam tolerated him with the same sweet profanity-laden disrespect that she tolerated me with. He just laughed, flexed his huge muscles at her, and swatted her on the butt. Pam would squeal like a little girl, and then cuss him out like a sailor. We were one little happy *albeit odd* family—except for one thing. Even though The Kev loved Pam and me, he was head over heels, cuckoo crazy in love with Gemma. As for how Gemma felt? I'd have to say overwhelmed and alarmed.

"He's hot, but he's weird," Gemma said, hiding from The Kev in my bedroom. "He told me I wasn't all human," she hissed.

"What did you say to that?" I asked, staring at my ceiling and looking for the little ugly monsters. Where in the hell were they?

"I didn't say anything. I punched him."

"Holy shit," I laughed, impressed that she got a shot in. I'd been fight training with The Kev for a while, and barely ever made a dent in him. "What did he do?"

"He laughed and congratulated me on my fabulous left jab."

"Awesome," I grinned.

"I suppose," she giggled.

We still hadn't seen The Kev's wings, but everything else about him was utterly magical. His main shortcoming was his choice in apparel. If he wasn't running around buck ass naked, which I had expressly forbidden, he put together the most hideous ensembles. Bless his heart.

Case in point—yesterday he wore a bright purple muscle T-shirt with gold spandex leggings, flip flops and an orange skull cap. I wasn't sure where he was locating these items and was afraid to ask. I had a very bad feeling that he and Pam had been shopping online with my credit cards while I slept.

Along with my daily tutoring at the Cressida House from Venus, who was quickly becoming a close friend, my fight training with The Kev had gotten serious. I've never worked so hard or been as sore in my entire life. I'd only taken The Kev down once and it had not been easy. He was so delighted when I bested him that he slapped me on the back and sent me flying into a tree, which I knocked down. It was a hundred year old oak.

As lovely as The Kev was, that bastard punched hard. Not only did I get a major concussion from the tree, I'd had two black eyes, two split lips, four broken ribs and a dislocated shoulder to prove it, and that was after only four days of training. Thank God I was a Vampyre or I'd be for real dead. Well, that and The Kev's blood. Fairy blood heals. Without The Kev's blood I'd be a mess. I was too new a Vampyre to heal very quickly.

The Kev let me drink from him whenever I wanted. Again, strangely enough, it wasn't sexual with the Kev even though I drank from his neck. Pam was not happy about me drinking so much Fairy blood, but she knew it was necessary for me to heal. Apparently the combination of Fairy blood and Angel blood was very powerful, and pretty much untested. When they thought I was asleep I heard her tell him he'd better train me "fuckin' good." According to Pam there were a lot of beings that would want me dead with the unimaginable strength and Magic I would soon have from all the celestial blood I'd been partaking in.

Between Venus' tutoring and The Kev's fight classes I knew more about bloodsuckers and ass kicking than I could ever want to in twenty lifetimes. I still hadn't revealed anything about Pam or The Kev to any of my new Vampyre friends—not even Venus.

They hadn't forbidden me to talk about them, but it just didn't feel right.

Since my disastrous decision about getting hypnotized left me dead, I had been following my gut ever since.

Chapter 7

Visiting a graveyard at 2:30 in the morning could indicate one of two things. I was drunk and really stupid. Or I was a Vampyre out to pay respects to my beloved recently dead grandmother and didn't want to fry my ass in the sun. I fell into the latter category.

"Why the hell is it getting colder?" I asked the crumbling sidewalk. Surprisingly, it didn't answer. With all the unbelievable occurrences in my life, I half expected the damn sidewalk to strike up a conversation. It was June for Christ's sake. It wasn't supposed to be cold. I hurried my pace, wondering if it was going to storm, and ended up right in front of Nana's huge gravestone. I shivered and got a creepy feeling that I wasn't alone. I looked around to make sure no one was about to witness how bonkers I'd become.

"Nana?" I whispered. Nothing. If at first you don't succeed...blah blah blah.

"Nana?" Still nothing. Shitfire, I was getting spooked. Why in the hell should I be nervous? I was a Vampyre for God's sake. I was a bloodsucking fiend! Right?

Right. I was at the top of the stinkin' food chain!

Right?

Right. I was not afraid of anybody!

Right?

Wrong! What the fu...?

With the grace of a cow, I dove behind Nana's grave into a shallow hole. I heard people walking and talking. Nobody sane should be out here at this time of night except me, and my sanity was debatable. Pam was right. I was a wimpy, pansy-ass

Vampyre. Why in the hell did I think it was a good freakin' idea to visit a graveyard in the middle of the night? Did I learn nothing from the hypnotism Vampyre fiasco? I peeked out and observed three of the most beautiful people I'd ever seen nearing my hidey-hole. Shit.

There were two women and one man. He had the finest, most asstastically perfect backside I'd ever seen in my life. I started to stand up to get a better look, but common sense prevailed and I stayed put. Thank you, Jesus. What the hell was wrong with me? An ass is an ass is an ass.

The trio stopped about six feet from where I hid. They stared at each other with a razor sharp deadly focus. It was as if invisible walls held them back from one another. They completely ignored me. Again, thank you, Jesus. Because I clearly had a death wish, I shifted ever so slightly to get a better look.

Mr. Beautiful Butt had gold eyes with shoulder length golden blonde hair to match, high sculpted cheekbones and pale flawless skin. Right out of a freakin' romance novel. His lashes were full and long. He was tall, had a rockin' bod, and a drool worthy ass that I couldn't seem to rip my eyes away from. He had full kissable lips, and did I mention that his butt was insane? It was packed into some well-worn jeans with some scuffed up Doc Marten boots, topped off with a just-a-little-bit-tight black T-shirt that clung to his oh-so-muscular top half. He was simply the best looking man I'd ever seen in my entire life and I had this crazy feeling I knew him. There was no way. I would have never forgotten him if we'd met before.

Red—scary female on the left—was gorgeous. Wild dark red curls flowed down her back and her eyes were a bluish silver. Holy cow, this Vamp-vision was like having binoculars for eyeballs. Her skin was pale and luminous and her mouth was full and pink. She was long and lean with a great rack. Normally, all that would make me jealous, but noooo. What was killin' me was that Red was Prada'ed out. Prada from head to toe. She was even wearing this season's thigh high stiletto boots. I would die for those. Oh wait, I can't do that. I'm dead already.

Brownie—scary female on the right—had the PMS look. I was very familiar with that one, although I guess that PMS was now a thing of my past. Anyhoo, Brownie had chin length, curly, shiny dark brown hair. Her skin was pale mocha and her amethyst eyes had that same glittery glow as the others. Her cheekbones looked as if they had been cut in stone. Brownie was stunning. She was smaller in stature than Red but held her own. She wore a low cut Betsy Johnson dress with insane platforms.

Where did these girls shoe shop?

Their silence was scarier than if they were screaming. What in the hell was going on here? I sunk lower into my hidey-hole.

"Haven't seen you in several years," Red snapped at my boyfriend.

"That has certainly been a pleasure," he grinned. Be still my heart, could he get any hotter? "Last time I saw you, several of your limbs were missing," he said.

Now that was random. Maybe my bionic Vampyre hearing had a glitch.

"That would be thanks to your no-good, son of a bitch, Jane-Austen-Wuthering Heights-loving boyfriend," Red hissed at my *gay??* lover. Damn it to hell, there was no justice.

My gay prince laughed at Miss Prada. "Ah my lovely sister, I'll admit to many things over my many centuries, but experimentation is your hobby, not mine. I can guarantee you he is not my boyfriend."

Thank you, Jesus.

"You're both an embarrassment." Brownie finally spoke, sounding as bored as I would at a knitting seminar.

"She speaks," he said.

"Screw you," she countered.

"Been there, done that, Honey Bunch," my man parried back.

Brownie laughed derisively. "You wish," she quipped, still managing to sound bored.

God, who does she remind me of?

"Speaking figuratively, not literally, my dear sister."

What the hell? All of these people—and I used that term loosely—were related? If they were, they either have different mothers or different fathers...or maybe they're step-siblings. Because clearly I'm just that stupid, I stood up. Bad, bad, bad idea. The beautiful redhead stared at me, almost confused.

"There's someone here," she said, stating the obvious.

All of a sudden there were three sets of glittering eyes on me. I finally knew what thick silence felt like—it felt wrong on every level. I struggled to find my voice. Unfortunately, I found it. "This is a lovely cemetery, don't you think?"

"She can see us?" Brownie hissed. She didn't sound so bored now.

"Impossible," my future boy toy muttered, "we're cloaked."

Before I could blink he was in front of me, so close I could barely function. He smelled really good. His eyes blazed gold and slowly turned to a brilliant emerald green. He stared steadily at me. A shudder ran through my body.

My first compulsion was to touch him. I lifted my hand and lightly ran my fingertips along his jaw line. He jerked back as if burnt and began to laugh. "My God, it didn't work."

I knew something was really not right here. This was not normal conversation. These were not normal people. I was fairly sure these were *my people* and I didn't want anything to do with them.

These Vampyres were not like the vapid idiots who visited me the other day, nor were they interesting and nice like the Vampyres at the Cressida House. These were dangerous psychos, dressed to kill, *probably literally*. Oh. My. God. *These were the Rogue Vampyres I was warned about! Shit, shit, shit.*

I was not drunk or asleep. But I was clearly in tons of trouble. Wouldn't it just figure, the first time I find anyone attractive in like a year, he turns out to be a cuckoo-cuckoo killer Rogue Vampyre. A crazy, mortal-killing bloodsucker that had friends who had ripped his sister's limbs off.

Fuck. I couldn't catch a break if it bit me in the ass.

And what in the hell was that all about anyway? Ripping limbs off? Did they grow back? Did she get them surgically sewn back on? They looked too normal to have been sewn back on. Crap, why were they staring at me? Did I say any of that out loud? I needed to get the hell out of here.

"Who do you belong to?" Brownie demanded.

I had no idea what she was talking about. Did I have an owner? Like a dog? These Vampyres must be from some other kind of Vampyre club, because unless I was mistaken that was not how it worked in Kentucky, or anywhere else in the good old U S of A for that matter. That bullshit ended with the Civil War.

Wait, did she think I was a hooker? I didn't look like a hooker. She looked more like a hooker than I did in her big ass platforms and her boobies hanging out of that seriously cute Betsy Johnson. God, I'd love to have that dress. I would look great in that dress. I bet it cost a fortune. *Shut up. Shut up.* I didn't have an answer to the question, which was rare, so I said nothing.

Red stepped closer to me and the air got cooler. "She's very pretty," she cooed. "I smell Vampyre, but there's something else."

"She's gorgeous." Mr. Hottie's gaze lingered on my mouth as he spoke then snapped up to my eyes. "But that's neither here nor there. Who made you and what are you?" he demanded.

I was starting to get pissed—and careless. "I'm a female," I told Mr. Hot Pants, "and as far as I know my mommy and daddy made me."

"Obviously," he laughed. His eyes raked over my body with appreciation. "But I'm in no mood for games. I'll ask you again—nicely—one more time. Who made you and what are you?"

I had no idea what they wanted me to say. My pissed-off reaction was shifting to scared-silly. I was so terrified I felt rooted to the ground. How weird was that? I'd heard people say it but I never believed it until now. My feet would not move. I wanted to run, but there was no chance of that. Brownie was by my right shoulder, Red was by my left, and Prince Starting-to-Be-UnCharming was in my face. I knew I was going to die. How unfair was that? I'd already died once this month. *Shit.*

He wrapped his large hand around my throat and very calmly stated, "Why don't I give you a few choices to make this a little easier for you, pretty girl? Are you a Vampyre-Witch, Vampyre-Ghoul, Vampyre-Demon, or Vampyre-Shifter?"

"Ghoul and Shifter are out," Red threw in. "I would be able to sense that."

Brownie, not to be out done by the rest of her psycho kin added, "Who sent you and why are you here?" She punctuated it by squeezing my arm so hard I was surprised the bone didn't snap.

"Oh my God," I blurted, "you people are nuts." I started to laugh. Knowing absolutely I was going to die, I still couldn't help myself. Prince UnCharming dropped his hand from my throat. If I didn't know better, I'd say he was shocked.

"Clearly..." I went on, very noticeably raking Mr. Smarty Pants up and down with my eyes. Turnabout is always fair play and he was hot. If I was going to die I may as well enjoy looking at the eye-candy before he ripped me apart.

"Clearly you are all very good-looking, well dressed Vampyre people who must have escaped from an extremely expensive insane asylum. I don't know if I like being a Vampyre yet, but if I'm going to end up like you, go ahead and kill me. I want out." I was definitely heading toward hysteria and entering the land of bizarre cheerleader voice. "You people are batshit crazy. Witches? Ghouls? Demons? Shifters? You forgot Mermaids and Trolls and the Tooth Fairy. I'm just going to leave you to what you were doing. Limb-ripping or whatever. So please step away from me and I'll go."

Nobody moved. Much to my chagrin I started laughing again.

"Is she laughing at me?" my ex-boyfriend asked.

"No," Red interjected, "Us. Did she just say Tooth Fairy?"

"Yes, I believe she did." He tried to suppress his

amusement.

"Does she have any idea who we are?" Red asked.

"I'm going to go with a no on that one," her brother replied.

Brownie was not happy. "This is not good, not good at all," she barked. "I think we should kill her."

"We can't kill her," Red snapped. "We don't know what she is, who she belongs to, or why she's here. So, if we kill her we could end up banished for centuries. She has not threatened our lives. Trance her, Ethan," she ordered.

Ethan? His name is Ethan?

"I tried," Ethan said. "It didn't work."

"What do you mean?" Brownie was shocked.

"What I mean, Lelia," Ethan condescended, "is that she doesn't trance. She can also clearly see through our cloaking."

That juicy tidbit set them all off as they yelled at each other about what to do with me. This was absolutely ridiculous. If I was going to die, I may as well go out fighting. What the hell were my choices? I wracked my brain to think of what I could say that would satisfy them enough to let me leave or kill me quickly.

"I'm an Angel-Vamp," I shouted over their argument. That shut them up, and if I'm not mistaken, scared them.

"Prove it," Red growled.

"Um..." Well, now I was screwed.

"She can't prove it, Raquel," Lelia said. Ethan just stared at me, a slight smile playing on his all too perfect face.

"It's not that I can't," I bluffed, "it's that I won't. Since you all seem so interested in what I am, I'd like to know what exactly you are. Besides certifiable," I added quietly.

Not quietly enough. Red...*oops*, I mean Raquel knocked me to the ground with a force that startled me and hurt like hell. I cried out as she straddled me and slapped me hard across the face. I felt my lip split and my cheek start to swell. I struggled but was no match for her. Lelia, formerly Brownie, held my arms down and I could swear both of their eyes were glowing like emerald green flashlights.

"Enough," shouted Ethan, grabbing the girls like they were rag dolls and flinging them into nearby graves. I struggled to my feet and tried to run, but Ethan held me tight to his chest. God, his chest was amazing. I wondered how it would look and feel without the T-shirt in the way. What in the hell was wrong with me? He was not that hot, plus he wanted to kill me. Well, he *was* that hot, but he was still going to kill me.

I watched in shock as Red and Brownie, or rather Raquel and Lelia stood up and brushed themselves off as if nothing had happened. They should have been decapitated after the way their heads hit those crypts. I was sure I was hallucinating. Raquel grabbed her arm which was grotesquely twisted behind her back and popped it back into place. The huge gash on Lelia's cheek healed as I watched. They must be old to heal that fast.

"That's it, Ethan," Raquel screamed. "You could have knocked my arm off and I don't have the time or the patience to grow a new one, Asshole."

Well, there was one question answered.

"So let her go," she continued, "because now I'm going to kick your ass. It's about time you knew what it felt like to be legless."

Lelia laughed and clapped her hands. "I'll hold the little Angel," she said, grabbing me from Ethan.

He turned on her quickly and snarled, "If you hurt her, you will be permanently dead. Do you understand me?"

Lelia blanched. I suppose he wanted to kill me himself after he was done ripping his other sister's legs off. Lelia quickly nodded to Ethan and loosened her vise-like grip on me.

"Bring it," snapped Raquel.

"As you wish," he growled.

They began to circle one another like predatory animals. They were both so very beautiful and so very deadly. At least they were off the subject of killing me, but now they were more intent on killing each other. I glanced around the graveyard and wondered if there was any way to escape. This absolutely sucked. I was about to witness some limb-ripping, and then I was going to die...for real. Just as they were about to attack each other, something changed in me.

I could feel it in my body. Heat surged through me. I could see everything around me glowing in sparkling golds and peaches. It was wonderful. I smiled and flicked my fingers and a breeze laced with glitter lifted my hair off my neck and hugged my body. Lelia was blown away from me and I was free. I felt strong and beautiful. Plus, I was no longer scared. Part of me knew I'd jumped off the Bridge of Sanity and part of me didn't care.

My three new friends—I use the term very loosely—stared in awe. Lelia and Raquel huddled together and backed away while Ethan advanced on me, wonder and desire in his eyes. My fangs descended, as did his. Oookay, a little freaky, but strangely hot. Was this the Vampyre sign for "I'd like to get you naked"?

As much as I wanted to see where this would lead, Ethan scared the hell out of me, and still possibly wanted to kill me. I backed away from him and he stopped. His gaze never left mine, and a new kind of heat started searing its way through my body. I knew he could sense what I was feeling because I knew exactly what he was feeling.

God, this Vampyre crap was complicated. Just when I thought I had a handle on my power some new freaky wrinkle got thrown in.

Suddenly I was barraged with images from his head—very naked, very explicit images of what he wanted to do to me. Oh. My. God. He was bad. Really good, but really bad. I'd never done half of that stuff he wanted to do. If his visions were accurate, he was quite something naked. Had I still been capable of blushing, I would have been a deep crimson. He grinned at me and ran his tongue across his lips. The tongue I wanted on my lips, in my mouth, not to mention other places like on my...wait...*what is wrong with me and when did my inner slut take over?* I swear to God, I wasn't usually this much of a ho-bag, but all I wanted to do was jump the crazy killer Vampyre and have my way with him. How in the hell was this man making me feel this way without touching me? Why did I feel such a connection to him?

A soft breeze blew up around my body, whipping my hair and lifting my skirt. Ethan's gaze slipped from my face to my legs. Thank Jesus I had good panties on. Wait...Why the hell did I care what kind of panties I had on? Five minutes ago the son of a bitch tried to kill me. Lord have mercy, I'd almost gone commando. That would have been bad.

I lifted my hand and flicked my fingers again and a glittery breeze engulfed me. Ethan began to come towards me again with a very determined look in his eyes. This both excited and scared the bejesus out of me. His intention was clearly carnal as evidenced by the lust in his eyes and the enormous bulge in his jeans. I caught myself moving towards him. While a huge part of me wanted to tackle the gorgeous killer and make him see God, the saner part of me somehow prevailed.

I flicked my fingers three more times, flinging glitter wildly around me. I knew with every fiber of my being that I needed to leave this place *now* or I would not be responsible for what I did. Having sex with a strange killer Vampyre in a graveyard while his sisters watched was just not my usual M.O. no matter how mouthwatering the Vampyre might be. Ethan stopped and tried to reach for me. I stepped back and heard him ask, "What is your name?"

I looked into his beautiful eyes and said nothing. He took a step closer. My body began to tingle with anticipation...and then I vanished.

Chapter 8

I woke up in a pile of bodies on my bed. Mine, Gemma's, Pam's and The Kev's. What the fu...?

"Um...guys? As much as I love all of you this just seems wrong. Like against the law wrong."

"Oh my God," Gemma jerked awake, grabbed my face and started crying. "Astrid, you're alive!"

"Of course I'm alive...at least as alive as a dead person can be," I said, pushing The Kev off of me. "Why wouldn't I be alive?"

Pam rolled herself off of my bed. How in the hell did we all fit on my bed? "Well, Assmunch, when you showed up last night you were convulsing in a funnel of Fairy Glitter. You had just transported yourself, which only Angels or Fairies should be able to do, and your eyeballs were rolling back into your head like a rabid dog. Call me nutty, but we were a little concerned."

"Krumecaca!" The Kev woke up and shouted with great joy. He tackled me in a hug, possibly breaking a rib. "My goodness of the sakes," he yelled, "we were so worried with the crazy sparkles and the crazy hairdo and your eyeballs rolling around in your head like a wild animal with the rabies and..."

"Thank you," I cut him off, "enough with the scary Astrid imagery. I get it."

Pam walked over to my vanity and sat, or rather copped a squat on my little stool. The Kev was pacing. To my horror he was wearing a red, white, and blue Speedo....and nothing else. Bless his heart.

Pam rested her head in her hands. And The Kev, despite his wrong-on-every-level clothing choice, looked gravely serious.

58

"What?" I was getting uncomfortable. "Why are you acting like somebody died? Oh shit, did I kill someone?"

"Hell no," Pam bellowed. "Sit your skinny ass down and shut up."

I obediently walked over to my bed and curled up next to Gemma. She put her arms around me and stroked my hair.

"Did anyone see you disappear?" Pam questioned, wringing her hands.

"Yes." I hesitated, remembering the effect that the gorgeous Rogue Vampyre had on me. "Three Vampyres."

"Fuck," Pam shouted as The Kev's pace picked up. He ran his hands through his hair and mumbled to himself.

A lead ball sat in the pit of my stomach. My vision blurred as my eyes filled with tears. "What? What did I do?"

"Did you know these Vampyres? Were they from the Cressida House?" she asked.

"No," I sniffled. "I didn't know them. I don't think they were the good kind." Although...one of them *did* have a crazy good ass. What the hell? Talk about inappropriate thoughts. I needed to erase him from my brain. "If I had to guess, I'd say they were the Rogue Vamps I was warned about." I got up and reached for the phone. "I need to call Venus and tell her."

"No!" The Kev tackled me to the floor.

"Get. Off. Me." I ground out, positive he'd cracked a rib. The Kev gently picked me up, sat me on the bed with Gemma and patted my head like a dog. My eyes, now a bright emerald green, bored into Pam's. "Tell me what in the hell is going on."

Pam looked up to the heavens for a long moment, then at The Kev, and then finally back at me. "You have powers that Vampyres are not supposed to have. Ever. I am assuming you will need these powers for your path in life, but it would have been a fuckload better if nobody knew about them."

"Call me crazy," I snapped, "but wouldn't that have been a good thing to tell me?"

"Little Wienersnitchzel, we did not know you were that powerful yet. It should have taken decades for you to be at such a high level." The Kev shook his head in confusion.

"Why?" Gemma asked. "There has to be a reason why she can do what she did."

Pam's brow furrowed, "I'm not sure. The Angel and Fairy blood have something to do with it, but I have never seen anything like this."

"What about her sire?" Gemma stood up and started pacing with The Kev.

"My what?" I asked.

"The Vampyre who made you," Gemma said. Of course Gemma, the supernatural junkie, would know more Vampyre lore and lingo than me.

"That's it!" The Kev shouted, slapping Gemma's tush lovingly. She blushed furiously, looking quite pleased with her discovery and The Kev's love pat.

"You're right...it has to be her maker. She must have been one old and powerful motherfucker. That's the only way to explain it," Pam said, relieved to have an explanation. "That, coupled with our blood, has made you the Bionic Vamp."

"Is it reversible?" I asked hopefully.

"Nope," The Kev and Pam answered together.

"It will only get stronger," Pam added.

"Why is her power such a problem?" Gemma asked.

Wait a minute. Was she scooting closer to The Kev?

"I'm not a hundred percent sure it is," Pam said, rummaging through my drawers. "For whatever reason power always ends up being a problem. It will make our Assnoodle a target for Vampyres who will want to use her gift for their own gain, possibly even kill her out of fear. You," she pointed at me, "are not ready to defend yourself against a Vamp with two hundred or three hundred or even five years of experience."

"What in the hell is my gift?" I asked.

"Assbutt, I don't even know. Right now you can transport and throw Fairy Dust, which can freeze or confuse people. Hell, tomorrow you might be able to fly and turn people into toads. It's anybody's guess at this point." Pam shook her head.

Oh my God, this was bad. I did not want to be some crazy powerful Vampyre that would cause other Vamps to want to kick my ass or kill me.

Pam found some lip-gloss and tried it on, checking herself out in the mirror. Clearly unhappy with her choice, she went back to rummaging.

"Anyway," she said, spritzing herself with my expensive French perfume, "you need to lay low. Don't go to the Cressida House except for your lessons with Venus and don't offer up any information about last night."

"What if they ask?" I said.

"Why the fuck would they ask? They don't know anything about it."

Pam found my nose hair clipper and turned it on.

"True, but what if they do?"

I watched in utter disbelief as she stuck my nose hair clipper up her nose. Not only was that disgusting, it was totally unsanitary.

"I'm an Angel, Assface. What do you think? That I'll tell you to lie? If—and only *if*—they ask, then tell them."

"Okay," I snapped, "that's all I wanted to know."

Pam rolled her eyes, went back to her nose, and got busy.

Chapter 9

After a lot of consideration, several more human artery lessons, and some life-threatening encouragement from Pam, I finally drank mortal blood.

From Gemma.

To make Pam happy.

And to continue to live another day.

If you asked The Kev, he'd tell you that Gem wasn't totally mortal. He wasn't sure what she was, but he was convinced she had "the Magic." I was convinced he had it bad. I caught The Kev practicing a Michael Jackson medley, crotch grab and all. Ahhh, the lengths a Fairy would go to impress a woman.

If The Kev was correct about Gemma, I still hadn't had mortal blood. God only knows what secret superpower Gemma's blood would give me. Magic or mortal, Gemma tasted yummy, just like a best friend should.

"What does it feel like?" I asked, licking the punctures to stop the bleeding and handing her wrist back to her.

"It kind of tickles, in a fuzzy way."

"Does it feel sexual?"

"No. Does it to you?" Gemma asked, wiping a blood smear from my mouth.

"Not at all." I lamented the fact that my blood drinking may never be a sexual experience for me, or for anyone else.

Gemma tucked her hair behind her ears and hummed a few bars of *'Rock with You'*. "Dude, maybe you just need to suck the right guy to make it all hot and steamy."

"Possibly," I agreed, envisioning a beautiful blonde Vampyre with gold eyes and a huge...*don't go there*.

I'd been daydreaming about him constantly, about how his lips would feel pressed against mine. I wondered if he really looked that good naked, and I couldn't get his scent out of my nose. Forget my nose. I couldn't get him out of my head. He was my every other stinkin' thought. I was obsessed with Ethan, the Evil Rogue Killer Vampyre.

With great effort, I pushed him over to the far left side of my mind. It was useless to lust after someone I'd never see again anyway. I hadn't told Gemma about him. I knew if I did, she'd latch on like a pit bull and not let go. I hadn't dated anyone in a while. A long while.

According to Gemma, who never lacked for dates, that was a bad thing. Secretly I agreed with her, but outwardly I simply pretended not to care.

I didn't date much. Apparently all men were losers and only good for one thing. My mother had beaten this nifty little fact into my brain since birth, ensuring I would be wary of the opposite sex. It had worked.

My mother couldn't bother to remember my father's name.

My mother's father had died in Vietnam. By the time she was an adult, she couldn't be bothered to remember his name either. I knew that hurt my Nana, but my mother was an odd duck, and a cold, unhappy, and very angry woman.

She had a mother who loved her, despite her shortcomings, and a daughter who adored her. A daughter who in adulthood had racked up several thousand hours of therapy, trying to figure out why her mother didn't love her, along with why she couldn't maintain a relationship with a man for more than two weeks.

You'd think after that upbringing I'd harbor some extremely nasty feelings for her. I didn't. I didn't exactly worship her anymore, but I didn't hate her. Sadly, I couldn't ratchet up enough emotion to feel much of anything for her.

On the other hand, if I were really honest with myself, unfortunately there was still part of me that thought I could make her love me. Ahhh, those wonderful childhood fantasies.

Gemma held up her other wrist, snapping me out of my walk down dysfunction lane, "Do you want any more?"

"Sure," I said, hunkering down.

Gemma turned the volume back up on my brand new flat screen plasma TV, compliments of the Vampyres at the Aurora and Lucern Houses. In a matter of three hours they had completely repaired my house and brought me all new furniture.

I was tempted to invite Muffy and Paris over and let them

have at it in my kitchen. I could use some new appliances.

***

Holy hell. I jerked awake trying to figure out where I was. This Vampyre crap was messing with my sleep. What time was it? What in the hell was I doing here? Wait...I was home...in my bed. I was okay. I had just taken a nap.

I was home in my own bedroom and I'd had the dream. Again.

Damn that Lady in the Tomb. She usually only popped into my dreams once a month or once every few months. Now she was popping in every other night. I was getting closer to getting her out of that tomb. I supposed if the dream kept rearing its bizarre head, I'd have her out of there by the end of the week.

I considered going back to sleep, but the movement on my ceiling caught my attention. Rachel, Ross, Honest Abe, and Beyonce were tap dancing. I'd named my monsters. I figured since I'd arrived in Crazytown, I may as well take off my coat and stay a while. It was odd. Out of all the little monsters living on my ceiling, the four of them really stood out. It started slowly with a shy nod and a wave, and then progressed to a full on dance party by day five.

I decided after a week and a half of bonding, and dancing, that they deserved better than just being called 'monster'. Hence their names, given because of their uncanny resemblance to their historical counterparts. I loved them and they loved me. No one could take them away, not even my mother.

My little ugly babies didn't eat, poop or bite. They lived on the ceiling and disappeared when anyone else was near. They were my three inch tall bundles of love. They were perfect and they were tremendous dancers. Their tango demonstration last night nearly brought me to tears of laughter. I hadn't told anyone about them yet. I was afraid they would go away if I revealed their existence. I'd already given up so much. I wouldn't take the chance of losing my monsters.

They often foreshadowed my evenings ahead. Tonight they were agitated. Very agitated.

They were slapping themselves and making high-pitched clicking sounds, which was like a cross between a cricket on speed and those wind-up teeth that chatter. The sounds were new. The more we interacted the more we could communicate. They loved when I flicked my fingers and shot breezes of Glitter Magic at them. They ate it up. Literally. They ate it, and then they ran around screaming and laughing like little drunks.

Their agitation tonight was unsettling. "I wish you guys

could talk," I muttered, getting dressed. I pulled on a super cool hot pink Juicy sweat suit that hugged my bottom just right and my brand new gold sequined UGG boots. My monsters approved. Their clapping and whistling made me giggle. I bowed. "Thank you, thank ..."

"Who in the hell are you talking to?"

"Shit," I yelled, jerking around and slamming my head on the bed frame so hard I saw stars. "How many times have I told you to knock?" I hissed at Pam, who looked like hell warmed over. "What's wrong with you?"

"Your mother is here."

My little monsters screamed bloody murder and disappeared back into the ceiling. I quickly glanced at Pam to see if she'd heard them, but she gave no indication that anything was out of the ordinary.

"Are you sure?" I panicked. I paced my room frantically. I felt my fangs descend and my eyes go green. This was not good.

"Yes," she replied, equally as panicked.

"Wait." I stopped. "How do you know it's my mother?"

"What do I look like to you?" Pam demanded.

"Oprah Winfrey?" I replied, confused by the question.

"Oh for fuck's sake, I'm an Angel. I know these things," she yelled.

"Hold. On." I said with excitement, "Can you see the future?"

"Not down here I can't," she muttered, running her hand through her already frightening hair. "My boss...that would be GOD to you...much to my great disgust gave you imbeciles free will. So even if I could see the future, it can change on a dime because you idiots are as flighty as gnats."

"But you can see it up there?" I insisted, pointing to Heaven.

"Sometimes," she carefully replied.

"Did you see any of this before you came down?" I waited.

"Only up until three days ago." Pam sounded so tired. "Now I occasionally have visions, and I know your mother being here is not a good thing."

"Can she see you?"

"No. Not if I don't want her to," Pam said.

I was shocked, "You mean you can control that?"

"Of course I can, Asswad. I am more powerful than you will ever know. Now suck your fangs up, turn your eyes back to gold, and get your sorry ass down to your kitchen and..."

"Hello, Astrid," my mother said from my doorway. "Who are you talking to?"

"Shit," I screamed, slapping my hand over my mouth and lowering my eyelids 'til they were mere slits. Please God, please God, please God—don't let her have seen my fangs. I could explain my eyes away as contacts, but there was no way to explain two inch razor sharp fangs.

"That's a lovely way to greet your mother," she said as her eyes narrowed. How did she do that? I felt like I was thirteen and got caught looking at naked guys on the Internet.

She tucked her perfectly coiffed hair behind her diamond studded ear and crossed her arms across her perfectly appointed chest. There she stood in her chic summer Chanel suit, pearls and low heeled pumps. Subtle makeup, light perfume and a slight tan. As Pam would say, *absofuckinlutely perfect.*

Pam watched my mother's every move with a look of utter disgust and revulsion. I supposed Nana had filled Pam in on my mother while they were hanging out in Heaven.

My mother was a beautiful untouchable ice queen. She was blonde, fair skinned and had huge violet-blue eyes framed by unnaturally long lashes, high cheekbones and a Cupid 's bow mouth. She looked crazy young for her age, which I happened to know was forty-six. More often than not, people thought she was my sister. She had me when she was sixteen.

As a child, I often wished she had given me up for adoption, but then I wouldn't have had my Nana. I'd have gone to hell and back for my Nana. How my Nana spawned such a frozen piece of work is beyond me...but she did. My mother's name was Petra, which was perfect. It meant stone.

"You're looking quite good for someone who was so sick," she said, taking in my messy room with displeasure.

"Thank you, Petra," I said with my hand still covering my fangs. Go up, go up, go up...they did. Thank you, Jesus.

"Oh darling, you don't have to call me Petra," she laughed. Her laugh reminded me of ice breaking from limbs after a huge winter storm. The kind that looks beautiful, but kills.

Darling? What the fu...?

I looked around the room, convinced there had to be someone here she was trying to fool with her loving mother routine. Nope, just me, her, and an invisible Angel.

"I...I thought that's what you wanted me to call you, so...um, no one knew you were my mother." The small, childlike voice that came out of my mouth disgusted me. Oh shit, I was going to cry. God, I hated myself. I was a grown woman. Why did I let her do this to me?

"Oh, don't be silly," she trilled. "I'm your mother...*your mommy*," she smiled.

Did Pam just growl?

Who in the hell was standing in my bedroom? It looked like my mother, but it definitely was not my mother. My mother had never been loving in any way. Ever. All sorts of impossible things had happened lately, though. For God's sake, I was a Vampyre with a Guardian Angel and my own personal Fairy. I suppose Martians could have come down and inhabited her body...or maybe she'd changed.

She put her arms out and approached me. I cautiously took a step closer. I awkwardly moved into her arms. It felt uncomfortable and wrong.

"Sweetheart, you feel so cold," said my concerned mother with a bizarre satisfaction in her voice.

"I'm fine." I tried to return her smile, but old habits were hard to break.

Her smile was still plastered on, but being so close to her I could see it didn't reach her eyes. *Alrighty then, she was still my mother.*

"I came by to tell you something," she said, gracefully but firmly disengaging herself from me. Crap, I didn't realize I was holding on to her. Would I never learn? She circled me, examining me like a car or a horse.

"Being sick agrees with you, Astrid," she said, "you have never looked so good in your life." Why did her compliments always feel like a slap? "Yes...you look good, but a bit pale. Maybe you should get some sun, Astrid. Don't you think you should get some sun, dear?"

"Well, I...um," I stammered. I felt caught like a deer in the headlights.

"Oh, but you shouldn't go out in the sun, should you, Astrid?" she asked, pointedly.

"What do you mean?" I whispered. Did she know? How could she know? People didn't even believe in Vampyres.

"I mean, people like you shouldn't go out in the sun...the sun will age you. It will give you sun spots and cancer," she laughed.

Was she screwing with me?

"Actually, Astrid darling, that's why I'm here," she said. "I have cancer and I'm going to die. I'll probably be dead within the week. My will is in order, so you have nothing to..." She stopped.

I was laughing. Like a hyena. What in the hell was she talking about? Cancer? Dying? In a week? She looked like a million bucks. Cancer, my ass. With extreme effort I pulled myself together.

"Petra...I mean, Mother...I am so sorry, but if that's a joke it's awful. Is there something you want?"

Ice settled in the pit of my stomach. Shit, she was getting pissed. She tilted her head to the left. Left equaled pissed. Right equaled ballistic.

"Mother, come on," I said, trying desperately to lighten the mood, "if you want something from me, just ask. You don't have to tell me you're dying to get me to do something."

If I could breathe I'd be hyperventilating. If looks could kill I would be lying dead on the floor right now.

"I am not lying," she ground out through clenched teeth. "I don't want anything from you. I have never wanted anything from you. You are a stupid, directionless girl. At least now you've done one thing right and I would hope that you won't fuck that up too. I'll be dead by Friday. Everything is in order. I'd like to say my goodbyes now and not be bothered with any soul-searching or last minute bonding."

I blinked. Did she say fuck? I had never heard her say fuck. It sounded so odd. Don't get me wrong, the emotional beating she just dished out coupled with her bizarre death wish was painful, but I was used to that. I'd just never heard her say fuck.

She walked to my bedroom door. She stopped, not bothering to turn around. "When I'm gone, I hope you'll remember me fondly. I'll try to visit you in your dreams. Look for me."

She left.

Was she high? Oh God, please don't let her into my dreams. I have enough problems trying to get that poor woman out of the tomb. I didn't need some bipolar demon mother telling me what a pathetic disappointment I'd been while I slept. What was she talking about—*done something right?*

My little monsters had been correct. This day sucked.

Chapter 10

The hardest part about being a Vampyre—forget the not smoking part, I didn't even miss it much anymore—was that Black Raspberry Chip ice cream, as well as chips and salsa were no longer part of my daily existence. I had always claimed that Black Raspberry Chip was better than sex. Even though I couldn't eat it from the carton anymore, I stood by my statement.

To that point, I discovered something earth-shattering tonight.

Whatever Gemma ate I could taste in her blood! It didn't work with Pam or The Kev—just Gem. I was beginning to think The Kev might be on to something. Gemma did have *the Magic*. So as Gemma happily scarfed down her second pint of Black Raspberry Chip, I happily scarfed down Gemma.

I licked Gemma's wrist, closing the punctures. "God, I feel drunk."

"Me too," Gemma giggled. "I haven't eaten that much sugar in one sitting in years!"

"Unfortunately I'm not drunk enough to forget about Petra's impending death schedule."

"Do you believe her?" Gemma asked, examining her wrist.

"I have no clue what to think. Oh God, did I take too much blood?" I asked, concerned.

"You can't," she said.

"How do you know?"

"I'm not sure." Gemma licked the spoon, put it back in the carton and started humming '*ABC*'.

"Her blood replaces itself immediately," The Kev said with pride. *Did he just run his hand over her bottom?*

69

"Are you sure?" I asked him.

"Yes, I'm sure. It's nothing I can explain, it's just something I know." He smiled down at Gemma and touched her hair. She blushed.

Could she not see that he was wearing obscenely short teal running shorts? Teal *women's* running shorts? He'd paired these with a sunshine yellow wife beater and a royal blue bandana on his head. This was the finest example of *love is blind* that I'd ever seen.

"Watch it," Pam snarled, entering the room and shoving me off the couch with her big ol' butt. "Gemma is not human. I don't know what in the hell she is, but it ain't mortal." She picked up the ice cream and took up where Gem had left off. "You know what that means for Assssstrid here?" she demanded from all three of us.

"No," I groaned, "but I can just bet you're gonna tell us."

"Yes, Assbag, I am," she said with a mouthful of Black Raspberry Chip. "It means you still have not had mortal blood and I have absofuckinlutely no idea what we may have turned you into."

"Well," The Kev hesitated, looking everywhere but at Pam, "she's shown strength—at times equal to mine—but she can't maintain it," he quickly added.

"What did you say?" Pam bellowed at him, slamming the ice cream down on the coffee table.

"She can't maintain it," he insisted.

"You," she pointed at The Kev, "are a two thousand year old Fairy. There is no way in hell she can come close to your strength."

"She shouldn't be able to, but she can," he muttered, fussing with his do-rag.

"You're two thousand?" I asked. "I thought you were fifteen hundred."

"Oh, for the gosh of sakes, everyone shaves a few hundred years off their age after a certain point. Just ask Pam."

"Don't ask Pam nothin'," she spat. "You freakin' Fairies are so full of shit. You should have told me she was as strong as you. Give me your hand."

I did.

She produced a wicked-looking blade out of thin air and sliced into my palm before I even knew what happened. Gemma shrieked and tried to save me from further butchering, but The Kev held her back. I screamed in pain and tried to grab the knife from Pam, but it disappeared as quickly as it had appeared.

"Look at your hand," Pam demanded, snapping me out of

my pain-induced haze. While it definitely bled, it was closing up immediately.

"Oh my God," I gasped. "I heal like an old, old Vampyre."

"Yep," Pam said, staring daggers at The Kev. "How much Fairy blood has she had?"

"A lot," he admitted, "but she needed it. I beat her up good." He smiled gently at me, like a proud father. "She's an excellent fighter now and she is controlling her Magic beautifully. As soon as she has weapons training she will be able to go against the best. Eventually she will be unbeatable. She will become a master."

"She'd better," Pam grunted, "because with all her fuckin' bells and whistles, quite a few Vamps are going to want a piece of her."

"We don't know that for sure," The Kev said hopefully.

"Yes...yes, we do," Pam said so quietly I almost missed it.

Gemma sat on the couch looking pale and confused. I suppose I'd be thrown for a loop if I watched my best friend get sliced and found out the guy/Fairy I was crushing on was two thousand years old. I mean, what the fu...?

Not only that, I knew she was having a tough time with my friendship with Venus. I needed to get them together, but both of them were being butts about it.

"Okay, both of you need to relax your cracks," I said to The Kev and Pam. "I'm strong and magical and loaded with the potential to have every Vampyre I meet for the rest of my very unnaturally long life want to kick my ass or kill me. Whatever. What I'm concerned and freaked about is my mother."

"Oh good God, that woman is pure evil." Pam threw her hands in the air and fell back on the couch.

"She scares The Kev," he muttered, pacing around the room.

"Do you think she knows?" Gemma asked me.

"I do. I really think she knows I'm a Vampyre, but that's impossible."

"No," Pam said. "It's not impossible, and she definitely knows."

"Is she really going to die on Friday?" I could feel the tears welling up. Why did I even care? She wouldn't give a shit if I died.

"You're right, she wouldn't," Pam said.

"What? You can read my mind now?" I practically screamed at her.

"No," she said, reaching out for me, "your face."

I went to her. Pam had been more of a mother to me in the

month I'd known her than Petra had been my entire life. Pam's love may have been filled with wicked-looking knives and swear words delivered at decibels guaranteed to make your ears bleed, but it was real and from her heart. No matter how disrespectful and bratty I was with her, I adored her and loved her fiercely.

I curled myself up in Pam's lap. I thought about sinking my fangs into her for comfort, but I felt like a tick after feeding from Gemma.

"Is she going to want me to change her into a Vampyre? Is that what she meant by not fucking up?" I sniffed.

"No," Pam said quietly. A quiet Pam was not something I was comfortable with. I listened carefully. "No," she repeated, "she can't become a Vampyre. It would destroy her."

"How do you know that?" I asked, confused.

"Trust me." She turned me so our eyes met. "I know."

There was more to this story, but Pam only revealed what she wanted, when she wanted.

"Is this one of those Angel things?" I asked, not daring to press it further.

She considered me carefully. I could tell she was weighing how much to say. She settled for, "Yes."

"Well then, what am I not supposed to fuck up?"

The Kev put his head into his hands. Gemma put her arms around his shoulders and held him tight. Pam stared into space.

"I wish I knew," she said. "I really fuckin' wish I knew."

Chapter 11

My monsters were shocked and appalled. This was not part of our normal routine. They were pissed at me for waking them up at 8:00 AM. They shouted and screamed and flipped me off. Who knew that a change of schedule would turn them into such cranky little turds? I returned the middle finger salute and rolled out of my bed with superhuman, or rather, super non-human effort. I wasn't happy to get up either. I was in the middle of a very graphic sex dream about that bad Vampyre. I just couldn't get rid of him.

Getting up in the morning for a new Vampyre was a terrible thing. A very terrible thing. We were supposed to sleep during the day because we were stronger at night. We weren't dead during the day and alive at night. We were dead all the time—we just liked to sleep when the sun was up because we tended to get crispy.

I was going back to work at the senior center today. I was informed that if I took anymore sick days from my art classes, my very old and talkative students were coming to my house to take care of me. That alone scared the shit out of me. So I was going in. I was fairly sure I wouldn't eat anyone. Pam assured me I would be fine.

I tried to get an evening meeting, but apparently people over eighty-nine hit the hay at 6:00 PM sharp. Right about the time my monsters and I usually got up.

Pam laughed as I entered the kitchen. I couldn't blame her—I'd be laughing too if I wasn't so damn tired. I had on sweat pants and tennis shoes, a long sleeve turtleneck, a big floppy hat, sunglasses and my old boyfriend's soccer goalie gloves from high school. To make things worse my face, the only skin exposed, was covered in thick white sunscreen. I was hot, as in sweaty not sexy. It was June, for God's sake, and I was dressed for winter weather. However, the floppy hat and sunglasses slightly evened up my outfit's chances for qualifying as summer attire.

Who was I kidding? I looked like a dork.

Thank God Almighty other Vampyres weren't out during the day. I'd die if one of them saw me looking like this. Especially Ethan. *Stop thinking about him. He's a bad, bad Vampyre. I just wish I didn't feel all tingly when I pictured his face...or his butt.*

"Well, Asscan," Pam gloated, "I don't envy you." She laughed and put down copies of my tax returns. Was nothing sacred? "You should probably think about a new career."

"I'd make a great night watchman," I snapped.

"There's always phone sex," she offered.

"Yep," I replied and nailed her with a pillow. I grabbed my new Prada purse, and the keys to my old Toyota and headed for the front door.

"Have fun with the old folks," Pam yelled after me.

I saluted her with my middle finger and left. I could hear her laughing all the way to my car.

***

"Did you get your boobs done?" Charlie asked, reaching out to cop a feel.

"No, I did not," I said, swiftly moving out of Charlie's grab range. "And if you try to grab my boob again I will yank that toupee off your head so fast you won't know what hit you."

"Awww, come on, give an old geezer a break," he moaned, adjusting his false teeth and giving me a cute leer.

I slapped a wad of clay in front of him and moved on to the next row. Being back at the senior center felt good. I loved these cranky old bastards. Well, most of them. I could even kind of pretend I wasn't a bloodsucking Vampyre for a couple of hours. Well, except for the fact I was covered in sunscreen and covered up like an Amish woman. Thank Jesus most of the class was practically blind. "Where are Martha and Jane?" I asked, dreading the answer.

No one said a word. They feebly beat on their clay and avoided eye contact with me. Oh shit. My stomach dropped to my toes. I hated those old bitches, but..."Did they die?" I asked in a tiny voice.

"Too mean to die," an old gal whose name I could never remember yelled from the back of the room.

"They're on the crapper," cute little Niecey informed me. She was about four and a half feet tall with a shock of white hair that stood straight up on her head. "Been there for two days."

A few in the class snickered. WTF?

"Do the nurses know?" I asked Niecey.

"Yep, said it's their own damn fault," she grinned, shaping her clay into a penis.

"Okay, um...why's it their fault?" I asked, removing the phallus from her hands and giving her a new hunk of clay.

"Because they're gonna try out for American Idol," she told me, as if that made sense.

"I like cheese," Charlie yelled.

"That's great," I told Charlie. "What does sitting on the toilet and trying out for American Idol have to do with each other?"

"Your bosom looks wonderful," Niecey said, ignoring my question and creating another penis. I had to stop letting them play with clay. "We were so worried about you. That skinny bitch subbed for you and told us she hoped you got fired for cussin' all the time."

"What the fuck are you talking about?" I was gonna rip that skinny, skank born-again loser a new one. She'd been after my job for months.

"Yay," Charlie yelled. "I just won five bucks!"

"Fine," Niecey huffed, handing the money over.

"Told you she'd say fuck within the first ten minutes!" Charlie was thrilled. I noticed he'd made a set of knockers with his clay, or maybe it was testicles.

"Shit, did I say fuck?"

"Five more bucks," he shouted.

Oh my God, he was taking bets on my potty mouth...and winning.

"Niecey, why'd you take a bet you knew you were going to lose?" I asked, handing her some paper and charcoals and removing another clay penis from her hands.

"Charlie's cute," she whispered. "I want to get in his pants."

Had I had still been able to eat, I would have thrown it back up at the mention of Charlie in a sexual way. He had no teeth and no hair and was fond of grabbing any breast within reach. "Oookay, that sounds like a plan. Can you tell me why Martha and Jane have been in the bathroom for two days?"

"Laxatives!" She burst into laughter.

"Explain," I said, grinning. I had no idea what in the hell she was talking about, but her laugh was contagious.

"I can't," Niecey snorted, unable to stop.

"They snuck into the kitchen and ate all the pies," Mrs. Jenkins, a bulldozer of a little old lady shouted, throwing her clay at Charlie. Clearly he'd tried to adjust her lady bits.

"And?" I prompted, moving Charlie to the corner for his own safety.

"They have big plans to be rock stars on American Idol, but since they ate too much pie they felt fat," Charlie said, placing his hand on my ass. I took Charlie's hands and tied them to the chair with craft yarn. "Dang it, Astrid, how am I supposed to get some if I'm all tied up?"

"You're not supposed to get anything in here except art lessons," I snapped. "Finish the story."

"Can I touch your butt again if I do?" he negotiated.

"Possibly."

"Great!" he grinned. "They felt fat from the pies and have a tryout coming up, so they took an ass-load of laxatives to get skinny before they become stars."

"Did you intend that pun?" I asked.

"What's a pun?"

"Oookay, let me get this straight. Martha and Jane are trying out for American Idol, stole and ate pies from the kitchen, felt fat, took a wad of laxatives to get their figures back and are shitting their brains out as I speak."

"She said shit," Mrs. Jenkins bellowed. "I win ten dollars."

I ignored her.

"That's about right," Charlie said. "Can I touch your butt now?"

"Sure." I untied his hands and let him touch it for three seconds. "Aren't they a little old to try out for American Idol?" They were ninety if they were a day.

"Don't let them hear you say that," Charlie whispered. "I only have one gonad left because I told them the same damn thing."

"Has anyone checked on them?" I scanned the class.

"Nope, I'm not going near the ladies' restroom," Niecey said, still laughing.

"Hear it smells like road kill in ninety degree weather on that side of the building," Charlie added and then blanched. The room went silent and I knew the killjoys had arrived.

"Hello, Astrid, we hoped you'd quit," Martha said, gripping the door with her gnarled old claws.

Holy hell, they looked bad. They never looked good, but today they looked particularly not good.

"What in the hell happened to you?" Jane barked. "You

look like a shiny albino."

Of course Jane and Martha's vision was outstanding...these two could suck the life out of anything. Considering I didn't have one anymore...life, that is...I decided to play.

"I have a sun allergy. Heard you two had a little poopchute problem."

They cast an evil glance around the room. "No, we're fine," Jane snapped. "What sort of unnecessary crap are you teaching us today?"

"I wouldn't use the word crap if I were you. I'd think you'd had enough of that," Niecey muttered under her breath. Charlie gave her a thumbs up and she blushed with delight.

"Shut up," Martha hissed. "You are all worthless bags of flesh. We are going to be stars and leave you to rot in this disgusting redneck hellhole."

"Well that's lovely," I smiled. "Are you going to join us today? I'd be happy to push a table over by the door, just in case you have to make a run for it."

"Your days are numbered, you foul-mouthed piece of trash." Jane shook her fist at me.

God, it would be so easy to flick my fingers and leave them bald and toothless and in their underpants. I was pretty sure using my new bloodsucker powers against old human ladies would be frowned upon, no matter how vile they were.

"Good thing you got an inheritance from that grandma of yours, because you're gonna need it when they fire you for disgusting behavior and lack of skill," Jane spat.

"She didn't have a brain in her head, leaving you all that money. Stupid woman," Martha added.

That was about all I could take. I'd been putting up with their shit—*pun intended*—for years. They could say whatever they wanted about me, but my Nana? Game over. They want to hear foul-mouthed? No prob.

"Okay, well since I'm out of a job here soon why don't you have a seat and work with your clay. If your old, saggy asses are too sore from shitting your brains out, you can stand. The assignment is to create a piece of fucking art that means something to you. Something that tells us about who you are. Niecey has made a penis and Charlie is working on some boobs, or possibly testicles. Mrs. Jenkins, what are you working on?"

"A whip and handcuffs," she replied, giving me a wink.

"Oh my God," Jane gasped, "this is sinful."

"These aren't boobs or testicles," Charlie chimed in, holding his mound of misshapen clay up. "They're ben wa balls!"

"That's wonderful," I said, giving him a high five and

letting him touch my butt again.

"You are a spawn of the devil and probably a Democrat," Martha shouted. She turned a very unbecoming shade of purple.

"Maybe," I grinned, "but in my class, there's a separation of church and state and bullshit. So I'd suggest you sit down, pick up your clay and make something that is a part of you...or was a part of you."

"Like a pie or a pile of shit!" came a voice from the back of the room. Damn, I needed to learn that gal's name...she was hilarious.

Surprisingly, at the end of my class I didn't get fired, but the powers that be did ask me to watch my mouth. So much in my life was changing so fast that my little job at the senior center felt like the last part of me that was hanging on to my humanity—and I needed that.

Chapter 12

There were people in my house and they were very unhappy. Unhappy with me? Unhappy with each other? Shit, after the day I'd had, could I not have one normal evening? Ever?

It smelled like lemons and grapefruit. Normally yummy smells, but not tonight. They were acrid and bitter. I was beginning to identify scents with their matching emotions, a very handy talent for someone with my bionic sniffing abilities. What I was smelling now qualified as jealousy and a little anxiety, mixed with distrust.

I plastered myself against the wall moving slowly to my den, worried that the emotions might be aimed at me. God forbid I'd need to defend myself. The Kev was convinced that I would be one of the great Vampyre warriors of my time. The Kev also thought silver stretch pants were high fashion.

I rounded the corner expecting to see zombies or werewolves or some other unbelievable entity like that, but it was worse. It was Gemma and Venus.

Together.

Gemma and Venus sat on opposite sides of the room and eyed each other warily. I felt like I'd gotten caught cheating with two guys at the same time. I hadn't planned on them meeting each other without me present, but this kind of situation was par for the course in my life lately.

Venus was surrounded by garment bags, shoe boxes, and shopping bags all labeled Prada. Gemma was armed with chips, extra hot salsa, and an available wrist. What were the odds? Two of my favorite people with my favorite things in the world, and I had to choose? Shitballs.

I knew if I truly had to choose, it would be Gemma. Even though Venus and I had become very close, Gemma was my best friend. I prayed that I wouldn't have to choose. I was sure we could work all this out. Maybe my confidence came from the fact that I was a materialistic bitch who wanted my cake (Venus and the Prada) and to eat it, too (Gemma and the chips and salsa flavored blood).

"Hey guys," I yelled, hoping the sheer volume of my voice would distract them from their intense staring contest. No such luck. Damn, volume always worked for Pam.

"Hey hot mammas," I shouted as loud as I could, "I see you've finally met! That's fantastic!"

Well that did it. They stopped staring at each other and refocused their killer laser beams on me. They stared at me like I'd grown three heads and dangly parts. Both of them started to speak at once. I heard...

"I got hot salsa and the Warrior Prince is a formal taco stand. I brought clothes in shades of Black Raspberry Chip ice cream kind of melted but the stilettos should fit and it doesn't matter how much blood you drink because you don't have to wear pantyhose in the summer because if you get full they itch."

They stopped and glared at each other.

"Oookay, that was seriously confusing, especially the part about the Warrior Prince being a taco stand," I laughed, trying to thaw the icy chill in the room.

Ahh...nothing like laughing alone. Again.

"Okay look, I can't deal with this shit right now. My morning consisted of getting my ass and boobs grabbed by an eighty-eight year old man while his wannabe gal pal made clay penises. That was nothing compared to the two mean old bags who took wads of laxatives due to an overconsumption of stolen pie. Of course they did this because they felt too bloated for their American Idol audition. They're ninety."

Silence. What in the hell did I have to do to catch a break? Time for a new approach.

"Gemma, I love you. I've loved you since we were four," I said to a smiling Gemma, but before Venus could pitch a fit, I continued. "And Venus, I am adoring you tons, and really quickly too. Normally it takes me years to trust somebody, but I let you in immediately. I plan to love you for hundreds, even thousands of years." Venus smiled and shot Gemma a *nanner* look.

"Hold it right there, little missy." I busted Venus. "Don't get too uppity. While Gemma may be mortal, she's also something else. What *exactly*, I have no idea, but she could potentially be with us for hundreds or thousands of years. I personally hope like crazy that she will be. So we shall become a trio."

They both groaned.

"That's right...we will be the Three Musketeers of the Vampyre and Whatever-Gemma-Turns-Out-to-Be-World." I clapped my hands three times and did a cheerleader herkie jump, causing both of them to gape at me in horror.

"Screw you," I defended myself. "I was really good at those in high school. I have the trophies to prove it." Doubling over in pain I muttered, "Shit, I think I pulled something."

"Dude, that was twelve years ago," Gemma blurted, trying to muffle her laughter. Venus didn't even try. She just started guffawing. Of course, this gave Gemma permission to lose it, and she did. Which in turn, led them to high five each other and roll all over the floor laughing uncontrollably.

"It wasn't that funny," I shouted. My outburst only served to make them laugh louder and harder. God, if I'd only known that maiming myself would have brought them together, I'd have damaged myself sooner.

"Are you through?" I asked them. The joy they were taking in my self-inflicted bodily harm was starting to piss me off.

"Are you okay?" Venus asked, lying on the floor with Gemma's head on her stomach.

"No, I'm not," I said, limping to my couch. "You two need to get up and be kind to me," I pouted. They both crawled over and sat on either side of me.

"Gemma and Venus," I said, "now that you've bonded over my pain and humiliation, we're all going to be friends."

"Fine," they said in unison.

"Actually," Venus volunteered, "I've researched you, Gemma, and I'm aware of your love of Prada. It seems equal to Astrid's." I cleared my throat and gave Venus the eyeball. "Mine too," she giggled. "I may have a little something in here that might interest you..."

Venus dug through the bags, pulled out a beaded clutch and a black miniskirt from this season *worth a small fortune* and handed them to Gemma.

"Oh. My. God," Gemma gasped, grabbed Venus by her shoulders and laid a big wet one on her cheek. "I am deeply, irrevocably, and materialistically in love with you." I watched her wheels turn. She got even more excited, if that was possible, "Venus, what was your favorite food?"

Venus paused for a moment, surprised at the odd question,

"Well, I've been a Vampyre for over two hundred years. When I was a mortal, food wasn't very good."

When in the hell wasn't food good? She caught our gazes and looked down.

"I was a slave ...food was sparse." She paused and regrouped. "But I do remember grapes. I had them once or twice and they were delicious."

Gemma and I sat in silence. My vision blurred as my eyes filled and I noticed Gemma's nose turn red. Sure signs that we were about to cry.

"Stop," Venus said, putting her hand up, "it was a long time ago, and even though my human life was hell, I avenged myself and my brothers and sisters sufficiently. Trust me, those who treated me and mine like animals died like animals."

I supposed I was getting jaded about death. Possibly because I myself was dead, but I gotta say Venus' story had a happy ending for me.

"I want to do something for you," Gemma said to Venus and then quickly left the room.

"Is she okay?"

"You bet," I grinned. "She is going to blow your mind." Venus looked alarmed. "In a good way," I quickly added.

Gemma came back to the den with both red and green grapes in a bowl, "Which ones do you remember?"

"Is this a joke?" Venus growled. "You are aware I can't taste any of that." Her fangs descended and her eyes glowed green. I was glad I was seated between them. Gemma wouldn't stand a chance against a two hundred year old Vampyre. Come to think of it, neither would I.

"It's not a joke. Which ones? Red or green?" Gemma asked without an ounce of fear or concern.

"Red," Venus said, trying to calm herself.

Gemma popped a bunch of red grapes into her mouth, chewed and swallowed, "It works with Astrid," she told Venus with her mouth full. "I'm guessing it will work with you too." She popped a few more grapes into her mouth and wedged herself in next to Venus. She held out her wrist. "Drink."

Venus cautiously took her wrist, brought it to her lips and bit. Almost immediately her eyes grew wide and tears soon followed. She took several long swallows and reverently released Gemma's wrist, closing the wound with her tongue. Venus dropped to her knees before Gemma and whispered, "Thank you."

"You're welcome." Gemma hugged her. "You can't tell anyone. I don't want a group of Vamps on my front porch with their favorite food in hand."

"You have my word," Venus laughed, wiping her eyes. "By the way, you're only a small percentage human."

"How do you know?" Gemma asked.

"Your blood gives me an unusual rush. I feel more powerful." Venus was awed even further by Gemma.

"Do you know what she is?" I asked excitedly.

"No, that's not one of my gifts. The only Vampyre capable of definitively identifying species by blood is our King," Venus said.

"And he comes by...what? Every century or so?"

"Pretty much," Venus laughed.

"You know what?" Gemma interjected, "I'm just getting used to the fact that I may not be what I thought I was. I'm not sure I'm ready to know what I am."

"Got it," Venus said.

"So," I eyed the bags and boxes, "what are all those things for?"

"Don't you mean who are all those things for?" Venus teased.

"Yes," I said slowly, "that is what I meant, but I didn't want to seem like a materialistic Prada whore."

"But you are a materialistic Prada whore," Gemma chimed in. Venus grunted in agreement.

"True," I admitted, "but being one and copping to it are two entirely different things."

"They're for you," Venus happily informed me.

Oh my God, somebody was screaming bloody murder. I whipped my head around to Gemma. Her mouth was closed. Venus? Mouth closed. Me? Not so much. Need to stop screaming now.

"You done?" Venus asked, tentatively removing her hands from her ears.

"Yes," I answered, not quite sure if I was telling the truth. "Is there a reason for my windfall of Prada?"

"Oh yes, my friend," Venus answered, sounding serious. "I am here to formally invite you to the Cressida House in the Haven of Kentucky. You are to be inducted and accepted into the North American Dominion of Vampyres."

"What exactly does that mean? I thought I already belonged to the Cressida House."

"You do. This is your formal induction because the Prince will be here. Basically it means you get dressed up in really hot clothes and go to a great party."

"Cool," I smiled, "do I get to keep the clothes?"

"You bet," she grinned and continued. "You will be presented to the Warrior Prince at the Congregant tomorrow night."

"What's a Congregant?" Gemma asked.

"It's a trial," I answered her. "Wait, tomorrow night?"

"Yep," Venus said to me and turned back to Gemma. "It is a trial, but it's much more. At the Congregant Vampyres with grievances may bring them before the Warrior Prince to be mediated and those accused of crimes will be sentenced."

"To jail?" Gemma asked.

"To death," Venus replied.

"Good God," I butted in, "there's no chance I'll get sentenced to anything by trying to become a member of your club, is there?"

"No," Venus laughed and tossed me a garment bag.

The three of us started flipping through the Prada as Venus got us up to speed on the bizarre world of Vampyre politics. The Warrior Prince would also be adding to his Elite Guard unit during the Congregant. This was one of the most prestigious positions a Vampyre could aspire to, especially one from the Cressida House.

The Cressida House's main function was to train Vampyres to protect the Warrior Prince and the Royal Family. The Elite Guard consisted of thirty Vampyres, but word had it they were going to increase the number to thirty-four, possibly because of the Rogue Vampyre activity. God, that reminded me, I had never told Venus about the Vampyres I saw in the graveyard. I was sure they were Rogues. If I told her, I'd have to explain too many other things that Pam and The Kev didn't want me to share. Shit.

"In order to join the Cressida House, a Vampyre must swear their loyalty to the Warrior Prince with a blood oath," Venus said solemnly.

"Wait," I said, forgetting all about the Rogues and dropped a smokin' hot strapless black Prada dress to the floor. "I thought a blood exchange between Vampyres meant they were mated."

Venus laughed and picked up the small fortune I'd so carelessly discarded, "No, you're only mated if you drink from each other. A blood oath consists of slicing palms and grasping hands with the Warrior Prince." She paused, thinking. "It is intimate, but it's not even close to mating."

"Thank God," I said, slipping on a pair of drop dead stilettos. "Do I look good enough to go to the ball and meet Prince Charming?"

Gemma giggled, but Venus' tone was serious, "Astrid, you cannot make light of the Warrior Prince. He is the most trusted and sacred leader we have. He is fair and kind and very ethical in a world where that's very uncommon. It's okay to be silly with me, but that's as far as it can go. You can get in unspeakable trouble for talking ill of him. Soon you will love him and honor him as I do."

"So we just slice palms and high five?" I teased her.

Venus rolled her eyes and nodded. "The Prince can drink directly from a subject during initiation. It would be considered an honor above all honors. It is very rare," she continued, "and has never happened in the North American Dominion and probably never will."

"What if he did drink from someone?" Gemma asked.

"Well," Venus thought for a moment, "among other things they'd be halfway to a mating."

"How romantic," Gemma gushed.

I rolled my eyes, "So our Warrior Prince isn't mated? Is he ugly?"

"No," Venus practically spit, "he is definitely *not* ugly. The farthest thing from it. He is beyond gorgeous and beyond unavailable according to one of his top guards."

"Oh, so he's gay?"

Venus choked. Gemma slammed her on the back.

"Oh my God," Venus gurgled, "he's as straight as an arrow. His guards are male and female. The top aide I'm referring to is a female."

"He's not mated to her?" I asked.

"Nope, and she's been guarding him for over a hundred years," Venus gossiped.

"Get. Out. Of. Town." I laughed, "That man is one hundred percent available."

"What do you mean?" Gemma asked.

"If he had wanted to mate with his security *female*, he already would have. I mean...my God, if I dated or schtupped a guy for over a hundred years without a commitment that would make me a pathetic loser!" I was on a roll. "I'd have kicked his ass to the curb after fifty years."

"Dude, you are so right," Gemma agreed, slapped me a high five and hummed '*Wanna be Startin' Somethin'*.

"Venus, don't leave me hangin', baby," I said as I put my hand up for her to slap.

"You are one crazy Vampyre," Venus laughed as she slapped me five.

"But you love me, don't you?" I challenged with a big, shit-eating grin on my face.

"I do," she laughed, shaking her head. "God help me, I do."

Chapter 13

You are H-O-T hot, I thought as I hung out in the Grand Foyer of the Cressida House, admiring my babysitter.

"I'm sorry?" he said with a twinkle in his gorgeous blue eyes.

Oh hell, did I say that out loud? Shit, shit, shit. I mean, he's gorgeous, but I don't want him to think I was checking him out...even though I was. That would be sexist and wrong and rude. God, what in the hell is wrong with me? He is not a piece of meat. He is a very nice, very handsome Vampyre guy who is showing me the ropes and he's going to think I'm a crazy slut. I can't believe I said the hot thing out loud.

"Actually you didn't," he grinned. "One of my gifts is mind reading."

"Holy hell," I gasped, mortified. "Did you hear all of that?"

"Yes," he laughed. "And thank you."

"Oh my God," I pleaded. "Is there an off switch?"

"Yes," he said slowly, "but with where your mind seems to be going, I'm loath to tell you."

"Please?" I gave him a flirty smile. He returned the favor with a killer smile of his own. Were those dimples? Damn it, I loved dimples.

"Alright, but there's a price," he teased.

"What's the price?" I asked, hoping it had something to do with my lips on his.

"If you keep having thoughts like that," he informed me, grabbing his chest as if his heart was breaking, "there's no way I'll let you close me out of your mind."

"Sorry," I giggled. Damn, he was beautiful and sweet and

86

silly with a fantastic ass and...

"Enough! You're killing me," he grinned. "Close your eyes."

I did.

"Now visualize heavy metal doors, similar to garage doors. Reach for them and slowly pull them down. When you have closed all the doors, visualize heavy metal locks and lock them."

I did.

"Is that it?" I opened my eyes in surprise.

"Yep," he smiled, "that's it."

"Is it working?" I asked.

"I don't know. Think of something wickedly sexual, something I would absolutely have to react to...and we'll see."

Were all male Vampyres were perverts? I envisioned something very naked, very sweaty and very vocal between the beautiful Vampyre and myself. I watched him closely for a reaction. Nothing. Thank God.

"What if I want you inside me?" I asked.

"Oh my sweet, you only have to ask," he said. His eyes turned green and he laughed.

"Shit," I blurted, "that came out totally wrong. I am so sorry. I didn't mean inside...I mean, um, I meant my head. Inside my head."

"I know what you meant," he sighed, "but a man can always hope."

If I could still blush, I'd be a tomato.

"If you want me inside you," he teased as I rolled my eyes in embarrassment, "just unlock the doors and open them."

"It's that easy?" I asked.

"It's that easy," he replied with another beautiful smile. "Now Astrid, do you know what to do when you go into the ballroom?" he asked, changing the subject.

"Kind of," I said, "but I'm at a loss."

"A loss?"

"Yes," I said slowly, "you know my name, but I don't know yours."

He paused and stared at me for a long moment. "Do you promise not to laugh?" he asked, the twinkle back in his eyes.

"With a set-up like that, I'm not sure," I said, really liking this guy.

"Would you like to guess?" he asked.

"Rumplestiltskin?" I teased.

"Nope."

"Herman?"

"Definitely not," he shot back. "It's Heathcliff."

"Really?" I tried to stifle my giggles.

"Really," he smiled. "My mother was a huge *Wuthering Heights* fan, and also a good friend of Emily Bronte."

"My Nana loved Emily Bronte too. So you must be...?"

"One hundred and forty," he answered, watching my face for a reaction. He got one.

"Sorry," I stammered, "it's hard to wrap my head around that. You don't look a day over thirty," I added hastily.

"In mortal years, I was twenty-seven when my father changed me."

That stopped me. "Your father?" I was astonished. "Vampyres can't have children."

"It's a long story. He fathered my sister and me when he was mortal. He and my mother were changed when we were babies. My mother didn't make it. My father was devastated, but he raised us and loved us. He waited until my sister and I were in our twenties and then gave us the option. We took it."

"So your real biological family is still alive?" I was awestruck.

"Yes," he said with pride, "other than the Royal Family, we're the only biological Vampyre family."

"Just don't tell me your sister's name is Catherine," I joked.

"Okay," he said sheepishly, "I won't."

"Get. Out. Of. Town." I started laughing. "You're kidding!"

"Nope, it's Catherine. She goes by Cathy...you can meet her later. And yes, we take a lot of crap about our names. She is one of the Elite Guard for the Warrior Prince, as am I."

"Where's your dad?" I asked this one hundred and forty year old man who looked my age.

"He's the leading scholar of Vampyre History and resides with our King. I believe they're in Italy at the moment. They'll be visiting the North American Dominion within the month," he said, taking my hand and leading me to a settee.

"Astrid, when you enter the Grand Ballroom," Heathcliff coached, "keep your eyes downcast until the Warrior Prince speaks to you."

I was so glad he couldn't read my mind, because that sounded like backward-ass feudal bullshit to me. Venus told me I had to behave, so behave I would.

"Okay Astrid," he said. *God, he was dreamy.* "Someone will be out for you shortly. I have to go in now." He squeezed my hand and turned to leave.

"Heathcliff," I called after him.

"Yes?"

"Where do you live?" *Hell, could I be more transparent?*

He stopped and smiled, clearly delighted with my question. "I live wherever the Warrior Prince lives, but we stay in Kentucky often." He winked at me, turned and left.

God, why couldn't I have a boyfriend like that? I was sure I'd just embarrassed myself. There was no way someone who looked like that didn't already have a girlfriend or ten or twenty.

Why in the world were all the Vampyres so good looking? Everything about the Vampyre world was exquisite—the Vampyres themselves, their homes, their clothes, their asses. For God's sake, there was another one at the top of the stairs. From this distance he looked like a Greek god come to life.

The Cressida House might be gorgeous, but nowhere near as stunning as the Vampyre descending the Grand Staircase. God, this one may be better than Heathcliff. His name had to be Romeo or Fabio. He was the finest looking man I'd ever seen. Talk about hot; that guy could melt the polar icecap. He was so hot, he could melt panties...so hot that he could...wait. Holy hell, I knew him. Shit, shit, shit.

It was Ethan. My heart bounced around in my chest like a Ping-Pong ball. He was headed my way, the crazy Rogue killer Vampyre I'd been fantasizing about day and night. How in the world did he look better than I remembered? That wasn't fair. Whatever. It didn't matter how good-looking he was. It couldn't erase the fact that he tried to kill me.

I frantically glanced around the foyer. Why wasn't anyone around? If I ran he'd definitely notice and if I transported away, I'd probably be put to death by the Prince. Either way I end up deader than I already am. Shit, can't I ever catch a break without being killed? Maybe he won't see me if I stand really still. *That's stupid.* Please God, let him walk right by and not notice that I'm standing next to the door that he's moving toward. Please, please, please...damn.

He stopped dead in his tracks about six feet from me. He started at my stiletto clad feet, sliding slowly up my bare legs, pausing at my breasts that were firmly hugged by my black strapless Prada. From there his eyes traveled lazily to my neck, my lips, and finally my eyes. I saw delight and something I couldn't define flash in his beautiful gold eyes as recognition hit. He recovered quickly, much quicker than I did.

"Hello Angel, you've been on my mind," he said, walking toward me.

"Interesting. My mind erased you—*and* Angel's not my name. Gotta go," I mumbled, moving down the hallway at a sprint. Away from the ballroom and away from him. I'm supposed to meet the freakin' Warrior Prince, not get murdered by a hot Rogue Vampyre.

Door, door, door...where in the hell was a door? If I could find a closet or a bathroom...wait. Did they even have bathrooms here? I mean, they don't use them. For a place so huge you'd think they'd at least have a stupid closet, for shit's sake.

I quickly glanced over my shoulder. Great, I'd lost him. At least one thing had gone in my favor. Now I just needed to find a...door! Thank God! I threw myself into what turned out to be a bathroom, evidenced by the toilet I tripped over.

"Crap, that hurt," I muttered, getting up off all fours and turning on the light. I glanced in the mirror, hoping that they had a special one that a Vampyre's reflection showed up in.

Nope.

"Okay..." I explained to no one as I adjusted my dress. Sprinting, strapless dresses and stilettos didn't go well together. "I'll just stay in here for a few minutes and then find my way back. Hopefully Mr. Hot Pants Killer will be gone. I can meet the Prince, slit my wrist, get this stupid medieval bullshit over with and get the hell out of here."

"Sounds like a plan."

"Holy shit," I screeched, hopping my butt up on the counter. Very poorly thought out move on my part as my ass landed in the sink. How did I not know he was in here? Damn, I sucked as a Vampyre. "Did you even think about knocking?"

"No," Ethan grinned. "I find the element of surprise to be helpful, Angel."

"I told you that's not my name," I insisted. I tried un-wedge my rear end, but a butt in a sink is a butt in a sink.

"No, it may not be," he said, moving just a little bit closer, "but that's what I think I shall call you."

"What are you doing here?" I asked, changing the subject and hoping I didn't look as ridiculous as I knew I did. "Did you and your Rogue friends get caught?"

He stared at me in amazed confusion for a moment. "Are you serious?" he asked.

"Of course I am, you dork."

"Oh, little Angel," he grinned with delight, "I'm not the Rogue. I'm the Rogue's worst nightmare."

"Really? How very Rambo of you," I offered flatly. *What was he? Some kind of Vampyre police?*

I was trying to keep my eyes on his face when they desperately wanted to roam his whole body, followed by my hands, then my mouth. *Whoa there, Nelly.*

"So then I suppose you're in trouble for ripping your sister's limbs off?"

He laughed. *Help me...*he was even more beautiful when he laughed.

"I'm always in trouble, Angel," he said, running his hand through his hair and watching me closely.

What was it with this guy? Heathcliff was as good looking as Ethan, but ol' Heath didn't make me want to rip my panties off. I couldn't think straight when I was near this bad Vampyre. Damn it, if my ass wasn't stuck in the sink I could make another run for it. He stopped inches from me. My insides started to tingle.

"You're a mystery, little Angel." With strong hands, he gently lifted me out of the sink and settled me on the counter. He slowly and deliberately ran his hands down my thighs. I had a burning desire to open them, trap him between them and make him see Jesus. *What the fu...?*

I knocked his hands away and pressed myself against the mirror. I was hoping to put more than just a few inches between us. This murdering Vampyre was making me consider things no nice girl should ever consider—sex in a sink, for one.

He moved closer. I squeezed my eyes shut and pretended he was Charlie from the senior center. Not. Working. Shitfire. The seniors didn't smell like he did. If he didn't smell so damn good, I wouldn't feel the need to knock him to the ground and ride him 'til he was blind.

God, he really smelled like Heaven. I opened my eyes to find the sexiest killer alive a mere thought away from my lips. His eyes had changed from gold to green. He slowly ran his fingers down my neck and along my collarbone. I felt my nipples harden. His eyes flashed a brilliant green, and his lazy grin almost made me pass out. I was quite certain that he no longer wanted to kill me.

"Why are you here, Angel?"

He was so close I got confused. He was literally jumbling my brain. Was that his special Vampyre power, or was I just in heat? If he ran his fingers any closer to my traitorous boobs, I was going to have multiple orgasms. He smiled as if he knew what I was thinking.

"I have to go see your Warrior guy. Prince, thing...guy....um..." I mumbled.

"You must be in a lot of trouble."

To my great dismay, I leaned into him. His lips feathered across mine and he made the sexiest sound I'd ever heard. Holy hell, he was making staying clothed very difficult.

"Why do you say that?" I gasped. He barely touched me, but if he did it again he was going to get slammed to the wall and manhandled by me. He'd probably love it, but I knew I wouldn't be able to face myself in the mirror ever again. Wait...I couldn't see myself in the mirror anyway. What if I just...NO. Ethan was a bad, bad sex-on-a-stick Vampyre man who tried to kill me. Am I so hard up that I need to suck face with a criminal? Well...

"Come back to me, Angel." Ethan snapped me out of my fantasy with a twinkle in his eyes that led me to believe he definitely knew everything I was thinking. Shit. Was he a mind reader too?

"Why do you say I'm in so much trouble?" My voice sounded husky and far away. "You don't even know if I did anything," I said, frantically trying to close and lock the garage doors in my brain. All these Vampyres with *gifts* were killin' me.

"Doesn't matter. You're his type," Ethan said as his lips moved to my neck. *Can't think, can't think, can't think.* I moaned.

My body melted as he lightly nipped and kissed my neck. I felt all noodley and he grabbed me before I fell back into the sink. Ethan pulled me to the edge of the counter, effectively lining up my lady parts with his very impressive man parts.

"What do you mean?" I whispered. I was quickly losing control of my modesty, not that I had that much to start with. But even I realized wrapping my legs around and pressing myself closer to a man I barely knew didn't look so good. A man who until two minutes ago I thought might want to kill me. I didn't even care. As crazy as it sounded, this psycho made me feel safe...or at least mind-alteringly horny. But what the hell did I know? I'd gotten hypnotized at a strip mall.

"You're the Warrior Prince's type," he whispered into my ear, sending shivers straight to my girlie parts. "He's been dead for so long, it's rare for any woman to make him feel like a man." He nipped my earlobe and I gasped. *Dear God, I couldn't remember my name. What's my freakin' name?* "He's too powerful, too feared—they treat him like a god instead of a man," he continued to whisper and I continued to try to recall what people call me. "I don't think you're afraid of anything." He ran his lips along my jaw, back to the corner of my mouth. I shuddered. What in the hell was he babbling about? Fear? Who?

His eyes bored into mine with an intensity that scared the hell out of me and made me want to tackle his ass at the same time, "I believe you could make him feel alive again."

He grabbed my legs and inched me even closer. This was getting serious and I still couldn't remember my stupid name. No getting away this time, even if I wanted to. I didn't want to. I was crazy happy right where I was. I wove my hands into his hair, cupped the back of his head and pulled his lips to mine. His lips were soft and anything but gentle. He bit at my bottom lip, sucking it into his mouth. He teased my tongue with his own, sending little shockwaves through my body and waking up my very bad girl from her slumber. He tasted even better than he smelled. The pressure of him against me sent a hot heat coursing through my body. Turns out kissing a Vampyre was better than sex with a human one hundred times over.

Sex with him would be...deadly. Maybe literally, but I couldn't bring myself to care. I just wanted to...but I can't. Oh God, I still didn't know my name. My brain cells flew out of my head with every touch, every lick every...Oh. My. God. His hands moved down and roughly grabbed my ass and ground me into an erection so impressive I damn near fainted. There was no doubt that he wanted me as much as I wanted him.

My barely-there thong was soaked and my body had taken over for my brain. Much to my great shock *and secret delight* I was grinding and writhing against the gorgeous Vampyre and I even...wait.

Astrid! My name is Astrid.

I was on the verge of breaking every rule I'd ever made for myself, but the gorgeous Vampyre was having a difficult time holding onto his control too. The sounds that were coming from deep in his body made my brain skitz out. I answered back with my own moans of pleasure. I melted against him, pliant and oh so willing. I knew if I died right now, *I mean for real dead,* I'd die happy.

The power I felt over him was as intoxicating as his kiss. I could do this forever. *Whoa. What the fu...? No, no, no. This is wrong...*The burning in my gums led me to believe my fangs decided to show up and I wanted to bite him. Bad. That's right, I wanted to bite him and drink from him. I wanted to sink my fangs into him and claim him as mine. Mine, mine, mine, mine, mine.

But that would mean something...damn it, what did it mean if I bit him? If he hadn't sucked out all my brain cells I could remember why it would be a bad idea.

Whatever. I was done trying to listen to my rational self. It was time to throw him to the floor and ride him like a cowboy. I didn't care if the whole ballroom came out and watched me have sex in a bathroom with a killer Vampyre.

But wait...we were clearly not on the same page. Why did he stop? What in the hell was he saying? The pre-coital ringing in my ears made hearing anything but moans virtually impossible...was he actually talking? *For real?*

"The Prince will want you."

"What?" *The Prince will what?*

"He will want you more than he's ever wanted anything in his whole life. He will want you in his bed. Naked and pinned beneath him."

I froze.

"That's disgusting," I practically spit. I pushed Ethan the Greek god, the man of every sexual fantasy I'd ever had, off of me. He stumbled back, surprised by my strength.

"What are you, his wingman? Scoping out new Vamp-meat for Prince Jackass? Taking me for a test run, you jerk?" I hissed, trying to block out the fact that less than a minute ago I was ready to get naked and sink my fangs into this asshole and claim him for eternity.

Before I even saw him move, he was back up in my face, his body flush with mine. *Brain cells, brain cells, brain cells, why have you forsaken me?*

His eyes bored into mine, "Little Angel, I would suggest you be careful. Not everyone is as lenient as I am when it comes to bashing the Prince."

"Your Prince sounds like an oversexed asshole rapist," I gasped, trying to get Ethan off of me. My struggles were embarrassingly pathetic.

What in the hell was wrong with me? This asshole, while rubbing all over me, was informing me that I would be having sex with his even bigger asshole Prince. First he tried to kill me, now he was ready to pimp me off to his almighty Lord and Master.

Why in the hell was I still turned on by him?

"I'm not sure there is such a thing as oversexed and he's definitely not a rapist," he laughed, cupping my face between his very large hands. "I assure you, the Prince can be an asshole, but he has never taken an unwilling woman to his bed. Ever."

I pushed him away again, and again he seemed surprised by my strength. Uh oh, I needed to pull back or he might start asking questions I couldn't answer.

"You should take heed, little Angel," he said, "he gets what he wants...and he will want you."

"Well, he can't have me," I told him.

He thankfully seemed to be ignoring my power for the moment. What was I thinking? He saw me disappear in a cloud of Fairy Glitter in the graveyard.

"We shall see, little Angel, we shall see."

He ran his fingers lightly across my collarbone and down my arm. His sexy smirk was back. "I'll be seeing you. Soon."

"Don't bet on it."

He kissed me lightly and then he was gone. My hand went automatically to my lips and the rest of me went boneless. Thankfully there was a sink to catch my fall.

Chapter 14

After three tries I found my way back to the ballroom foyer and was greeted by some very attractive, no-nonsense Vampyres. They said very little and made me feel uncomfortable. Screw 'em.

After standing there in silence for what felt like an hour with the most boring Vamps I'd met yet, it was finally time to go. I entered the Grand Ballroom as if I were walking to the guillotine.

What a freakin' crazy day...and it wasn't even over. First, I'd flirted with a beautiful Vampyre named Heathcliff, who turned out to be five times my age and probably thought I was easy. Second, I'd been willingly molested by a very sexy and dangerous Vampyre who definitely assumed I was easy. Now I was going to slap bloody palms with another guy who hopefully knew nothing about my loose morals...although according to Ethan this Prince guy was going to want to do me. Not gonna happen. I was done with Vamps. They were nuts. Well Heathcliff seemed nice.

As we made our way in, there was a Vampyre on either side of me and one directly behind me. No escaping now. My eyes were downcast and I had no idea where I was going. Thankfully I was sandwiched between the ridiculously serious Vamps, or I'd have walked into a wall. The marble floors were very pretty and very clean.

Thank Jesus for my nose. At least I could get a sense of what was going on by the scent in the room. The smell thing had taken some getting used to, but it had been worth it. I'd learned how to turn it off when I was around garbage or other foul smelling things, and I'd almost mastered how to focus on one person or area. It was very handy for assessing human or non-human intentions. I could smell anger, sadness, jealousy, arousal, hatred...all kinds of emotions. Right now the overriding emotions in the ballroom were curiosity and excitement.

I could smell Venus. She smelled like jasmine mixed with a touch of vanilla. She was happy and nervous for me. It was comforting to know she was close by. Hard to admit, but I was scared. This was all so formal and unfamiliar it made my stomach churn. It felt like a movie, and I was the dumb heroine on the verge of an event that would change her life. Permanently. *Crap.*

Focus. You're a Vampyre and you have to do this. If I turned and ran, I'd probably be punished...by death. Fuck, life was so much easier when I was an art teacher who smoked. Just sniff people—get your mind off of dying. Thankfully I could smell Heathcliff. He was spicy with a hint of brown sugar. He was glad to see me again. I sensed anticipation and attraction from him. Heathcliff was so solid and kind. Not like that disgusting Ethan at all. Why couldn't ol' Heath be part of the Vampyre sandwich surrounding me? I wanted to look up and find him, but I didn't dare.

And then it hit me. There was a scent in the room that overwhelmed all the others. It made me angry and confused. I recognized it at once, as if I'd always known it. Ethan was in this room somewhere. I so needed to stay away from him. He smelled like Heaven. Clean laundry right off the line, summer breezes with hints of orange blossoms and sex. He also smelled dangerous. The scent was indescribable, but it was very masculine and very hot.

I assumed he was one of the Elite Guard with Heathcliff. He'd have to be, to know so much about the Warrior Pig's, *whoops, Prince's* sexual habits. He seemed to know way too much. What did he do? Watch? All of these Vampyres were perverts. Ethan was probably the biggest pervert of them all. No matter how good he smelled or how hot he was, he was a jerk. Next time I saw him, I'd tell him. With my luck, he and Heathcliff were best buds. That would suck.

My Vamp sandwich was guiding me to my knees. Nobody said anything about kneeling. Shit, it was seriously difficult to kneel in a super short dress and stilettos. I couldn't believe I had to kneel to the Warrior Idiot. I grabbed the elbows of my totally not-hilarious escorts and made them help me down.

These Vamps clearly worshiped their Pervert Prince. So did Venus. So did Heathcliff. Wait...something wasn't adding up.

Ethan had to be full of it. Just because he was a sexist asshole, didn't mean the Warrior Prince was too. Did it? He could have been lying to me about the whole sex with the Prince thing.

I had no idea why he would have done something so awful and stupid, but he must have. Maybe he got off on scaring the new Vamps. He was such a total asshole. I could only imagine what would happen if anyone knew what he had said about the Prince. He would be punished. Speaking blasphemously of the Prince was punishable by death. Not that I would tell—Ethan was far too pretty to die. Furthermore, I could hold it over his head for eternity. I grinned at the thought of having something on him. That would teach him not to screw with the heads of newbie Vampyres.

Venus loved and respected the Warrior Prince. I trusted Venus more than I trusted Ethan. My brain cells evaporated around Ethan. You couldn't trust someone who brought out your inner slut. Thousands of Vampyres couldn't be wrong. In such a violent society, the Prince would have to be extraordinary to have the loyal following that he did.

Speaking of violent, I felt the chilled handle of a jewel-encrusted knife being pressed into my hand. It was heavy, and I'm sure worth more than my house. This was the knife I would slice my hand with to prove my loyalty to the Warrior Prince. I wondered if I got to keep it. Gemma and The Kev would be so impressed. I would slice my palm as he sliced his, then we would join hands and mix our blood. Our lives would forever be intertwined. I would pledge to guard his life as I would my own. I really thought all of this would piss me off, but suddenly I felt excited and nervous and ready. God, what if I did something stupid? Please, please, please let me get through this without doing anything embarrassing. Let me make Venus and Heathcliff proud.

I sensed about six hundred Vampyres in the ballroom to honor their Prince. He had to be amazing. He couldn't be the sexual predator that Ethan made him out to be. If anyone was a sexual predator, it was Ethan, although I'd bet most of his victims were more than willing. God knew I was. When I met up with that bastard again, I'd just nod politely and ignore him. I was safe as long as I wasn't alone with him. If he got me alone I'd knee him in the balls and run like hell.

Mr. Humorless on my right began speaking. I kept my head bowed.

"My Liege," he said, "I present to you Astrid of the Cressida House in the Haven of Kentucky. We ask His Excellency to accept this humble servant into the North

American Dominion. She would be honored to co-mingle her blood with yours and to pledge her loyalty to you and the Royal Family. If it is your desire to bestow the gift of citizenship upon Astrid, please call to her. She has come to serve."

Mr. Stick-in-the-mud paused. This was C-R-A-Z-Y, crazy. I'd come to serve? Humble servant? What in the hell was wrong with Vampyres? My babysitters were pulling me to my feet, and as told, I kept my head down. I wanted to giggle. This was too damned serious. I felt like I was in church with all the kneeling and standing and bowing of heads.

"Astrid of the Cressida House," said a male voice. A familiar male voice. A very familiar male voice. No way...No, no, no. What the fu...? I wanted to stamp my feet and scream. This could not be happening.

Instead of turning around and running out of the room, or finding a silver stake and ramming it through my chest, I raised my head. Slowly. Praying that I was wrong about what I knew I wasn't wrong about.

"Do you swear your loyalty to me? Will you be my humble servant and...serve me?" The voice was amused, his words laced with double entendre.

I felt my eyes go green with fury when they met the breathtaking gold of his. He smiled that sexy smile, and before I could stop myself I embarrassed my entire House and possibly the whole North American Dominion. Not to mention I put my life in incredible danger.

I called him an asshole. To be more precise, I used the F-word, with an 'ing' before the asshole part. That was when my three escorts tackled me.

***

"Get off of her," Ethan, The Warrior Prince of the North American Dominion roared.

"My Liege," I heard a woman speaking urgently to him, "she has no right to desecrate you in that way. She will be dealt with and punished accordingly. I will deal with her myself."

What in the hell did that even mean?

"She had every right," Ethan said, dismissing her with his tone and a wave of his hand. He addressed the pile on top of me. "Remove yourselves from her at once and bring her to me."

The chaos and snapping fangs were surreal. I had no clue what was happening. Were they going to kill me? I was terrified, pissed, and in severe pain. The burning in my thigh was due to the dagger sticking out of it. The beautiful blade that I was set to slice my hand with was embedded deep in my thigh. A small side effect of being tackled by a gaggle of Vampyres, and it hurt like a bitch. Furthermore, they completely ruined my Prada dress. Knife in thigh? Fine. Lying asshole Prince? Whatever. Torn Prada? Unforgivable. Unfortunately, I did what was becoming very natural for me. I let it all hang out. Pam would kick my ass later, but her right hook was the least of my worries at the moment.

I lifted my hands and let the glitter fly. I'd freeze every last one of their undead asses and make a run for it. This was not one of my better plans. Damn it, if they hadn't screwed with my dress none of this would have happened. It would take more Magic than I had to immobilize that many Vamps. There were six hundred of them. I only froze the Vampyres within twenty feet of me. Bizarrely, they didn't just freeze. They were definitely frozen, but they were also dangling helplessly in the air. I wasn't quite sure how I did that, but it worked. Of course the dangling Vampyres discouraged any others from getting too close. I suppressed a totally inappropriate giggle at the sight of fifty or so Vampyres floating in the air like helium balloons.

"Angel," Ethan said to me, "let them down. They will not hurt you."

"They already did," I shot back, referring to my bloody mangled thigh that was healing as I spoke. "And why in the world should I believe anything you say? Oh, and by the way, my name is not Angel," I yelled at him.

"Look at me," he said.

I refused.

"Look at me," he repeated.

I refused again.

"Please...look at me, Angel,"

I did. My first mistake.

"I will not let them hurt you. I will not let anyone hurt you ever again."

There was a collective gasp throughout the ballroom. Ethan's golden eyes bored into mine with such an intensity that I felt a little drunk.

"I want proof," I told him. He was too good at this and I had too much to lose. Like my life.

"Let me come to you and I will give you proof," he said. His eyes never left mine for a moment.

I sensed hatred being shot at me from somewhere to his left. Scanning the group surrounding him, I found her. If looks could kill I would be so dead right now. Five bucks says she was the one who wanted to deal with me and punish me. Yikes. She had to be the girlfriend, and she was beautiful. Not only was she beautiful, she was the female version of Heathcliff. Please don't tell me the pathetic loser that had been schtupping Ethan for a hundred years was Cathy. This did not bode well for so many of my future plans. She was furious and, quite honestly, looked a little unstable.

"Ethan," she said to him, "I don't think..."

"Let me come to you," he repeated, cutting her off and ignoring her. She stepped back, humiliated.

"Yes," I told him, "but only you."

"It will only ever be me, Angel," he said, striding towards me. Again with the collective gasps. What in the hell was he talking about *only me*? He was crazy. Why did I trust him? Why? Why? Why? Because I was an idiot, that's why.

He was so close I could touch him, but I wouldn't give him that satisfaction. His eyes flashed with disappointment and I turned away before I changed my mind and jumped him or punched him.

"Let them down, Angel," he said gently.

"You said you had proof," I told him, refusing to look at him or to back down.

"Are you absolutely sure that you want proof?" he asked.

"Yes," I said, slowly glancing up.

"One hundred percent sure?" he asked, smiling wickedly.

"I think so." Mistake number two.

"Very well then," he said, turning to address all the Vampyres in the ballroom. "Astrid of the Cressida House, known as Angel only to me," he paused, letting that one sink in, "will become a member of my Elite Security Force. As you can plainly see, she is gifted and has the ability to protect me in...creative ways." With a smirk, he indicated the fifty of his warriors floating in the air around him.

The silence in the room was palpable, and he continued. "I also believe that she is the Chosen One. The one from our Prophecies. The One we have waited for."

Again with the collective gasps, but this time I joined in. What on earth was he talking about? Chosen what?

"That's not possible, Your Highness," Cathy quickly retorted. "She must be one with the Angels and Fairies. She must be able to control Demons."

Ethan, with his back to her, quietly demanded, "Do you have knowledge that she cannot do these things?"

"No, my Liege, I do not." She wasn't backing down.

"Then I would suggest you keep your opinions to yourself." He was very polite, but there were daggers sticking out of every word. Good God, remind me never to get on his bad side. He was very still—he looked inhuman, like a beautiful furious statue.

"Yes, my Liege." She backed way down.

Before my eyes, he went from deadly Vampyre Prince back to sexy, lying piece of shit. Scary Vampyre Leader Guy was gone. He was Ethan again.

"Was that the proof?" I asked.

"No," he replied.

"What's the proof?" I asked, getting exasperated with him. He grinned and my tummy flipped.

"This is."

It happened so fast. I couldn't have stopped him if I tried, and sadly, I didn't try. In an instant his fangs elongated and he yanked me to him. There was a searing pain in my neck as he bit me. My skin ripped like paper and the sound that left my lips was inhuman.

I was falling through the rabbit hole like Alice in Wonderland. He wanted to kill me, and this time he would succeed. I was so stupid. His arms were like steel vises holding me immobile against his body. Why did I let him come near me? He'd been nothing but bad since the moment I met him. I screamed again. Every nerve ending in my body was pushed to its limit. Everything was getting dark and a loud ringing pierced my ears. Why wouldn't Venus or Heathcliff save me? I thought Venus was my friend. I would save her. From above myself, I heard the sobs rip from my chest. I struggled against him to stop the burning exploding through my body, but he was too strong for me and the blood loss was blocking my Magic. From the sounds he was making, he was getting some perverse sexual satisfaction from killing me. I hated him.

What a horrible way to die...at least I had good underwear on. Wait, something is not...oh, no. The pain slowly subsided and turned into something else, something far worse. He still drank from me. I knew this was significant, but for the life of me, I couldn't remember why.

The pain was replaced by a heat that started low in my abdomen and slowly wound its way through me. Strong hands were roaming all over my body touching me everywhere, and I mean everywhere. Stroking, teasing, pinching, squeezing, probing...Oh. My. God. He wasn't trying to kill me, but it would have been better if he had. It was hazy as to exactly when my screams turned into moans, but they did. Oh God, if he didn't stop soon, my moans would turn back into screams. That would be bad. Crazy, embarrassing bad.

I was sure Cathy wailed *"No!"* at some point, and through

my blurry vision I thought I saw Heathcliff hold her back. He looked so sad and disappointed. I couldn't understand why. I couldn't understand anything. And then I exploded.

Ethan pulled his fangs out of my neck right after I had the best orgasm of my life in front of a ballroom filled with hundreds of Vampyres. Hatred didn't even begin to cover what I felt for him. He bit into his own tongue, leaned into my neck and licked the puncture wounds he'd made, officially co-mingling our blood. I was weak, pissed, dizzy and bizarrely satiated, like I'd just had great sex for three hours.

As much as I hated him, I had to admit that was one fantastic...no, wait. Oh shit, no...what just happened? Was I halfway mated to him? If he wasn't already dead, I would kill him.

"What in the hell did you do?" I yelled.

"What I was meant to do," he informed me smugly. "What I wanted to do from the moment I laid eyes on you." He leaned in and continued his crazy talk at a whisper, "I did what I've never even been tempted to do to anyone else in my entire five hundred and twenty-two years."

I stared at him, my mouth agape. I wanted to slap him. Then he mouthed something to me. I wasn't positive, but it looked like *You're mine*. He was grinning from ear to ear, speaking in full voice again, "You wanted proof? You have it. No one will ever harm my intended mate. It is punishable by death."

The ballroom exploded into applause. I assumed they were clapping for the Prince. For the Prince's joy at being halfway mated to the crazy Vampyre girl with powers that could suspend them midair if she didn't like what they had to say. That was flat out strange. If bloodsucking and orgasms equated to engagement announcements, this Vamp world was more screwed than I thought. My chest was tight and I wanted to run. I had to get away from all of these insane dead people. Especially Ethan. I looked around and tried to find Venus amidst all the jumping, cheering, whistling Vampyres, but it was impossible.

I did spot two people who had not joined in on the celebration...Heathcliff and Cathy. She was staring at the floor and he stood stiffly beside her. I caught his eye and held his gaze for a moment. He looked away. I barely knew him but I felt as if I'd betrayed him. When did my life get so fucking complicated?

I wasn't sure if it was the blood loss or the fact that I was halfway mated to someone that had tried to kill me, lied to me and gave me an orgasm in front of six hundred Vampyres, but I was fading fast.

But a promise was a promise. Right before I blacked out, I stretched my fingers out to the floating, applauding Vampyres and released them. I vaguely remember hearing thuds and groans as everything went black.

Chapter 15

Oh my God, it was so soft. I moaned and sank farther down into my bed. My bed had never been so cozy. I stretched and snuggled deeper under the covers. When did I buy such amazing sheets? How in the hell did I afford them? I didn't remember owning such soft, gorgeous sheets. They had to be at least a thousand thread count. Shit...I didn't own soft, gorgeous, thousand thread count sheets or a bed this huge...which meant this wasn't my bed. I was in someone else's bed...naked. *What the fu...?*

Think, think. Where was I? I was at the Cressida House to get initiated and then I got drunk and went home with some random Vampyre. No, that wasn't even possible. Number one, I didn't drink. Number two, Vampyres couldn't get drunk because they only drank blood. Alright, that scenario was out... I remembered Heathcliff. Sweet, handsome Heathcliff and then...what happened after that? It was on the tip of my brain. I saw Ethan, and then...oh shit.

It all came flooding back to me in a hurricane of mortification. Dangling Vampyres, screaming orgasm, pissed off girlfriend, gaping hole in thigh, ruined Prada dress, halfway mated to an extraordinarily beautiful, crazy, scary, lying bastard Warrior Prince.

Maybe if I closed my eyes it would all go away.

I tried.

It didn't.

Son of a bitch, how many things could go wrong for me in two months? I died *and* I'm engaged? All this because I quit smoking? Really? Movement on the ceiling caught my eye. To

105

my great joy, there were monsters up there. Not my monsters, other little ugly babies. I waved. Maybe they could help me escape.

"Hi," I whispered, just in case anyone was around. "I'm Astrid. Some of you live at my house."

They stopped dancing and stared at me, shocked and pleased to be noticed. They began to wave and shriek and show off. I giggled and threw some Glitter Magic to them. They ate it and went bonkers.

These guys were bold. They were trying to jump off the ceiling and come down to me. I was sure that was a very bad idea. The Vamps already thought I was a freak. I didn't want them to know I was a monster magnet.

"No, no." I pointed at three of them who were ready to go. "You stay." Thankfully they did. Amazing. Something that actually listened to me.

The little monsters were so special. I was delighted that they lived on ceilings everywhere. I debated getting out of the bed and dancing with them, but decided against it. No telling who would walk in, plus I was naked and I wasn't sure where I was. As their dancing hit psychotic levels, I realized they were not a good escape plan. I was assuming I was still at the Cressida House. Hopefully in Venus' room...although this looked a little opulent for a regular Vampyre.

The bed was a huge, hand-carved, four poster work of art. The wood was dark and rich. The bedding was covered in olive and cream brocades with thick down comforters in dark navy. Everything was insanely soft and expensive. There must have been twenty pillows on the bed. Definitely not Venus' room.

I sat up and really looked around. The rest of the suite followed suit. There were thick Persian rugs, and dark wood furniture mixed with chocolate leather chairs and couches. A huge stone fireplace dominated one wall. The curtains on the floor to ceiling windows looked like they belonged in a French Renaissance castle, but the *pièce de résistance* was the chandelier. It was stunning—tier upon tier of the most exquisite crystal drops I'd ever seen. I loved anything that sparkled, and this put everything I'd ever admired to shame.

The more I thought about it, the more I was convinced this was his room. How did I get here? I could only guess. Why was I naked? I didn't want to know. Did I need to get out of here? You bet.

"Hey guys," I questioned my new monster buddies, "do you know where my clothes are?"

"Over there," a female answered.

"Oh my God." I was flabbergasted. "You guys can talk?" They were far more advanced than my monsters. They were flipping, punching each other in the head, running in circles and screaming. Well, a little more advanced. There was so much commotion I couldn't figure out which little cutie had spoken.

"You need to stay still," I told them. "Whichever one of you little dudes spoke to me needs to do it again." Maybe they could help me escape, but more importantly, I bet they could tell me how to teach Rachel and Ross and Honest Abe to talk. Beyonce was another story. She had issues.

"Come on, please," I begged. "When did you learn to talk? Did someone teach you?" If they would tell me their secret, I could talk *with* my babies instead of *at* them.

"Let me see...it was about two hundred years ago and my mother taught me," Venus said, staring at me from the doorway.

"Shit!" I screamed. "You scared me to death."

The monsters shrieked and disappeared.

"That's impossible," she replied coldly, "you're already dead." Her arms were crossed over her chest and she wasn't liking me much.

"Who were you speaking to?" she asked.

"Um...nobody?"

She was silent. She slowly walked into the room, grabbed clothing off of a chair and threw it on the bed.

"Friends don't lie to friends," she stated flatly.

"Friends didn't lie to friends," I said, and she snorted. "Certain friends were really scared and freaked out, so they didn't lie...they omitted. Certain friends had other friends from different species that arrived before friends who are accusing friends of lying. Those other friends told her not to tell certain things." I was confusing myself.

"There is no reason in hell I should have followed that, but somehow I did." Venus said, walking toward the bed. "Were you just talking to those certain friends?"

"No." God, how to explain this..."Actually, the certain friends who told me not to tell certain things don't know about the friends I was just talking to."

"Jesus Christ, Astrid," Venus grabbed her head. "I can't keep up with you. To tell you the truth, I'm not sure I want to." She turned to go.

"Wait!" I was desperate. I was losing my mind. My hands shook and I wasn't sure if I wanted to cry or scream or punch something. Everything was spinning so far out of control I didn't know how much longer I could hold on. As panic threatened to overtake me something warm and sweet rushed through me, straight out of my fingertips. Something in me clicked. It was Pam. The panic was gone. I felt Pam's love envelope me. I couldn't see her, but I could feel her spirit inside of me. She was letting me know I could talk to Venus and it would be okay.

"Please stay with me," I begged.

Venus slowed and turned back to me, shaking her head, "Astrid, I..."

"Please." I could feel the tears coming.

"All right," Venus said slowly. She walked back to the bed, sat on the edge and waited.

"Venus, I need your word that I can trust you."

She moved to the bedside table and retrieved a dagger. The same jeweled dagger I stabbed my thigh with. Why in the hell was that in here? She sliced her palm and handed me the knife, I sliced my own. Shit, that hurt. Venus didn't even flinch. I wish I could say the same. She grasped my hand and our blood co-mingled.

"What you tell me, I will guard as if it were my own," Venus told me, "and you will do the same."

I nodded and patted the bed. "You'd better sit."

She did.

I started at the beginning. I told her how I got changed by the big blonde Amazon without my knowledge or consent. I described how I came home and found Oprah, who turned out to be my foul-mouthed, nosey, fiercely loyal Angel named Pam. How from there I was graced with my style-challenged Fairy, who was a doppelganger for Arnold Schwarzenegger. How he had taught me in a very short and very violent time how to fight to the death and how to control my Magic.

Then I explained my monsters. They started out as cracks in my bedroom ceiling, but the longer I stared, the more alive they became. My monsters were so ugly they were cute. They were about three inches tall and looked like tiny people. I suppose I thought of them as my babies. The babies I would never have now that I was a Vampyre. I loved them.

"I was afraid if I told someone about them, they'd go away," I admitted. "I've lost so much already. I couldn't bear losing them too."

"Is that who you were talking to?" Venus asked, trying to wrap her head around my crazy story. I was just thankful she didn't run from the room screaming.

"Yes and no," I explained, "they were similar monsters, but they weren't mine. Turns out they live on ceilings everywhere," I smiled ruefully. I was still nervous she was going to bail on the insane Vampyre girl.

"Can I see them?" she asked.

"I don't know." I looked up. The monsters were back. "I don't know," I repeated. "Can you?"

Venus looked up and stared at the ceiling. Hard. "No, I can't."

I glanced up and wondered why in the hell I could see them. They giggled and waved and stomped on each other's heads. I realized I didn't care why. I was grateful I could.

"That's okay," I consoled her, "you're strong and don't need them."

"No," she replied, examining me strangely, "you don't need them either. They need you." She took a huge pause and continued searching my face. "You *are* the Chosen One," she whispered, dropping to her knees next to the bed.

"Get up, you're freaking me out," I blurted, yanking on her arm.

"Astrid." Venus was excited. She grabbed me and hugged me hard. "You are. You are the Chosen One."

"No," I gasped, trying to peel her off of me, "I'm not. I don't want to be the Chosen One. I'm still not a hundred percent sure I want to be a Vampyre. I am a materialistic Prada whore who teaches art to old people. There's no way I can be the Chosen One." I paused. "What in the hell is the 'Chosen One'?"

Venus' excitement freaked me out. "The Chosen One is beloved by Angels and Fairies and can control Demons."

"I don't know any Demons," I yelled at her, "except for Ethan."

"Don't you see?" she went on, ignoring my slam on her Prince, "Angels and Fairies don't ever even acknowledge Vampyres. Our breeds only come together in times of war...and hopefully then it's as allies, because Angels and Fairies are the fiercest warriors in the Universe."

I was still confused.

"Angels and Fairies are from the Light, from life," Venus explained, "and Vampyres are from the Dark, from death." She touched my face. "You are the Light who lives in the Dark. You will save us."

"Holy shit." I threw myself back on the bed. "I thought I was crazy. Did you not get the part that I don't know, and therefore cannot control, any Demons?" I had her there.

"Your monsters are Demons," she simply stated.

Oh fuck.

"I don't want to deal with this right now," I told her, overwhelmed. "You can't tell anyone about this, Venus."

"I won't," she promised. "Eventually you will have to tell

the Prince."

"He's already figured most of it out," I said morosely and filled her in on the glitter-filled disappearing act in the graveyard. "The only part that would be missing for him would be the Demons."

I realized I'd forgotten to ask the most important question of all. "How in the hell am I supposed to save everybody?"

"The Prophecy doesn't say, but I do know it involves our King somehow," Venus replied.

Well, that just pissed me off and made me want to cry. "Heathcliff told me the King will be in the North American Dominion within the month. Does that mean I have to save everybody this month, as opposed to next month?" I tried for a lame joke. Venus didn't bite. I didn't blame her. It sucked.

Ignoring my rapidly deteriorating sense of humor, she went on, "I hate to broach another touchy subject," Venus was treading carefully, "but would you like to discuss The Warrior Prince?" She tried to suppress a grin. She failed.

I was gonna kick her ass.

"No," I shouted. "I do not want to discuss him. Ever."

"You're halfway mated to the most powerful ruler of all the King's children. Not to mention the fact that he seems to have gone cuckoo crazy over you. In all my two hundred years as a Vampyre, I've never seen him like this. No one has. You will have to deal with this sooner rather than later," Venus informed me.

"He's a liar and a cheater and he tried to kill me. I. Hate. Him. I find him unattractive and rude. He's an asshole and a bastard..." I trailed off.

Venus just stared at me.

"All right, fine." I gave up. "Yes, I'm attracted to him, but he didn't ask me to mate with him—he just did it. I hate that. I don't even know him. I can't get mated or married or whatever to a stranger, no matter how hot he is or how good he smells."

"Vampyres often recognize their life mates the first moment they see them or scent them," Venus said with authority. "They are fated for each other. They have an uncontrollable mental and sexual bond. I'm fairly sure Ethan recognized you."

"No, he didn't," I shot back at her. "The first time he saw me, he and his sisters tried to kill me."

"But he didn't," Venus fired right back, "and he stopped his sisters from killing you."

"Yeah...so?"

"Nothing." Venus was smug. "I'm just sayin'...that's all."

"You are aware that you suck, and all of you people are

perverts?" I informed her, wanting to slap that superior look off her face.

"Yes...yes I am," she smiled. "By the way, you're one of *those people* now."

I rolled my eyes. "Anyway, I can't be his mate because I think I have a connection to Heathcliff too. At least he's a gentleman."

"Ooo," Venus scrunched her nose. "That could be awkward."

"No duh."

"He has a sister..." Venus started. I cut her off.

"Yes, that would be Cathy. The Cathy that has been schtupping Ethan for a hundred years," I said. "Yep, I put that all together when I noticed a female Heathcliff trying to kill me with her eyeballs." I paused and sighed. "I suppose Heathcliff is out of the picture for me. I never get the nice guy."

Venus rolled her eyes at me. "The other one ain't so bad."

"Why do I have to be with anyone at all?" I whined. "Can't I just save the world and then go on about my business?"

"No," Venus the Party Pooper said. "You are now part of the Elite Guard. Your life is not your own anymore."

"What?" I shouted. Venus cut me off.

"No," she firmly announced, "you cannot get out of it. As a member of the Cressida House, we are here to protect the Royal Family. Period."

"I can't," I stammered, "I teach art to old people and I...you know have, um, stuff..."

Venus laughed and punched me in the arm. Damn, she punches hard. I punched her back harder and remembered I was naked.

"Do you have any idea why I'm naked?" I asked her.

"Nope."

"Do you know how I got here?"

"Yep."

"Did he bring me here?" I shut my eyes. If I couldn't see anything, I could pretend nothing happened.

"Yep."

"Do you think he...?" I mumbled.

"No way," Venus said. "I know you think he's an ass, but he has more honor than any Vampyre I've ever met."

"That doesn't say much for Vampyres," I laughed.

"I'm not saying he didn't look," she grinned, "but I would bet my life he didn't touch."

"You have way more faith in him than I do," I told her. "Why don't you mate with him?"

"Oh, he's pretty and all, but he's more like a father to me. Besides, I like the *brothers*."

I started laughing. "Oh my God, you're racist?" I threw a pillow at her.

"No, I'm not," she giggled, "a girl likes what a girl likes!" She threw the pillow back at me. "I like the same kind of man my mama liked!"

I froze. Petra...it was Friday. I had to go to her.

"Venus," I choked out in a panic, "I have to get out of here."

"You can't," she said, "Ethan will have a fit."

"I don't give a damn what he'll do. It's Friday...my mother..." I couldn't continue.

"What?" Venus asked.

"My mother, Petra is supposed to die today." Venus looked at me askance. "I know, I know, I'm not sure if I believe her, but I need to go to her. I need to offer to change her. I need to save her if she'll let me."

"You can't," Venus sympathized. "You'll kill her."

"Pam said the same thing. Why?"

"Once a woman has borne a child," Venus explained, "she will not make it through the change."

"Is that one hundred percent for sure?" I asked, looking for a loophole.

"I don't know, but I wouldn't try to change her if I were you," she replied.

"You're not me."

"True, although there is an old wives' tale about sacrificing Royalty, or maybe it was an animal, in order to attain immortality. I can't remember how it goes, but only Vampyres would know that tale and we don't need it—we're already immortal."

"Oookay, that's just weird on every level," I said flatly. "If there's even a remote chance to save her, I have to try."

Why did I feel so compelled to save her? Was it simply because she was my mother? No, it was far more complicated than that. I was that pathetic idiot that was still after her love and approval. At least I wasn't in denial. "Venus..."

"No," she said.

"Please cover for me," I begged.

"Are you trying to get me killed?" she gasped. "There's no way to sneak you out of here. There are guards everywhere, especially on this floor." Venus shook her head vehemently. "Even if we did get you out of the house, there are security guards all over the property."

"I don't need to leave this room to leave the compound," I

told her calmly. She was a nervous wreck. "I just can't have you ringing the alarm bells when I leave."

"Astrid, you're killing me," she said, dropping her head into her hands.

"Venus, why don't you go find someone for me to eat," I told her. "Please take your time. I'm extremely picky about my meals, especially considering I've never had mortal blood before."

"You've never..." She was shocked.

"Shut up," I cut her off. "It is what it is. It will probably take you about an hour to find someone appropriate. Do you understand me?" I asked her, making sure she understood. She nodded unhappily. "Do you think anyone else will be checking on me?" I began to dress quickly.

"No." Venus paced the room and wouldn't make eye contact. God, I hoped she would keep my secret. "He's on an investigation with some of the Guards. There's been more Rogue activity."

"All right then, you should go." I squeezed her hand.

"Please be careful, Astrid," she said. "He will be destroyed if anything happens to you."

Her statement surprised and secretly delighted me. I looked at her for a long moment...then I disappeared.

Chapter 16

I felt like a burglar. I didn't want to be here. I wasn't wanted or welcome, but here I was. Again. Begging to be slapped down for loving someone who didn't love me back. I was pathetic, but I wouldn't live with regrets. No one can say I didn't try. I may suffer severe wounds to my ego and heart, but being a Vampyre had its advantages. I had thousands of years ahead of me to do therapy.

"Petra? Mother?" I called out.

Nothing.

Surprised and relieved that I wasn't exhausted from teleporting, I stood and waited. Pam was right, I was getting stronger. I didn't know if that was a good thing or a bad thing. I just knew I was grateful for it right now.

I smoothed down the crisp, cotton, fitted white halter over the black raw silk capris and admired my insane platform wedges. All Prada. Every thread, button, snap and zipper on me was Prada! The material felt like heaven on my skin. Being a Vampyre made my body and senses hypersensitive. I was in love with whoever chose this outfit for me. It had to be Venus, or maybe it was...no, there's no way he would know I would love all this. What in the hell was Venus going on about *knowing your life mate*? I thought back to the first time I met him. I knew I was attracted to him, but was that it? Did the fact that I couldn't take my eyes off of his ass mean he was my mate? Could you base an entire relationship on being obsessed with an ass? I didn't even know him...and he didn't know me.

I couldn't think about that right now, mostly because my mind went immediately to an X-rated place when I thought about him. A naked, sweaty, scream-filled, bloodsucking, orgasmic place. I needed to dial down my inner slut.

"Astrid, what are you doing here?" my mother asked me.

"Shit," I yelped. My mother was better than a cold shower for getting rid of my loose morality concerns. "You almost scared me to death."

"Is that really possible, dear?" she asked calmly, staring me down.

She certainly looked spectacular for someone that was going to die from cancer today. So pulled together in her Tory Burch flats and her sweet little Armani shift.

Hair? Perfect.

Nails? Perfect.

Makeup? Perfect.

Beautiful, and as cold as ice.

"How's the cancer going, Petra?" I asked her, trying to goad her into some sort of emotion. I didn't care what. Just something.

"Cancer's a bitch, dear," she replied. "Terrible way to die."

"Mom, what's going on?" I snapped. "Are you really sick?"

"Do you really care?" she murmured. Damn, she was evil.

"Unfortunately, I really do." I felt the tears welling.

She totally ignored my need for comfort and put more distance between us. God, did she not have one maternal bone in her body? She fussed with pillows and brushed imaginary lint from the couch. Then she heaved a huge put-upon sigh. "Look, Astrid, I thought I made myself very clear the other day. I have no desire to bond with you or make up for any of the wrongs you perceive me to have committed. You didn't turn out at all like I expected. I have a very hard time believing you're the one. You're just so pathetic and weak. To put it mildly, you're a grave disappointment." She laughed at her double entendre.

I wanted to crawl out of my skin. My mind was so crowded with hatred and regret and shame, I couldn't even follow what she meant. Did she think I was the Chosen One too? How would she even know about that? I wanted to run away from her. I wanted to hit her and hurt her like she hurt me. I wanted to destroy her. I wanted her to hold me. Most of all, I wanted to destroy myself for still caring about her, although I was fairly sure if I hung around much longer she'd successfully do that for me.

I swallowed every bit of pride I had left. "I came to offer you immortality...if you want it."

She said nothing.

"I know you know what I am," I continued talking. I was sure if I stopped the world would end. "If you'd like me to change you, I will." With little left to say, I stopped and waited for Armageddon.

She glared at me with hatred. *What the fu...? Would I ever win with her?*

"You can't change me, you stupid girl. I wouldn't trust you with my life. You would kill me permanently," she spat.

The ceiling hissed and moved. We both looked up. Could she see that? Did she know about monsters? Did she have her own?

Her ceiling was covered in monsters. They weren't small and silly like my monsters. They were big, angry and evil. They undulated in and out of each other, like a macabre orgy. I wondered what a blast of my Glitter Magic would do to them and decided it was best not to find out. They were scarred and bleeding. It was difficult to look at them. Some had pus and sickening liquid leaking from their wounds. It dripped down from the ceiling, coating the furniture and floor. Most had horns protruding from their heads and they all had claws. Some were missing limbs and several seemed to be functioning without heads.

The ones that were not wounded were taking great pleasure embedding and twisting their claws into the wounds of the less fortunate. They had razor sharp teeth with bits of what appeared to be bloody flesh hanging from them. I may be gross for drinking blood, but I was small potatoes in the repulsive department compared to these guys. Movies couldn't come close to these atrocities. They examined Petra with a patient hatred while they evaluated me with a hungry curiosity.

"Um...Petra, can you see that?" I asked her, keeping my body very still as not to startle them.

"Of course I can," she snapped. "They're mine."

"Oookay." I glanced over at her. "They don't seem to like you much."

They hissed viciously at her right on cue. She looked bored. Who was she? Better yet, what was she? She couldn't be human and be able to see all this. Could she?

One of them yelled at her in a language I couldn't even begin to identify. Petra stiffened and watched the bloody monster with narrowed eyes. Her glare didn't affect him at all. She hissed at him and he continued to scream at her.

As he screamed he slowly took on human features. His tirade was turning him human. Kind of. A gross, bloody human with razor sharp teeth and huge claws. His horns came along for the ride too. He was massive and disgusting. Next thing I knew, the thing was standing next to my mother.

He stood about six feet, six inches tall, and his burnt, bloody body bulged with muscles. He watched me closely.

"Astrid," my mother smiled evilly, her eyes narrowed to slits as she clapped her hands like a happy child, "Meet your father."

Holy shit, was she serious? "My father is a monster?" I gasped.

"A Demon, you imbecile," she snarled, "not a monster. There's no such thing as monsters."

That was debatable, I thought as I looked at the woman who gave birth to me. My father stood next to her, wheezed some kind of internal goop and stared at me. Beneath all the blood and oozing sores he was kind of...well, maybe a little...sort of...

Nope. Who in the hell was I kidding? He was horrible. Hideously butt-ass ugly and he smelled like hell. Literally. He smelled of sulfur, burnt hair and charred flesh.

He bared his teeth. Dear God, was he trying to smile at me...or was he getting ready to eat me? I knew Vamps were immortal and all, but I was almost sure even I, the Chosen One, couldn't survive being eaten by a Demon. I really didn't want to die today. I had too many things left I wanted to do.

Number one on the list was to wrap my legs around Ethan and screw him until neither of us could walk. *What the fu...? Where did that come from? Why was he in my head right now? He needs to get out.* I quickly shoved him to the back of my mind and watched my bloody daddy closely. Any sudden moves and I was so out of here.

Petra leaned into him and stroked his oozing face with her perfectly manicured hands. Something wasn't quite right about that. As long as I'd known her, she hated anything dirty or messy. Just goes to show you how love can change a cold, heartless bitch. She actually cared for someone. God, that tore me apart in unexplainable ways.

He slapped her hand away and grunted violently at her.

"Can he speak English?" I asked her.

She laughed at me, "He speaks everything, you little pathetic piece of..." Before she could finish her loving description of me, he slapped her so hard he knocked her out and her body flew across the room. She looked like a broken doll lying on the floor beneath the window. I moved to go to her, but my, um...father put up his hand.

"No," he ordered. His voice was ragged. It sounded painful, like he was speaking through shards of glass. "She's done enough damage this time around." He watched me back up towards the door. "Stop," he commanded. "I want to touch you. Come to me."

Bizarrely enough, I didn't think he was going to eat me or hit me. I could tell he really did just want to touch me. I looked into his eyes, which were gold like mine. They were the only human-looking thing about him. I walked to him. If I concentrated on his eyes, I could almost pretend he wasn't the most frightening and disgusting thing I'd ever seen.

I stood in front of him. Inside I was a trembling mess. Outwardly I was calm.

"Are you afraid of me?" he ground out, his razor sharp teeth clicking grotesquely as he spoke.

"Yes, I am," I told him truthfully. "Are you really my father?" I had to know.

He examined me closely. His breath was putrid and it was all I could do to stand my ground. He slowly raised his hand. I could tell he was trying not to scare me. It was a little late for that. He reached out with his bloody hand, touched my face and replied, "Yes."

He backed away from me and went to my mother, picked up her crumpled body and gently laid her on the couch.

"What is she?" I asked him.

He paused and considered my question. "She's a bitch. A horrible, horrible bitch." He looked down at her and laughed. "But she's my bitch."

With that, he clapped his hands and the Demons slithered off the ceiling and moved toward Petra. He yelled something in an unfamiliar language. I didn't need to understand the language to know what he said. Licking their bloody lips, they surrounded her and they ate her.

The screams of joy were something I would never forget. Thankfully their grotesque bloody bodies covered the gruesome brutality of what they were doing.

I gagged and fell to the ground. I closed my eyes and put my hands over my ears. I wasn't about to wait around to see if I was next. Without saying bye to Daddy, I transported the hell out of there and went home.

Chapter 17

I didn't stop, I didn't pass Go...I teleported, and then I ran.

I ran straight into Pam's waiting arms and I broke. A dam burst inside of me and rushed from my damaged spirit with a vengeance. I pulled away from Pam's embrace. I had to move. I couldn't stay still. My head was a mess and my insides felt raw. I paced frantically. My fists opened and closed at an alarming speed. I wanted to jump or run—instead I fell to the floor and beat on it.

And I cried. I cried for myself. I cried for my mother, who I hated and loved with such a confused passion it was painful. I cried because her death was so horrific and because part of me didn't care. I cried for my Nana, who I missed more and more each passing day. I thought time and distance dulled pain. They didn't.

I cried for Venus because she used to be a slave, and for Paris Hilton because she was such a freak. It pained me to think about other people being as judgmental as I had been. I cried for Cathy, because she loved someone who didn't love her. I knew about that. I cried about Heathcliff. After everything that had happened, I didn't know if I would ever get a chance to know him and he seemed like such a kind and beautiful person.

I cried for my monsters and worried they would become like my mother's Demons. It killed me that I would never have children because I wanted someone to love so badly. I wanted to be a real mother to someone. I would have been so good at that. I cried because the father I'd imagined in my dreams was so much better than the monstrosity that had sired me.

I cried because Rogue Vampyres were killing innocent

people and because I used to be innocent. Maybe that was my path, I thought wildly. Kill the Rogues. I didn't even care if I died in the process.

I cried for Pam because I loved her so much. I knew there was much more to her story than she let on.

And I cried because I was worried I would outlive Gemma, and I didn't want to. I cried because The Kev was so sweet and his love for Gemma was so beautiful.

My blood-laced tears ruined my pretty white halter. My track record with Prada was not so good lately. First the dress, now the halter. That made me cry too.

My tear ducts had almost run dry, but there were still enough bloody tears to cry in confusion. I wanted Ethan. Now. I wanted him to hold me and comfort me. I wanted to lay my head on his chest and wrap my arms around his body. I wanted him to whisper to me and I wanted to fall asleep in his arms while he played with my hair. I could not begin to understand why I wanted or needed a man I barely knew, but I did. With every fiber of my being, I did. Maybe he was mine...and I was his. Was Venus right?

Oh. My. God. In my jumbled mess of a brain, a horrible reality occurred to me. She wasn't right...she wasn't even close to right. That bastard didn't want me. Ethan didn't want me for me. That son of a bitch wanted *the Chosen One*. He'd waited five hundred twenty-two years - not for me, but for the Chosen One.

Please God, just kill me now. How much more did I have to take? Petra was right about one thing...men were bad. I knew my heart was breaking. The unconditional love I wanted would never be mine. Not from my mother, not from a child and not from Ethan. Why did Ethan's betrayal hurt more than the others? Nothing made sense anymore. I fell back to the floor and the flood gates reopened for business.

***

"Astrid, are you okay?" Gemma rubbed my back and pulled my head to her lap.

"How long have I been here?" I asked, dazed.

"Um...about six hours," she said, smoothing my hair away from my face and kissing my forehead. "You sobbed and moaned for about five hours, and you've been sitting here comatose for the last forty-five minutes or so." She paused. "Pam told me what happened."

"How does she know?" I asked, sitting up.

"She had a vision," Gem replied quietly.

Well, now I knew why she was waiting for me. "Did she see my daddy?" I asked Gemma, wincing at the memory of him.

"Yes, Asscrack, I did. Damn, he's one ugly motherfuckin' Demon," Pam said, resetting herself on the couch.

"Oh my God," I shouted. "Does that mean I'm half Demon?"

"Technically yes, Asswad," she said, "but the fact that The Kev and I raised you since you turned should negate your Demonic traits."

"Demonic traits would be...?" I asked, against my better judgment.

"Oh, you know..." *Was she grinning at me?* "You know," she continued, "eating people, killing without discretion, blowing things up, mass murder, wreaking havoc. Stuff like that."

"Shit," I screamed. I scanned the room for something silver to shove through my chest.

"Don't fret, Assbutt," Pam laughed. "I'm certain there ain't no evil Demon left in you. You drank too much Angel and Fairy blood to be anything but good, good, good. Besides, not all Demons are bad. I do believe this means you have to kiss my big, fat, sexy ass for the rest of your long life."

"Kill me now," I begged. She was right though...I would kiss her butt 'til the end of time. She and The Kev had saved me from being something that had no right to exist in a civilized world...or any world, for that matter.

"I gotta say," Pam announced, "your daddy has got to be the most butt-assed, fucked up ugly I have ever seen. How your momma did the wild thing with him is beyond my imagination. And I've got one hell of an imagination," she bellowed.

Holy God, that visual had never occurred to me. I started to laugh, and I couldn't stop. I was now the proud owner of an image that even one hundred million years of therapy would never erase.

"Pam, you suck!" I yelled at her, moving in to tackle her on the sofa.

She defended herself by smothering me in a bear hug. God, she smelled yummy. I sank my fangs into her neck. She hummed and rocked me like a baby while I ate. Petra's ugly death seemed so far away from my home full of love.

Whenever I drank from Pam, my brain swirled in colorful circles. My body tingled all over and I felt calm and happy. Sometimes little sparkling fireworks went off if I kept my eyes closed. The Kev said I was a bad eater, because I let all my defenses down when I drank. I wouldn't have known if the world ended when I ate. Clearly that's why I didn't realize a certain someone was standing two feet from me.

"Um, Astrid..." Gemma was flustered.

I ignored her. I was too blissed out drinking from Pam. I wouldn't interrupt her during sex. *Okay...yuck.* Did I just equate drinking from Pam to sex? I needed to get laid. Soon.

"Astrid," she tried again. I ignored her again. I was still totally grossed out by my sex analogy. I wondered if I could Green-Eye a human into having sex and then Green-Eye them into forgetting about it. Shit, that was so complicated.

"Angel, you really don't have to do that," an all too familiar voice volunteered suggestively. "I'd be more than happy to accommodate you."

I could hear the grin in that son of a bitch's voice. Damn it, he was a mind reader. I slammed the garage doors in my head shut and I heard him chuckle. I slowly pulled my fangs out of Pam's neck and made eye contact with her.

"Do we have company?" I asked her.

"Yes, Asswad, we do," she said gleefully, "and he is one fine-looking piece of ass."

I rolled my eyes. "Can he see or hear you?"

"I'm letting him see a shimmer of me. I look like a sparkly mirage. And no, Shithat, he can't hear me," she said as she stood up and dumped me to the floor.

Crap, that was not graceful. *Did she just call me Shithat?* This was not how I had envisioned my next rendezvous with Ethan. I quickly stood and turned to face him. I almost fell back on the couch. He was so stinkin' beautiful. If I'd been human, my heart would have stopped.

He wore Prada from head to toe. Black pants and a black fitted shirt. Were all Vamps Prada whores? The color made his skin look like polished alabaster. His hair was a sexy messy and his eyes sparkled beneath his ridiculously long lashes.

I wanted to go to him. I wanted to trace his lips with my fingers. I wanted to run my hands all over his chest and those muscular arms. What I really wanted to do was grab his butt. His perfectly beautiful, assorific derriere. I held myself back. It was not easy.

Why was I holding back?

He was clearly open to the idea of being thrown to the floor and ravaged. He tilted his head to the side and let his eyes travel down to my chest.

"Do you like the outfit I picked for you?" He smiled and ran his tongue along his bottom lip.

"I have no idea what you mean," I huffed. No way did he pick this out. I vaguely recalled promising to be in love with whoever chose this. Following the direction of his eyes, I looked down and realized I was a crazy, bloody hot mess. Shit, shit, shit.

I scrounged up as much dignity as I could muster and politely informed him, "If you'll excuse me for a moment, I need to change."

"Do you need any help?" he asked, equally as polite.

"No, thank you," I primly answered, walking past him and trying not to notice how delicious he smelled.

"Hi, I'm Gemma," I heard as I slunk down to my room. "And you are..."

"Ethan," he informed her. "The Warrior Prince of the North American Dominion and Astrid's mate."

A scream flew out of me before I could slap my hand over my mouth. I heard him laugh as I ran the rest of the way to my bedroom. I ripped through my closet looking for something to wear that would make him so sorry that he couldn't have me.

Ever. I was not his mate, and he couldn't make me.

Nothing. I could find nothing to wear.

"Screw this," I said to no one in particular and grabbed my favorite pair of old holey Levis and a black camisole top. I put on blue sequined Converse and flopped back on my bed. Maybe if I didn't go back out, he would leave. Who was I kidding? That douchebag wanted to own me.

My monsters were very busy chastising me. They clearly did not approve of my outfit choice. Beyonce and Rachel were miming puking, while Ross and Honest Abe cried hysterically and pointed to my closet.

"I don't care," I told them. "All of you are lucky I didn't put on sweat pants and a big paint splattered T-shirt."

They screamed in horror.

"Oh for God's sake." I leaned off my bed to find something on the floor to throw at them. "You guys are so not the boss of me and I can..."

"Who are you talking to, Angel?"

"Shit," I yelled, slamming my head on my bedside table. "Has *anybody* ever heard of knocking?"

He stood in the doorway, casually leaning against the frame and evaluated me. He looked so big in my small room. His exam started at my sequined Converse, which made him smile, to my jeans, which made him raise an eyebrow, to my camisole, where he stopped. I suppose he decided to take a break and stare at my girls. I felt my nipples harden under his gaze and quickly crossed my arms over my chest. He grinned.

"Why are you here?" I asked him. I sat up and pulled some of my comforter around me.

"For you," he said.

"I don't need you," I snapped. God, what in the hell did my hair look like? I'd transported twice, watched my mother get eaten, and cried for five or so hours. I couldn't be looking my best. Wait. Why did I care? I didn't. I was glad I looked like a piece of crap. He could take that and shove it up his...

"You look beautiful," he said, "and although you may not need me, I need you."

Damn those mind readers. I must not have shut my brain doors properly.

"You need to go home," I told him. Flattery was going to get him nowhere.

"I came here because I felt your pain, Angel," he said, moving into my room. "It almost incapacitated me."

"You can't feel my pain."

He watched and said nothing. I felt trapped in his gaze. This was so not fair. I could feel my desire for him taking over all the rational arguments of why I should boot his ass out.

"I feel everything you feel," he said, walking to my bed.

"That's impossible." I moved to the far side of my bed, putting as much distance between us as I could.

"Nothing is impossible," he said gently. "You and I are Vampyres. You have an Angel living with you. I sense a Fairy here somewhere, and I can't quite put my finger on it, but your friend Gemma is not a human. Most importantly, you are the Chosen One."

"I'm not ready for all this."

"Ready does not factor into the equation, Angel. Life happens whether we are ready or not—the only choice or control we have is whether or not we will rise to meet its challenges."

"How'd you get so smart?"

He laughed and sat down on the edge of my bed. "Because I'm five hundred twenty-two years old." He leaned over and took my hand in his. He started rubbing delicious little circles on my palm. This did not bode well for rational decision making on my part.

"Angel, when I drank from you I took part of you into me. You are inside me. When you feel joy, I feel joy. When you feel sorrow, I feel sorrow. When you feel like your world is being ripped apart..." He paused, letting the sentence finish itself. He watched me closely. "That's why I came. I came to take care of you. Please let me take care of you."

"You don't want me." Oh. My. God. Was I about to cry?

He sat up. "You have no concept of how much I want you." His tone and the look in his eyes sent shivers through my body.

"It's not me that you want," I insisted.

"What are you talking about?" He was bewildered.

"You don't want me, you want *the Chosen One*," I said.

"You're one and the same," he laughed, clearly confused by my logic.

Why couldn't I accept that it didn't matter why he wanted me? The fact that he wanted me should be enough, but it wasn't.

"If I weren't the Chosen One, you wouldn't want me."

Now I was crying. Great.

"Oh baby," he said, gently gathering me to him, "I'd want you even if you were the devil incarnate."

"Really?" I blubbered.

"Really. I knew from the moment I saw you," he said, tucking my hair behind my ear and running his thumb along my cheekbone. "You're so beautiful, so strong," he whispered, cupping my cheek.

God, this felt so right. I was so small and soft against his hard body. I leaned into his hand and very slowly, very tentatively wrapped my arms around his body. I felt him contract under my hands and heard a soft moan escape his lips. He guided my head to his chest and gently laid us back on the bed. I closed my eyes and breathed him in. I could feel him doing the same.

"What do I smell like to you?" I asked quietly.

"You smell like heaven, like wind and rain. You smell like promise and desire and hope and a little touch of brown sugar." His voice was husky and I could feel my body tightening. God, he was good. If I weren't so exhausted from transporting and crying for five hours, I'd be tempted to slip my clothes off, straddle him and make him beg for mercy.

He chuckled, "There will be plenty of time for that," he said.

Damn it, I think my brain doors have a defect.

"You are mine," he whispered, running his hand through my hair. "You were meant to be mine. You will always be mine."

"Aren't people going to worry about you?" I mumbled, snuggling closer. I could barely keep my eyes open. "Should you go home?"

"I am home, Angel. You are my home," he said.

I smiled into his chest and fell asleep.

Chapter 18

She was going to die if I didn't help her. The voice inside the tomb was not weak or sickly. It was strong and melodic and very insistent.

"Astrid, you have to help me," she begged.

"How do you know my name?" I asked, thrown by the familiarity.

"Because you are part of me," she replied. "Push the stone, Astrid. Help me, please. You're the only one."

"Why does it have to be me? I'm not strong enough," I insisted. I started to cry. I should get help. Big men... or the police...or a crowbar.

"You are strong enough," she said simply. "There's not much time left." In that moment I knew she was right. I was strong enough. She was going to die if I didn't get her out. Now.

I walked slowly toward the tomb, my hands outstretched. I could feel the tingling in my fingertips. It quickly spread down my arms, through my chest and into my legs. My heart was pounding inside me, my stomach felt twisted and it was hard to breathe. The wind picked up and blew my hair wildly around my head. I was inches away.

"Push, Astrid," she gasped.

I placed both of my hands on the tomb and began to push. The tomb started to crumble under my fingers. The stone turned to cold, hard diamonds...beautiful, sparkling sharp ice that sliced into my hands. My hands bled, but I did not stop. I was so close. The blood ran from my hands, down my arms and seeped into the soft white cotton of my shirt. The stunning diamonds were awash in my blood. I knew if I pushed just a little more...I could... The pain was becoming intolerable. Every nerve ending in my body was on high alert.

That damn dream was getting weirder and weirder, and when in the hell did my bed get so lumpy and hard? Prying my eyes open was an impossibility. I'd cried so much they were fused shut. I rearranged myself and realized my sheets had grown muscles and hair. Really soft, sexy hair and muscles that made my fingertips tingle. It was definitely not the tomb lady.

Feigning sleep, I crawled on top of the hot Vampyre in my bed and noticed two things...we were very topless and he was very happy to see me. Hmmm...should I stay or should I go? I should go. Definitely go. Right? No, I should absolutely go...

I opened my eyes and tried to slide off his body, but his arms were like steel bands keeping me pinned where I was. My very aroused body was having an internal bitch fight with my good girl brain. My body was winning...

Wait a freakin' minute. What in the hell was I doing? Just because he was hot didn't negate the simple fact he tried to kill me and then he half-Vampyre married me, *without my permission,* in front of six hundred Vampyres. Not to mention I'd had a screaming Big O in front of said Vampyres, ensuring I would not be able to maintain eye contact for years...possibly centuries.

He was an egotistical, hot, obnoxious, sexy, bossy ass. I should hump a tree before I did the nasty with him.

But he's so damn hot...

My mind flew back to the graveyard and the visions of what he wanted to do to me. I didn't think half of it was even legal. A slow heat started between my legs and began to move quickly through the rest of my body. The right corner of his mouth lifted and I knew I was gone. All of the excellent reasons I had come up with vanished. I was staring at the most beautiful man I'd ever seen. I was face-to-face, *not to mention body-to-body,* with every fantasy I'd ever had.

"Hello, pretty girl," he murmured as he pressed his lips to mine.

My arms, clearly controlled by my raging hormones, found their way around his neck as my lips parted underneath his extremely insistent ones. He moaned his approval as his tongue began a very deliberate exploration of my mouth.

"Wait a minute," I demanded, untangling my mouth from his. "How did I lose my shirt?"

"I couldn't sleep."

"So getting me partially naked helped you sleep?" I narrowed my eyes and tried not to focus on his perfectly ripped chest.

"No," he grinned. "But it made staying awake a lot more fun."

"You do realize you're a pervert."

"Agreed," he said, cupping the back of my head and

drawing my lips back to his.

He was making me dizzy and I tried to pull away, but apparently that wasn't part of his agenda. He held me firmly against his rock hard body. I couldn't move if I tried. Squirming would only make the mouthwateringly large problem pressing against my tummy bigger. Anyone else would have received my knee to his man bits, but with him...all I wanted to do was press my body even closer.

He slowly made his way from my mouth to my neck. *Ohhh my God.* "Ethan," I gasped.

"Yes, Angel?" he answered, lightly scraping his fangs along my neck.

I cried out and he flipped me over, pinning me to the bed with my arms over my head. *Damn, that was hot.* All of his hard was pressed against all of my soft. My body jerked underneath his and his eyes went an even more brilliant green. I hadn't been this turned on...well ever. If I could just...wait. Small house. Too many people here. Makes me scream. Pam will give me hell...

When his mouth moved slowly and deliberately down my body, my brain completely fritzed out, to my body's delight. My mind was a jumbled mess and my body had hatched its own plan. I arched wantonly toward him. His controlled dominance made my thinking erratic and the slickness between my legs was more than obvious to both of us.

"Look at me," he said, taking my chin in his large hand and forcing me to stare into his beautiful eyes. "Do you know what you do to me?" he demanded, lowering his lips to mine and kissing me senseless.

I writhed beneath him. His eyes were blazing green and I knew mine matched. He tore his mouth from mine and ran his open lips form my jaw to my breast. My back arched up and his chuckle of delight sent shockwaves right to my core. I had never wanted anyone so badly in my life.

"You are beautiful," he murmured before taking my painfully hard nipple into his mouth. He drew hard and I whimpered, arched higher, and wordlessly begged for more.

I rubbed myself against his hard, sexy body. I wanted him. I wanted to be controlled by him.

I wanted the decision of becoming his mate and having sex with him taken out of my hands.

I wanted him to force me...I wanted to be blameless in a decision I knew I wanted to make. It went against everything I was taught and everything I thought I knew about myself...everything I *believed.*

He nipped and sucked until I saw stars. He pressed the

lower half of his body into mine, creating a rhythm that made me see Jesus. I felt my fangs descend and I pulled Ethan up by his hair until we were face to face. I slanted my mouth across his and drew his tongue into my mouth. He dug his fingers painfully into my hips and increased the speed of his undulating body. I cried out. It was perfect...that mind-numbing sensual place that mixed pleasure and pain.

He groaned into my mouth, cupped the back of my head with one hand and my ass with the other and flipped us over. I wanted to get closer. I wanted to be completely naked and I wanted him inside me, but I wanted more. For the first time, I was conscious of thinking like a Vampyre, not a human. It was scary and liberating.

I slid my lips along his jaw and down his neck. I could feel the blood rushing through his veins. With the tip of my tongue I traced the arteries in his neck, loving the taste of him. My fangs burned and I knew what I had to do. What I wanted to do. What I needed to do. His body tensed beneath mine. Through his jeans, I felt his erection grow bigger.

I scraped his neck with my fangs and his body jerked.

"Angel," he moaned.

I laughed and lightly punctured his neck with my fangs, without drawing blood. I loved the sound his skin made when I bit into him. It popped. It was different from Pam or The Kev or Gemma. It was right. I knew it with every fiber of my being. As my body writhed on top of his, I reached down and ran my hand up and down the length of him. He was beautiful and mine. I moved in to take what I wanted.

He moaned and drew my head back to his neck. All I could focus on was his skin...the breathtakingly beautiful, smooth pale skin on his neck. The place I would bite him and drink from him and make him mine. Mine. Mine for eternity. It was so clear to me. I had never wanted anything so much. I would mark him and finish what he started...

Wait.

I gasped and jerked back. What in the hell was I doing? Just because my lady bits were on fire didn't mean I should make a decision that would last a lifetime...*a really long lifetime.* Would I be doing this if I wasn't half naked? Or if he wasn't so freakin' hot? Was I about to let my need for an earth-shattering orgasm dictate the rest of my undead life? Um...yes. Yes, I was.

"I can't," I said. I rolled off of Ethan and buried my head in my hands.

"You're right."

"No, Ethan, I really can't...wait. What?"

"You're correct. As much as it pains me...and it does," he said, referring to the unavoidably large bulge in his pants, "this is not how it should happen."

"So, I guess you don't want me," I teased.

"Oh, I want you," he moaned and chuckled. His green eyes glittered dangerously. My insides jumped, not with fear but with lust, and I wondered if I had been an idiot not to claim him. "Letting you pull away from me was the most difficult thing I've done in all my years."

"First of all, you didn't let me do anything. I did it myself," I informed him. "I just didn't think you were that into it."

He pulled me into his body and pressed me against some hard evidence to the contrary.

"I'm into it, Angel," he grinned, "but more importantly, I know that you're into it."

"Am not," I laughed, trying to get out of his embrace.

"Are too," he said, grabbing me and trapping me underneath him. "Just because you can't bite me yet," he informed me with an evil twinkle in his eyes, "doesn't mean I can't bite you." He leaned into my neck.

"Not fair," I screeched, trying to wrestle him off of me.

"So not fair," he agreed, "but so going to happen." He grinned as his fangs elongated.

I gasped in total delight, struggling only to entice him further.

"What in the fuck is going on in there?" Pam bellowed from the hallway.

"Could you hear that?" I asked him.

"Yes." He had the strangest expression. "Who was that?"

"My Angel, Pam," I said. "Are you okay?"

"Yes," he paused, "I just had a...I think..."

A flash of pained confusion passed his face, and then it was gone.

"It's nothing," he smiled and shook his head. "Probably the blue balls I feel coming on, damaging my brain."

I laughed and kissed him. "So, what are we doing?" I asked.

He considered me and my question for a moment. A slow, sexy smile spread across his beautiful face. "We're going to get to know each other and I shall court you."

I grinned. "Court me?"

"Yes, Angel...court," he proudly informed me.

"Um, Ethan," I said and rolled my eyes, "you're kind of showing your age."

"Yes," he grinned. "I am."

"Are we *courting* exclusively?" I asked with narrowed eyes.

"I don't know." He watched me carefully. "Are we?"

"If this is going to be fair, it shouldn't be exclusive," I told him.

"Are you seeing someone else?" His eyes flashed green and I saw a streak of possessiveness that scared the hell out of me and turned me on with a vengeance.

"Nooo," I said, messing with him, "but I might. I'm new to this whole Vamp thing. I don't even know what's out there yet."

He did not like that. I watched the muscle in his jaw clench. He controlled his jealousy, but with effort. God, he was so easy to bait. I could twist him in knots.

"Well, Astrid, I suppose if you don't mind watching me with other women...we can do it your way." He crossed his arms over his naked chest and waited for my hissy fit.

"I don't mind at all," I lied through my teeth. If he thought I was going to throw a fit in front of him, he had another thing coming. I would simply wait until he left. I grabbed my shirt with shaking hands and yanked it on. What in the hell was going on? Why was I so furious at the thought of him with someone else? Not just furious...murderous. "It's probably a good idea. I really don't think we're suited anyway. So you should just go get laid by a bunch of Vampyre floozies and I'll..."

Faster than I could blink, he was on me. I was flat on my back, trapped under the man I wanted to be trapped under.

"Astrid, the only Vamp I want to get laid by is you. And I'm quite sure the only Vamp you want to get laid by is me."

"Someone's a little full of himself," I snapped.

He gave me a lopsided grin and my insides melted. Just the sight of him was a punch to my gut and my heart. Crap.

"This will be fun, Astrid. I look forward to winning you. And make no mistake...I will."

He leaned in and kissed my very willing, traitorous lips and left. I tried to find my voice, but it was gone. I wanted him to win...I think. But he was going to have to work very hard.

Chapter 19

Wandering around the art room at the senior center, I tossed out all the clay phalluses and boobs. Didn't want to scare my potential replacement. The interviews were going to start in thirty minutes. I'd never interviewed anybody in my life. Ready or not, I had to grow up. Why in the hell they wanted me to interview my replacement was beyond me.

I didn't want to quit but I had a few new issues...Daylight was a problem, although not as much as it was initially. Apparently my body behaved like a five to six hundred year old Vamp. Sunlight sensitivity wears off with age and it was becoming less of an issue for me, even though I'd only been dead for a month. That pissed Venus off to no end. Even with her black skin, she burned like paper in a fire when she was exposed to the sun.

The main reason I couldn't teach anymore was time. As an Elite Guard I had to train day and night. Ethan was hell-bent on preparing me for whatever the Chosen One was supposed to do, although no one seemed to know exactly what that was. Turns out, training was for my own safety as well as the safety of everyone around me. Certainly my weapon skills had a long way to go.

For instance, if you threw a dagger it shouldn't end up embedded in the head of someone on your team. I was sure Cathy thought I did it on purpose. I solemnly swore on my life that it was an accident. Not a good way to become friendly with someone who already hated me. Thank God we were Vampyres, because a human wouldn't have lived through that one. Apparently the Chosen One had to know how to do it all. Not that they believed I was the Chosen One. Hell, I wasn't even completely convinced.

If I were them, I would be skeptical too, but I had no intention of proving anything to anybody. Ethan and Venus knew my particulars. Neither one had felt it necessary to enlighten anyone. Fine by me. And good God, I had new powers emerging every day. Ethan and Venus didn't know the half of it. The Kev and Pam wanted me to keep some of it under wraps.

"Damn it," I muttered, finding a full scale clay model of male genitalia sitting on my desk. I quickly shoved it in a drawer. "Holy shit, what is that?"

Under my desk was a large pile of what appeared to be dog poop. Charlie had one hell of a sense of humor...I hoped. I crawled under my desk. It didn't smell and God knew I had a bionic nose. I was loath to touch it just in case it was real but petrified...It wasn't real. Damn Charlie, I was going to get him back for this one.

"Excuse me," a child called out. "Is anyone here?"

Oh crap, a child? A child was here to teach art to a class of penis-loving seniors? Maybe if I stayed under my desk she'd leave.

"Hello?" she said. "Hello? Anyone here?"

I waited.

"Hello?" She was getting louder. She was not giving up. This child did sound vaguely familiar. She smelled like insecurity and sadness—not dangerous at all. She was lonely. I crawled out from under my desk with a big smile plastered on my face. *Wait. Where in the hell did she go?*

"Astrid?" a tiny voice said from behind me. How did someone get behind me? I was a Vampyre for Christ's sake. I whipped around and came face to face with the child—*well, kind of* since she was about seven inches shorter than me. It was Paris Hilton.

"Holy shit, Paris," I gasped. "You about scared the life out of me."

"That's not possible." Paris Hilton chuckled at her own joke. "You're already dead."

She slapped me on the back and I went flying. Damn, she was strong. I righted myself before I took down a huge pile of charcoals and paint and turned to find her prostrate on the ground before me.

"Oh for God's sake, get up," I told her.

"You are the Chosen One," she said reverently, not budging.

"Chosen shmozen. Get your ass up," I barked. "Why are

you here?"

"I want to teach art. My specialty is pastels, but I adore sculpture and watercolor, too."

"You do realize these are seniors in the class?"

"Oh yeah, I love old people," she said, pulling on her straggly black hair.

"What do you mean by that?" I asked, worried.

"What do you mean, *what do I mean?*" She was confused.

I felt bad saying it, but I liked most of the class and I had a responsibility to them. "Well, um... I mean, do you like them or do you *like* them?"

Shit, I was starting to sweat.

"Oh, I get it," Paris giggled. "You mean will I eat them?"

"Yes," I shouted, both relieved that she figured it out and frightened of what her answer would be.

"No," she assured me, "old folks don't taste so good."

"Great. Good to know."

"So do I get the job?" she asked.

"Okay, here's the deal," I said, eyeing her narrowly, "you got Charlie who likes to touch all women inappropriately. You got Niecey, who stands about four feet tall and is secretly in love with Charlie the Ass Grabber. Mrs. Jenkins is a bulldozer who likes to make whips and handcuffs out of clay. Charlie usually sticks to boobs. Niecey can't help herself but create out of proportion replicas of the male anatomy. There's a hilarious gal in the back whose name I can't remember and she likes to throw art supplies. But...the main problems are Martha and Jane. They are horrible, nasty, mean women. I'm unclear why they even come to the class, but they do. They've made my life a living hell for several years and they will do the same or worse to you." I stared at her long and hard. "How would you deal with all that?"

"Hmmm," Paris said thoughtfully. "I suppose I'd have Charlie model nude for the class. That would keep him away from the privates and Niecey might have a better chance of sculpting a more realistic penis. I'd make sure the gal in the back never works with knives or scissors since she is fond of launching things. I'd let Mrs. Jenkins think she's in charge, and as for Martha and Jane...Are they conservative, or religious?" she asked.

"Both."

Paris grinned happily. "That's easy! I'd trance them into only being able to utter liberal or sacrilegious statements."

"Oh my God, can you really do that?" I asked, impressed.

"Hell yeah. I could also zap them bald."

"Great! You're hired," I said, praying to Jesus I wasn't making a huge mistake. Paris was so excited she grabbed me in a bear hug so tight I was sure she was breaking every bone in my upper body.

"Let go," I gasped.

She did. I fell to the ground in agony.

"Oh my God," she shrieked, "I am so sorry. I got excited and I...oh God." She dropped to a fetal position and began to roll around on the floor. I momentarily forgot my own pain and watched the most bizarre reaction to anything I'd ever seen in my life.

"Um...Paris," I said.

"Yes?" She stopped rolling and looked at me.

"Are you gonna do that if something goes wrong in class?"

"Um...no?" she asked.

"No," I told her. "Under no circumstance can you ever do that around the seniors."

She was shocked, "Really?"

"Really," I replied, beginning to wonder if I was high.

"Another thing," I continued, "if you physically destroy the classroom, I will kick your ass from here into the next century."

"Good to know...good to know," she told me without an ounce of sarcasm.

"Oh, and Muffy is not allowed in here. Ever." I could just imagine the shit storm that would ensue if the Muffster showed up.

"You don't have to worry about her. She can't go out in the sun at all."

"You can?"

She nodded. I was surprised. She was only about ninety or so in Vamp years.

"I can tolerate it quite well," she said with pride.

"So the Vamps that changed you and your...comrades...were really old?"

"Oh no," Paris said darkly, "they were young, but they didn't turn me."

I stared at her. "Oookay, you lost me. If they didn't turn you, who did?"

"Prince Ethan turned me."

What the fu...? Why would Ethan turn Paris Hilton? No offense, but...

"I'm sure you're wondering why," she said slowly.

Son of a bitch, another mind reader? I shut my brain doors and regrouped. If everybody could read minds, why couldn't I?

"I am curious," I said gently.

She started rocking from one foot to the other. Back and forth...back and forth. I could smell her uncertainty and fear, her anger and her sadness. "Those other Vamps, the bad ones, changed everyone in the freak show...everyone except me. Muffy almost escaped—she's a contortionist." She stopped and stared at the ceiling. "They beat me for several days, but for some reason I wouldn't die. I wanted to...I really did, but I just kept on living."

She fiddled with her T-shirt and pushed her hair behind her ears. "It angered them I wouldn't die. They wouldn't give up. They just tried harder." She tucked her concert T-shirt into her leggings and wrapped her slender arms around her body. "They increased their efforts. They were so furious that Muffy almost got away and that I wouldn't die so they..." She looked up and continued without emotion. "So they burned me and took turns raping me...repeatedly. When that didn't work, they cut my throat."

If I'd had a beating heart it would have stopped. As it was, whatever was in there broke. I felt so much anger I was numb. I couldn't say anything. All I wanted to do was to gather her into my arms and rock her, but she wasn't finished.

"Eventually they left, and for some god-awful reason I was still alive. The Elite Guard arrived and found all of us, including what was left of me." Her sweet voice was so soft now I had to lean in to hear her. "Prince Ethan found me. I was disgusting. Anyone else would have simply found me beyond repair...but not the Prince." She smiled a little. "He gave me a choice—he would help me die, or I could become a Vampyre and join his Dominion. He told me he would be honored to have someone as strong as I was as one of his people. Anyone who had survived what I had deserved to live. He said he would care for me like a daughter, and he always has."

"Why were they only banished? Why weren't they put to death?"

"Because the Prince gave me a gift," she said with pride. "He banished them so I would have the pleasure of killing them. I trained for a year and when I was ready, I had his permission and blessing to go after them. And I did."

Boy, I was getting really desensitized to death. The end of that story made me so happy I almost clapped. I walked to her and took her little damaged body and wounded spirit into my arms and I did what I had wanted to do. I rocked her like a baby while she cried.

When she finished I sat down with her on the floor.

"Oh, I've got one little problem," Paris said, wiping the

pink tears from her cheeks.

"What's that?" I asked.

"I got kicked out of my House and I don't have anywhere to live at the moment. Can I move in with you?" Paris asked.

"Um, no. Absolutely not. Out of the question...but I think I might have an idea."

Chapter 20

Tonight when I woke up my monsters were in bed with me, cuddled up like warm puppies—minus the fur. They came off the ceiling a few days ago, but only a few minutes at a time, 'til now. Our relationship was progressing, what with the sleepovers and all. Ethan would be so jealous.

I had always assumed Ross and Rachel were a couple, and that Honest Abe and Beyonce were a couple. But if sleeping positions were any indication, all my monsters were gay. Beyonce and Rachel were very tangled up in each other, while Ross and Honest Abe were spooned up sweetly. It did make sense. The boys had always been far more concerned with my ensembles than the girls. They also had better taste.

Cuddling with my monsters delighted me. I liked playing with Ross' hair—it felt like Velcro. Beyonce was a great singer and some of the sounds she made were beginning to sound like words. All of her songs seemed to be about her vicious mother. We did have that in common. Honest Abe gave me arm tickles by *very* lightly running his razor sharp claws up and down the inside of my arm. Rachel was my girl...she would play with my hair for hours on end.

I loved feeding them breezes of Glitter Magic and watching them run around my bed like tiny drunks on speed. I didn't even find them unattractive anymore.

"You guys are beautiful," I cooed, tickling Ross' fat little belly. He screamed with joy and blew me kisses.

"Dadadadadadablablabla," Rachel told me urgently. All the monsters froze and stared at her in horror.

Oh shit.

"What?" I asked, stupidly thinking I could understand. Why in the hell couldn't I understand? I was half Demon for God's sake.

"Dadadadadadablablabla," she repeated. Honest Abe smacked her in the head and they all began to wrestle and punch each other. Ross kept running over to hug me and then dove back into the fray.

I sighed and wondered if their brawl indicated a bad night ahead. I had a ton of stuff to do on this fine evening and I didn't need any unplanned drama.

I picked up my brawling babies and tossed them back up to the ceiling. Ross didn't want to leave me. I gave him a kiss and promised to be back soon. He reluctantly let me lob him back up.

I pulled on some black yoga pants, a hot pink jogging bra, some fabulous sparkly, silver beaded flip-flops and put my hair in a ponytail. I adjusted the girls, slapped on some lip gloss and I was ready to go. I had fight and weapons training at the Cressida House in a couple of hours and I'd found the less clothing I wore, the better. First off, too much clothing can encumber movement. Second, the less I wore, the more distracted the male Vamps got. It was a lot easier to take down a distracted Vamp than a focused one.

That left me about three hours to get Paris Hilton all settled, but I needed to eat first.

***

"What do you want, Assbutt?" Pam yelled as I sidled up to her on the couch. "Can't you see I'm in the middle of my program?"

She didn't like people to bother her or to talk or move during Jerry Springer. Of course, she was excluded and allowed to shout her head off at the desperately pathetic people who enjoyed displaying their backward-ass screwed up lives on national television. It was more fun to watch her watching the shows than the shows themselves.

"I'm hungry," I told her, crawling into her lap. She gathered me to her without missing a beat of her program.

The Kev and Gemma joined us, looking suspiciously flushed. Hmm...maybe that two thousand year age difference wasn't such a big deal anymore.

"Hello, my strudel cheeks," The Kev whispered. He too was in fear of Pam's right hook, frequently dealt out when anyone spoke during Jerry Springer.

"What are you doing tonight?" Gemma whispered.

"Oh for fuck's sake," Pam groused, "you people can talk.

I've seen this one four times already. It's not his baby." We turned our attention to the TV. "You see that dumbass in the blue shirt?" she asked. We nodded. "He's gonna try to choke his cheating hooker of a wife, and then that fine lookin' bald security guy is gonna come out and pound his ass. I really like me a nice, beefy bald guy with big muscles."

Sure enough, she was right. Blue shirt got an ass-pounding from the bald beefy guy.

"I'm going over to Nana's house. I'm going to let Paris Hilton live there for a while," I told Gemma. "Then I have weapons and fight training at the Cressida House."

Did she have a hickey on her neck?

"Back the fuck up." Pam started laughing. "You're letting Paris Hilton live in your Nana's house?"

"Yes, and she's taking over my teaching job at the senior center," I added defensively.

The Kev winked at me. "You have the balls that are big," he chuckled. Good God, was he wearing a muumuu?

"Holy hell, child," Pam laughed, "have you lost your mind?"

"You know what?" I shouted, "I like her and she knows a lot about art and she got kicked out of her House because...." I realized I had no idea why she was ousted from her Vampyre sorority and I had a feeling it was better that way. "I know she's weird-looking and talks like an eight year old and seems to enjoy breaking furniture, but she's had a really hard life and death," I informed my open-mouthed crowd. "I want to take care of her. She makes my non-beating heart hurt. Pam, you're going online to buy her some clothes in size zero that are not black and don't have a rock band on them. Gemma..." I held my hand up to stop her before she could speak. "I have plenty of money with my inheritance and I'll feel a lot better spending it on someone other than myself."

I really, truly felt like I was going to hurl. I knew this was an impossibility for Vamps, but nonetheless, the thought of relocating Paris to Nana's house seemed like a good idea until I actually said it out loud. I had to sit down and put my head between my knees. I was dizzy, but I knew I was right. I looked up, expecting more crap from the nutty people I considered my family. They all smiled with love and pride. Nary a swear word passed Pam's lips. She put her arms out and I cuddled back up into her ample and beautiful lap.

"You're a good girl," she said as she rocked me. I sank my fangs into her neck. Gemma curled up next to me and rubbed my back. The Kev sat at my feet and rested his head on my shins.

How did I ever get so lucky?

***

The house smelled like Nana. I hadn't been back since I'd become a Vampyre and had my new nose. It smelled like freesia and lilies with a hint of brown sugar. Like Nana. It smelled so good, I wanted to cry. For a while after she died, I couldn't come back here at all. I kept expecting to find her, and everyone would realize what I already knew. She wasn't really dead. That never happened.

I took a deep cleansing breath and stepped back into reality. I wandered around the house. It felt good and safe and real to be here. The rest of my life was spinning around me like a deadly tornado. I was having horrible nightmares about Petra. Pam wasn't convinced that she was dead. I, on the other hand, was sure she was dead. Being eaten by Demons clearly meant death...although who in the hell knew. Maybe she wasn't mortal. Maybe she wasn't dead.

"Astrid?"

"Hey, Paris." I quickly wiped away the tear rolling down my cheek.

"You okay?" she asked, her arms full of suitcases and art supplies.

"I'm fine." I smiled and relieved her of some of her load. "You really are an artist."

"Yeah, I'm not that good, but I love it," she said, dropping her suitcase and looking around. "This house is pretty."

"I know," I muttered, wondering what Nana would think of me installing Paris Hilton, the violent little Vampyre, in her home. A small tickle of warmth settled in my stomach and bounced all through my body. *What the fu...?*

"Oh my God." I grabbed the back of the couch for balance.

"What?" Paris shrieked, pulling a wicked-looking knife from her bag. She slammed me down on the couch and sat on me, ready to defend me.

"No, Paris. It's not bad. Nana wants you here," I grunted, positive she'd crushed my ribs.

"Who's Nana?" she asked, still unwilling to relinquish her weapon or her seat on my back.

"My Nana, my grandmother," I groaned, shoving her off.

"She's not going to mind sharing her house with a Vampyre?" Paris asked skeptically, putting her knife into her belt.

"No, she'd dead."

"Great! When can I meet her?"

"Not our kind of dead. For real dead," I said quietly.

"Oh." She fidgeted with her stringy hair and stared at the rug. "I'm sorry. I can still smell her. Brown sugar and flowers...she was good."

"She was." I gingerly moved to the other side of the room. Her protection was going to kill me, or at least break something. "So anyway, you're going to live here and if you fuck the place up I will kill you. For real dead."

"Got it."

"She loved me and she would have loved you too," I told her as I dragged her suitcase to the guest room.

"I'm not really what you would call lovable," Paris muttered as she followed me down the hallway.

I stopped and turned. "You are lovable, Paris. You deserve love and so do I."

"Well, um...okay."

"Good. That's settled. There's a stupid car coming to pick me up, so I have to go. But as lovable as you are, just remember I will destroy you if you fuck with Nana's house."

"Roger that," she grinned.

I grinned back and wondered for the umpteenth time if all my brain cells disappeared when I died.

Chapter 21

I left Paris happily puttering around Nana's living room and waited for my ride to the Cressida House. The Vampyres were so formal with me that it was humorous and alarming. They insisted on a car and a driver. They also posted guards outside my house. I would lay odds that Ethan was behind it.

Those that believed I was the Chosen One often dropped to their knees in my presence. Most just bowed their heads. All of it made me hyperaware of how different I was. I supposed many of them were still afraid of me after witnessing the Dangling Vampyre Show.

To complicate matters further, their Prince was a-courtin' me, so even if a Vampyre found me attractive he wouldn't dare show it. No one would challenge the Prince. He was revered, adored and feared. That made it a little difficult to date. I debated whether or not Ethan had forbidden any male to come near me. They all ignored me, except one—Heathcliff. His attraction was mixed with frustration and anger that made me sad and uncomfortable. He refused to spar during training and went out of his way not to touch me, but I could feel his eyes on me constantly.

It was very difficult for a Vampyre to hide attraction due to scent. His lust was easily detectable and it wasn't one-sided. I was attracted to him too, but it was so confusing and complicated. If I was meant to be Ethan's mate, why did I feel this connection to Heathcliff? Not only did I feel this for him, it extended to his sister Cathy. I wanted her to like me. I wanted to be friends. Of course, nailing her in the head with a dagger last week didn't help matters. She wanted nothing to do with me.

She, unlike her brother, sparred with me every chance she got. I found myself going easy on her. This, of course, infuriated her. Heathcliff was a beautiful fighter. He was strong, precise and deadly. He was a superb mind reader and could also fly. I couldn't fly, but I could transport. None of them could do that. Vampyres were not supposed to be able to do that. Then again, I wasn't just any Vampyre—although God knows I wished I were.

Ethan hadn't been participating in training. This was good on several levels, the most relevant being I couldn't think straight around him. As far as fighters go, there was none better. He was the strongest, fastest, most deadly Vampyre of them all. No one wanted to tangle with him. He fought like a force of nature. He was a force of nature. I didn't think he would have reacted well to the Heathcliff situation. To top it all off, I had guessed it correctly—way back when, they were best friends. Couldn't get much worse.

The car pulled up, a sleek Mercedes sedan. I got into the front seat. They could pick me up all they wanted, but I refused to ride in the back seat. I refused to behave as if I was better than whoever they'd chosen to drive me that day.

"Hello, Astrid," Heathcliff said. My stomach dropped. *Why in the hell didn't I get in the back? Shit, shit, shit.*

"Heathcliff," I nodded and stared straight ahead. My voice sounded tiny.

"How are you tonight, Astrid?" he asked.

"I'm okay. How are you?" Small talk was going to suck.

"I'm not so good, Astrid. Do you know why I'm not so good?" he asked.

"No," I whispered. *Oh help me, God. This was not something I could handle right now.*

"I'm not good because you're very close to mating with my best friend who also happens to be my Prince, and I want you for myself. That puts me in a rather bad situation, don't you think?"

He certainly got right to the point.

"Um...yes." I wanted to be anywhere but stuck in close quarters with him. I could transport home but that would make me a chickenshit. I was not a chickenshit.

"Astrid, look at me."

I slowly turned my head and looked into his killer blue eyes.

He pulled the sedan over and stared at me.

He was absolutely beautiful. Where Ethan made me feel out of control, without the ability to reason, Heathcliff made me feel calm and happy. I knew I was safe with both of them, but I began to panic. I was attracted to two men. Really attracted. This was so not good. I felt a little lightheaded, and I wasn't sure if I was going to giggle uncontrollably or cry.

"Sometimes," he continued, "if a fire starts with an explosion, it burns out quickly. Everything in its path gets destroyed, turned to ash. Then it is gone...forever." He watched me closely. "If it starts out with a spark, even a small one, and slowly picks up heat it can develop into something beautiful and meaningful. A healthy fire, full of warmth and love...and it will last."

Kill. Me. Now. He was making sense. Did it matter that I didn't feel the sexual attraction to Heathcliff that I did to Ethan? I did find Heathcliff attractive. My God, who wouldn't? Was it even real what I felt for Ethan? Would we crash and burn? Did I really want to be part of the Royal Family? It was hard enough to make friends just being the Chosen One. Heathcliff was attracted to me before he knew I was the Chosen One, but his motives could be suspect too.

"Is this about your sister?" I asked, praying it wasn't.

"What are you talking about?"

"Are you trying to take me out of the running so Cathy can still be with him?"

"Again," he said, looking at me like I was nuts, "what are you talking about?"

"Don't your sister and Ethan..." I trailed off.

"Do my sister and Ethan have sex? Is that what you're asking?" I could feel him staring at me. I looked at the floor. "The answer is yes, occasionally, from what I understand..." He stopped, debating whether to go on. He went on, "...with the knowledge that when they find their true mates, their relationship is over and they will become friends." I knew he didn't want to tell me any of that. "My sister can look out for herself. Trust me, my intentions toward you have nothing to do with my sister. My intentions have everything to do with me and how I feel about you."

"Are you asking me to mate with you?" I whispered.

"No," he said, taking my hands in his, "not yet. I'm asking you to give me a chance. I'm asking you not to mate with anyone yet." His eyes burned a shimmering green. "We have a connection. It may not be as crazy as the other one, but it's real and it cannot be ignored. I just want you to give me a chance."

Damn Vampyres, they were so beautiful it was hard to deny them anything. This one was making too much sense.

"I'm...I wish..." *What in the hell was I trying to say?*

He smiled gently at me. "I'm so sorry to hear about your

mother."

"Thank you," I murmured. He was probably the sweetest man I'd ever met, apart from The Kev. Kind, gentle, good and so pretty...I think he's prettier than me.

"That's not possible," he smiled with those dimples. "You are the most beautiful woman I've ever seen."

Shitfire. Mind readers.

"Heathcliff, that's not fair," I laughed and quickly closed the doors in my head. His spicy, brown-sugary scent was making me feel a little slaphappy.

He chuckled, "I love how you say my name, and just so you know, I'm not always nice." He smiled a killer sexy smile and I was glad I was sitting, because I felt my knees go a little weak. "Anyway, all's fair in love and war."

"How old were you when your mom died?" I asked, abruptly changing the subject.

"I was eight and Cathy was three," he told me, pulling back a bit at the unexpected detour.

"Do you remember her?"

"Yes, I remember her well. She was beautiful inside and out. She had wild, dark curly hair and sky blue eyes. She had a lovely mouth, kissed us constantly, and she sang like the angels in Heaven."

"She reminds me of my Nana," I said wistfully.

"Your Nana?"

"My mom's mom," I sighed. "I adored her. She raised me. Not my mom. My mother was...um....well, not so much into being a mother. Your mom sounds a lot like my Nana, right down to the singing voice of an angel."

"Where is she? I'd love to meet her," Heathcliff said.

"She died last fall." I looked down and fiddled with my yoga pants. When I looked up he was staring at me so intently, if I still had breath it would have caught in my throat.

"You've had quite a few changes this year," he said, reaching out to touch my face. If that wasn't the understatement of the century.

I laid my hand over his as he placed it on my cheek. "Heathcliff, why do women die during the change if they've borne a child?"

"We don't know. It may have something to do with the fact that a mother is from the light. She has created life and we are from the dark," he said slowly, "but it's a bad death...very prolonged and very painful." He shifted uncomfortably. "Vampyres were not organized for thousands of years. It's only in the last three hundred years or so that we have become internationally connected. We didn't share information. We lived in hiding for the most part and our government, The Royal Family, was only accepted as law by some."

He slid his hand down my face and arm and gently took my hand in his. "Many Vampyres tried to change their mortal wives only to have devastatingly tragic results, but they didn't know. Many Vampyres..." he paused, debating how much to say. "Many Vampyres who inadvertently killed their wives harbor a great resentment to our King."

"Why?" I wasn't following.

"Because he knew about this, yet he never spoke of it. The King's first wife was Queen Paloma. She's the mother of Princess Lelia, the Monarch of Africa." *The gorgeous Betsy Johnson wearing Vamp who wanted to kill me in the graveyard.* "He loved her above all the others. She was strong and fun-loving as the stories go. She could hold her spirits well and trade stories with the men that would make them blush. She wanted the King to change her. She loved him so fiercely that she wanted to spend eternity with him, and he with her. They did it in secrecy. Her death was horrific and went on for several weeks...weeks filled with excruciating agony. The King wanted to kill himself, but she would not hear of it. She made him promise to go on, vowing to come back to him someday."

"Has she come back?"

"Not yet," Heathcliff said sadly. "He still waits for her. After her death, the King was so devastated he told no one for one hundred years what they had done or how it turned out. He never tried to change another one of his wives."

"He had multiple wives?" *Holy shit, did Ethan have a bunch of wives too?*

"Yes, that was an acceptable practice then, but most Vampyres practice monogamy, and when they find their true mate the point of multiple lovers is moot anyway."

Thank you, Jesus. "Did any of them know why he wouldn't change them?" I was fascinated.

"No, and some were filled with great anger because of this. He changed all eleven of his children, but none of his wives. One of his wives in particular tried repeatedly to get him to change her. She resorted to begging, then eventually blackmail and attempts on his life."

"Oh my God." This was better than Jerry Springer. "What happened to her?" I asked.

"She was banished, and died after a while. It was her child who was supposedly killed," he said.

"Do you think the King did it?" I loved me some Jerry

Springer behavior.

"No, absolutely not," Heathcliff said. "He loves all of his children to distraction. He searched for over a hundred years for Juliet. He still holds out hope that she is alive."

"God, that's sad...and weird," I said.

"I've always found it odd that we have never found proof of her death," he said.

God, he smelled good. "Well, it would be awfully difficult to hide for five hundred years, dontcha think?"

"That would depend on your gifts." He tilted his head to the side and looked me up and down slowly. "Someone like you could get away with a lot." His eyes twinkled.

"Whatever do you mean?" Was I flirting? Yep, I was flirting.

"Well," he said and moved toward me, "if you didn't want to be somewhere, you could transport." He kept moving closer. His scent was making me giddy. "For example," he inched forward, "if you didn't want to be here, with me...right now...in this car...wearing very little..." His eyes flashed green as they roamed my body. "You could disappear," he whispered.

Our lips were mere inches apart.

He was right. I could disappear, but I didn't want to. I wanted to be here in this moment with him. The gorgeous green of his eyes was almost making me forget about Ethan. Almost. I'm not sure a tsunami would make me forget about Ethan. I felt a bit like I was cheating, but Heathcliff was right. We did have a connection and it was strong. I owed it to myself and to him to find out what it meant.

"I want to give you a chance," I whispered. I felt my eyes go green. He grinned at me with those killer dimples. Those dimples could make a girl faint.

We leaned into each other very slowly, eyes locked, and we kissed. His lips were warm and soft and sweet. He cradled my head in his hands and deepened the kiss. He definitely knew what he was doing. I kissed him back, but...

We pulled apart and looked at each other in surprise.

"Let me try that again," he said, trying to mask his confusion.

"Okay," I agreed, re-situating myself so our bodies were closer. Maybe that was the problem. He leaned in and I let my lips part underneath his. I wrapped my arms around him and tried pressing my body into his.

Oh. My. God. Who was laughing? What the fu...? It was me. I was laughing? Wait...he was laughing. Thank God it wasn't me. Wait...Why in the hell is he laughing? Did I kiss funny? Shit, I was laughing. We were both laughing.

Clearly this is not working.

"What in the hell was that?" Heathcliff leaned back in his seat, still laughing and put his hands over his eyes.

"I don't know," I giggled.

"I felt like I was kissing my sister," he groaned.

"Me too," I said, punching him in the arm.

"I feel like your sister?" he asked, mortified.

"No," I stammered, trying to suppress laughter, "not my sister...my brother."

"Oookay," Heathcliff said, "clearly our connection is not sexual."

"Nope," I agreed, "it's not."

"What is it then?" He searched my face for answers.

"I have no idea, but the connection is there. It's real and it feels good."

"Maybe we're supposed to be friends," he said quietly.

"Yes, but it's more than that...although it's definitely not lovers," I said, wishing I knew exactly what I meant.

He smiled, but it was sad. "Definitely not lovers," he agreed. He took my hand in his and he squeezed it. This time there was nothing sexual behind it.

"Whoever you fall in love with will be the luckiest woman in the world," I told him.

"Ahhh, but she won't get my whole heart," he said. "A part of it shall always belong to you."

I wanted to cry. Why in the hell do I never end up with the nice guy?

Heathcliff chuckled, "Astrid, your brain doors are open."

"Crap."

"Astrid, just so you know, Ethan is a nice guy. He's one of the best. He is the finest man I know."

I looked down. I didn't want to discuss Ethan with him. I had no idea what I was going to do about Ethan. Even though there was nothing romantic between Heathcliff and me, he'd given me a lot to think about where Ethan was concerned. Nice guy or no, Ethan and I might be too combustible.

Heathcliff took my chin in his hand and gently lifted my face up to his. "We are connected. I believe we are connected for eternity," he said. "We will care for each other, we will have each other's backs, and we will never betray one another. We will love each other as brother and sister."

He pulled a small dagger from his boot and sliced his palm. I took his dagger and did the same. We joined hands and we mixed our blood. It was right.

Afterwards I wrapped my arms around him and laid my head on his chest. "How's Cathy going to feel about this?" I asked.

I felt his body shudder at the thought. "She'll get used to it. Eventually."

Chapter 22

Fight training at the Cressida House was ugly and painful. The training facilities were top notch, including a huge gym with every machine known to man. There was a boxing ring and a three mile indoor circular running track.

The training center also encompassed a very large empty area covered in mats for sparring. There was an observation deck on the north wall about forty feet up. It was accessible from an outside set of stairs. One building contained a shooting range and a cavernous room filled with weapons—swords, daggers, katanas, throwing stars, guns and then some.

The weapons building also housed an area used for knife throwing. I spent many hours there after I nailed Cathy in the head. Thank you Jesus, I was getting more proficient with daggers and swords. I really didn't want to kill one of my comrades by accident.

After the car kissing debacle, Heathcliff decided it was okay to spar with me. That would have been fine, but the son of a bitch punched as hard as The Kev. If I didn't have healing powers, I'd be dead on the floor. After the third punch to my head, which may have caused brain damage, I understood why he was in charge of the Elite Guard.

"Are you okay?" Venus whispered as she pulled me to my feet.

"Fucking awesome," I muttered, getting up for another round. I was going to wipe the floor with Heathcliff's ass soon. I just needed to live through his attempt at wiping the floor with mine.

Venus, much to my great delight and relief, was also chosen

to be a new Guard. She was present along with the other new recruits. None of them really spoke to me. Actually, most of the Vamps in general stayed away from me. I couldn't tell if they were scared of me or just showing respect to the Chosen One. Whatever it was, it made me feel bad.

The majority of the existing Guard, including Ethan, was out on patrol, but several were here to put us through our paces. Cathy, looking thrilled to see me, was here along with Samuel, Luke and David. I loved that all the senior male Guards had Biblical names. I wondered if that was a requirement.

The veterans stretched us. While that may sound lovely, it wasn't. It was freakin' excruciating. Having a two hundred and thirty pound Vampyre push your leg up over your head with all his weight behind it sucked. Bad.

"Son of a bitch, Samuel," I grunted. "That kills."

"Not as much as the razor stubble on your leg is killin' me," he laughed and pushed harder.

"You're a shithat," I shouted through the pain. I was sure Samuel was going to pull one of my legs out of the socket and right off my body.

"What the fuck is a shithat?" he asked, truly puzzled.

"I have no clue," I moaned as he yanked my body into a pretzel.

Not everyone was intimidated by me, and Samuel certainly wasn't. I think that's why I liked him so much. He couldn't have cared less if I were Queen of the World or just some random Vamp off the street.

He was a big, good-looking guy with mocha skin, spiky black hair and long, lean muscles. His nose was a little crooked and he had a wonderful jagged scar that ran along his left cheekbone. It made him look dangerous. Hell, he was dangerous. They all were. He had intelligent dark brown eyes, the speed of a cheetah, a beautiful smile and an infectious laugh. Everyone loved Samuel, especially the ladies, from what I understood. He took great pleasure in repeatedly explaining to me that the Chosen One should be able to kick his ass. Clearly that hadn't happened yet.

"You are such a pussy," Samuel yelled gleefully as he put me in a chokehold.

"You are a son of a bitch, Asshat," I tried to yell back, but it came out all muffled due to my head being trapped in his armpit.

"God," he shouted, "you are the wimpiest recruit I've had in over ninety years."

He forcefully threw me to the mat. As he was about to body

slam me, I quickly rolled to my left, hopped up and gave him a round house kick to the head. He staggered back, grinning like an idiot.

I realized I was grinning like an idiot too. Who knew violence could be so much fun? "I've had about enough of your shit, you dress-wearin', backward-ass momma's boy," I panted, egging him on.

"Ooooo, sticks and stones..." he yelled and flipped me off, still grinning from ear to ear.

He ran at me with speed that almost made him disappear...almost. I dropped down to my right. I threw my leg out and undercut him, sending him flying. He landed with a thud on his back. With swift aggression I didn't know I possessed I pinned him *and* elbow slammed him in the face. The crunch was horrific and blood spurted everywhere. Samuel moaned and rolled around on the floor as he tried to adjust his nose and realign his cheekbones and eye sockets.

"Oh my God," I screamed and dropped to the ground to help him. "I am so sorry."

He was laughing. He grabbed me in a bear hug and bled all over me. "I am so proud of you," he gurgled through the blood. "You are finally close to kicking my ass."

"I'd say that was more than close." I was so relieved that he wasn't mad or dead.

"Astrid, you have to stop holding back," he said. It was difficult to take him seriously with all the blood gushing from his face.

"Samuel, you're my friend. I don't have too many of those and I don't want to hurt you."

"You can't, Astrid," he smiled, wiping his blood off of my face. "Short of you setting me on fire, removing my head or putting a silver stake through my heart, you can't permanently hurt me. We're Vampyres. We heal." He ruffled my hair and pulled me to my feet. I was amazed at how quickly his face was mending back together.

"How old are you, Samuel?" I asked. He had to be old to heal that fast.

"One thousand and three."

"Holy shit, you're older than dirt!"

"That's right, little girl, and I have been waiting for the Chosen One for a long time. I assumed when he or she came along, I'd finally find a good fighting partner. But noooo," he laughed. "Who knew she'd be such a fucking weak little peckerhead?"

"That's it," I yelled, putting Samuel into a headlock and

swinging him around like a doll. "I've had enough of your shit, you redneck jackass." I threw him across the room with such force I knew I broke both of his legs and possibly his back.

When and how did I become so violent...and when did I start to enjoy it?

"Now that's what I'm talking about," he grinned through his excruciating pain and gave me a thumbs-up. "If I were the real bad guy, you would have incapacitated me enough to stake me or decapitate me. I am so proud of you!"

I smiled at my crazy, very injured friend. I was sure it would take him at least a day to recover from what I had just done. I ran over and propped him gently against the wall. He squeezed my hand with pride and I kissed him on the forehead. I was torn between feeling really bad and really good. I turned to find the rest of the Vampyres in the room gaping at me in shock. Fucktard...they all wanted a piece of me now. I looked around and made eye contact with each one of them. It was do or die time...

"Who's next?" I asked.

Cathy stepped forward. "I am."

I looked down at the floor and took a moment to regroup. If I had thought it through, I wouldn't have asked that question. I would have challenged Luke or David or even Heathcliff, but I didn't think and now I was stuck. Samuel gave me a gentle push toward the mat. I looked to Heathcliff and he nodded.

Cathy intercepted the look and grunted in disgust. "Come on, you stupid holier-than-thou bitch. Come and try to get a piece of me." She was crazy. "Your silly little outfit won't distract me, dear," she said, looking pointedly at her brother.

There was power in stillness, so I walked to the center of the mat and waited. I stood quietly and claimed my space. Cathy circled me, dissipating her energy because of her anger and pride. I kept my eyes on her and my knees slightly bent, ready to spring.

The fighting techniques that we had to master were a mixture of martial arts and pure brute strength. One of the favorites included Dim Mak, also known as the Death Touch. This technique would kill a mortal instantly, but didn't kill Vampyres. It could knock them out or delay their reaction, which provided valuable staking or decapitating time. Iaido involved swords, specifically the katana. Ninjutsu involved throwing knives and stars. That was the one I had a little trouble with—*just ask Cathy*. And then there was my favorite, Capoeira, which was very dance-like yet still very aggressive.

Katanas, throwing stars and daggers seemed to be the

weapons of choice, but we had to be excellent marksmen too. Guns were not considered honorable, but Vampyres were very practical. Unfortunately, in today's world they were necessary. Several of the older Guards, my buddy Samuel included, were outstanding archers. However, I had tricks up my sleeves that they weren't aware of. That was why I fought so hard not to lose control. I was fairly sure I could kill every Vampyre in this room with Magic, and I really wished that was not the case. I didn't want the responsibility that came with my power.

Thankfully, The Kev had taught me how to separate Kill Magic from Damage Magic. It wasn't easy. I had accidentally killed a robin in my backyard when I was practicing and I cried for three hours. Let me assure you, it wasn't a pleasant death for the bird. I was positive whoever decided that I was the Chosen One had made a terrible mistake. If I had trouble killing a bird...I refused to finish the rest of the thought.

The Kev assured me that a killing machine that was capable of compassion, like me, would be one of the ultimate warriors of all time. I didn't understand his logic, but I prayed he was right. I had a bad feeling about whatever trouble was headed my way. I had no idea if I would be up to the challenge.

Cathy was getting impatient and I let her. Too much aggression led to carelessness and mistakes. She should know better. "I know why you're holding back," she jeered.

I just stared.

"You're afraid of me," she smiled. It wasn't pretty. "You know if you give it your all and I win...which I will...you're nothing. You're less than nothing, and Ethan will soon know it."

Several of the Vamps in the room laughed uncomfortably.

I stayed silent.

"Are you going to fight me this time, *Angel*?" All the Elite Guard gasped. Ethan was the only one allowed to call me Angel. I couldn't have given a shit, but the fact that she said it was serious business. No one messed around with the Prince's edicts. She clearly had a death wish.

I didn't want to hurt her. I knew she would heal, but for some reason hurting her was abhorrent to me. She clearly didn't feel the same way. Why on earth I felt protective of her was beyond me. It wasn't about Ethan anymore, and it certainly wasn't because she was sweet or defenseless. Maybe it was because she smelled so similar to Heathcliff. I suppose scent ran in the family. I couldn't figure out my reticence.

"Jealousy is ugly," I told her calmly. My plan was to set her up, piss her off, let her pound on me and be done with it. I would not fight back.

"You bitch," she screamed, attacking and knocking me to the ground. One of her hands was around my throat and the other was slapping me viciously across the face. "Fight me," she growled. "Damn you...fight me," she begged.

She was crazed and desperate. I could feel blood dripping from my lip and my eye was swelling shut. God, that hurt. I looked into her eyes. She needed to fight me more than I needed to not hurt her. Fine. She wanted a piece of me? A piece of me she would get.

I turned over and flipped her off of me. I flicked my fingers and sent her flying across the room at about fifty miles an hour. She hit a huge stack of chairs. It sounded like a bomb going off, echoing ominously throughout the room. I was sure that couldn't have felt good, but she was right back up and coming at me like a runaway freight train. She was so angry, it made her sloppy. I sidestepped her and gut punched her at the same time. It was a little difficult to see with one eye swollen shut and the other on the way there, but I hit my target. Hard.

She roared in frustration and pulled two very sharp, curved daggers from her belt. I was assuming they were steel and not silver. We weren't allowed to use silver during practice, but who the hell knew with Cathy? Silver was extremely painful for us, and of course deadly if run through the heart. I could stick steel or wood or copper straight through my heart over and over and not die, but silver...not so much. I quickly protected myself. I touched my hands to my chest and a glittery breeze shot out all around me, shielding me from all weapons including bullets. I heard Heathcliff gasp. I caught his eye for a moment and he stared at me in awe.

Cathy screamed and threw down her weapons. "What, you can't fight the normal way, you whore?"

She did not just call me a whore. I was a lot of things, but a whore was not one of them.

She was on my last nerve. I needed to take her ass down before my other eye swelled shut. I released the protection wall around me with a flick of my fingers. I did an aerial cartwheel right into her and scissor-kicked her in the head, taking her down to the floor before she even knew I moved.

I pinned her face down on the mat. I held her arms twisted behind her back and I dug my knees viciously into her hamstrings. As she screamed in agony I leaned down and head-butted her. *Shit, that hurt.* Whatever. It made her shut up.

I leaned over and whispered to her, "I am not a whore. Maybe a bitch, but definitely not a whore. I would suggest you remember that in the future, *Cathy*."

She tried to spit at me, but missed. "You'll kill him." She was crying.

"What are you talking about?" I hissed. She was starting to piss me off.

"If you mate with him, you'll kill him."

"Yeah, I heard that part," I barked. "What in the hell are you talking about?"

"You're the Chosen One," she grunted. "Vampyres and Demons and God knows what else will try to kill you for the rest of eternity."

"So what?" I yelled, twisting her arms tighter and pulling her shoulder out of the socket.

Whoops.

"If you mate with Ethan and you die, he does too, you stupid, selfish bitch," she gasped in hellish pain.

That stopped me. I let go of her and kicked her torn and battered body away from me. Why hadn't anybody told me that? That couldn't be right.

I slowly turned to Heathcliff. "Is that true?" I asked so calmly that I scared the hell out of everyone. I couldn't see him clearly through the swelling and the blood. I had split my scalp open when I head-butted Cathy and blood was running down my swollen face. This was definitely not my best look.

"Is it?" I yelled.

"Yes," Heathcliff said, "it is."

"Why in the hell do you people have so many goddamn stupid rules?"

Heathcliff looked down at the floor along with the rest of the Vamps in the room.

Well, my little Demons had been correct...this had turned out to be a clusterfuck of a day.

157

Chapter 23

I vaguely recalled Heathcliff carrying me to Venus' room. I knew I had collapsed, what with the blood loss and all my new stress. Venus helped me undress and bathed me. I was too tired and too weak, plus one of my eyes was still swollen shut.

Venus' room was cozy and inviting. She favored shabby chic—big overstuffed furniture in soft cottons and fuzzy chenilles mixed with thick crushed velvets. The patterns were faded cabbage roses in peaches and pale pinks mixed up with equally faded tulips and daisies in lavenders and periwinkles. Her walls were a pale celery green covered in crazy cool folk art and Aboriginal Dream art. None of it went together individually, but together it was perfect. Just like Venus.

The gashes on my head and lip had closed and were healing, but I was covered in dried blood and bruises. Venus washed my hair in lemon-scented shampoo and filled the tub with hot water and bubbles. It smelled like heaven. She was so gentle. I felt like a baby, a very happy and well-loved baby.

"Astrid," Venus asked, "do you want to stay in the tub?" She had drained out the dirty, bloody water and was refilling it with hot, lemony-smelling suds.

"I'll stay in here forever," I told her, sinking lower in the bubbles. She giggled and put an ice pack over my eyes. The swelling was going down. I could tell because I could see out of them now.

"Is Cathy okay?" I asked.

"Physically she'll be fine. Mentally, it's anybody's guess," Venus snorted in disgust.

"Is this all about Ethan?" I wondered aloud, taking the ice

pack off and sinking even lower in the tub.

"It can't be," Venus shrugged and handed me a big bottle of blood. "Compliments of Gemma," she smiled. "Chips and extra hot salsa!"

"Yesss." I gulped it like a starving person, dribbling some down my chin in my haste. I loved my friends.

"Anyhoo, Miss Manners..." Venus chided, wiping the blood from my face with a washcloth as I sighed happily. "From what I recently heard, Cathy and Ethan have not been...well, you know...intimate in about twenty years. Knowing they were not meant to be mates, he ended it and encouraged Cathy to look for her true mate."

"And?" I asked.

"Clearly she hasn't done that yet," Venus laughed and ran a brush through my hair.

"Heathcliff thinks they still sleep together," I told her.

"Heathcliff wants you, Astrid," she shot back.

"Did," I said firmly. "Not anymore." Venus raised her eyebrows and finished cleaning my poor battered face. "So if it's not about Ethan, why does Cathy hate me so much?"

"I'm not sure. Maybe she's still hung up on him," Venus offered. "Come on, let's get you dressed."

Wrapped in a fluffy towel, I followed her to her room and collapsed on her bed.

"Look, after what I found out today..." I paused and carefully considered what I was about to say. "I don't think I should mate with Ethan. Ever. I had no idea so much was at stake."

"Don't you think that's something you should discuss with me, Angel?" Ethan asked, leaning against the doorframe of Venus' bedroom.

"Holy hell," I screamed. Curling into a tight ball on Venus' bed I held my towel firmly in place. "Oh my God, do you *ever* knock?" I yelled at him.

Venus looked down and tried to hide her grin. She still couldn't get over the way I spoke to her Prince.

Ethan smiled and tilted his head to one side, making me want to slap him...then screw him. "Door was open," he grinned. "Venus, would you mind giving us a moment, please?"

"Not at all, my Liege." Venus winked at me as she left.

"I'm naked," I informed him.

"Interesting."

"You have to leave so I can get dressed."

"No."

"No?" I repeated, narrowing my eyes at him.

"No." His eyes changed to a beautiful emerald green and I could feel mine doing the same. "You are breathtaking," he said.

"I'm a bloody bruised mess," I retorted. God, he made me a nervous wreck.

"No," he disagreed, "you are the most beautiful woman in the world."

"Well, that's lovely and all, but I'm still naked and you still have to leave," I told him, reaching for the corner of Venus' quilt to ensure more coverage.

"It seems we're at an impasse." He sat on the edge of the bed, making my quilt grab unsuccessful. "How about a compromise?" he suggested.

"Last time I agreed to some vague idea of yours I ended up halfway Vampyre-married to you," I snapped and attempted to move away. Of course, the almost boob-reveal kept me anchored to my spot.

He threw back his head and laughed, and I swear to God I contemplated a strip tease and a lap dance. Damn it, he didn't play fair. How in the hell was I going to get out of here without offering myself up on a platter to him?

"How about you let me dress you?"

I considered his suggestion. Could I make this work to my advantage? Probably not, but it did sound intriguing.

"Will you keep your clothes on?" I asked, kind of hoping he'd say no.

"Of course, and I won't touch your skin at all...unless you ask me to," he replied smoothly.

While the thought was appealing, the reality was alarming. The minute his hands came close to my girlie parts I knew I would beg. He was such an egotistical pig. I wanted to make him suffer.

"No," I said. "That doesn't work for me, but I suppose you could watch me dress. You can look, but you can't touch."

His smile was positively feral and I shivered. God, how stupid was I?

"That sounds delightful, Angel. Shall I pick out an outfit?" he asked

"Um...yes." Clearly I was really, really stupid. "Wait, this is Venus' room. I don't have any clothes in here. Shit."

"Oh, but you do," he informed me, going through a pile of clothes on the chair.

"Where did those come from?" I asked, eyeing the pile suspiciously.

"My little Angel, you may not live here yet, but I am quite prepared for you when you do come to me." He grinned and pulled out the sexiest and most obscene panties I'd ever seen. He coupled them with a drop dead Prada halter dress and thigh-high stockings.

"Fine," I said, calling his bluff. "Leave them on the edge of the bed and go to the other side of the room."

"As you wish."

Damn it, I could do this. I would give him a case of blue balls that would make him double over in pain. I'd make him pay.

I got off the bed slowly and smiled, letting the towel fall to my feet. His sharp intake of breath made me giddy. I had never been so brazen in my life . . . or death, for that matter. Ethan shoved his hands into his pockets and I enjoyed watching him try to stay put. Locking my eyes with his, I ran my hands over my breasts and down to my hips. His eyes were blazing and his fangs descended, as did mine. I was enjoying torturing him. Unfortunately, I was also torturing myself. This was beginning to seem like a very bad idea.

I reached down and grabbed the scrap of silk he considered underwear. Moving in slow motion I bent over and stepped into them, making sure he had a very fine view of my entire backside. He groaned and dropped into a chair. He gripped the arms so tightly his knuckles were white. Damn, this was fun.

"You're a tease," he said, grinning from ear to ear.

"Honey, I'm just getting started," I purred, sliding the panties up my legs.

"Call me that again," he said gruffly, coming partly out of the chair. The tension in the room was thick and I was beginning to think I was in way over my head. I could feel the dampness between my legs and my breasts felt heavy and swollen under his gaze.

"Call you what?" I asked, settling the barely-there panties to their correct spot with shaking hands.

"Say 'Honey' again."

"Really?"

"Really. You've never called me anything sweet before. I like it," he replied and stood.

"Honey, sweetie, snookums, sex-pot, if you take a step closer, you'll be breaking the rules," I said, grabbing the halter dress and quickly stepping into it.

"What's the punishment if I lose?" he asked, advancing on me.

"Um...well shit," I screeched as I got my foot caught in the hem of my dress and I tripped forward into a set of very strong arms. "This wasn't part of the plan," I muttered and tried to twist away.

His hands on my bare skin ignited a fire down below. My naked breasts were pressed against his chest and my head was spinning. One hand slid down to my ass and neatly ripped away the sorry excuse for underwear he had chosen. If I could have found my voice, I would have yelled *Fuck me*...thank God my ability to speak had taken a vacation. His fingers continued their exploration to the area between my legs that made my knees buckle. He hissed as he felt how wet I was and reached further, immediately finding the spot that made me go partially blind. His long fingers expertly massaged me in circular motions. I cried out and writhed against him.

"Ethan," I gasped.

"Yes, Angel?"

"You're supposed to be on the other side of the room." I grabbed his shoulders so I didn't drop to the floor like a sack of potatoes.

"I was being a gentleman," he whispered into my ear as two fingers slipped inside me.

"Oh God," I moaned, pushing my body further down on his hand. "How is this being a gentleman?"

"You tripped and I caught you," he said. He lifted me up with his unencumbered hand and took me to the bed.

"You're not playing fair," I cried, trying unsuccessfully to calm my writhing hips.

"All's fair in love and war," he ground out as he captured my mouth with his, making any further protest impossible. His lips and fangs moved to my neck. His tongue played with my veins and I shuddered. His hand was moving like a high-speed vibrator and I shrieked. I was spiraling out of control, and I loved every second. I bucked on his hand like a champion bull rider and I had absolutely no control of the screams leaving my body.

"Oh my God, Angel," he whispered against my ear, "I have never wanted something so badly in my life. You belong to me, to no one else. Mine."

How in the hell did it feel like he had ten hands? Every inch of my body was a live wire ready to explode. My core was literally throbbing and words were replaced by screams and moans. He buried his fangs in my neck at the same time that he pressed down on my clit with the heel of his hand.

I detonated.

I vaguely heard him chuckle right before he sank his fangs into my nipple.

I cried out from the burning pain of his bite and tried to jerk away, but he held me fast. He drank from me while he plunged his fingers in and out of me. I thought I was done, but he had other plans. My body tightened to the point of pain and gripped his fingers like a vise. The rhythm of my hips increased to a frantic pace and I screamed over and over again as my world exploded into the loudest, most earth-shattering orgasm I'd ever had. My voice was raw and hoarse. I was sure speaking would be gone from my skill set permanently. Ethan held me and kissed me all over as I came down from my second orgasm in less than ten minutes.

"Oh my God," I whispered with what voice I had left, "that was..."

"Amazing."

"Um, yeah," I giggled.

"My Angel," he smiled, brushing my wild hair out of my face, "I am amazed by you. You are everything I want and more. I have waited so long for you."

"Ethan..." I looked down. I knew if I looked into his eyes he would know I was lying. "I don't want to mate with you."

He went as still as a statue. "Look at me."

I refused.

"Look at me," he repeated harshly.

"I can't," I said, trying to get off the bed but he pulled me close and held me still. Where in the hell did all my super Vampyre strength go? I supposed I would have to admit he was stronger than me.

"Angel, I know what happened during training today," he said quietly.

"Then you know why I can't mate with you."

"When I first drank from you, I knew who you were and what you were and what the risks were. I have no regrets, nor will I. Ever. You belong to me. You are mine and I will be yours." His golden eyes searched my face and his thumb gently traced my cheekbone.

"Ethan...I..."

"Stop," he commanded. "If you can tell me you don't want me and have no desire to become part of me, then I will leave you alone. Forever. Can you tell me you don't want me?"

He waited.

"No," I whispered, "I can't tell you that."

"I thought not," he said smugly. "So I will wait for you. You'll come to me when you are ready. But make no mistake, Astrid, you will come."

"I kind of already did," I muttered, looking away. "Ethan, it seems like you got the raw end of the deal." I'd just had several massive orgasms and he'd had...um, none.

"I wouldn't say that," he laughed. His eyes flashed and turned back to a brilliant emerald green. "But we'll take care of my end of the deal when you come to me willingly, with no reservations about how you feel about me. When you agree to be my mate."

"Are you sure?" I asked as I ran my hand over some very hard evidence. "I am quite willing."

He removed my hand and rolled off the bed. "I will have you," he said, "and when I do, it will be because you are mine. Forever."

With that remark he left the room, shutting the door behind him. I heard him laughing joyfully as he went down the hall. I was grinning from ear to ear. God, I adored that beautiful, conceited asshole. I might even love...

Stop. Don't go there. Do not fall in love with him. He didn't love me, he just wanted me. I quickly yanked on my dress and decided to go commando because the panties were toast.

"How ya doin'?" Venus grinned as she came back into her room. "I certainly hope you changed my sheets."

"Oh my God, Venus," I burst out, "we did not do that."

"Uh huh," she smirked.

"We. Did. Not. Do. It." I insisted and she snickered. "Why don't you believe me?"

"Well," she began, enjoying herself immensely, "your dress is on backwards, everyone in the entire mansion heard you screaming, and I just passed the Prince in the hall looking like the cat that ate the canary."

"Oh shit." I ungracefully righted my dress and slipped my feet into my sparkly beaded silver flip flops that thankfully weren't destroyed during my training ordeal. How was I going to face anybody here ever again?

"It gets worse," Venus said, trying not to laugh.

"How in the hell can it get any worse?" I hissed. All I seemed to do in front of my Cressida brothers and sisters was have really loud screaming orgasms with their Prince. First my initiation—now this.

"The King and his entourage arrived about a half hour ago," she said. I was speechless. This was a bad, bad, bad day. My potential father-in-law heard me screaming like a porn star angling for an award. "Ethan is with his father now," Venus said.

"You're joking." I felt sick.

"Astrid," Venus said, recognizing the symptoms of my impending panic attack. "Vampyres aren't uptight about sex like mortals. It's very natural for us. We're very sexual beings."

"I didn't have sex with him," I yelled.

"Then I'd hate to be within earshot when you finally do have sex," she laughed.

"He won't have sex with me until I mate with him," I said, peeking into my dress at my breast to see if he'd left puncture marks. Nope, all clear.

"Are you serious?" Venus was shocked.

"Yep...as a heart attack."

"What will you do?"

"I have no idea. I do know that I'm not walking out of this room and risking a meeting with the King," I said. "I'd rather go to a tanning bed."

Venus laughed, zipped up my dress and smacked me on the butt. "I would suggest you get moving then, because I can hear some Vamps headed this way to retrieve your sorry, screaming ass to present you to the King."

"See ya," I said, flinging my arms out and creating a glistening wall of glitter dust around me. I felt the Magic envelope me...and I disappeared.

Chapter 24

"Brad Pitt called," Gemma said, channel surfing.

I grabbed the mail and flipped through it. Nothing but bills and junk mail

"Again?" I was disgusted. This was the fifth time Brad called today.

"He's not going to stop until you call him back," she laughed.

"Oh. My. God." I yelled, "I'm so not in the mood to deal with Brad Pitt today."

I was still trying, without much success, to block out my scream-a-thon at the Cressida House. I hadn't even told Gemma about it. Speaking of it aloud would somehow make it more real.

"How about Angelina?" she asked, ducking to avoid the pillow I threw at her.

"She called too?" I couldn't believe this. What kind of evil had I done in my past to deserve this?

"Three times." Gemma bit her lip to stifle her laughter. Why she derived such pleasure from my pain was beyond me.

"Fine." I stomped my foot like a preschooler. "I'll just go down there and put a stop to all this bullshit."

"Go get 'em, killer," Gemma laughed, and ran from the room before I could find something else to throw at her.

***

Why in the hell was Brad Pitt so insistent on seeing me, and why was Angelina involved? Something didn't add up here.

He'd already informed me of my mother's unfortunate demise in an explosive private plane crash. No survivors. No remains. Huh...that was convenient. For the life or death of me, I would always wonder how she made that work out. I suppose if you're married to or screwing a Demon, you can make almost anything happen and make anyone believe it.

I had a whopper of a headache. I thought Vampyres were immune to human ailments like headaches. Some were. Obviously, I wasn't. My headache was named Brad Pitt and it was hitting me right between the eyeballs. Why, you may ask, would anyone in their right mind be angry that Brad Pitt was calling? I mean, come on, everybody wants them a little Brad Pitt...right?

Wrong! He wasn't *the Brad Pitt*, just *a Brad Pitt*. That's right, Brad Pitt from Bowling Green, Kentucky. He was a good ol' boy, ambulance-chasing lawyer with a severely receding hairline, greasy comb-over, beer gut, and bifocals, who happened to share a name with a really good-looking movie star.

He believed the similarities went beyond the name. Clearly he drank. Staggering as it may be, he thought he was sexy and interesting and that every woman in town secretly wanted him. He was wrong. Nobody in town wanted him, including his wife, Angelina.

That right there was one of the most alarming parts of the story. He had married a rather large balding gal named Tammy Sue Jinkers, but had made her legally change her name to Angelina Jinkers. Her entire family balked when Brad tried to persuade all of them to switch to their surname to Jolie.

She was a hoot, and if you listened to gossip, pretty loosey-goosey. Legend had it, with a few drinks in her, she'd go home with anything that could walk and had dangly parts. Six months ago at the Bingo Marathon, she had a few too many and informed all within earshot that Brad wore her panties and liked to be spanked. There was so much wrong with that I couldn't even begin to dissect it.

When they had first moved to town four years ago there was mass hysteria. All the townsfolk showed up bearing gifts and casseroles for Brad and Angie and their brood of children. All the local news stations came down, and by God our little local paper was there to cover the happening. Lexington and Louisville even sent crews down to our little podunk municipality. Then Brad and Angelina arrived, and boy, were people pissed.

I didn't see it, but legend had it that Martha and Jane threw casseroles at them, they were so furious. Knowing the old biddies, I was apt to believe that story was true. I felt sorry for our new neighbors until I found out the fake Brad Pitt planted all the stories that led us *stupidly* to believe the real Brad Pitt was moving here. Gemma read that the real Brad Pitt had finally had to take out a restraining order on our big, fat, greasy Brad Pitt. She also said that our local Brad Pitt's aura labeled him as very untrustworthy and downright skeevey.

His ego was as big as his gut, and his gut was big. He was a lardass lawyer, and of course Petra had retained his services. I was sure she got a good laugh knowing I'd have to deal with him, his bad breath and his wandering hands after her death.

Brad Pitt's office space hadn't been updated since the 1980s. Due to my super keen sense of smell I detected Taco Bell, B.O., Old Spice aftershave and bad breath.

To my great surprise and horror, Martha and Jane were Brad Pitt's new receptionists.

"If you don't have an appointment, Astrid," Martha snapped, "Mr. Pitt won't be able to see you."

"Free health care for everyone," Jane grunted and then slammed her own head down on the reception desk.

"I'm sorry, what?" I grinned, sure that I had misheard.

"Jesus wears a thong," Martha hissed and turned a shade of red I'd never seen.

Holy shit, had Paris Hilton already gotten to them? This was awesome.

"Moses liked sheep," Jane screeched. Martha slapped her and stuffed a wad of paper in her mouth.

"Equal rights for gays," Martha moaned. "All the rich people should give all their money to the poor, and Jesus ate pork in a tube top." She threw herself to the floor and yanked on her own hair.

Jane fell on top of Martha and proceeded to spew liberal and sacrilegious nuggets of wisdom.

"Well, hidey hodey ho, Astrid," Brad Pitt yelled from his office doorway. "You are lookin' miiiiighty fiiiine today, girly girl."

"Thank you, Brad," I said with disgust. "Why in the hell do you keep calling my house?"

"Well, little darlin', why dontcha come on into mah office and we can have a little chitty-chat," he leered.

God, he was foul...so foul that he actually gave me a tremendous idea. I should use some of my powers for the good of mankind. Shouldn't I? Yes...yes, I should.

"I'd love to rendezvous in your office with you, Brad," I purred.

He looked so confused that it was difficult not to laugh. Clearly no one had ever responded positively to his disgusting come-ons. After today no one would have to ever hear one again.

I sauntered past as he watched my butt with great appreciation.

"Martha and Jane, hold all my...what in the fuck is wrong with you two?" Brad bellowed as they wrestled all over the floor.

I glanced over my shoulder. "They're dating."

"Well, if that's not the goddamned grossest shit I've ever heard," he muttered. "Just hold my calls and don't you dare teach none of that lesbo shit to Angelina. She's already loose enough." He shut his office door behind him, licked his lips and gave me a big, skanky, good ol' boy grin. Brad Pitt of Bowling Green, Kentucky defined the word asshat more than anyone I'd ever met. He was vain, disgusting, and sexist.

"So, girly girl," he said, flexing his muscles, "why dontcha sit your pretty little hiney down. We done set up that memorial for next Saturday just like you requested."

"I didn't..." I started.

"I know you didn't think we could do it, but we did, sweet cheeks! And boy, are them some sweet cheeks," he guffawed and pointed to my ass so I wouldn't mistake his compliment. My stomach roiled. "We got that there message from 'Petra's daughter'. Like we didn't know who you was." He laughed and sucked in his gut, which if I'm not mistaken—and I'm not—made him pass gas.

"What are you talking about?" I was confused and asphyxiated at the same time. Bad combo.

"Don't you play coy with me, you little sweet potato." He had spittle in both corners of his mouth. "We got that big ol' six foot by eight foot poster of your momma that you sent over and Angelina had it mounted just like you wanted."

"Uh huh," I mumbled. Who in the hell was pretending to be me? Was Petra alive and screwing with everybody?

"I took one good look at that poster of your momma and...God rest her soul...I would have really liked to have mounted her! No offense," he said.

"None taken," I replied. "Tell me again when I called to request this."

"Well, lemme think." *This could take a while.* "I'm a guessin' it was about two...or four or maybe it was three days ago. We got a real kick out of that fake accent you used on that there message you left."

"Do you still have that message?" I smiled at him and ran my tongue slowly over my lips.

He about choked on his own saliva he got so excited. "Naw, once we listen to something the machine eats it. Besides..." He made sure his comb-over was still in place. "You told us to erase it after we wrote down all your orders."

He slithered his big ol' butt closer to me on the couch. "But here's the big news, little dumplin'." He moved closer. "Your momma left you forty million fuckin' dollars!" he shrieked like a game show contestant on *The Price is Right*.

What the fu...? "What?" I was in such a state of shock I didn't realize Brad Pitt was fondling my right boob. As soon as I did, I punched him in the head and he went flying across the room. It was a good thing Ethan wasn't here. Brad Pitt would be dead.

Forty million dollars. Where did she get forty million dollars? That couldn't be right. Could it?

"Are you sure about that amount?" I demanded.

"Yep," he whimpered from the floor. "You have one hell of a left hook."

"Thank you."

"Yer welcome." He got up and sat in the chair across the room from me. I guess you could teach an old dog new tricks. "The check will be ready next week, and right over there on my desk..." he pointed tentatively "...are all the details for your momma's memorial next Saturday."

I grabbed the folder and slowly approached him. He got lower and lower in his chair. Time to do some good for mankind.

"Sit up," I barked. He did.

I didn't know if this would be hard or easy. I was a little nervous, but he deserved it. He was a boil on the butt of the universe, and it was high time he was lanced. I let my eyes go green and I stared deeply into his little beady ones. He went slack-jawed and was more unattractive than usual. How was that possible?

"You will never come on to any woman other than your wife ever again. You will treat your wife like a goddess, and you will be at her disposal twenty-four seven. You will get rid of that skanky comb-over and you will brush your teeth more often."

This was fun!

"If you ever say anything inappropriate to a woman in this lifetime, your testicles will itch horrifically for a week. If you persist, your balls will fall off, followed by your dick. You will donate a third of your income to local charities."

I thought for a moment. Was there anything else? Nope, that pretty much covered it.

"Yes," he said, still tranced.

"Good." I let my eyes go back to amber gold and I waited. If this was successful, I might have a new calling in life. As he came out of his stupor, he looked confused, but quickly refocused.

"Well, Miss Porter, again please accept my condolences on your mother's untimely and tragic death." He gave me a fatherly smile. "The check should be here next week, and the memorial should run smoothly. I will review the details again myself. I must say it's quite a beautiful sendoff you have planned for your mother. Please let me or my lovely wife, Angelina, know if we can assist you further."

"Thank you Mr. Pitt," I smiled, satisfied with my work but still confused about who arranged all this. "Please give my best to Angelina."

I left his office and approached a grunting Martha and Jane.

"Teachers should get paid more and gay marriage is the answer to my prayers," Jane shouted and then punched herself in the head.

"The Pope wears a miniskirt and I worship dogwood trees!" Martha choked out, turning a mottled purple.

I smiled. Being a Vampyre so did not suck.

Chapter 25

I walked out of Brad Pitt's office feeling good, and saw something that made me feel even better. He sat across the street on the steps of the only bank in town. His chin rested in his hands and he had that sexy half-smirk thing going on. I think I'm in lov...What in the hell am I thinking? Close the brain door, close the brain door...he can hear me. *Shut it!*

I looked around and wondered where all of his guards were. He was too important to be traveling without protection, although from what I had seen he was stronger and more deadly than any Vampyre in our compound, and the Vamps in our compound were the best of the best. I didn't spot anyone, and my eyes were good. Good enough to clearly notice he was the hottest thing I'd ever seen in my life.

He grinned and my knees almost buckled. *Damn him.* I stopped about thirty feet away. I gave him the eyeball and put my hands on my hips. He just kept grinning as he stood and waited.

I shouldn't go. I should stand my ground. I absolutely should not go. If I go, I might have to jump him in public... I should not jump him in public. I should do it in private. Wait. I shouldn't jump him ever. Anyway, he should come to me...*but I wanted to go to him.* Nope, I'm not going.

While I argued with my inner slut he made up my mind for me. He picked me up and carried me to the most expensive-looking car I'd ever seen. I wrapped my arms around his neck and my legs around his waist and laid a big wet one on his beautiful lips. He tasted so good.

"Did you have fun in there?" Ethan inquired as he carried

me across the street to his car.

"I did," I said, ducking to avoid knocking my head on the door as he dumped me into the passenger seat while copping a major feel of my butt.

He got in the driver's side. "You know, you were right. I almost did come in there and kill him when he touched you." He was very serious.

"Oh my God," I yelled, hitting him. "You cannot go around killing people for me. I am perfectly capable of doing that myself."

He laughed. "But you wouldn't have killed him, would you?"

"No, I wouldn't have. He's an idiot, not a danger. Big difference," I told him, putting on my seat belt.

He watched me and smiled.

"Oh," I giggled. "Habit...guess I don't really need this anymore."

"You are still so beautifully human." He touched my face, drawing me to him.

Every touch, every look, everything about him sent electricity and need coursing through my veins. His lips were so close to mine. I wanted him to kiss me.

"How's the 'dating other people thing' going for you?" he asked with what I would have to label as mock sincerity.

"It sucks," I told him, running my tongue along his lower lip. "No Vampyre will come near me because of you." I saw no need to say anything about Heathcliff. We did not go on a date and although it turned out to be very special, it was not romantic.

He made a sad face. "I'm sorry to hear that." He was gloating.

"How's it going for you?" I realized in that moment I really wanted to know. Holy shit, was I jealous? I never got jealous. Ever. I wanted to rip her eyes out. Whose eyes? I had no idea, but if he told me he was seeing someone else I'd kill her.

"It's going fine," he said, revealing nothing.

I narrowed my eyes. "What exactly does that mean?"

"Well..." He took the longest pause in the whole wide world, loving my jealousy. I was going to cry. "I don't need to date anyone else. I already know who I want and I have every intention of getting her." He kissed my eyes. "And making her mine," he said as he kissed my nose, "for eternity." He kissed my lips, then pulled back and looked right into my soul. "Soon."

"Well...okay then," I said, mollified.

"Okay then," he said, starting the car.

"Where are we going?" I asked, kind of hoping he'd say a hotel.

"On a date," he grinned, "but we could go to a hotel after if you'd like."

"Get out of my head," I snapped.

"Can you not read my thoughts?" he asked, enjoying himself way too much.

"No, I can't. That one time in the graveyard I could. You must remember that," I snarked, "the time you tried to kill me?"

"I had no intention of killing you, Angel. I had every intention of doing something else with you, but you disappeared. We never have discussed how you were able to do that." He arched an eyebrow at me and waited. That look brought other Vampyres to their knees. He could be very scary. If I were easily intimidated that eyebrow thing would have scared me to death, but as it was it just made me want to make out with him really bad.

I wondered how much to reveal. He already knew quite a bit. "Angel blood," I said slowly. "My first feeding was from my Angel, Pam. The Magic comes from my Fairy, The Kev."

"The Kevin is your Fairy?" Ethan was shocked.

"Yes, is something wrong with that?" He had better not trash The Kev. I'd kick his ass. How did he even know about The Kev? He pulled the car over and stared at me. "What?" I said, getting uncomfortable.

"He lets you drink from him?" He was awed.

"All the time," I replied. Where was this going?

"You drink from him, but not from me?" Jealous Vampyre Boy practically shouted.

"I'm not in danger of being mated to him for eternity, Little Mister," I shot back.

"Did you just call me Little Mister?" The shock on his face was priceless.

"You betcha I did, Little Mister." I was positively gleeful.

"Do you have any respect for me at all?" he demanded.

"Tons," I smiled.

"All right. I was just clarifying." He rolled his eyes at my total lack of respect for his authority. I knew that he loved that I treated him like a regular Joe, but it frustrated him at the same time. He was used to getting his ass kissed.

"I guess that it would be so awful," he said, pouting, "to be mated to me. To be mine."

I could not believe one of the strongest and most respected Vampyres in the world, the Prince of the North American Dominion, was jealous and pouting. Over me. This was the best day ever.

"I'm not saying it would be awful," I told him. "Quite the opposite, I'm sure." He started to perk up. "But I need to know you better and you need to know me better."

"Will you show me your cheerleading jumps?" he asked, biting his lip to keep from laughing.

Venus and Gemma were so going to die.

"Only if you run buckass naked through the Cressida House professing your undying love for me," I snapped.

"Fine, I'll do it," he said, calling my bluff.

"You so will not," I laughed.

"I so will too." He grabbed me and brought his lips to mine.

"Screw you." I tried to push him away.

"Love to," he said.

"Wait," I said, torn between satisfying my curiosity or my libido. "Why is it such a big deal that The Kev is my Fairy?"

He shook his head and smiled, refusing to untangle himself from me. "The Kevin is the most beloved and feared Fairy in history. He is the finest warrior to come along in the last two thousand years. People faint in his mere presence. My guess is you're not even remotely scared of him." I nodded my head in agreement. "He doesn't give his protection or his tutelage to Vampyres. I can only recall one other Vampyre that he has taken under his wing, so to speak," he grinned.

"Who?" I asked.

"Me," he replied. "Has his fashion sense improved?"

"Get. Out. Of. Town. You trained with The Kev?"

"Yes."

"He punches like a freight train and no, he dresses like a blind man. If he ever left the house I'd be embarrassed."

"Oh, he leaves the house," Ethan assured me. "I wouldn't be surprised if he were quite nearby."

"Hello, my little Krumecaca," The Kev bellowed from the back seat on cue.

"Shit." I jumped and slammed my head into the passenger side window. Ethan winced in sympathy. The Kev just laughed and threw a little Glitter Magic to heal the bruise that was fast forming along my cheekbone.

"My Prince." He joyously slapped Ethan on the back. "How in the hecks are you doing?"

I turned back to look at The Kev. He was clad in tight salmon-hued flannel PJ bottoms and a cherry red wife beater with pink sponge rollers in his hair. Before I could ask, he explained.

"Gemma likes my hair wavy," The Kev said, pointing to the

rollers.

"Why don't you use Magic?" I asked.

A wicked grin spread across his beautiful Fairy face. "Because it's way too much fun to give to you the embarrassment." He winked at me. "Also it distracts you when we fight."

"You cheater!" I smacked The Kev and two of his pink rollers flew out. "Oops, let me fix that." I climbed over my seat into the back and I heard Ethan moan. I took my time and I made sure he got a really good look at my ass.

"You're killing me, Angel." His eyes were bright green.

"I'm trying to, Your Highness," I laughed and rerolled The Kev's hair. "Why are you here, The Kev?" I fixed several rollers that were about to fall out.

"I have come to you because I had the thoughts that you would be hungry," The Kev said mischievously. "I also think I would enjoy to watch my other favorite beautiful Vampyre get jealous," he laughed. Ethan did not.

"I am hungry." I was being careful. "Um, is that...?"

"No," Ethan snapped. "I will not allow you to crawl into some Fairy's lap and suck on his neck, no matter who he is." God, Vamps were territorial.

"Oh, my dear Ethan..." The Kev leaned forward and took Ethan's face into his hands. "She is the little sister of my heart. I love her like a child, the same way I love you. Astrid's path will be very difficult. She needs what I can offer her and I am here to prepare her." He paused. Sometimes his English was so good, I wondered if he was screwing with us the rest of the time. "She is the Chosen One, and it will not be easy."

"Absolutely not. She is mine and I will give her what she needs," Ethan said, defying The Kev, which was either really brave or really suicidal. The Kev grinned from ear to ear as if he expected Ethan's reaction and quite enjoyed it. "Very well," The Kev bellowed joyfully. "I am sure she is in the hands that are good."

"She is," Ethan replied in a clipped tone. I could feel him watching me. Ethan confused me. My love for The Kev was simple...a no-brainer. He was kind and gentle and there was nothing sexual to muck it up. Ethan was another story. There was so much sexual to muck it up it was hard to see clearly, but I was beginning to. I was falling... *No. I wasn't falling. I was already in love with him.* I was fairly certain part of me knew it from the first moment I saw him. Being in love with him scared me to pieces. I had ruined every relationship I'd ever been in. Partially thanks to my mother, but mostly thanks to myself.

My God, everything was getting too complicated, and I had a feeling that I was in the lull before the storm. It was going to get a lot uglier. How had I not gone insane? A month ago I didn't know Vampyres existed and now I was their Chosen One. I should be a blubbering idiot. I was sitting in a car with a Vampyre and a Fairy, and not just any Vampyre or any Fairy...the head honcho Vampyre and Fairy. My daddy was a Demon. I still had a hard time wrapping my mind around that one. Thankfully, I had my own personal Angel and Fairy or I might have taken after Daddy and started eating all the townsfolk. Who in their right mind would believe that a whole bunch of paranormal beings would choose the backwoods of Kentucky as their home and like it?

Checking myself into a facility was an option, but for some reason I was calm. Totally calm. I suppose tomorrow someone could let me know that werewolves and leprechauns exist and I could self-combust...or how about trolls and mermaids?

My life was careening out of control, but the only thing that unsettled me was Ethan. You'd think being spawned by a flesh-eating Demon or the fact that I was supposed to save the world would freak me out. Nope. The thing that scared me most was that I was in love with the Prince of the North American Dominion and I had no idea if he loved me back. I knew he wanted me, but lust and love were two different animals altogether. I wanted both.

The Kev took my hands in his and began speaking to me telepathically. Ethan was not included.

"Your heart may not beat, but you still have one, my liebchen. If you are not true to it, you will die a death more permanent than the one you live in now." I started to cry. He sweetly pushed my hair back from my face and continued. "It's okay to be scared, strudel princess, but not okay to run away from what will make you happy and complete." He took my face in his hands. "Don't you find it unusual that the two Vampyres in this car are the only two I have ever molded and made strong? Personally, I would wonder if there's a reason for that."

He winked at me before disappearing in a cloud of Fairy Glitter.

"What did he say to you?" Ethan asked.

"How do you know he was talking to me?"

"I could feel it," he said, watching me from the front seat. Even the small amount of distance between us made me feel lonely for him. What in the hell was wrong with me?

"Did you hear him?" I was alarmed.

"No, he blocked me," he said with disgust. "Far better than

you do, I might add."

I sat still and stared at him. He was so beautiful and so strong...and so mine, if I let myself go. If I followed my instincts, I'd crawl back to the front seat, bite him, drink from him and love him until the end of time.

"I wish you weren't the Chosen One," he said quietly.

"Why?" I was shocked. "Don't you think I'm capable of doing whatever the hell needs to be done?" Damn it, every time I was close to committing to him, he did or said something stupid.

"It has nothing to do with that." He angrily dismissed that notion. "Of course I believe you will succeed." He closed his eyes and ran his hand through his hair. "I wish you were not the Chosen One because I don't want anything to happen to you. I would not want to go on anymore without you. I have never been so happy in my life. You couldn't care less that I'm the Prince of the North American Dominion. You were attracted to me when you thought I was a Rogue Vampyre." That clearly delighted him. He reached back and put his hand under my chin, forcing me to look at him. "I wake up every day thinking about you, go to sleep thinking about you, and you are on my mind every minute in between. I can't wait to be insulted, teased and kissed by you. I cannot wait until we make love for the first time, and the second, and the third. You make me feel alive. Mostly I wish you were not the Chosen One so you would believe that I want you for *you*...that I have fallen head-over-heels, no turning back, in love with you."

I was speechless. My body felt light and airy and I was shaking. And then I did it. I followed my instincts.

I crawled over that seat, threw myself into Ethan's arms, and sank my fangs into his neck as I made him mine.

Forever.

Chapter 26

"Oh my God, Ethan," I gasped as I withdrew my fangs from his neck. "Something is happening to me." I was having a beyond overwhelming need to get naked, followed by getting him naked and violently making love to him.

"It's okay, Angel." He white-knuckled the steering wheel. "When Vampyres mate, they have to consummate the bonding. Their bodies demand it."

He put the car into drive and floored it.

This was news to me. I was dizzy and horny. I leaned over and put my head between my knees, hoping to eliminate some of the pressure building up inside of me. Bad idea. Leaning over made the crotch of my pants hike up and press against part of me that did not need to be touched if I was going to be able to hold it together.

"Ethan," I moaned, "I don't think I can..."

"You can." He touched my back and a bolt of electricity shot through me, causing me to orgasm. I screamed. The orgasm should have given me relief, but it didn't. It made it worse.

"Don't touch me," I ground out through clenched teeth, "unless you plan to follow through."

"Trust me," he said, his voice thick with lust, "I plan to follow through. Over and over and over. Just hold on—we're almost there."

"Where is *there?*" I asked, gripping the dashboard as if my life depended on it.

"Cressida House." He glanced over. His eyes were greener than I'd ever seen them and he was more beautiful than he'd ever been.

"No, not there! They all heard me yesterday. The only thing I ever do is have screaming orgasms with you at that House," I yelled at him.

He laughed. "God, I love you. My suite is soundproofed, Angel. Besides, sex in the Vampyre world is very different."

"Yeah, yeah, yeah...heard it before," I snapped. "I love you too, you jerk, but I'm sick and tired of not being able to make eye contact with anyone."

"You love me?" he asked, slowing the car to a stop.

"Yes, I love you," I shouted. "Do you really think I'd become your mate if I didn't love you?"

"I didn't know."

"Well, I find that incredibly insulting," I told him. "If I wasn't so goddamned horny, I wouldn't let you have any tonight. Clearly that's not gonna happen." I was shaking all over now. "Can't you drive any faster?"

He laughed his insanely sexy laugh and put the car in drive. And what do you know? I orgasmed. Again. This was getting ridiculous and I was getting teary. The pressure just kept building. "Ethan, *please.*"

"We're almost there, baby," he said, his voice unsteady. "I had no idea it would be like this."

"This has never happened to you?" I asked, turning away from him. Looking at him was dangerous. If I had another big O, I was sure I would die.

"Never." He swerved into the Cressida House drive at eighty-five miles per hour and screeched to a halt on the lawn, tearing out seventy-five to one hundred feet of manicured grass and bushes.

"Oh my God," I cried out, "your dad is here."

"Don't worry about him. He's going to be thrilled." He had me out of the car faster than a human could blink, whipped me up into his arms and headed for his suite. Of course, every Vampyre I'd ever met was hanging out in the foyer.

"Get out of my way," Ethan bellowed. "Astrid and I have mated."

Holy shit, he may as well have just yelled, "Watch out, Astrid and I have to go screw so we don't explode and die." I was never setting foot in this House again. What in the hell was the muscular, bald beefy security guy from Jerry Springer doing here? Was he a Vampyre? Wait, that wasn't the same guy...but he looked a lot like him. No, this guy was way better looking. Pam would luuuuurve him. We paused briefly in front of him. God, he was magnificent looking. He had eyes looked just like...*oh shit.*

Ethan bowed to him. "Father, this is Astrid. We've just mated. I'll see you in five or six hours."

Kill me now.

"That's wonderful, son," the King laughed joyously. "Astrid, I look forward to meeting with you...later."

The entire foyer of, oh...I don't know...about forty or fifty Vampyres burst into laughter and applause. Was this really happening? Were they truly celebrating the fact that I—or rather their Prince—was about to get laid?

Yes...yes, they were. Vampyres were so damn weird.

I wasn't positive, but I think Ethan flew up the stairs. Thank God for that because I wasn't going to last much longer. A door slammed shut. I couldn't have told you where we were because I didn't care. The only thing I knew for sure was that I was alone with Ethan and he was mine.

"I can't wait," I gasped, clawing at his clothes.

"Neither can I." He literally ripped my clothing from my body. "You went to see Brad Pitt without a bra on?" He was incredulous.

"I never wear a bra." I pulled his jeans and boxer briefs down and came face to face with the largest penis I'd ever seen in my life. My insides clenched and I thought I might faint. I wasn't sure I could handle him. Good God, had I come this far only to realize sex with Ethan would tear me in two? The sane part of me wanted to run and the horny side of me wanted to try him on for size. I didn't realize I was frozen and staring until I heard him clear his throat.

"Problem?" he asked suggestively.

"Um...no," I whispered. "It's just that...oh, what the hell..." I trailed off and grabbed the oversized monster.

"Oh my God," he gasped, pulling me to my feet and pressing his naked body against mine. "Angel, I need you," he moaned.

"Yes," I readily agreed, feeling light-headed and out of control. He pulled me to his bed and threw me on my back. He stood there naked, looking beautiful and deadly and mine. He was the most exquisite man I'd ever seen, just looking at him made my body sing. I was about to orgasm again without him even laying a hand on me.

He slowly, with carnal intent, kissed and nipped his way down my body. He paused at my breasts and marked me with his fangs 'til I screamed and begged him to fuck me.

"Spread your legs," he demanded. No more nice. No more gentle. No more soft. "Open for me, baby," he said as he parted my legs with his hands and blew on my most intimate places.

"You are perfect." He lowered his head and made me see Jesus with his tongue.

"Oh Ethan...I don't think..." I cried out and clamped my legs around his head trying to make him stop.

Startled, he looked up at me from between my legs. "What's wrong?"

"Um....well, I'm not very experienced with this kind of, um..."

"But I am," he grinned. His eyes sparkled and his lips glistened with my moisture.

"Well, that's certainly a big turn on," I huffed and tried to escape, picturing him with hundreds of hot sexy Vampyre sluts.

"Trust me, I'll turn you on," he whispered so sexily I lost brain cells, erasing the images of other women.

His hands were like manacles around my thighs and any thoughts of anything else were obliterated. This was not nice or romantic or simple. It was violent, sexy, and hard. It was changing me at some fundamental level.

As I screamed and moaned, and fought to gain dominance over the beautiful inhuman man possessing me, a trigger flipped. Suddenly, I was just like him, violent and sexual and no longer human. I wanted him more than I wanted to live. I would die for him and destroy anything that would threaten him in the slightest. He was mine. Period.

His fangs pierced me in places I had no idea were proper to bite and I returned the favor, making him shout in pain and pleasure. The line was so fine, I couldn't discern it anymore. And I didn't want to.

In a flash, his fangs were in my neck and his body was on top of mine. My body convulsed and he wasn't even inside me yet. I lost count on the mini and major orgasms wracking my body and started to beg.

"You're mine. Your body. Your mind. And your soul," he moaned into my ear and I shuddered.

"Please, Ethan," I gasped, writhing under him in wanton invitation. "Please."

"Please what?" he ground out, grabbing my hair and making me stare into his blazing green eyes. "Tell me what you want."

"You. I want you," I cried.

"More specific," he demanded, grinding his body against mine.

"Fuck me. Oh God, please fuck me."

"As you wish."

His smile was pure sex and frightening, but it was

everything I never knew I wanted or needed.

"Open for me."

I spread my legs for him. He took my hand and placed it on his engorged cock. "Put me where you want me," he said gruffly.

He was like thick steel covered in silk, hard and smooth at the same time. I was so in love with him, and as unsure as I was of his size, I also had no intension of stopping. Ever. I guided him to where we both wanted him to be. He pushed the head of his shaft into me and I gasped.

"God, it feels so good," he moaned, one hand grasping my ass and the other tangled in my hair, forcing me to lock eyes with him as he breached me slowly.

"Oh God," I gasped, "don't stop." I was right. He was huge and I was not.

"Mine," he groaned as his fangs descended.

He filled me to the point of pain, but his fingers on my clit forced my body to accept him as he methodically pushed more of his beautiful body into mine. He filled me to capacity and beyond, yet I wanted more. I wanted all of him. The thin line between pain and pleasure blurred to the point I was unsure what it meant. They were so intertwined that I lost sight of myself and became part of him. My core throbbed and I writhed beneath him, begging and crying. My body demanded satisfaction without care for the consequences. I lost all control and arched my pelvis up, pleading for more. My unspoken need undid him. He roared, and with a deep and violent thrust, he buried himself inside of me.

I screamed.

I was flying. My heart and my mind were with him, but my body tightened in protest. I felt him press at my womb. The orgasmic agony ripped through me and suddenly shifted. The pleasure overrode the pain and a slow sensual burn consumed my entire body. I bore down and gripped him inside of me, never wanting to let go.

"Mine," he growled. He was triumphant, his eyes blazing a beautiful green.

He moved in and out of me with inhuman speed. I was physically at my limit, but unwilling to stop. I needed more. I met each thrust with an abandon I didn't know I was capable of. My control had snapped and I didn't ever want it back. I knew it would be amazing, but I didn't know it would be perfect. I knew it would be good, but this was beyond. A fiery heat erupted as our bodies met. I needed him closer. I needed him deeper.

My nails raked across his back drawing blood, and I kissed

him everywhere—neck, chest, shoulders, and lips. It was animalistic and inhuman and I loved it. We branded each other over and over. I no longer knew who I was without him. I spiraled toward an orgasm that would either make me see Jesus or kill me.

"Angel," Ethan gasped, "bite me."

My fangs descended and I leaned into his neck as his body possessed mine with a speed and a force I had never known. I bit into his neck and began to drink. He did the same. The explosion that rocked my body was nuclear. I was flying higher than I could have imagined. I couldn't stop coming...it was the monster of all orgasms. My brain was skitzed and spots of brilliant color danced in my vision. Although I was spent, my body refused to obey. Ethan stiffened on top of me and then released himself. It was powerful and beautiful and felt like nothing I'd ever experienced. He had made me his and I had made him mine in every way possible.

"I love you," I gasped, running my hands through his hair and gently kissing his swollen lips with my own. "We should, um...probably get cleaned up and go downstairs to your father."

Ethan laughed and smoothed my hair back from my face. "I love you too, my Angel, but we're not going anywhere," he said, tracing my collarbone with his finger. "We've only barely gotten started."

"You can do it again?" I was shocked.

He was delighted. "Oh baby, I'm a Vampyre. I can direct where I want the blood in my body to go." He grabbed my hand and guided it to his rock-hard penis.

"Oh my God," I gasped and giggled.

"Are you ready to go again?" he asked, caressing my breast.

"I'm not sure," I lied with a smile as a slow heat coiled low in my body.

"I believe I can help you be sure," he said with a wicked grin, moving down my body and burying his face between my legs.

I shrieked as shots of electric pleasure pulsed through me as his tongue did things I'd never known a tongue could do.

"I'm getting pretty sure," I gasped.

"That's good." His voice was gruff as he slid back up my body. "Because I'm very sure I will never get enough of you."

Chapter 27

Eight hours and forty-five minutes later...

I wasn't exactly sure how I was able to walk. I'd had more sex in the last eight hours than I'd had in my entire life thus far. Drinking Ethan's blood, as old and as strong as it was, helped me recover some, but it was still a miracle that I could move. Quite honestly, I was surprised he could walk.

About four hours into our sex-a-thon, Ethan presented me with a ring. A six carat, square-cut pink diamond surrounded by white and pink champagne diamond clusters. I almost passed out, being the materialistic gal that I was. Pink diamonds were the rarest in the world. The ring had belonged to Queen Paloma, the King's first wife. Ethan's own mother, Queen Antonia, had died in childbirth with Ethan, so Queen Paloma raised Ethan along with her own daughter, Princess Lelia. She had been the one in the Betsy Johnson dress and great shoes, who had tried to kill me in graveyard.

The Queen had given the ring to Ethan over five hundred years ago making him promise to give it to his mate when he found her. Queen Paloma told Ethan that his mate would be the Chosen One and that their life together would be both complicated and beautiful.

"Why did he have so many wives?" I asked, gingerly pulling on some clothes from the stash Ethan had bought for me due to the fact that what I had been wearing yesterday now lay in shreds on the floor.

"It was very common then. There was a high mortality rate. A King had to give the world many princes and princesses. If I had to pick his mate though, it was Queen Paloma," Ethan told me. How in the hell did he always look so perfect? I watched him button his black shirt and marveled at his beauty. "I am nowhere near as beautiful as you are, my Angel. You are exquisite. Every inch of you is absolutely ravishing and totally mine."

God, he could fluster me. A pulsing heat beat between my thighs. A change of subject was in order or I was going to throw him down and molest him. Again.

"Get out of my head." I narrowed my eyes at him and he grinned. I grinned back. "Wait...he couldn't have been a Vampyre when he fathered you."

"He wasn't. He was a regular king with many wives and eleven small children. No one is clear on how he was changed, not even my father himself. We knew of Vampyres, Demons, Angels, and Fairies, but we had never encountered any. After he was turned, he went into hiding for a year, terrified that if he stayed he would harm or kill everyone that he loved."

"Did he?" I asked.

"Yes." Ethan paused and then continued slowly, "He drained his brother. Killed him during his first thirst."

"Oh my God." I felt horrible for the King and for his brother. Remembering my pain and desperation before I fed for the first time, I was so grateful Pam had been there to feed me. I could have easily killed a mortal in that awful state.

"My father was devastated." Ethan took my hand. "He adored his brother. That's when he left. He didn't know the first hunger was the worst. None of us did."

Ethan pulled me over to one of the leather couches, sat me on his lap and continued the story.

"During his absence we encountered Demons and Fairies. The worst and most dangerous was Abaddon, the King of the Demons. He showed up and repeatedly tried to seduce my father's wives in his absence, hoping one would kill my father. This would have let Abaddon assume his reign. The King of the Demons might even have been successful with one of them, but Queen Paloma had his number, so to speak. No matter what face he chose to show himself in to the wives, she banished him back to Hell every time."

"Why didn't Abaddon just try to kill the King himself? Why get a wife to do it?" Again I was confused.

"The story is a bit complicated," he said. "The King's death must be at the hands of someone emotionally and physically connected to him. Abaddon was neither. The Demon had to be personally responsible without physically committing the murder, if he wanted to gain control of the Upper World. Therefore, one of the King's wives was a perfect choice. Trust me, the Demon could be very beautiful and very persuasive. The person who destroyed his plans was Queen Paloma. She fought him every time."

"She sounds amazing," I said with admiration.

Ethan smiled. "She was. She was as beautiful as she was tough. We all adored her, especially my father."

"Did that make any of the other wives jealous?" I always wondered how the Mormons did it. You never really heard much about Mormon wives offing each other.

"No," he said, "it was quite common to be in marriages like that in those days. My father took very good care of all of his wives. They wanted for nothing."

"Oh, come on." I punched him in the arm and realized my entire upper body was sore, too. How in the hell was my upper body sore? Oh wait...maybe the handstand position had something to do with that. I knew that was risky, but Ethan had been so impressed..."You can't tell me that every wife was happy with that arrangement. There had to be some Jerry Springer stuff in there somewhere."

Ethan raised his brows at my aches and pains, or maybe it was my referencing Jerry Springer. He began to massage my back and neck. God, that felt good. "There was some strife, but that didn't come until my siblings and I were in our twenties."

"Mmm," I moaned. I was in heaven. First sex and then a massage. It didn't get much better.

"At the time," he chuckled as I snuggled closer, "we did not know how or why Queen Paloma had died. We didn't find that out for a hundred years."

"Didn't he try to change her?" I asked.

"Yes, that's when he realized that women who had borne children could not be changed," he said sadly.

"Why didn't he say anything? So much heartache could have been avoided had he spoken out."

"He was too devastated," Ethan replied. "It's a decision he regrets every day of his life. Many women died because their husbands didn't have the knowledge that my father had. Several hundred years ago when everything became known, the monarchy was almost destroyed."

"So which wives got all pissy?" I asked. Heathcliff had told me some of it, but Ethan had been there. I had to admit that it was weirding me out a little that I was Vampyre-married to someone who was over five hundred years old, but damn, you'd never know he was older than dirt in the bedroom. He was a total rock star in the sack. I didn't even know people did some of the stuff we did. I couldn't wait to do it again.

"Um...Angel, I can hear you," he laughed.

"You have got to get out of my head," I snapped.

"That's very difficult now that we're mated. We're more connected than any two people could be. You're mine and I'm yours."

He leaned in and nipped at my neck sending little electric shocks through my body.

"Stop," I giggled, "I want to hear more of the story."

"Fine." He rolled his eyes and continued. "He changed all of his children, but none of his wives. None of the wives challenged his decision except one. She was furious. She begged and pleaded, but he stood firm. At the time I felt bad for her. I, too didn't understand why he wouldn't change her." He twirled my hair between his fingers. He had no idea how many points he was earning. I loved having my hair played with. That was definitely worth a blow job.

"Angel," Ethan moaned, "your train of thought is going to make me strip you naked and have my way with you again."

"Whoops," I laughed. "Will this sexual thing ever fade?" I asked, not knowing if I wanted him to say yes or no.

"Nope, from what I've been told it gets more intense with time and familiarity."

"Oh my God," I gasped, "we'll end up killing each other."

"I could think of worse ways to go," he smiled, running his tongue along my shoulder. I shuddered.

"Wait," I said, pulling out of his embrace. "So is that the wife that got banished?"

Ethan sighed and realized he was not going to get into my pants until my curiosity was satisfied. "Yes, I no longer felt sorry for her after she tried to kill my father. Apparently, Abaddon had regaled my father's wives with a tale of how to attain immortality without becoming a Vampyre, but only one took the bait. If they sacrificed the King, drank his blood, and ate his flesh, they would live forever."

"Oookay," I gagged, "that's disgusting."

"Oh, but that's not all," Ethan continued, "the murderer must rip out the heart of the Vampyre King, and present it to the Demon King. This action ensures that King Abaddon will rule both the Upper and Underworlds. Abaddon is the most viciously evil of all the Demons, although all Demons live in Hell for their own wicked reasons."

"Is any of that true?" I was shocked. Vampyres and Demons were sickos. Wait. I belonged in both of those categories. What in the hell did that make me?

"I have no idea," Ethan said. "It's never been accomplished...not that it hasn't been tried. So my father banished his wife, the mother of my sister, Princess Juliet. Juliet disappeared about twenty-five years after her mother was banished. We've never been able to find her."

"Was Juliet angry with the King?" This was fascinating.

"No, we never thought so. She seemed lost after her mother was banished, but she was well loved by the other wives and all of her siblings."

"So how does The Kev figure into your life?" I asked as I straddled him, making it difficult for him to think.

"You're so asking for trouble." Ethan grabbed my hips and pulled me closer.

"I so know that," I grinned, winding my fingers into his hair and putting my lips to his ear. "How did you meet The Kev?" I ran my tongue along the edge of his ear and sank a fang into the lobe. God, his blood was delicious.

Ethan moaned. "He was sent by an Angel in the Heavens to train me to protect my father." He was losing control quickly. "I was so surprised to see the form he took this time." He cupped my bottom with one hand and started to unzip my dress with the other.

"What do you mean, form?" I demanded and he stilled. "What are you talking about? What form?"

"What?" He was confused. "What do you mean, what form?"

"You said it," I told him trying unsuccessfully to crawl off of his lap. I knew this was important. "What do you mean about The Kev's form?"

"Oh," Ethan laughed, "you lost me there for a moment." Clearly all the blood had left his brain and traveled south. "The Kevin doesn't really look like Arnold Schwarzenegger." He tried to kiss me, but I was having none of it.

"What do you mean?" I snapped. "Of course he looks like Arnold Schwarzenegger." That stopped him.

"Oh baby," he said, "Angels and Fairies rarely show their true form. They are so beautiful it is impossible to look at them. They can choose any form they like."

"You are kidding me." I was astounded.

"Nope," he smiled at my shock.

"You're telling me that The Kev doesn't look like Arnold Schwarzenegger and Pam doesn't look like Oprah Winfrey?"

Ethan started laughing. Hard. "Your Angel took on the visage of Oprah Winfrey?"

"Yes, she did," I said, getting pissed at him. "Why in the hell is that so funny?"

He couldn't stop laughing. He was starting to make me laugh. "I don't know why I find that so amusing, I just do. She must have a hell of a sense of humor."

"She does," I said with loving pride. "She also has a mouth like a sailor."

"Oh my God." He was still laughing, "I want to meet her."

"I'm not sure she'll let you see her. She seems to have an aversion to Vampyres."

"Most Angels do," he said, calming down. "She doesn't have an aversion to you."

"No, she loves me," I told him.

"I do too." His eyes turned green and his fangs descended.

"Oh no, no, no," I said, trying to squirm away even though I could feel my own eyes turning green and my fangs descending.

"Oh yes, yes, yes," he insisted, tearing open the front of my dress. "God, I love that you don't wear a bra." His mouth quickly closed over my very erect nipple.

I squealed with delight, threw my head back and gave in to the sensations. Oh hell, what's another hour or two going to hurt?

Chapter 28

I was so nervous to sit down with the King I thought I was going to pass out. Ethan had more clothes sent up for me, due to the simple fact that all my clothing had yet again been shredded in a sexual frenzy. Of course the new stuff was all Prada. This time it was a body-hugging, midnight blue strapless dress and a kick ass pair of black stilettos. The fabric felt slippery and sexy on my skin. Mortals were really missing out on the Vampyre sensory overload thing. At least I knew I looked good on the outside, even though my insides were churning. Turns out, I had nothing to worry about. Who knew I was going to fall in love with the King within the first two minutes of being near him? I was jealous of Ethan and his siblings. I had always imagined a father just like the King.

"You are absolutely lovely," the King laughed happily and enveloped me in a bear hug. He smelled wonderful. He held me out at arm's length and studied my face. "May I?" he asked, indicating he'd like to sample my blood.

From anyone else that request would seem either sexual or repulsive, but from the King it was completely inoffensive, almost sweet. I nodded. He produced a beautiful but wicked-looking dagger from his belt and gently sliced my palm. He brought it to his mouth and licked. He considered for a moment, rolling my blood around on his tongue...

"You are strong yet compassionate. You are very capable of killing, but it is not your first choice. Your strength and skill with Magic will be unparalleled." His golden eyes sparkled like jewels. "You are gifted beyond reason, and I would hazard a guess that you have only scratched the surface of your abilities.

You are much more than just a Vampyre, my little one."

Oh my God, he knew I was half Demon. Damn, I'd forgotten he could identify species by blood. He paused and I could swear he looked right into my soul. "You are the One," he whispered. "You are the Chosen One. We have waited so long for you, my beautiful child."

He squeezed my hand and looked down at the ring on my finger. God, he really did look like the beefy security guy on Jerry Springer that Pam liked so much, only way better. He was bald and muscular. He had incredible cheekbones and his golden eyes were magnetic. His lips were full like Ethan's and his lashes were impossibly long. It was a little strange that he didn't look much older than Ethan, but that's just the way it was with Vamps. Forever young. Pam would fall over dead for this guy. I'd bet money that she would give up her aversion to Vampyres for him.

"Ah, Ethan..." The King had tears in his eyes. "You've given Astrid Queen Paloma's ring."

"Yes, Father, she is my mate."

"Do you love her?" he asked his son.

"Completely," Ethan told his father while staring directly at me. My knees went weak.

The King gently took my face in his hands. "Do you love my son?"

"I do."

The King leaned in and kissed my forehead. "Then it is right that you wear the ring," he smiled and released me. "You two have my blessing."

"Thank you, Father." Ethan looked at me with pride and love. I could not remember when I had been this happy.

"Your Majesty," I said.

"Father," the King corrected me, "please call me Father." I couldn't hide my delight at the honor of his request. It made Ethan and the King laugh. Great, now I was embarrassed. "What is it, my daughter, my Chosen One?"

"About that Chosen One stuff...do you have any idea how I am to serve you?"

"No," he sighed, "I don't, but I can feel that the time draws near. There is more Rogue activity in this particular part of the world than ever before. This does not bode well for the mortals or for us. Our anonymity is why we can exist. Without it we will be destroyed."

"Why this part of the world?" I asked. "Why Kentucky?" It didn't make sense to me why beautiful, glamorous Vampyres would be drawn to Kentucky. Don't get me wrong, I loved

Kentucky. To me it was paradise, but it wasn't exactly the mecca of sophistication.

"Don't you know?" Ethan seemed surprised by my question.

"Clearly I don't, Mr. Smarty Pants, or I wouldn't be asking. Let's see, I've been a Vampyre for what? A month?"

Oh my God...I slapped my hand over my mouth. I was mortified. I didn't really want the King to know how rude I could be right off the bat.

"She has no respect for me," Ethan sighed with amusement in his voice and lust in his eyes.

The King chuckled. "Ahhh, she reminds me of my Paloma. Astrid, to answer your question, it's the caves."

"The caves? Mammoth Caves?" I was confused.

"Yes, Mammoth Caves and the Diamond Caverns are an epicenter of paranormal strength. An apex, if you will, of natural immortal power."

"I love the caves," I said.

"Of course you do, that does not surprise me." He smiled and touched my cheek. I leaned into his hand. Who knew I was so starved for parental affection? I pulled back in embarrassment as he continued. "The caves began forming about ten million years ago during a time of great paranormal activity. The limestone deposits in the caves trapped the earth's natural Magic and fed it. That enabled the power to grow and strengthen for eternity."

"Normal people go there every day." I was shocked to learn all of this.

"Yes, they do," the King sighed. "The caves opened to the public in 1816. It's made it more difficult for us, but not impossible. The strongest areas are those that the mortals have not discovered or mapped. There are hundreds of miles of cave that the mortals know of, but hundreds more that they will never find. There are portals to Heaven and Hell in the Diamond Caverns. Many immortals of different species are attracted to this area."

"Is that why I see Demons everywhere?" It flew out of my mouth before I knew it was coming.

"You see Demons?" Ethan was surprised.

Uh oh...the jig was up. "I do," I said slowly, "but they're not all evil."

Ethan snorted. "All Demons are evil—period."

"Well, she's definitely the Chosen One!" The King clapped his hands like a child. "Can you speak to them?" he asked. Ethan looked at his father as if he were crazy.

"Yes, I have four of my own," I told the King. Ethan watched me with an unfamiliar look in his eyes. "Mine are my babies. They wouldn't hurt anyone. I love them and they love me." I knew I was getting defensive.

"Not all Demons are from Hell." The King assured me while clearly making a point to Ethan. "Some are fallen Angels looking for good deeds so they may return to Heaven. Some are tortured souls who committed suicide and must do earthly penance to redeem themselves in the eyes of God."

"Do we believe in God?" I whispered, hopeful and scared at the same time.

"I don't know if you do, but I certainly do." The King smiled at me. "How can you look around this beautiful world and not believe in God?"

"Do we have souls?" I sounded like a child to my own ears, but these were questions I had been too intimidated to ask until now. If I was very possibly going to die for these Vampyres, I wanted to know exactly where I stood and what I was.

"We do have souls, child," he reassured me, "and we will answer to God on Judgment Day, same as anyone else. We just have a much longer time to rack up sins than your average mortal."

"I have to tell you something." I hesitated and realized I should have told Ethan all of this before I mated with him. Oh my God, he hates Demons. Will he hate me? But I'm not a Demon. Okay I'm half, but Pam said I wasn't a Demon. Does that count? He had a right to know what I was before he was stuck with me for eternity. How in the hell was I supposed to know he was prejudiced against Demons?

Again, I have screwed up another relationship. I guess I'll be headed to Vampyre divorce court. I felt sick. I was in love with someone who hated what I was.

"Yes, my daughter?" the King waited.

"Right before my mother, um...died two weeks ago, she introduced me to a Demon. A bad one and she said...well, I mean, told me..." God, there was no easy way to say this. "She said he was my father."

The room was silent. Ethan's anger was palpable.

"What was your mother?" Ethan demanded coldly. It was the first time I was afraid of him since our encounter in the graveyard. He was no longer the man I'd just spent hours making love with. He was the Prince of the North American Dominion and I was but a lowly subject with whom he was furious.

"Mortal, I think." My voice came from far away.

"Is that possible?" he snapped at his father.

"Anything is possible," the King said, looking at me intently. "After your change, you were raised and fed by an Angel and a Fairy, correct?" he asked.

"Correct," I told him. "My Angel is Pam and my Fairy is The Kev."

"My goodness," the King smiled and took my hand, "they sent down the big guns for you." When he touched my face, he made me feel safe and cared for. "There is no problem...you are not evil. You are who you are supposed to be. You are the Chosen One."

God, he made me feel better. I'd spent my whole life thinking there was something wrong with me and that I wasn't good enough to win my mother's love, that I was unlovable. I had that same feeling in the pit of my stomach when Ethan got so mad. If the King could love a half Demon, I could only hope Ethan would do the same.

"Don't you think," Ethan said between clenched teeth, "that you might have informed me that you were a Demon before we mated?"

"Are you serious?" I gasped.

"Completely," he said, his voice cold.

Oh my God, he was such an asshole. I was filled with rage and humiliation and embarrassment. I wanted to sob, or to hit him, but mostly I wanted to run away. If he did not want me, I did not want him. "Your Highness," I spoke with icy calm, "it's half Demon, not Demon. But you're right, I should have told you...just like you should have told me you were going to severely limit my dating options before you bit me in front of six hundred Vampyres. Next time you sink your teeth into somebody you should probably do a better background check."

I was amazed at my ability to sound cold and mean when all I really wanted to do was beg him to love me.

"Limiting dating options and being a disgusting spawn of the Devil are two entirely different things. Don't you think?" His voice dripped with sarcasm and anger. I barely recognized him.

"No, I don't think," I hissed.

"That's right...your kind doesn't do much thinking."

My cold, dead heart was truly broken. I wanted to die for real. Instead, I held my head high and looked the son of a bitch right in the eye.

"According to my Angel and my Fairy, their blood negated any Demonic tendencies I may have had. So you see, Your Highness, I am not considered a Demon. Back to your original concerns though, you're right. I should have told you I was a disgusting half Demon, and on the same note you probably should have told me that you were a hateful, bigoted half-asshole!" I yelled.

Oh my God, was I crying? Shit, I was crying.

I tried to take the ring off and throw it at him, but it was stuck on my finger. I cried out in frustration and I narrowed my gaze at him. It finally seemed to have an effect. He still looked furious, but he was also very upset and uncomfortable. Good.

"We are no longer mated," I hissed. I was losing it fast. "I don't want you and you don't want me. We are done!" My non-beating heart was shattered. I backed up quickly as he started to come for me. What the hell? Did he want to kill me on top of destroying my life?

"Don't you dare come near me," I screamed. That stopped him dead in his tracks. I threw my hands in the air and in a cloud of Fairy Glitter...I disappeared.

***

"She's a feisty one, isn't she?" The King said, brushing the magical glitter off of his suit.

"How can you be so calm?" Ethan yelled at his father. The King just stared at his son. "Oh my God, what have I done?"

Ethan dropped down into a chair and put his head in his hands. The King patted his son on the back.

"She can't do that, can she?" he asked.

"Do what, my son?" the King asked.

"She can't break the mating. She can't leave me."

"No," the King said gently, "she can't break the mating. Once the relationship is consummated, it is permanent. Unbreakable, except through death. As far as leaving you...that she can do, but you would still be mated."

"She's mine, whether she knows it or not," Ethan muttered. He paused for a moment. "I don't think I handled that well."

His head dropped back into his hands.

"No," his Father agreed, "I don't believe you did. You may think she's yours, but I'm quite sure she would not agree. Does it really bother you that she is half Demon?"

"For a moment it did. My God, I've hated Demons for over five hundred years...and then I realized that I wouldn't care if she were half the Devil himself. I'd still love her." He paused. "What do I do now?"

The King considered his son's options. "I suppose you could start by begging."

Chapter 29

I walked slowly toward the tomb, my hands outstretched. I could feel the tingling in my fingertips. It quickly spread down my arms, through my chest and into my legs. My heart was pounding inside me, my stomach felt twisted and it was hard to breathe. The wind picked up and blew my hair wildly around my head. I was inches away.

"Push, Astrid," she gasped.

I placed both of my hands on the tomb and began to push. The tomb started to crumble under my fingers. The stone turned to cold, hard diamonds—beautiful, sparkling sharp ice that sliced into my hands. My hands bled, but I did not stop. I was so close. The blood ran from my hands, down my arms, and seeped into the soft white cotton of my shirt. The stunning diamonds were awash in my blood...I knew if I pushed just a little more...I could... The pain was becoming intolerable. Every nerve ending in my body was on high alert, screaming for me to stop.

If I could just push harder... I felt silk, soft slippery silk, between my fingers. Her dress....I was touching her dress. I was so close to her. I knew I could save her. I needed to pull her out. I looked down and watched my blood turn her beautiful, sheer, green silk dress to crimson. She was laughing with joy... She was so proud of me. I had waited my whole life to hear her tell me...

OUCH! What the fu...? I opened my eyes. My little monsters were standing on my chest covered in bloody diamonds, looking confused and alarmed.

"Oh my God," I cried, "are you guys okay?"

I frantically brushed the bloody diamonds off of my babies and checked them for injuries. Ross had a jagged cut on his forehead and Honest Abe's shoulder was sliced open. Beyonce and Rachel looked upset but fine. The boy's gashes were not deep, but they were definitely bleeding. Why in the hell were bloody diamonds in my room? That was a dream. Wasn't it?

I picked up a handful of diamonds and stared at them as they turned to a fine powdery dust and slipped through my fingers. I thought I was okay with all the Magic and craziness in my life, but this one was a little unnerving.

"Dink," Ross pointed to his little forehead.

"I know, baby," I cooed, holding him in my palm and running my thumb through his Velcro hair. It had just been in the last week that we'd been able to fully communicate with speech. It thrilled me. "You dinked your little head. Mommy will make it better." I went to wipe the blood away with my finger and they all started screaming, scaring the hell out of me and making me drop Ross onto the bed.

"No, Mommy," they shrieked. "Dink, dink, dink!" They mimed licking Ross' forehead and Honest Abe's shoulder. *What the fu...?* They wanted me to drink from them?

"Drink?" I asked them.

"Dink, dink. YESSS!"

They were doing back flips and grinning from ear to ear, slapping each other with high fives and kissing me all over my face. I giggled and squeezed Ross' fat belly. He screamed with joy and proceeded to tackle Honest Abe, who in turn tried to slap Rachel in the back of the head but missed and nailed Beyonce. Of course Beyonce got pissed and kicked Honest Abe in his little Demon nuts. Honest Abe doubled over and moaned in agony while Beyonce laughed hysterically. Rachel just looked confused and Ross cupped his own balls, in defense or solidarity...I didn't know which.

"I can't drink from you. I might hurt you," I told them. Now there was an irony considering what they had just done to each other.

"DINK, DINK, DINK," they chanted, jumping up and down on my bed. They sounded like the Munchkins from The Wizard of Oz, or me after I sucked all the helium out of a balloon.

I picked up Ross and brought him eye level. "Are you sure?" I asked. I would die if I hurt him.

"Yesssss, Mommmmy," he said, kissing all my fingertips. The peanut gallery below was still chanting "Dink, Dink, Dink." I gently ran my tongue over Ross' wound. He tasted amazing, like Skittles and Sweet Tarts. He purred like a happy kitten.

The minute his blood entered my system something strange

happened. Bolts of heat shot through my body, down through my toes and out through my fingertips. It was violent. I started to convulse, but it quickly turned into a gentle hot wave churning inside me. It didn't hurt, just felt surreal, floaty and powerful. I wondered if I was crazy to trust my Demons. No, I was not crazy. I did trust them. With my life.

Ross stared at me, his little golden eyes shining. He gently touched my chin. "Take moooooore, Mommy, you need more. I make you strong." He licked my face and rubbed his Velcro hair on my cheek. His cut had almost closed. I carefully ran my tongue over it again and had an identical reaction. As I came down off the bizarre high from Ross' blood, I could hear Honest Abe impatiently babbling.

"Me next, Mommmmy, MEEEEEEEE! My turn, Mommmmmmy," he yelled frantically, jumping up and down like a Mexican jumping bean on crack. I picked him up and slowly licked his shoulder, being careful not to hurt him. He tasted different from Ross, but just as wonderful. His blood reminded me of watermelon Jolly Ranchers. I was shocked as my body started levitating off the bed. The ringing in my ears was almost deafening, but I could still make out the joyous cheering from my baby Demons.

"More, more, more, Mommmmmy," they whooped. So I did. I licked again from the quickly healing shoulder wound of my little Honest Abe. He kissed me with delight as I levitated even higher.

He crawled up my face, over to my ear and whispered, "You can flllllyyyy now, Mommmmmy. I give you flllyyy." He giggled and kissed me again.

I floated back down to my bed and realized I had controlled that. If I visualized what I wanted to happen, I could make it happen. I tried again. I closed my eyes and pictured myself flying around my room. I opened my eyes and I was doing it! I laughed and did back flips in the air as easily as if I were underwater. My little cheering section whistled and shouted.

I shot some Glitter Magic down to them and they went ballistic. I floated back to my bed and happily watched my Demons have fun. They were showing off like crazy, doing every trick they knew. Then all of a sudden they froze.

I looked around my room in a panic. Was someone here? No, it was just us. I looked back down at my babies. Beyonce had stepped forward and was clearing her little munchkin throat. She had taken up poetry and I could feel one coming on. The others were right to freeze. Beyonce had been known to beat the snot out of anyone who even breathed during one of her poems. She reminded me of Pam.

"Between this world and the next,
There's only one way to kill,
A magic secret blown in the ear,
Do not cave into yourself,
Be strong like a rock and save us."

She finished and took a bow. All the other Demons clapped like their lives depended on it.

Holy shit, what in the hell was that? If that was a foreshadow, it was bad. I wasn't clear if Beyonce was talking about her past, or my future. I had a feeling it was my future, considering all the gifts I'd been receiving today.

"Mommmmmy, say with Beyonce," she shrieked at me.

"Oookay," I said.

"Say it, say it, say it." They ran in a circle flapping their little arms like birds. I started and they joined.

"Between this world and the next,
There's only one way to kill,
A magic secret blown in the ear,
Do not cave into yourself,
Be strong like a rock and save us."

We finished and they just stared at me. "Will Mommy remember?" Beyonce asked me.

I realized then that the poem was definitely about my future.

"Yes, I will," I told her. They looked at one another and seemed satisfied with my answer. After that, they began to pummel each other joyously. Rachel pulled herself out of the fray and shyly approached me.

"Rachel give Mommmeeeey present?" she asked.

God, she was cute. "Okay, baby," I told her.

"Rachel's present will hurt Mommmmmy, but she needs it. Okey dokey, Mommmmy?" she inquired, showing me her razor sharp little claws which were glowing a gorgeous sparkly iridescent silver pink.

What the fu...? Today had to go down as the weirdest day of my life.

"Okay Rachel, how long will it take you to give Mommy your present?" I asked nervously.

She giggled, "Rachel go fast. Me no like to hurt Mommy." She jumped up on me and made her way to my chest. She settled herself under my right collarbone and went to work.

Holy hell! Hurt didn't even begin to describe it.

The pain felt like hot poisoned lava burning my skin.

I shut my eyes tight and with super Vampyre strength

willed myself to stay still. I tried to count but all I wanted to do was die.

Finish...

God, please...

I was falling off of a cliff made of fire. A flock of sad beautiful white birds flew by and looked at me, but they didn't try to save me. Angry voodoo dolls shot bloody fire arrows at my body, and Elvis was dancing on my grave. Naked? *WTF?* I realized I was inside Rachel's mind and it was not a real good place to be. Then it stopped.

"Finished, Mommmmmy," Rachel whispered. I opened my eyes and all four of them stood quietly on my chest, watching me.

"It's a tattoo?" I asked Rachel. My voice sounded scratchy and far away. I didn't have the heart to tell her that tattoos didn't last on Vampyres. I was too scared she would try again.

"Angel Wings. Rachel give Mommy Angel Wing tattoo!" she trilled. "If Mommmy touches it, she gets more stronger."

Well shit, I didn't need to be any stronger than I already was, but I figured I'd try them out. I gingerly touched my wings. They felt hot to the touch. I shot some Glitter Magic at my Demons. It blasted out of my fingertips like bullets and knocked my little babies clear across the room. I freaked and ran to them only to find them laughing like hyenas and screaming.

"Again, again," they screeched.

God, they were tough little suckers. I scooped them up and gently kissed each one of them. In my hands, I held four amazingly powerful little creatures who loved me. They shared their gifts with me because they loved me...just the way I was.

I looked down at myself and realized I was still in my Prada dress and the kickass stilettos and I started to cry. I hated Ethan so much. I was no longer mated to him. He was no longer mine and I was no longer his. I felt broken, like I'd experienced a death. Why did it hurt so bad? I'd only known him a month. Why did it feel like my heart had been shredded? I cried harder. The mating probably didn't even count because I was a Demon. I should have known it was too good to be true.

Men were bad. I will never forget that again. That was the only thing that my mother had ever been right about.

I would do my duty though. I would prove my worth to the King and do whatever I had to do to save him and his people, and then I would leave. I would fulfill my destiny as the Chosen One, and then I would disappear.

I would never lay eyes on the Prince of the North American Dominion again. I'd go to Europe or Australia, or maybe I'd die while I was saving everybody. I really didn't care. My heart was broken and all I had left was my pride. He had already taken my heart. He could not have my pride. Ever.

"Asscrack?" Pam yelled, banging on my door. "Get your sorry butt out to the TV room, fast. We've got business to take care of and Jerry Springer comes on in thirty-eight minutes. So haul ass!"

God, I was happy to be home. I was safe. I knew what to expect here...Jerry Springer, swear words and unconditional love. I quickly changed into some awesome jeans, my favorite pale coffee-colored camisole, a thick brown belt and some rockin' dark brown Doc Marten combat boots. With my pale skin and fangs, I looked very Vamp chic. I glanced back at the stilettos and the dress crumpled on the floor and felt my eyes fill up. *Stop.* I would not cry for him anymore.

I had to stop loving people who didn't love me back. I was so empty on the inside, but time and distance from him would heal that. I was a Vampyre, damn it. I was going to live for God knew how many years. I would meet hundreds and thousands of guys that would make Ethan look like the asshole that he was. I plastered a big fake smile on my face, threw my shoulders back and left my room.

But I really didn't believe a word of that shit. Help me, Jesus.

"Pam? The Kev? Gemma?" I yelled as I hurried down the hall, "I've missed you so..." I stopped dead in my tracks. Gemma was sitting on my couch between two people I didn't know. A statuesque black woman, whose beauty was so riveting it, was ridiculous. She looked about thirty. Her skin was a creamy, dark mocha. Her lips were full and her eyes were an amethyst purple. They were shaped like a cat's and were fringed with long black lashes. She had a big bosom and long legs. She was beyond stunning.

The man though was a joke. I was sure my eyes were playing tricks on me. I thought Vampyres were beautiful? They had nothing on this guy...although I personally thought Ethan was prettier. No. Stop. Ethan was dead to me. The man on my couch had blonde hair and the bluest eyes I'd ever seen. He had the face of a god and the body of an Olympic champion. I felt like a total shlub in front of these strangers. Gemma looked different too, even more beautiful than usual. What in the hell was going on?

"What the fuck are you staring at, Asswipe?" The gorgeous woman on the couch bellowed at me.

"Pam?" I was in shock.

"Who in the hell else would I be, dumbass?"

The man on the couch chuckled and smiled lovingly at me. "The Kev?" I asked.

"Yes, my Krumecaca, it's me." His accent was gone! Imagine that. He put his arms out and I ran to him.

"You guys look...um...well..." I didn't want to say the wrong thing.

"I look fuckin' hot is how I look," Pam yelled, yanking me off The Kev's lap and onto hers. Damn, she was strong. "Let me look at you, child." She examined my collar bone and nodded with satisfaction at my tattoo. "It's about time those little bastards branded you."

"You know about my Demons?" *Did I have any secrets at all?*

"Of course I know about them," Pam shouted. How could someone so beautiful be so loud and obnoxious? "I know everything, jackass. They're Fallen Angel Demons and they're under my jurisdiction." She pressed on my Angel Wing tattoo.

"Tattoos don't last on Vampyres," I told her.

"That one will," Pam informed me, "that ain't no normal tattoo."

I'd heard everything now. I turned to Gemma who sat quietly watching me. "How long have you known about these two super models?" I asked her.

"Not long," she laughed, "but I had a feeling because of their auras." She looked at The Kev and blushed. He put his arm around her possessively.

"Is there anything I should know?" I poked her with my combat boot-covered foot. She looked up at me and I was amazed. Gemma's eyes were a sparkling glittery silver and her skin had an otherworldly glow. She looked like a magical Fairy Princess.

She smiled, took my hand in hers and gently pulled me down on the couch. She was trembling. "Dude," she whispered and giggled. "It's all insane. I am totally in love with him." She looked at The Kev, who gently kissed her. I squeezed her hand, willing her to go on. "I know what I am now and although I'm scared...I can do it."

I swallowed hard when Gemma took my face into her warm loving hands. "You are the reason I can do it. Your bravery and the way you've kept your humanity when it would be so easy to let it go, makes me believe I'll be okay, too. I love you so much, Astrid." She started to cry and lovely silvery diamond tears slid down her lovely face.

"What are you?" I whispered, wiping her tears away.

"It's what I will be. I'm not there yet," she said.

"Can you still be a Prada whore?"

Gemma laughed, "But of course...once a Prada whore, always a Prada whore."

"Thank God," I muttered. "So?"

"So, I am the reincarnation of the Fairy Queen."

"For real?" I asked.

"For real," she replied.

"Immortal?" I held my breath.

"Yep," Gemma squealed.

Oh. My. God. This was the best news in the world. It almost eclipsed the fact that I was single again. Gemma and I could be friends for thousands of years. Literally. "Are you guys totally sure about this?" I hadn't even realized reincarnation was possible. Then again I hadn't known Vampyres or Demons or God only knew what else was possible either.

"Yes, we are very sure," The Kev said. "She died about seven hundred years ago in the last major war with the Underworld. I have been waiting for her for a long time." He was so obviously in love with her. I hated myself, but I felt a pang of jealousy.

I wanted Ethan to love me like that. Wait. No, I didn't. I didn't want him at all...ever. Besides, he didn't want me. I would never think about him again. Good luck with that.

"What do you mean you're not there yet?" She looked like a Fairy Queen to me.

"Well..." Gemma started.

"For fuck's sake," Pam groaned, "you people are taking too damn long, and my program is about to come on. She has to break the four Mortal Strings before she becomes the Queen again."

"Mortal Strings?" I asked.

"If you'd shut your cakehole," Pam bellowed, "I'll finish." I bit my lip to keep from laughing. She may be beautiful, but she was still nasty. "The first string she had to break was feeding a Vampyre." Pam pointed at me. "That was you. The second was falling in love with a Fairy...that was him." She pointed at The Kev. "Then of course she had to fuck the Fairy."

I burst out laughing as The Kev and Gemma looked mortified to have their sex life discussed so crudely and bluntly by Pam.

"The fourth Mortal String," Pam went on, enjoying everyone's embarrassment, "well...we don't know what in the hell the fourth Mortal String is. She'll just have to figure it out like she did the others." Pam sat there for a moment and then looked at Gemma and The Kev. "Does that about cover it?"

"Yes." The Kev was still blushing. Gemma was simply in

shock. "That covers it."

"What's on your hand?" Gemma asked me, quickly changing the subject.

I held up my hand and showed them the six carat Pink Diamond that was stuck on my finger. Pam gasped, "You mated with Ethan?"

"How did you know that?" I asked her.

She looked taken aback for a moment, but regrouped quickly and shouted, "Because I know everything, Asscrack."

"I did mate with him...then I broke it." *Holy hell, it hurt to say that.*

"Why?" Pam demanded. "Don't you love him?"

"That doesn't matter," I said defensively. "He doesn't want a half Demon for a mate and I forgot to tell him about that before I bit the bastard."

Pam started laughing, "Damn, you are the right woman for him." She shook her not so Oprah-like head and smiled, "You ain't no half Demon. Well, technically you are, but you were raised by..."

"Yeah, yeah..." I cut her off. "He knows all that and he doesn't want me and I don't want him either."

"Tough," she yelled gleefully, "you can't just decide it's over."

"Well, I did," I informed her, daring her to disagree.

"Maybe, maybe not," The Kev said quietly. Pam narrowed her eyes at him. If I were The Kev I'd be scared, but he just smiled at Pam and pinched her cheek. "Astrid, I have a gift for you, but you cannot use it in haste. If you do you will regret it greatly." I wondered if this gift would be as painful as Rachel's. "It's a wish. You may use it to dissolve your mating or you may use it for whatever your heart desires."

"I already dissolved my mating," I insisted.

"Of course," he replied.

"Can I use it to wish for more wishes?" I joked.

The Kev laughed. "No, you can't. I would be very careful. Do not use it too quickly, for once you use it, it is gone." His tone became serious. "This wish can create life or cause death. This wish extends far beyond the mortal world."

Oh My God, I could use this wish to see Nana again. Or to have a baby. That one was impossible since my indoor plumbing was non-functioning. The Kev was right. I would not use this wish quickly or unwisely.

"Thank you," I told him. "I will use it carefully."

"Good girl," The Kev said, taking me into his arms. "When you use the wish say, 'Hear Me, O Fairies' and then state your desire." I nodded. "You need to feed from all three of us now. Our time with you is limited."

My stomach lurched and my eyes welled up. I had a feeling they would be leaving soon because they had gone back to their true forms.

"What about Gemma?" I was falling apart.

"She has to go, but she will be back." He pulled me close and I fed from him.

Just as Jerry Springer started, Pam pried me away from The Kev and took me on to her lap. "Pam," I was still sniffling, "you would love the Vampyre King. He looks kind of like the beefy, bald security guy from Jerry Springer, but better."

She laughed and drew me to her neck, "I've heard he's one hot piece of ass." God, she was profane.

Finally, I went to my Gemma, who was snarfing Black Raspberry Chip for me. I realized as I drank from her that Black Raspberry Chip ice cream was not better than sex with Ethan. This made me sad. That asshole had ruined me for all other men, and ice cream too. Maybe there were Vampyre Nuns. I may as well join an order and be celibate, rather than be disappointed the rest of my life. There was no comparing anyone to that jerk bastard.

I finished eating and put my head into my hands. Why was my life always so messy?

"Astrid?"

I looked up. Heathcliff was standing in my living room. I was alone on my couch and Jerry Springer was still spouting nonsense on the TV.

"Do you actually watch that?" he asked, smiling.

"No," I said, "well...sometimes. Why are you here?" I wondered where my family had gone and if they were gone for good.

"We've found the Rogues headquarters and we're going in." He handed me my katana, a dagger and several throwing stars. "Are you ready?"

I nodded. He had no idea. "Let's go," I said. Today was as good a day to die as any.

Chapter 30

Heathcliff seemed shocked I could fly. Hell, he'd pass out cold if I showed him the rest of my party tricks. He held my hand as we flew through the night. I felt safe with him. Furthermore, I'd never flown outside and it didn't appeal to me to run into a cell tower or, God forbid, a low-flying plane.

I could tell we were flying south, directly toward Mammoth Caves. *Shit, were we going to fight in the caves?* It was impossible to communicate with Heathcliff. We were traveling over a hundred miles an hour. It was insane. I had never felt so free in my life. As we came in for a landing, Heathcliff brought his legs down in front of him, kicking mine forward as he did so. We both landed smoothly on our feet in a field about a half mile from the main cave entrance.

"Thanks," I smiled, exhilarated from our flight. As giddy as I felt about flying, I was getting panicked about what was to come and who I was going to have to see. I looked around and saw my team of Samuel, Luke, David, Venus, Cathy and the rest. Princess Lelia and Princess Raquel, my two kind-of ex sister-in-laws who tried to kill me a while back in the graveyard, were also here. I noticed the redhead, Princess Raquel, giving Heathcliff the evil eye. Oh My God, I bet Heathcliff was the one that ripped her arms off all those years ago.

"Bastard," she hissed as she walked by him.

"Bitch," he grinned broadly, displaying his beautiful dimples. This seemed to piss her off greatly and delight him tremendously.

"Astrid," Princess Lelia cooed. The mocha-skinned beauty, approached me with a shit eating grin on her face and a wild sparkle in her amethyst eyes. Princess Raquel, composing herself from her exchange with Heathcliff, followed closely behind her sister. "Aren't you the sneaky one," Princess Lelia laughed. "I'm so glad we didn't kill you. That would have been a major cluster!"

Princess Raquel grabbed me by my shoulders and studied my face. "You really are beautiful. Welcome to the family, although you do have my sympathy for mating with my brother," she laughed and kissed me soundly on the lips. Clearly she hadn't spoken with her brother or she'd realize we were definitely not related.

He was here. I didn't see him, but I could feel him. My stomach was doing flips and his scent was making me dizzy. He was trying to get into my head to gauge my feelings, but I was not going to let him in. I was starting to come undone. I touched my wings and shut the doors in my mind. He was not welcome inside me ever again.

"Astrid," a child called out to me. I turned, but there was no child in sight. There was a beautiful teenage Vampyre girl in front of me. She had a rockin' layered bob, a stunning face and turquoise eyes. Turquoise, like the ocean in the Caribbean. I'd have paid big bucks for the jeans and spike-heeled boots she had on. Her top was one I'd been admiring in the Anthropologie catalog for weeks. Now that I could see it in person, I was definitely ordering it. I wanted to see what size she was wearing. I wondered if she'd let me try it on...

"Astrid," she said, smiling at me.

"Paris?" I choked out.

"Yes." She still sounded like a little girl, but she looked like a million bucks.

"Holy shit," I gasped. "What in the hell happened to you?" Paris Hilton was gorgeous. I grabbed her and swung her around like a three year old. "You are so beautiful!"

Was I screaming? Yes...yes I was.

"Niecey and the gal in the back of the art class whose name always escapes me gave me a makeover," she said shyly.

"Oh my God, I had no idea a beautiful girl was hiding under all that Goth shit."

"Are you happy with me?" she asked.

"Oh, Paris..." I put her down and took her hands. "I've always been bizarrely happy with you. You are amazing and strong and good. The only thing your makeover does is make the outside as beautiful as the inside. This is who you are. You don't need to cover up your beauty with all those black clothes and black makeup and...Wait, are you wearing contact lenses?" I marveled at her turquoise eyes.

"No," she said, embarrassed. "I used to wear black contacts. I thought it was cool...the old gals didn't," she laughed.

"Are you here to fight?" I asked.

"Yes, I would do anything for my Prince and my King...and for you," she added quietly.

I kissed both of her cheeks. "Be careful," I told her and moved away to find out the plan. I turned and ran smack into the person I was trying to avoid. I jumped back as if burned and saw the pain flash across in his eyes.

"She looks lovely," Ethan said, referring to Paris. "Thank you."

"Yes, she does," I snapped, "and don't bother thanking me. I didn't do it, my old ladies did."

I turned my back on him and tried to walk away. He grabbed my arm and hauled me up against his body. If everyone was watching, I was unaware. The only thing I could focus on was Ethan—the feel of him, the smell of him. My body automatically began to mold to his. *No. This was no time for my inner slut to take over.* I tried to jerk away, but he imprisoned me firmly against his body. What did he want from me? He'd already destroyed me. As much as I hated him, all I wanted to do was lean in, wrap my arms around him, and press my lips to his.

"Let me go," I hissed.

"Astrid," he said, his voice tight, "we need to talk."

"No, Ethan, we don't," I cut him off. "I will fulfill all my duties as the Chosen One and then I will go away from you. Away from all of you."

I thought he had already decimated my heart, but the pain I felt now let me know there was more damage to be done. God, if he didn't let me go soon there was no telling how I would betray myself.

"Angel, I lov..."

"Stop," I lashed out, disengaging myself from him. My whole body trembled. "You have to stop. You and I were a mistake." He flinched. "You were a mistake I will never repeat. I'll do my duty and nothing more."

Damn it, I was going to cry.

"Part of your duty as the Chosen One is to be mine," Ethan said quietly.

"Maybe at one time," I told him flatly. "Not anymore."

I walked away. And he let me.

***

It was unnerving to be in the caves at night. These were definitely not the caves that were open to the public. The caves went on for over three hundred and ninety miles, but the areas of extreme paranormal strength were way off the beaten path. They were on a path the mortals knew nothing about.

The plan was to spread out and take down as many Rogues as possible. Kill if we had to, but leave some alive for questioning. If there were humans, we were to get them to safety.

I was part of the Alpha Group. We would spearhead and be the first unit in. It was the most dangerous position. Alpha consisted of Samuel, Heathcliff, Cathy, Luke, Ethan and myself. I saw Cathy roll her eyes when I was called to Alpha Group. She was never going to like me. I could only hope that she would have my back if I needed her.

"No," Ethan said firmly, "Astrid will go with Unit Two. She has no combat experience."

I heard Cathy snicker.

"With all due respect, my Liege," Samuel cut in, "you're wrong. She is the deadliest weapon we have. She can do far more damage than all of us combined."

Samuel has the biggest balls I'd ever witnessed. Nobody second-guessed the Prince. Not to mention that Samuel was high if he thought I was stronger than a whole bunch of Vamps put together. Ethan looked down. His hands clenched into fists. He did not like to be challenged. However, I supposed if you were as old as Samuel you might know a thing or two. I was in no position to speak, but I knew I was ready for Alpha Group. I watched Ethan's internal debate.

"Your Highness," Heathcliff added, "Astrid is ready and we need her. Samuel is right."

Ethan looked up and his eyes bored into mine. "You will be with me." He left no room for argument. "We will move in groups of two. After ten minutes, unless someone signals, Unit Two will follow with Unit Three close behind. We have the element of surprise on our side. Move silently and quickly."

We wore small black watches on our wrists. They were mini computers with communication capabilities and alarm signals built in. Vampyres adored electronics. I almost asked if we had flashlights. Thank God that didn't pass my lips. I would have been thrown into Unit Five Hundred if I'd asked a question so stupid. Vampyres could see better in the dark than in the light.

The tunnels were unbelievable, truly one of nature's miracles. I reached out and ran my fingers over the calcite stalagmites and stalactites. They looked like crystals and diamonds hanging from the ceilings and walls and bursting out of the floors of the caves. No one, no matter how talented, could out-do Mother Nature. I could feel the power flowing through the currents in the air. It felt good and I felt strong

The six of us entered together and immediately split into our groups of two. I could make out sounds in the distance...screaming, laughing, gunfire and...slapping? I felt for my weapons and gently pressed my fingertips to my wings. I had a feeling I'd be using brute strength and Magic more than anything else.

"You will stay behind me at all times," Ethan informed me in a harsh whisper.

I yanked him to a stop and got right up in his face. In these tight quarters, my breasts were pressed firmly against his chest. I did my best to ignore the jolt of pleasure that ripped through me at the contact. "You are full of shit. I am the Chosen One. My job is to protect you," I hissed at him. "We will watch each other's backs and we will focus on the job at hand...not our problems with each other. Do you understand me?" I demanded.

His burning gaze made me fear I'd gone too far. I didn't want to fight him. I wanted to kiss him, but I didn't

"I understand you." His voice was terse. I could tell he wanted to say a lot more, but I walked ahead and didn't give him the chance.

We moved quickly together through the tunnels. I was losing my human self. My eyes turned green and my fangs descended. My senses sharpened. I was a Vampyre now and I was okay with it. It was the first time I think I truly accepted and embraced what I had become. I could see, hear and smell with more accuracy than I ever had.

As we moved closer to the noise, I could smell Vampyres and mortals. I scented anger, hatred, hunger, lust and fear. At first, I was unsure if the humans were alive or dead. From the agonized screaming I heard, I guessed that even if some were alive, it wouldn't be for long.

I kept one hand on Ethan so we didn't lose each other. We were moving very quickly. I planned to save humans, kill Rogues, and protect the man I hated. I realized that I would die for him. Happily. That's how much I hated him. Why did he have to be such an ass?

We neared what sounded like one of Dante's Circles of Hell. I could never have been prepared for what I saw. We came to a ledge about forty feet above the carnage below. The Rogue Vampyres were so agitated and involved in their feeding frenzy that they didn't scent or see us. I was able to take in the horrific scene.

It was dimly lit by torches. There were four or five mounds of human remains. They had been drained and some had flesh missing. They'd been eaten. There were fifteen to twenty bodies in each mound. The stench of rotting human flesh was revolting. I gagged and felt an anger begin to build in me like I'd never known.

There were about twenty Rogues down below and just as many barely alive humans. The Rogues were letting the mortals try to escape. It was sad and horrifying to watch the hope in those poor people. They ran around like caged rats, moaning and crying while the scum of the earth Rogues laughed maniacally and picked them off one by one.

I moved to enter the cavern, but Ethan held me back. *Not yet*, he mouthed and very quietly punched a code into his watch. We waited and he watched the sick activity below with a look of horror and disgust on his face equal to my own.

His watch beeped softly. He looked at me. There was a lot in that look that I had no time to decipher. He took my hand and whispered, "Let's go."

I touched my wings and pressed hard. I had no plans to leave any Rogue alive, not after what I saw they were capable of. We flew down from our perch at the same time as the rest of the Alpha Unit flew down from theirs. I had heard the term 'all hell broke loose' many times before, but I'd never seen it happen until now. Gut-wrenching screams erupted from mortals and Rogues alike as we took the room by storm. Fangs were snapping and blades were flying.

I tapped my chest and my shield surrounded me. No weapon could touch me. I wondered if I could extend it to my team. I knew I'd have to make physical contact with them to make it work. I was closest to Ethan. I quickly turned to him and watched him rip the head off of a Rogue Vampyre with his bare hands. Well, I supposed that was one way to do it. I touched him and cast the protection shield. He jerked once and then turned to me with awe in his eyes. He nodded. It worked.

I felt a blade slice up the back of my calf. *What the fu...?* How in the hell did a blade break my shield? I realized that by transferring my shield to Ethan it no longer protected me. There was no time to reset my shield around myself, nor did I want to. I wanted it around him.

I pivoted and shot hundreds of silver bullets from my fingertips into the heart of a female Vampyre who looked familiar to me. I squatted down to get a good look at her after she was dead. Did I know her? No, but she looked like somebody.

Holy hell...she looked like me.

I unsheathed my katana and cut her head off, just in case the silver hadn't shredded her heart. Without a thought, I quickly beheaded two more Rogues and pinned three others to the wall with Magic. The other two Units had arrived. I vaguely saw Paris and Venus kicking ass and taking mortals to safety.

I approached the pinned Vampyres with care and they eyed me warily. I had two silver throwing stars in one hand and my silver dagger in the other. *What the fu...?* Why did all these Rogue Vampyres resemble me? Dark brown hair, gold eyes, full lips, long lean bodies...but the worst part was the mole. They all had a mole high on their left cheekbone, just like me. Was I losing my mind? They seemed to recognize me. They grinned at me.

"Who are you?" I demanded, placing my dagger next to one of the male's throats.

"We are you, you stupid bitch," he spat as he laughed maniacally. "We are everything you could ever hope to be and more. It's about time you got your slutty whore-ass back home."

Oh. My. God. He was the second person to call me a whore in less than a week. This was not working for me. Like I told Cathy, I was many things, but whore was not one of them. He was not me. I was not like these things. I was a good person. I felt everything slip. My brain was racing and I needed to stop these monsters—forever.

Did my need to destroy them mean I was no different or no better than they were? My anger felt like fire inside me and I couldn't see straight. Without thinking I let my body take over. I wiped the smiles right off of their familiar faces as I shredded their hearts with my silver dagger. This did not even begin to quench my rage. I kept picturing them mutilating and torturing the humans, and in my fury I made them explode...*literally* explode with Magic.

How in the hell did I do that?

I turned and saw two approaching Samuel from behind. No one fucked with my Samuel. Before I could react, they ripped Samuel's right arm off. I aimed my throwing stars and took their heads off before they hurt him anymore. Samuel quickly turned and saluted me with his left hand.

"Goddamn, I've had that arm for over five hundred years," he shouted, grinning from ear to ear, before taking off after two Rogues trying to escape. The severed heads of his attackers rolled back to my feet and mocked me with their golden eyes. I kicked them away in disgust.

Was I supposed to be one of them? Had Pam and The Kev saved me from this?

I lowered my head and went inside myself and something clicked. I did know these people. I could have been like them. These Vampyres were part Demon, like me. They did not have an Angel or a Fairy. I closed my eyes and let my spirit seep out of me and enter them. Their souls were black, desolate, cold and angry. This is what I could have been. *There but for the grace of God go I.*

As I let all my fears go, somehow I let my spirit enter these horrible things that were so similar but so different from me. Burning, acid pain shot through my body and I doubled over, grasping at the limestone floor. My fingers began to tingle as I absorbed the Magic trapped in the rock. An eerie calm washed over me, creeping through every part of my body, replacing the acid with a gentle warmth that filled me. I knew what I needed to do.

With every bit of strength I had left, I stood up and looked at the bloody carnage around me. Several Cressida House Vampyres lay dead among the mortals and Rogues. I pressed my wings and I raised my arms above my head. I screamed, and flung my arms out from my body. The pain was...Oh my God, burning and burning. I was blind, the pain in my head excruciating... and then I heard it. It was music to my ears. I tried to smile, but it was more like a grimace. The entire cave rumbled like thunder, and every Rogue Vampyre, dead or alive, exploded into a million little pieces.

Everyone froze and stared at me.

The Rogues did not deserve to live, but did I? It was over and I had ended it. I felt strangely empty and sad. Of course there was no one left to question, but that was probably better. They may have known things about me I didn't want to learn. Maybe I just destroyed part of myself.

Shit...I wasn't sure an immortal lifetime of therapy would be enough to get rid of these new revelations and images.

Samuel ran to me, wrapped his left arm around me, and laid a huge wet one on my cheek. His right one had already started growing back. Venus, Princess Lelia and Princess Raquel were right behind him. I was numb and in shock.

Where was Ethan? Was he okay?

"That was the most amazing fucking thing I have ever seen in my long life. You are a freakin' Terminator," Lelia yelled as she group-hugged me and Samuel.

Raquel concurred, "Damn, I'm glad you're on my team. You are a walking, talking death machine. I thought I was good, but you could kick my ass."

"I never thought I'd hear that come out of your mouth. Ev-ah." Lelia laughed at her sister and hugged me some more. "Are you okay, Astrid?" she asked.

"I am," I told her. And I was okay. Tired, but okay.

I looked around at the carnage I'd caused and it shocked me, but I was fine with it. The dead Vampyres had begun to turn to dust. That was what we did when we died, within a half an hour after death a Vampyre's body disintegrated to a fine powdery dust. I had kept the majority of my people safe. I had saved the humans. And I had destroyed the bad guy.

"Why is your calf bleeding? No weapon should be able to penetrate your shield," Ethan said angrily. Everyone backed away from him. Everyone except me. He may be intimidating to some, but after what I had just done it would take a lot more than a pissed off Vampyre Prince to scare me.

"My shield was protecting you," I replied evenly, not moving an inch.

"Did you know you couldn't protect yourself if you extended your shield to someone else?" he demanded.

"Found out tonight," I snarked, looking him straight in the eye. Everyone watched our exchange with fascination. They still couldn't get over someone talking to their Prince like he was a person.

"You should have taken it back." He pierced me with his eyes, waiting for my reply.

"I chose not to," I said, walking away.

Shit, shit, shit, why did I say that? I may as well have said, *I love you and wanted to protect you,* or something equally as stupid like, *Didn't you know I'm attracted to things that hate me?* Just ask my mother.

"Come back here," Ethan said, "I'm not finished with you."

"Oh yes you are," I muttered, "and so am..."

"Somebody help me. Please," Heathcliff cried out from across the cave. Was he hurt? I'd be devastated if he died. I literally flew to him. It was Cathy. She had a silver dagger sticking out of her chest, but she wasn't dead...yet. Heathcliff was bent over her holding her completely still. The tension in his body was palpable.

"Stand back," Ethan commanded. We did.

"It hasn't shredded her heart," Heathcliff whispered. "If I can get her to the compound, they can save her." His eyes never moved from his sisters as he spoke and his body didn't move a millimeter.

"If you move her she'll die," Lelia said quietly. "We could

try to remove it here."

"No," Heathcliff was breaking. "You don't have the Touch...you'll kill her."

"There's no time to wait for someone with the Touch. She's going to die," Raquel said gently.

Cathy looked at Heathcliff with adoration. "I love you, my brother," she whispered. "Tell Father that I love him too." She smiled at him and he broke.

I had no idea what in the hell somebody with the Touch was. Some kind of Vampyre doctor? I watched Cathy and Heathcliff and I knew I had to do something. I was fairly sure I could get Cathy back to the compound without physically moving her and I could do it quickly. I moved in and squatted next to Heathcliff.

"I can transport with her. I'll get her to the compound in less than thirty seconds and then the...um...Touch people can save her."

"What if it doesn't work?" Heathcliff was shaking.

"She's going to die here anyway. Let me try."

He looked down at his sister. Her eyes had closed. "Please try."

"No," Ethan said. "No, I won't let you do it. You have never transported with anyone. It could kill you."

"And?" I challenged him.

"I said no, I won't let you do it."

"You don't 'let' me do anything. I do what I want, when I want. I want to save her, so that's what I'm going to do. Besides, Your Highness, we are no longer mated so if I die it will not affect you. I would assume your life would be easier if I were not around. Can't have any tainted Demon blood in the Royal Family."

"Astrid." Ethan approached me. He was not happy.

I pushed him back with Magic and everyone gasped.

"You are my mate and I am your Prince. You will not do this," Ethan informed me.

I laughed. "I dissolved our mating. You are not the boss of me."

I flung my arms out and Glitter Magic flew everywhere. I carefully curled myself around Cathy and we disappeared.

"What in the fuck was that about?" Princess Lelia yelled at her brother. "There's no such thing as dissolving a mating."

***

After Astrid disappeared, Ethan fell to his knees and began to pray.

Everyone around him froze and watched Ethan. If he didn't die in the next thirty seconds, that meant she had made it safely back to The Cressida House.

"Twenty-seven, twenty-eight, twenty-nine, thirty," Samuel counted, grinning. "Astrid did it!"

"Let's go," Ethan said.

Chapter 31

Where in the hell was I? In some bizarre alternate universe?

Jewel-encrusted torches bathed a huge white marble hallway in golden light. The floor was so shiny it looked wet. Floor to ceiling murals of Demons and Angels and Cherubs adorned the walls, some bloody and violent, some beautiful and peaceful. I felt tiny. The molding on both the floor and ceiling was a thick, burnished gold. Whoever lived here had the big bucks.

Was I dead? Where did everybody go? Did I transport to the wrong place? Shit, where was Cathy? Did I kill her?

"Hello," I called out tentatively. My voice echoed eerily though the grand hallway. "Is anyone here?" God, what a stupid question; of course someone or something was here...the torches were lit. What if this was a trap or a test? And if I failed everyone I loved would die...

Whoa Nelly. I was totally freaking myself out. What in the hell did I have to be afraid of? I was a Vampyre for God's sake. I was hopped up on a butt-load of Angel and Fairy blood, making me one screwed-up and moderately unstable magical force to be reckoned with.

But how could I be here? I could only transport to places I'd been before and I was fairly sure I'd never been here.

Oh my God, I was for real dead. I had to get out of here. I took off running at full speed down the marble hallway.

"Fuck," I yelled, flying backward and landing hard after I ran face first into an invisible barrier. So much for no pain when you were dead. That hurt.

Maybe I wasn't for real dead after all, or maybe I was on

another planet, or maybe my Demon daddy was going to jump out and scare me into a coma...

Coma? Why did I say coma?

Good God, I wasn't making any sense. I was confusing myself and I needed to...

"Baby Girl?" a familiar voice called.

I froze. Now someone was screwing with my head. I sat up carefully. If I'd been human, the violent run-in with the barrier would have killed me or at the very least knocked me out. Being a Vampyre, I only had a headache. I slowly scooted across the floor on my bottom, plastered myself against the wall and stayed low.

"Baby Girl?" the voice called again.

I was either for real dead or insane.

"Astrid," she said, "please say my name so I can come to you."

"Nana?" I whispered, not trusting myself to speak louder. I was tingling with fear and anticipation.

A sparkling orb approached me, not unlike Glenda the Good Witch's bubble in *The Wizard of Oz*. It floated down the hallway toward me, leaving what looked to be a glittery diamond dust in its wake. It might be coming to kill me or eat me, but it sure was pretty. Then it spoke.

"Hello, my Baby Girl," the orb said.

"Nana, is that you?" I asked the orb, realizing that in talking back to it I had indeed taken the train to Crazytown, gotten off, and bought property.

"Oh hells bells," the Nana Orb said. "I forgot to morph."

What the fu...? My Nana was a transparent glittery bubble ball that could morph? Dear God, was this what happened to people when they died?

"Nana," I croaked, "can I help you?"

"No, sweetie," she grunted. "Damn it to hell, I haven't morphed in a while. I can't quite remember how to do this."

I watched in morbid fascination as the Nana Ball bounced and quivered like Jell-O, throwing off the most unusually gorgeous sparkles I'd ever seen. I realized with delight that I was covered in her iridescent glitter.

"Sweet Baby Jesus," Nana yelled, "I think I've got it."

I tried to back away, but the wall was solid. The Nana Ball...Orb...whatever...began to grow. Quickly. Nana was moaning and groaning. It sounded painful.

"Are you okay?" I panicked. I'd already been through Nana's death once. I wasn't going to be able to handle it again. Could a ball of light die?

I'm good," she grunted and began to take on human features.

It was Nana. I could smell her...freesia, lilies and brown sugar. I smelled like brown sugar too. If I could breathe, I'd be hyperventilating. I was staring at my Nana. No wait, I was staring at the thirty-five-ish year old version of my Nana, and she was gorgeous. She looked just like she had when I was a little girl. It was strange to be almost the same age as my Nana, but I wouldn't have cared if she was a thirteen year old teenager.

"Nana?" I ached to touch her, but was terrified she'd disappear if I moved.

"Hi, Baby Girl." Nana smiled and extended her arms to me. I was crying and shaking. Never ever did I think I would get to hold my Nana again. Loving her as much as I loved her made this moment absolutely perfect.

"I've missed you so much," I blubbered.

"I know, Baby. Me too." She held me tight.

"Am I for real dead?" I asked her. "Are you?"

"Well," she laughed, "it depends on your definition of for real dead. I'm dead and you're undead."

"Does that mean we can be together?" I grasped her tighter. *Please say yes. Please say yes.*

"Only for a little while." She gently unwrapped me from her body and took my hands. "Your time on Earth is not done yet. You still have so much to do." She smiled and held my face in her hands.

"Where are we?"

"Heaven."

"Oh my God." I quickly slapped my hand over my mouth and waited for lightening to strike. Nothing.

Nana laughed and I got lightheaded. She was an Angel. She knew Pam...

"Nana," I was excited, "come back with me. I know you can. You sent Pam to me. By the way, she has a filthy mouth."

"She does, doesn't she?" Nana smiled and shook her head. "I can't go back with you. It's not my time yet."

"I don't get it." My eyes began to fill again.

"I've had several lives, little one," she said as she played with my hair, smoothing it away from my face

"Have I?" I asked, snuggling closer. She smelled so good, it was impossible to get close enough.

"No honey, this is your first go-round."

"How many lives have you had?" This was one of the weirder conversations I'd had, and I'd had plenty of weird lately.

"Two." She took my hand and led me down the grand hallway to a very simple and quietly beautiful sitting room. Everything was white and cream and beige. At first glance it seemed boring, but it was definitely not. It was rich and soft and safe. The furniture was overstuffed and reminded me of puffy clouds. I could stay here forever.

She sat me on one of the puffy cloud couches and continued. "The first time I died was about a hundred and forty years ago, and the last time was about five months ago." She watched me intently. She was trying to tell me something, but I had no idea what. I wanted to ask her, but the rules were different here. The air was thick with Magic and I knew in my gut there were more questions than answers in this place.

"If I'm here, where does everybody think I am?"

"Your body is on Earth. You are in a Heavenly form here," Nana told me.

"But I'm me. I feel like me." I ran my hands over my face and body.

"It's hard to explain, but your Earthly body is at the Cressida House in a coma, and your Spiritual or Celestial body is here with me."

My God, that's why I was having coma thoughts. Ethan knew something bad would happen to me if I transported with somebody. I wonder if he felt smug about being right or if he missed me. "How is my other body still alive?"

I pressed the bridge of my nose trying to ward off the panic attack that was coming on. Nana could tell I was on the verge and gathered me close.

"You left a very small amount of your essence on Earth, but it won't last long."

"So that's why I'm alive in two places?" This was nuts.

"That and the blood of your mate," she replied.

I pulled back and looked away. Why couldn't anybody get this straight? "I don't have a mate," I insisted, wrapping my arms around myself and staring at the floor.

"You do, my love," Nana said. "Look at me, child."

I did. God, she was beautiful. Uh oh...she had that look on her face. That look she got when I wouldn't eat my broccoli. Or when I tried to sneak out of the house in a see-through top and a micro mini.

"He doesn't want me." I ran my hand through my hair and looked up defiantly. "I'm half Demon. Ethan hates Demons." I turned away and tried to suppress my tears.

"You're not a Demon." Nana took my chin in her hand, forcing me to look at her. "Your father may be the King of the

Demons, but you are immune to your Demonic tendencies. Why do you think I sent you Pam and The Kevin?"

"Nana, Ethan doesn't care. He..." This was so embarrassing, trying to explain to your dead grandmother why the person you did the nasty with hated you.

"Astrid." Nana was firm, using that *I will take no bullshit* voice. "How long did it take you to come to terms with being a Vampyre?"

She waited. I said nothing. I wasn't completely sure I had come to terms. She forged ahead.

"I recall listening in on a rant that referenced blood breath, weird bun heads and the smell of the old lady bathroom at the country club."

"You heard that?" *Lord help me, what else has she heard?*

"Yes," she smiled. "I rather enjoyed Pam's confusion over the old lady bathroom thing."

"Nana, what's your point?"

"My point, Baby Girl, is that Ethan is over five hundred years old and has had horrific experiences with Demons. You didn't give him a chance to catch his breath and come to grips with any of this."

"He was an ass." I was not backing down.

"Yes, he was...and trust me it's not the last time he will be an ass, but he loves you. He tried to tell you and you ran away."

"Nana," I whispered, "I broke the mating."

"And just how did you do that, my baby?" Nana put her hands on her hips and tilted her lovely head.

"I told him we were no longer mated, that I didn't want him—that he was a mistake." I felt ill.

"Hmmm," Nana said, handing me a small glistening jewel that resembled an opal, "that's all well and good, but it's impossible to break a mating once it's been consummated."

She paused and looked pointedly at me. If I could still blush, I'd be purple.

"So Ethan is still my mate?" I felt giddy and elated and embarrassingly enough, horny. Gotta love my inner slut.

"Yes." Nana's eyes twinkled. "Ethan is still your mate."

"Does he really love me?" I needed to know. It was so hard for me to trust that someone besides my Nana loved me. Thanks, Mom.

"Oh yes, my child, he loves you and will never stop. He would die for you."

We were both quiet for a bit. There were so many things I wanted to ask her. I just kept staring at her, trying to memorize her. She was mine. My Nana. My Nana who was so kind and beautiful, and who smelled so delicious.

"Nana," I blurted. I'd almost forgotten. "Did I save Cathy? Did she live?" Oh dear God, I hoped so.

"Yes love, you did. She will be fine." Nana looked radiant and relieved. That was weird, She didn't even know Cathy. "I'm so proud of you and I wish to thank you."

How odd. Why would she thank...

Brown sugar. Oh. My. God. We all smelled like brown sugar. Me, Cathy, Heathcliff, Nana...

"Nana?" I searched her face, looking for clues. Everything was making sense. She said her first life ended about 140 years ago. That would be just about right. "When you died the first time, did you have a family?"

"Yes, Baby Girl, I did." She was excited. She knew I was close.

"Did you have a son and a daughter? Were you good friends with Emily Bronte? Should you be punished for saddling your children with names they could never live down?"

She was delighted and clapped her hands like a child. "I did and I was and I should. You are so smart, my love."

It all made sense. The intense connection I felt with Heathcliff. The disastrous results when we tried to be romantic. My desire for Cathy to like me. My need to save her when she clearly hated me. We were blood related. I wasn't exactly sure how. Siblings? Cousins? Nana was their mother and over a hundred years later she was my grandmother. I supposed that made them my aunt and uncle, many times removed? It didn't matter. My family kept getting bigger and bigger.

"Can I tell them?" I asked her.

"They already know. Heathcliff searched your house for things that would comfort you or possibly bring you out of your coma, and came upon our pictures. When you see them again, I'd like you to tell them how very much I love them."

"More than me?" I teased

"The same as you," she laughed and caressed my face.

"So you looked the same back then?" This was mind blowing

"Yes, very similar," she smiled.

"Are they upset?" This was crazy.

"Heathcliff is overjoyed. And Cathy, as you would expect, is wracked with guilt." Nana took me into her arms. "Astrid, you need to go back."

"Why?" I held her tighter. "I don't want to leave you. I just got you back."

"I will be in your life again, my child. All my cycles of life will involve you. You must go now. Ethan is dying."

"What?" My stomach dropped and I felt dizzy. "He can't die, he's immortal." I was in a full-on panic and started pacing the room. "He wasn't injured during the battle. Did someone hurt him?" My voice was loud and shrill.

"No," she said

"Then how? Why?" This could not be happening.

"He's feeding you, Astrid. Mated Vampyres must drink from each other to live."

"Yes...and?" I didn't get it.

"He won't drink from you because you're in a coma. He just keeps feeding you his blood."

"How long have I been in a coma?" I wasn't sure I wanted to know.

"Two weeks," she told me.

I tried to puzzle it out. "If he dies, then I die too."

"In most cases that would be true, but not in this case."

I stared at her, willing her to go on. My body was ice cold. Dread raced through me and I started to shake.

"Astrid, if a Vampyre dies while saving the life of his mate, the mate will live."

I dropped to my knees and started rocking. "Have to go...I have to go. I have to leave. I love him, he's mine. I have to go, Nana. Now."

"Astrid." She grabbed me by the shoulders and made me pay attention. "The stone I gave you will take you back to your body, but you will have to fight with everything you have to successfully rejoin the Earthly realm."

"Is it possible?" I asked her.

"Look at me. Look at yourself. Anything is possible." She stared deeply into my eyes. "Do you love him?"

"More than life itself," I told her, scaring the shit out of myself realizing how true that was.

"Then go save him."

I squeezed the stone, kissed my Nana and felt myself begin to fall. Faster and faster and faster.

Chapter 32

"Has anything changed?" I heard Venus ask.

"No," Ethan said flatly.

"My Liege," Venus hesitated, "may I have permission to speak candidly?"

"No."

"Please, Sire," Venus waited. Long moments passed.

"As you wish," he replied wearily.

"She would want you to feed from her. She would not want you to die. She lov..."

"Stop," Ethan harshly commanded. "I will do nothing that will harm her. I've done enough to hurt her already. Do you understand me?" His tone was clipped and frightening.

"Yes, Sire," Venus quietly replied and left the room.

She's right Ethan, I screamed inside my head. *She's right. Please drink from me. I love you. If you die, even if my physical body lives, the most important part of my soul will die with you. Somebody please hear me.*

I could feel his eyes on me, but no matter how hard I tried, I couldn't open mine to return his gaze. This was the worst possible prison. I could hear everyone...everything. I knew I was lying in a bed in a brightly lit room. I could feel their stares and I could do nothing. I couldn't move or speak. I couldn't respond to their touch. I couldn't utter a sound and I had no clue how to get back to myself. I caught faint traces of his scent and I could tell he was fading quickly from this world. Goddamn it. I needed to wake up.

***

There were people in the room, touching me, poking me.

"Don't hurt her," Ethan rasped.

"We won't, Sire," an unfamiliar male voice said. "I'm afraid there's little we can do for her. The Touch does not seem to be affecting her. We've never seen anything like this."

"Vampyres shouldn't be able to transport," a female voice muttered disapprovingly.

Ethan's voice was as cold as ice, and I felt the other Vampyre's fear vibrate through the room. "You can do nothing?"

There was silence. They were no longer touching me.

"Get out," Ethan roared.

I could feel him pacing, I could sense his anxiety and his weakening spirit. Why couldn't he feel me? He was a mind reader for God's sake. I used to have to force him to get out of my head. Nana said this wasn't impossible, but I didn't know what to do.

He gathered me into his arms. It was so warm and right. I knew his lips were on my forehead and I felt a dampness on my cheeks. Were those his tears? Oh God, please help me. Please. I smelled his blood as he slit his wrist and put it to my lips.

I tried so hard. I didn't know what I did to get back to him, but it didn't matter. I did it, and Ethan would be okay. I slowly reached up and pulled his lips to my neck. His body tensed. His beautiful eyes went green and his fangs descended. He smelled like Christmas and autumn air and life. I forced him into me. His fangs pierced me and ripped my skin like paper. My blood gushed into his mouth. His hands rediscovered my body and a ravenous hunger consumed me. He touched me, my face, my breasts, my hips, my stomach. I arched up against him, my body begged for more. Nothing had ever felt so good in my life. So right, so sweet, so hot, so delicious. I just kept swallowing and swallowing and swallowing...

Oh God, I hadn't moved at all. I was still trapped inside my useless body. He wasn't drinking my blood.

I was drinking his.

***

"Ethan this is madness." Heathcliff was angry. The room was filled with emotion...sadness, anger, regret, love...and I was still an immobile waste.

"You don't understand." Ethan sounded broken.

"No, I don't," Heathcliff snapped. His frustration was evident. "But I do know she won't want to live without you."

"How do you know that?" Ethan demanded, his anger felt like an inferno in the room. "She told me I was a mistake," he choked out.

God, I was an idiot. Why in the hell did I say that? When I went for the jugular, I really went for the jugular.

"Clearly you have no concept of how women think." Heathcliff stood his ground.

"And you do?"

"Better than you," Heathcliff challenged. "She didn't mean any of that. You rejected her. She spent her whole life being rejected by her mother. She was just protecting herself."

"And that's supposed to make me feel better...how?"

"I'm telling you she didn't mean any of that. Women are unstable and prone to unreasonable emotional outbursts. They don't mean half of the nonsense they say," Heathcliff blustered.

Oh, he did not just say that. My cousin or brother or uncle or whatever the hell Heathcliff was just took a dive off of the conversation cliff into the pit of he needed to get his ass kicked. Once I got out of my stupid coma, I was going to kick his ass into the next century. It was no wonder he didn't have a girlfriend, dimples or no dimples.

"Do you know this for certain?" Ethan sounded doubtful. Was he buying that crap? Wait, I wanted him to buy that crap and drink from me. As much as I would never ever admit it, Heathcliff was kind of right, but I was still going to kick his butt until he couldn't sit for a week.

"Yes," Heathcliff insisted. "There is tons of literature on this. I've read it myself."

"You do realize," Ethan said slowly, "that you sound like an ass?"

"Yes," Heathcliff sighed, embarrassed and defeated. "Yes, I do. I'm sorry...I just can't let you die. So many people need you. Astrid needs you. I know in my soul that she loves you and will be devastated if you die."

Go Heathcliff! I cheered inside my head. *If you get him to drink, I'll forget about all that male chauvinist bullshit you just spouted. Ethan, please listen to him. Please. Bite me, bite me, bite me...*

"Have you ever loved someone so much that your own existence is of little or no consequence?"

Heathcliff didn't answer. Ethan went on.

"I have conquered countries, civilizations, species...worlds. I have riches beyond the imagination, and the respect and fear of hundreds of thousands. It means nothing." Ethan's voice was flat and growing weaker. "Until she became mine, I was alone. I have been without love for over five hundred years. Many times during those years I thought I was happy, but I didn't really know what that meant until Astrid turned my world upside down. I never knew what it felt like to be whole. She made me feel alive, like a man...not some untouchable prince. And I fucked that up."

"Astrid made the choice to transport with Cathy," Heathcliff said.

"I know," Ethan sighed. "I just can't help but think the chain of events would have been completely different if I hadn't been so stupid and shortsighted."

"That's ridiculous," Heathcliff interjected. "Astrid is strong. Now that we know of the blood relation, there is no doubt in my mind that she would have done the same thing again."

"Maybe, maybe not." Ethan was unsure.

Oh for God's sake. Ethan was an ass, an egotistical ass. He had some gall to think if we'd been all lovey-dovey that I wouldn't have saved Cathy. Men were idiots. God, get me out of this coma so I can feed him and then slap him silly.

"Heathcliff, I have never been afraid of anything...ever. I'm afraid I will hurt her if I drink from her. I simply cannot take that chance. If..." he paused. "No...when she wakes...if she still wants me, then and only then will I take from her."

"I understand, my Prince," Heathcliff sounded defeated. "I really do."

***

"I couldn't get him to leave," The Kev told someone.

"What the fuck?" Pam shouted. "You are a two thousand year old Fairy and you can't get a five hundred year old Vampyre that *you* trained to leave the room?"

Pam was pissed like I'd never heard. She also sounded nervous.

"I don't understand why it's such a big deal," Gemma yelled at Pam.

Gemma had certainly grown some big balls, yelling at Pam like that. Maybe the Fairy Queen thing comes with a fantastic right hook or a death wish that leads to yelling at an Angel.

"Oh my God." Ethan was astonished.

"Shut. Up," Pam ground out at him. "Don't you say a word."

"But..." he sputtered.

"Not a fucking word," she bellowed at him. "You are not supposed to be here. I gave specific instructions that no one was to be in here when I arrived."

"Does he know you're...?" Ethan tried again.

"What part of 'not a fucking word' do you not understand?" Pam was not a happy camper. Why was she so angry at Ethan? "Do you want me to try to save her?" she demanded.

"Yes," Ethan begged.

"Can you keep a secret?" She stared hard at him.

"If I have to," he replied. "What are you?"

"I'm a fucking Angel with a foul mouth and a bad attitude. As much as I love you, and I do, I am not happy to see you right now. If you tell him anything about this, I will take you over my knee and beat your butt raw. I don't care if you're the ruler of the universe. Do you hear me, boy?" Pam shouted.

Was she talking to Ethan or was someone else in the room? Pam couldn't possibly be speaking to Ethan like that. Could she? *Damn it, why couldn't I wake up?*

"Pam, calm down. Yelling at him will not help," The Kev told her. "He is heartbroken and practically dead."

"For God's sake, Ethan, bite her," Pam exploded. "I will not sit here and watch either one of you die. That would put me in a very bad mood. You don't want to see me in a bad mood."

"Holy crap, this is a good mood?" Gemma muttered under her breath. The Kev laughed.

"I heard that, you little wannabe Fairy Queen. Don't you even think that I won't kick your pretty little ass," Pam growled and then refocused on Ethan. "You will drink from her. NOW."

"I will not." Ethan was cold and unmovable.

Come on, Pam. If anyone could scare someone into doing something, it was Pam. Clearly she knew him from somewhere. Maybe she and The Kev could physically force him. His bloodlust must be making him weak and needy. Shit, no one could force him to do anything. The Kev couldn't even get him to leave the room.

"I tell you what, you are on my last nerve, young man," Pam informed him.

"You said it would be complicated..." Ethan said.

Pam cut him off, "I said complicated, not over before it got started. So buck up and shut up. I've got work to do."

I felt Ethan relax for the first time in days. That made me happy. Magic began to fill the room. A warmth seeped into my toes and began to travel inch by inch up my body. The dull feeling of pins and needles started to pulse through my arms and legs, but I still couldn't open my eyes or move my body.

"Astrid." Pam was focused on me like a laser, "You have to fight. Come back, child."

Oh shit, Pam had called me Astrid instead of Assface or

Asscrack. This was serious. I was trying and praying. I was making deals with God and Buddha and all the Saints. I even threw Santa in.

The Kev and Gemma began to chant in a language I didn't understand. It was beautiful and melodic. I was floating into the music. It was misty and cloudy and a little ominous, but I knew I needed to be there. I was calling to them inside my head. Why couldn't they hear me? Then the pain started. Oh God...bad, burning, vicious pain.

"Listen to me, Astrid." I focused on Pam's voice. The more they chanted, the more excruciating it got, ripping through me, like daggers dipped in fire.

"Do not retreat," she ground out. "It will hurt like hell, but you have to walk through it." Pam was pissed. "If you don't walk through it, he will die and you will be stuck in this Limbo you're in right now. I know you can hear me. Walk out. NOW."

In my mind, I put one foot in front of the other and walked barefoot across the burning coals. I clutched the stone Nana had given me so tightly I felt it cutting into my hand. It began to heat up. I tried to drop it, but it had molded itself to my skin. My body began to shake and convulse.

"Hold her," Pam yelled to Ethan. His strong arms engulfed me as I kept walking through the living hell inside my head.

It would be so much easier to just die. This was too hard. I could die and go back to Nana. Wait, Pam said I would be stuck here and Ethan would die. My life sucked right now. Oh God, I couldn't move...hurt so bad. Please let me die...

"I love you, my Angel," Ethan whispered in my ear. "Come back to me. I'm no good without you. I'll make you so happy. I promise."

Pam joined the chant. I could feel my body, my real body, jerking and spasming. Ethan held me tightly as Magic whipped through the room bouncing off the walls and creating sounds resembling thunder.

I was close. I was so close. I pulled my ravaged body up and dragged myself toward an opening. I couldn't quite see it, but I knew it was there. My palms and knees were shredded from crawling through shards of jagged glass and I couldn't stop shaking. It was only a few more feet. I loved him so much...I could do this. I had to do this.

I gasped and moaned. I was raw and cold, so very cold. Scents overwhelmed me and cocooned me in a safe blanket at the same time. I smelled The Kev, Gemma and Pam, but most importantly I could smell Ethan. My love and my life. The reason I fought so hard to come back.

I slowly opened my eyes and there he was. I would never get used to how breathtaking he was. He had dark circles under his eyes and looked gaunt, but somehow it only enhanced his beauty. He reverently touched my face. Total adoration shone from his gorgeous golden eyes.

I still felt a bit like I was underwater as my lips curled into a smile. Pam, The Kev and Gemma surrounded us.

"I am so proud of you, baby," Pam said and gently stroked my cheek.

The Kev and Gemma leaned in and kissed me. I smiled my thanks. I loved my family so very much. I could feel Ethan's impatience—he did not want to share. The feeling was mutual.

I reached up and wrapped my arms around his neck and pulled him towards me. I pressed my lips to his ear. "I love you Ethan, now bite me already!"

He laughed with joy and then he did. Nothing had ever felt so good as his fangs in my neck.

Pam stared at Ethan and he looked up at her as he drank. She pointed at him and mouthed, *"Not a word"*. He nodded his head and my magical family disappeared in a breeze of Glitter Dust.

"I've missed you, Angel. Will you forgive me?" Ethan's voice was like a caress on my skin. His power and essence ran through me as mine ran through him. He was my other half and I wanted it no other way.

"I'll forgive you, if you'll forgive me," I said, running my fingertips over his beautiful face.

His eyes sparkled as he lowered his lips to mine and made me forget my name. Finally, everything was all right with my world.

Chapter 33

I opened my eyes, looked around the room and giggled. Vamps. Vamps everywhere. The mood in the room was light and airy. Happy and relaxed. My fellow Elite Guards were draped over couches, watching TV, sitting around a table playing games. Who knew Vampyres were obsessed with board games? They were playing Clue, but from their posture and faces you'd have thought it was a high stakes poker game. I remembered playing Clue repeatedly after a tonsillectomy when I was ten. Nana had been the best sport ever, but these guys had taken Clue to a whole new level.

Samuel looked very serious. I already knew from experience he was a bad loser. His arm had grown back completely. He named his new appendage Astrid in honor of my beheading the two Rogues who'd removed it. I felt honored...I think. Somebody Samuel's age should know better, but a bad loser is a bad loser. Period. David, Luke and Heathcliff seemed to be having more fun, although they eyed each other warily and kept Colonel Mustard in the kitchen with the rope close to their chests. Ethan sat in a chair across the room and watched me. I was bundled up in his big beautiful bed. Venus sat nearby flipping through catalogs and fashion magazines and Paris sat at her feet painting her toe nails.

I shot a look to Ethan and he winked at me. Oh help me, Jesus, my stomach got tingly and dropped to my toes. That man reeked of power and sex and he was mine. Mine, mine, mine. I was so tempted to fly across the room and tackle him that I had to grip the bed sheets to keep myself still. I could tell by the smirk on his lips and the green of his eyes that he knew exactly what I was thinking and very much approved. I had a bone to pick with my mate, but it had to wait until we were alone. The commotion at the game table knocked me out of my sexual stupor.

"You're cheating," David yelled at Samuel.

"How in the fuck do you cheat at Clue?" Samuel shouted back, slamming his cards down on the table. Heathcliff was laughing and Luke backed away, completely aware that Samuel and David were about to dance and it was going to get ugly.

"You looked at my cards, you bastard," David accused Samuel, as if he'd stolen national security secrets, not just peeked to see if Miss Scarlet did it in the library with the gun.

"You're full of shit," Samuel bellowed back. "You're just a pathetic player. No skill, no finesse."

"Take that back, you son of a bitch," David hissed at Samuel. "I have skill and finesse."

Oh my God, they were such girls. Skill? Finesse? For Clue? These Vampyres had too much time on their hands. Both men stood up, knocking their chairs over and circling each other menacingly.

"Enough!" Ethan told them, moving between them. "If you insist on behaving like children, I shall treat you like children. You two," he indicated Samuel and David "can go outside and beat the hell out of each other. If you destroy my suite or, more importantly, disturb my mate, I will beat the hell out of you." Everyone froze. Out of pure spite he joyously added, "And I will destroy the Clue game."

All four grown male Vampyres groaned like eight year olds. This was awesome. I filed the knowledge away for future blackmail use. I was sure he would beat them soundly if he thought they had upset me. As flattering as that may be, I just wanted a bit of peace and no injured friends for a little while. I didn't want any more appendages named after me.

I was so tickled by how dorky all these hot sexy Vampyres were, I didn't even notice the suite had gone silent and all eyes were on me.

"What?' I asked Venus.

"Oooklay at the Ooorday." she said, confusing the hell out of me.

Seriously, did she really just tell me to look at the door in Pig Latin? The cool factor of these gorgeous Vampyres was diminishing rapidly. I looked at the door and my gut clenched. It was Cathy and a man...a very handsome man...with the kindest eyes I'd ever seen. He was smiling at me and although I'd never seen him before, I knew him at once.

Heathcliff crossed over to his father, took his hand and began to lead him over to me. Cathy followed about five steps behind, her head hung low and her steps timid. She was breaking my heart. I was amazed at how much she looked like Nana. How had I not noticed it before?

"Stop," Ethan commanded. "I don't want her around my mate." He pointed at Cathy. Everyone in the room tensed.

God...talk about humiliation. "No, Ethan," I said. "It's okay. I want to see her."

Ethan's anger radiated out from him, bouncing off the walls of the room. Occasionally I was reminded that Ethan was like the President, Prime Minister and Pope all rolled into one. This was one of those times. I quickly moved to him and gently rubbed his arms and chest.

"It's okay, baby," I whispered. "You don't really mean that. Cathy has been loyal to you for over a hundred years. She won't hurt me." I put my arms around him to calm him down.

Cathy stepped forward and Ethan's entire body stiffened under my hands. The suite was drenched in his power and anger. "Don't take another step," he whipped out at Cathy between clenched teeth.

She gasped and I could have sworn Heathcliff growled. Sometimes I forgot that Vampyres were very deadly creatures. We were not human, and human emotions and ethics did not fit us very well.

"I understand your anger and reticence, my Liege," Cathy said quietly. "I deserve it, but I have come to beg forgiveness and humble myself to the Chosen One. To Astrid. I stand in shame of my behavior and request punishment equal to my digressions."

She dropped to her knees and went prostrate before us.

Ethan turned to Heathcliff. "I will not leave her alone with Astrid."

Heathcliff looked down. "As you wish, Your Majesty."

This was ridiculous. "Ethan, for God's sake, she's my sister, cousin, aunt two times removed or something like that. I know in my gut this is fine. I'd like some privacy with her, because I have a few things I'd like to say."

Ethan was torn. I think he also knew that Cathy would not try to hurt me, but he didn't usually reverse decisions after he made them. He'd also never had a mate before who could withhold panty privileges if she didn't get her way.

"Please," I smiled and opened my mind to him. I gave him a glimpse of all the things I would let him do to me and all the things I wanted to do to him. He smiled and looked at me with such heat in his eyes I came close to telling everybody to leave the room.

"Fine," Ethan conceded, giving me a look that implied he expected me to make good on all the visuals he'd just seen. I winked at him and he laughed. He was breathtaking when he laughed. Venus raised her eyebrows in shock and Samuel gave me a thumbs up, but I should have known my Vampyre stud wasn't finished. "You will wear your shield in her presence," he said. "Heathcliff, you and Sir James will stay in the room. If one hair on her head is mussed, I will destroy all of you. Understood?"

"Understood," Heathcliff replied stiffly.

Talk about overprotective. I didn't dare utter a word, fearing something snarky or smart aleck would fly out of my mouth and he would change his mind. He stared at me and waited. I touched my chest and activated my shield. Ethan seemed satisfied.

Everyone exited the suite, including a reluctant Ethan. I was left alone...with my family.

We all stared at each other. Now that we were alone, we didn't know what to say. It was strange and uncomfortable. It started slowly and no one could stop it as we began to laugh. At first it was that nervous, *oh my God, I'm laughing at a funeral* kind of laughter, then it morphed into joy. All the pent-up emotions and fear and excitement bubbled out, exploding into giddy laughter. Heathcliff, Sir James and I laughed until tears ran from our eyes. It was a perfect moment. Everyone laughed. Everyone except Cathy. Oh for God's sake, enough of this 'poor pathetic me' shit.

"Get up," I said to Cathy. She did. I circled her and she watched me with wary eyes.

"I would expect that you would want me banished," she began defensively.

"Then you don't know me at all." I cut her off and watched her squirm. "Try again," I challenged her.

She was so unsure. I wanted to help her out, but from past experience I was very aware of her pride. I waited for her to make the next move. I was not going to fix it for her.

She looked lost as she spoke. "I'm...grateful to you for saving my life and I beg your forgiveness. I am devastated about what happened to you." I watched her carefully. She was sincere.

"I'm not," I said, walking toward her and removing my shield.

"What?" She backed away from me.

"Stand still," I hissed. She did. "I'm not sorry. I'm not sorry about any of it. Not sorry about saving you and not sorry about what happened after, because I got to see my Nana, your mother. She was so proud of me. Proud of me for saving you."

They all froze and watched me and waited. Cathy was trembling. I thought they knew I had seen Nana, but their reactions proved otherwise. A myriad of emotions washed across all three of their faces, longing the most prevalent.

"Did she say anything?" Heathcliff was ashen and his voice was shaky. He looked like a child, insecure and desperately missing his mother. I realized, with great sadness, I'd gotten to have her many more years than they had. "Any message for us?" he whispered.

"Oh yes." I smiled at my friend. "She told me to tell you how very much she loves you all." God, it felt good to tell them that.

Cathy fell back to the ground and rocked back and forth as tears streamed from her eyes. Heathcliff wrapped his arms around her and wept with her. Sir James approached me. He radiated power and kindness and love. He extended his hands to me, I took them and a soothing warmth began to creep through my body.

His eyes sparkled with unshed tears. "Is she coming back?" he asked.

"She said it wasn't her time yet." I could feel my own tears escape and spill down my cheeks.

"Oh," Sir James said. A look of profound pain and disappointment crossed his beautiful face. He quickly looked away and regrouped. I had never realized that one short word could convey so very much. My heart tore for him, and for Heathcliff and Cathy...and for me. It was very clear how much this man and his children loved my Nana.

Sir James looked up at me and smiled. "We have waited many years for you, Astrid." He gently touched my face. "What a beautiful gift to have the Chosen One be part of our family. Part of the mother of my children. Part of the woman I have loved for over a century."

"I'm not technically related to you." I was devastated. I wanted this man to be my grandfather. I wanted him to be mine.

"Oh," he chuckled, "you most certainly are. I was married to your Nana. She and I were connected on unexplainable levels. What is of her blood is mine and what is of my blood is hers. You are as much mine as if I sired you myself, dear child."

I threw myself into his arms, practically knocking him to the ground. Damn, I've gotta watch that. Who in the hell knew that turning into a Blood Sucking Creature of the Night would be the best thing that happened to me.

"Astrid," he said, "there is much I know about the Chosen One's path. I believe I can help you understand yourself better. I also would greatly love to hear about everything from your perspective," he said. His dimples were identical to Heathcliff's. "We will sit together soon and educate one another."

"I would like that very much, Sir James," I said, relieved that somebody knew something about this Chosen One crap.

"Astrid, my child, what would you like from your sister? Or would it be cousin or possibly aunt?" He pondered the options. "Let's just say sister and leave it at that." I nodded and he continued. "What would you like from your sister in exchange for saving her life?" Sir James, my new grandpa, kindly asked. His beautiful blue eyes that were so much like Heathcliff's searched my face.

"Nothing," I told him truthfully.

"Ahh, I thought you might say that," he chuckled. "There must be something. The Prince is angry, and rightly so, due to my daughter's abhorrent behavior toward you. He will want a penance paid. I do believe it would be better if you chose that penance rather than him."

"You're right," I said, worried about what Ethan would do on his own. "I suppose if I had to choose something—I would choose for Cathy to like me." I watched her as I spoke. She looked up quickly and almost knocked heads with Heathcliff. She was so surprised that I giggled, and miracle of all miracles, she did too. "It's what I've always wanted even before I knew we were blood related."

"Oh my sweet child, blood related is such a clinical term," Sir James chuckled and caressed my cheek. "We are family."

He folded me into his arms. It felt like heaven. Heathcliff stood and joined the embrace followed very slowly and very tentatively by Cathy. It was a beginning. A good beginning.

Chapter 34

I knew he would be angry with me if I left, but I was angry with him. I'd been stuck in his suite for three days. It was a very nice suite, but stuck is stuck. No one would let me do anything. At first it was lovely, but now I was going batshit crazy. I was not the kind of person who did boredom well. I may be disorganized and somewhat directionless, but I was not lazy. Besides, I felt great. I was getting claustrophobic and that bastard had been avoiding me. Yesterday he muttered some lame excuse about it being too difficult to be near me because he wanted me so badly and was afraid of hurting me. Utter bullshit. I knew why he was running scared. He'd had some kind of past relationship with Pam and they'd rekindled it.

I couldn't believe they'd do that to me. Actually, I didn't believe they'd do that to me. There was no way. I knew I was being ridiculous, but I didn't care. There was something between them, but it didn't seem sexual. I was sure he was avoiding me because Pam made him promise not to say anything and he knew I'd wheedle it out of him. I was just pissy and bored and horny and lonely. It was a bad combination. Bad.

To make matters worse, the King seemed to be losing it. Ever since I'd come out of the coma, he'd been wandering around the compound looking for someone. He muttered constantly to himself and had a hard time focusing. Princess Lelia and Princess Raquel kept him under constant watch. They were worried. Ethan seemed worried too. Hell, everyone was worried around here. Ethan had a nifty way of handling it. He avoided his father as well as me.

I missed my baby Demons, my shampoo, my pillow, my

sweat pants and my sparkly Converse. Never in my life did I think I'd complain about wearing Prada twenty-four seven. A fine lesson in 'beware of what you wish for'. I wanted to be sloppy and comfy. I was jonesing for my old faded sweatshirts and my lime green Converse with some tight black Hard Tail sweats and a scrunchy.

Happily for me, tons of sweet little baby Demons lived on the ceilings of the Cressida House. They sang and danced and beat the snot out of each other to entertain me, but they weren't my babies. I needed Rachel, Ross, Beyonce and Honest Abe. I missed them terribly and they were probably worried sick about me. I needed to go home, even if it was just for a little while. Maybe I could just disappear for a couple of hours.

I ran around the suite and tried to find my shoes. As much as I missed my tennis shoes, the silver Prada platforms I'd been wearing were *hot*. Where in the hell were they? I crawled under the bed and searched.

"Astrid?" a child called.

"Shit," I yelped, nailing my head on the bedframe. Damn, was I bleeding? What was it with me and bedframes? Moreover, what the hell was it with people not knocking before they entered a room?

"Oh my God, are you okay?" she asked.

"I'm fine," I snapped, ready to rip the kid a new one. "I'd be a hell of a lot better if you could get some manners and knock on the ..." Oh dear God, it was Paris.

I quickly switched my tone before she started rolling around on the floor and freaking out. We needed to do something about that. "I'm fine, sweetie," I tried to convince a mortified Paris. "What do you need?" I attempted to hide the gash on my forehead.

"Are you bleeding?" she whimpered.

"Nope," I lied.

"Yes you are!" She dropped to a squat.

Oh shit, I didn't have time for this. I needed to get out of here. "Paris, if you roll around on the floor, I will kick your ass. Do you understand me?"

"Yes," she said, "but your head..."

"Will heal. I'm a Vampyre. Now, what I need," I explained, "is for you to crawl under the bed and get my shoes. I'm too big."

"Done." She got happy again. It didn't take much. "Oh," she yelled from under the bed, "I'm supposed to tell you that Brad Pitt called. The skanky one," she clarified as if I wouldn't know. "He said it was no problem to reschedule your mother's memorial for tomorrow night." She got out from under the bed and held my pretty shoes out to me. "And that he and Angelina got a big kick out of your accent."

"Dude, you're still yelling," I winced.

"Oh, sorry."

I ran my hands through my hair and took my shoes from her. "For God's sake, I didn't even call him," I muttered.

"Then who did?" she asked.

"Hell if I know," I sighed. "Maybe Gemma, but she doesn't have an accent. Anyway, Brad and Angelina know her." This whole Brad thing made my stomach queasy. Vampyres were not supposed to get queasy. I had a sick feeling that my mother was screwing with me. How in the hell could that be? I saw her get eaten for God's sake. Pretty hard to mistake your mother getting eaten by Demons while your grotesque Demon King daddy stood by and watched.

"Would you like me to...?" Paris stopped, embarrassed.

"Would I like you to what?" Hell, I wanted to get out of here. I loved Paris, but I wanted to leave and I couldn't disappear with her in the room. As loyal as she was to me, she was far more so to Ethan. She'd tattle on me so fast.

"Would you like me to go with you to the memorial tomorrow night?" She resembled a beaten dog, ready to be rejected.

"Of course I would." I looked at my beautiful and bizarre little Vampyre friend and I realized I did want her there. I wanted all of my Vampyre friends and family there. I knew that they all wouldn't be able to come because many had to be on patrol. More Rogues kept showing up and wreaking havoc. I was itching to get out and patrol again. I asked Samuel and Venus if the new Rogues resembled me, but every time I even started talking shop they changed the subject. They spouted some bullshit about me needing rest...blah, blah, blah.

"Yes, Paris, I want you to come. That would make me happy."

"Okay, great." She smiled like I'd given her one hundred million dollars. It made me sick to think of the way I'd treated her initially. I'd dismissed her because she was a freak. God certainly has a way of kicking you in the ass with irony. Who was the bigger freak now? Let me think. Hmm...that would have to be me.

"Wait a minute little missy, shouldn't you be teaching my art class now?" I raised my eyebrows giving her an imitation of my scary Ethan look.

"Whoops," she laughed and started for the door. Clearly I

lacked authority if my replacement thinks my scary look is funny and going to work is optional.

"Paris, wait," I said. She turned back at the doorway of the suite. "Have Martha and Jane been causing trouble?" I asked.

"Every day."

"Holy shit, are you okay?" I gasped, imagining all the hateful things they could have said. "I'll kill them if they hurt you."

Paris looked absolutely delighted by my violent protective streak. "Oh no, Astrid, they're fine. I like them."

"Good God, you do?" I was shocked. How could anyone like those hateful old cows? God bless them.

"Yep, they're not so bad. Plus their conservative Republican rants amuse me."

"You're a better woman than me," I grinned. Paris giggled, hugged me and left.

I pondered Paris' affection for the old ladies for a moment and decided very little made sense to me anymore. I pulled my pretty platforms on and flung my arms out, spraying the room with Glitter Magic, and disappeared.

***

Their little bodies wiggled like excited puppies. They yipped, squealed, licked and kissed me. I tickled their fat Demon bellies and fed them breeze after breeze of Glitter Magic. They all chattered at once in their little high-pitched Munchkin voices. Oh my God, I loved them.

After about fifteen minutes of utter ballistic chaos, they wore themselves out. They were lying in a panting heap on my bed. My small cozy bed in my small cozy house. I was so happy to be home, even if it was for a short while. I gathered their now calm little Demon bodies to my chest and cuddled them.

"I missed you guys so much," I cooed.

I realized Honest Abe was playing with my boob. That just wasn't working for me. I plucked him off my girls, set him up on my shoulder and told him "No, no."

I supposed I'd have to rethink his sexuality. Maybe he was more bisexual than homosexual. Wait—why in the hell was I concerned about Honest Abe's sexual preference? I had more important questions for my Demons. I'd been curious about a couple of things for a while and today was as good a day as any to get some answers.

"Um...Beyonce?" I started with her, figuring she'd be the most forthright. "What exactly do you guys eat?"

"Pizza," she informed me.

"Really?" I was so surprised.

"No," she screamed and began to laugh hysterically. Rachel, Ross and Honest Abe followed suit. They were laughing so hard I thought they'd throw up.

What in the hell was so funny? I tried again. "Oookay, clearly it's not pizza." I gave them the eyeball and they calmed down. "Do you drink blood?"

"Sometimes," Honest Abe said, inching back towards my boob. I plucked him back up and put him on my head.

I tried to grab Rachel, but she ran behind my knee. I settled for Ross. "Ross, do you eat animals?"

"Nooooo, Mommy, Ross no eat animals," he giggled. "Ross looooves animals. No eat. No eat."

Dear God please let the answer to this next one be no. "Do you eat people?" *Please God, no. Please God, no.*

"No, Mommy," Ross guffawed. "People too chewy!" He was laughing so hard he stopped breathing and started to turn purple. I smacked him on his little Demon back. He sputtered, coughed and thanked me. Unfortunately from his answer, I assumed he'd tried a person or two in his time. They were being vague about their culinary preferences. I needed a new approach.

"What if I guess?" I challenged them. They jumped up and down, grinning and clapping their hands. I took that as a go. "Okay, if you don't eat animals or pizza or...um....people, *thank you Jesus*, do you eat vegetables?"

"No," they chorused.

"Fruit?" I asked.

"No."

"Potato chips?"

"No," they screamed, laughing.

"Meat?"

"Yessssss," my babies hissed.

"Wait, if you don't eat animals or people, what kind of meat do you eat?" I was confused and alarmed. What other kind of meat was there? "Do you mean fish?"

"No! Meat, meat, meat," they chanted and ran all over my bed, slapping each other and giggling. Honest Abe kept getting dangerously close to my boobs and I kept flicking him away. He thought that was hilarious and kept trying.

"Good God, Honest Abe. You cannot play with my breasts. That's not appropriate. Do you understand?" I had him by the scruff of the neck. "What's gotten into you?"

He looked sheepish. "Me go to Big Sean's Booby Bungalow when Mommy was gone. Me love boobies!" he shouted with glee.

"Boobies, boobies, boobies," they all sang and kept rolling around on my bed.

Holy shit, my babies were going to strip clubs? I was gone for a week or two and they turned to pornography? Absolutely unacceptable. They weren't old enough to...wait a second.

"How old are you?" I demanded.

"Ninety-two," Honest Abe grinned.

"Me eighty-seven," Beyonce yelled.

"Me sixty-eight," Rachel piped in.

"Me fifteen thousand and three," Ross volunteered. *What?* I was speechless. He was older than Jesus. Literally. "Just joking, Mommy! Me seventy!" He was delighted with his little Velcro self.

"Fine," I muttered, "I guess you guys are old enough to go to a titty bar, but I don't like it. I find them offensive to women and totally skeevy. I'd prefer you do something more constructive with your free time."

I was going to use this as a teachable moment. Big Sean's Booby Bungalow? I'd never even heard of that one. The only two I knew of were out on the highway, Bare Assets and The Bowling Green Bush Company. I do have to admit that Big Sean came up with the best name.

"Don't be mad, Mommy. We eat there," Rachel informed me.

"You eat strippers?" I gasped. "I thought people were too chewy."

"Not strippers Mommy, we eat the bad things that love strippers," Beyonce chimed in.

"And that would be?" I held my nonexistent breath. *Please don't say drunk men or participants of bachelor parties.*

"Bad Demons," they screeched.

"Holy shit, you eat Demons?" That was disgusting. I felt myself gag remembering the lovely display at my mother's house.

"Only the bad ones, Mommy," Ross threw over his shoulder as he started doing a kind of *West Side Story* "Dance at the Gym" number on my pillow.

I sat up on my bed and pressed my fingers to the bridge of my nose, trying to ward off the migraine headed my way. I was worried sick that my babies were going to get themselves killed. There had to be something else they liked to eat besides Bad Demons. How could that even taste good?

"How can you tell a Bad Demon from a Good Demon?" I was getting panicked.

"Silly Mommy," Honest Abe yelled. "It's easy! We are Good Demons and your daddy is a Bad Demon."

"Yummy," Rachel hooted, "I want to eat Mommy's daddy."

"Noooo." Beyonce punched her. "I want to eat Mommy's daddy."

An all-out brawl involving the four of them ensued over who got to eat my daddy.

"Enough," I shouted. They froze. "First of all, my daddy is the most butt-ass ugly, smelly and disgusting thing I've ever laid eyes on. I can't imagine anyone wanting to eat him. On the flip side, he's large. I would imagine there's...um...enough of him for you guys to share." I felt my gag reflex kick in. They smiled and appeared to be satisfied by the compromise.

"Is Big Sean's Booby Bungalow the only place to find Bad Demons?" I asked.

"No," Ross was still dancing. "Jails and car dealerships are good too, Mommy." Ross walked up my arm and onto my chest. "Mommy, Bad Demons are everywhere. They keep coming through the Squish Hole and we eat them."

"Too many come," Rachel added, as she tried to braid Ross' Velcro. "Lately hard to eat soooo many Bad Demons."

"How many can you eat?" *Why did I continue to ask questions I didn't want to know the answers to?*

"Yesterday me eat twenty-seven," Beyonce informed me proudly, slapping her belly.

Wow, I had nothing to say to that. Nothing. I was tempted to ask what a Squish Hole was, but I was pretty sure I had that one figured out. It had to be a Portal between Earth and Hell. If it was something else...I didn't want to know.

I stood up and started tossing them back up to my ceiling. "I'm going to take a really long hot shower and try to wash this conversation off of me." They thought that was hilarious. "Look at me," I told them sternly. They did. "I love you and I will be devastated if anything happens to you. I want you to be careful when you dine. You got it?"

"Got it, Mommy," my babies screeched. "We love you too!" They pummeled each other for a few minutes and then disappeared. I shook my head and made my way to the shower.

Chapter 35

Oh my God, it felt so good to be clean using my own fabulous bath products. Not to be a snob, but as much money as those Vamps had, they had some sub-par bath paraphernalia. Although Venus had some good stuff, Ethan definitely did not. I'd just bring mine back with me.

Who in the hell had called Brad Pitt? Maybe it was Gemma. Where were they anyway? Gemma, The Kev and Pam were nowhere to be found. I'd be sick if they were gone for good. On top of missing them desperately, how was I supposed to eat? I'd still not drunk from a mortal—it just didn't appeal to me. I knew I could drink from Ethan. Thinking about that made my knees go weak and my imagination go wild. Thank goodness I wasn't hungry. I was feeling a bit nauseous. I supposed it was a hangover from my coma.

I sighed, dropped my towel and went digging through my drawers for some comfy clothes. I needed to get back to the Cressida House before I was missed. That could be a real shit storm. I had every right to leave, but I knew Ethan would be angry. Not because I left, but because I didn't tell him or take an army of armed guards. I was head over heels, no turning back madly in love with Ethan. I knew I didn't want to exist without him, but he was not the boss of me. I still needed to be able to run my own life. God knew I could defend myself. I could just scream and blow everything to smithereens.

Grinning, I grabbed a pair of tight black pants that I knew would drive him insane, but first I slipped on a barely there thong. I paired it with a whisper pink raw silk camisole that did very nice things for my very nice breasts, and then I added a rockin' pair of Prada wedges. He was going to stop ignoring me in a big way.

I threw a bag on my bed and started loading it with Converse, vintage T-shirts, my favorite jeans, a couple of Juicy sweat suits, some gold sequined Uggs and several really pretty tops from Anthropologie. I grabbed my flip flops, some colorful summer skirts, and a teddy bear that Nana had given me when I was eight. Soon I was zipped up and ready to go. I knew I shouldn't transport with a suitcase after what happened with Cathy. I'd drive back. God help me, I was going to get my ass kicked when they realized what I'd done, but I needed to see my babies. I wondered if I could get them to come back to the Cressida House with me.

"Rachel, Ross, Beyonce, Honest Abe?" I called. "Do you guys want to go on a field trip?" No answer. "Guys? What if I promise to introduce you to my dad sometime?"

"Who are you talking to?" a British woman asked.

What the fu...? British woman? I whipped around and was standing three feet from the big blonde Amazon who had turned me into a Vampyre. "Shit," I screeched. I slammed my body up against the wall, touched my chest and protected myself with my shield.

She laughed lightly and made her way to my vanity. She sat down and began rummaging through my nail polish. "So, how have you been?" she asked, smiling at me while she pocketed my favorite Chanel Gold Lame polish.

Was she kidding? That Amazon did not just steal a thirty dollar bottle of nail polish, did she?

Yes...yes, she did.

"What exactly do you mean?" I was very calm. "How have I been? Hmm, let me see...you turned me into a Blood Sucking Creature of the Night and left me for dead. That was awfully friendly of you and now you show up with some fakey British accent that you didn't have the last time and start stealing my shit."

"Oh, you saw that?" She was trying to play it off. Wasn't working.

"Who are you and what are you doing here?" I demanded. "Oh, and by the way, you can take my nail polish out of your pocket and put it back."

"I can see you're a bit upset." She stood up with my nail polish still tucked firmly in her pocket. "I'll come back another time." She went to leave.

"Oh no, you don't" I snapped. "Sit your Amazon ass back down. You're going to answer some questions."

She paused and examined me. I shivered. Something wasn't right with her. It was unnerving. "Aren't you a feisty one? I'd heard you were a dish rag and rather worthless."

What the fu...? Dish rag, my ass. I was so done with being insulted by dead people. "I don't know where you got your info, Blondie..."

"Julie," she interrupted.

I half expected her name to be Olga or Svetlana. "Oookay Julie. Clearly your informant was gravely mistaken and quite possibly a stupid dummy."

Crap, that sounded kind of middle school. Please tell me I didn't just say 'stupid dummy'.

"Clearly," she smirked, "definitely a stupid dummy."

"Well, um...okay. Who is your informant?"

"My mother," she calmly informed me, eyeing my Chanel Vamp and Dragon polish bottles.

No fucking way. I quickly crossed the room and removed all of my expensive polish, leaving her all the cheap shit to pilfer. "Your mother?" I questioned as I tossed about three hundred dollars' worth of nail polish into my little suitcase.

"And yours," she gave me a creepy smile.

"My what?" I didn't like the way this was headed. If this were a bad B movie, she'd tell me I was her sister and then she'd kill me. Wait...she had already killed me.

"Our mother, Astrid," she giggled. "We're sisters."

Jerry Springer, here I come. "Back the fuck up, Blon...I mean, Julie. Explain."

She smiled condescendingly and heaved a sigh as if I was mentally challenged. "Our mother, also known as stupid dummy, has lived several lives and had children each time."

"You're kidding." I felt a little sick.

"Do I look like I'm kidding?" She raised her very attractive eyebrows and waited.

"No." I felt defeated. "How many lives has she had?"

"A few."

"How many brothers and sisters do we have?" I asked.

"Several."

"Are we all Vampyres?" This was nuts.

"Mostly."

"Could you be any more annoyingly vague?" I was about over her.

"Possibly," she giggled again.

I closed my eyes, and tried desperately to ignore the reality of my life. Could it get any stranger? The answer was no. At least I hoped it was.

"It was you," I gasped, figuring out the Brad Pitt mystery. "You called Brad Pitt."

"Yes, Astrid, that was me." She rolled her eyes at how long it took me to figure that one out. God, she really was a bitch.

"Wait," I started laughing, "do you go around setting up memorials for her every time she dies?"

"Something like that," she replied, looking bored.

I stared at her. We looked nothing alike. We had to have different fathers. Of course we did. Didn't we? "How old are you?" I asked. She was eyeing my perfume.

"Older than you," she said, spritzing herself with the expensive bottle.

"You can't have that," I told her, "it's mine." *Was I twelve?*

"Fine," she huffed, "if you're not going to share, I'm leaving." She stood up and went for the door.

"I'm not done with you."

"Too bad, Astrid." She was so smug. "I'll see you at Mother's memorial tomorrow night. Perhaps you'll be more agreeable."

With that, she walked out of my room and left my house, with my nail polish in her pocket. She was a total bitch, had answered none of my questions, and had stolen my stuff. She was so going to pay for that.

Chapter 36

Driving back was stressful. I still felt sick. I heaved a huge sigh and tried to stop the storm of thoughts racing through my mind. I was glad I could tolerate sunlight as I watched the gorgeous Kentucky sunset rip through the sky. The blazing pinks and purples were in striking contrast with the huge orange sun that dipped lower and lower by the minute.

I had hoped to get back to the Cressida House before everyone woke up for the evening, but my unexpected guest had delayed me. Julie had pissed me off, but she had also scared me. I didn't want her in my life at all. Please God, let her move on after the memorial. I already had a sister. Cathy was my sort-of sister, and one pain in the ass difficult sibling was all I could handle.

I pulled up the manicured, tree lined drive of the Cressida House and was ushered straight through the guard gate. The Vamps on duty shook their heads in either disgust or pity when they saw it was me. Whatever it was, it didn't bode well. As I approached the manor house my stomach dropped. So much for getting back before my absence was noticed. I had a welcoming committee. Let me see, I spied Venus, Samuel, Heathcliff, Luke, David, Raquel, Lelia and a very unhappy Ethan.

Shit.

"Hey guys," I yelled, getting out of my junky car. I should buy a new one, but cars cost a lot of...Wait, I just inherited forty million dollars. I could buy a stinkin' fleet of cars. No one had returned my greeting. I tried again. Louder. "Hey friends, are you all going somewhere?" Volume always worked for Pam. Everyone looked slightly confused. It was working.

"It's a great night for a ...um...a run or...you know...a bonfire. Actually, fires are not our friend...being Vampyres and all..."

"Enough, Astrid," Ethan said quietly. Way too quietly. I shut up. "Where have you been?"

"I went home."

"This is your home now, Astrid," he replied tersely.

"No, Ethan," I countered, "it's not. I don't have a room here or any of my stuff. The mailman, the police, amazon.com and my newspaper delivery guy all think I live at 333 Montavesta Road, so..."

"Astrid, come with me," Ethan cut me off, took my arm and my suitcase and led me into the Cressida House. Venus winked as I passed which made me feel a little bit better, but Heathcliff shook his head like an older brother might when his little sister had done something really stupid. Why was it stupid that I wanted to go home? Did becoming a Vampyre mean I had joined some undead cult and couldn't be trusted on my own?

We walked silently through the mansion. After we'd crossed through the Grand Foyer and walked up the curved marble staircase, we stood in front of the intricately carved teak doors of the elevator and waited. It was difficult for me to get accustomed to the opulence of this place. I was used to a much simpler life. I stole glances at Ethan through lowered lashes. God, even angry he was the sexiest man I'd ever laid eyes on. I knew we were about to have it out, but all I wanted to do was strip him and tackle him.

Why couldn't I read minds? It was so unfair. I wanted to know what he was thinking. Clearly he was not pleased that I'd left, but had he noticed my butt in the tight black pants or how my camisole hugged my breasts just right? Or how just thinking about all this was making me dangerously horny?

Ethan led me into his suite, shut the door and began to pace the room. His power filled the large room making it small. "This is our suite." His eyes bored into me. "You are mine and this is where we stay when we are in Kentucky."

"You wait one minute," I shot back, getting louder and louder with each word that flew from my mouth. "I am not some possession you own or can control. You may run everything else, but you will never, ever control me. I am the boss of me. Not you!"

Was I suicidal? Yes. Yelling at the Prince of the North American Dominion was a big Vampyre no-no, but he was pissing me off big time. Maybe I would talk to him later when he wasn't being such a primitive jackass.

He grabbed me and hauled me up against his chest. He pinned my arms behind my back as I shrieked my displeasure. My breasts were planted firmly against him. I felt my nipples tighten and moisture pool between my legs. My inner slut was betraying me once again. Why on earth I was getting so turned on by his he-man behavior was beyond me.

"Let go of me," I hissed, trying to escape the steel bands of his arms.

"Not a chance, my love." His lips were inches from my ear and his voice sent shivers through me. "You are definitely mine and I am yours," he whispered. "You may not be my possession, but I plan to possess you. Every inch of you, for the rest of your very long life."

His lips brushed my ear and I started to tremble. "I don't know what I'm supposed to do," I shuddered as his lips made a hot trail from my earlobe to the corner of my mouth.

"I think you know exactly what to do," he replied lazily, nipping at my bottom lip.

"I don't know who I am anymore. I don't know what's expected of me. What you expect of me. What I expect of myself..." I trailed off and tried not to cry. I had a sick feeling in my stomach. Everything I was saying was so true. "I don't know how to be with you. It's too complicated," I whispered and started to cry.

"Shhhh," Ethan tangled his free hand into my hair. "It's not complicated. You have to let me love you, give me a little bit of yourself. Trust me."

"But I..."

He drove his point home, crushing his lips against my mouth, and pressing his body to mine. Trust him? Give myself to him? I couldn't even think straight. Actually, he might be right. Damn him. I struggled and successfully freed one arm, fully intending to deck him. My arm had a different idea. I pulled him closer and let my lips part under his assault. A growl of pure male pleasure escaped from him as he drove his tongue into my mouth.

I bit at his lips and tangled my tongue with his. All of my fear and anger and confusion from the last month came rushing out of me. I wanted to devour him the same way he was devouring me. It was aggressive, bordering on violent. We were spiraling out of control. Hard, fast and angry.

"Just so you know," Ethan groaned, digging his strong hands into my hips, "I noticed the pants and the top." He pressed himself against me and I could feel his appreciation for my efforts. His fangs scraped my neck and my knees gave way.

251

All chances for coherent thinking were gone. I couldn't remember my name, much less why I didn't want to strip him naked. His scent and his taste and the feel of his body against mine overwhelmed me.

I clawed at his clothes. "Make them go away," I demanded

"With pleasure," his voice was ragged with desire. My body pined for him. It took everything I had not to throw myself at him while he slowly disrobed.

"You're a tease," I hissed impatiently.

"Patience is a virtue," he chuckled and went slower.

"Not one of mine," I said, ripping at his clothes.

His body was glorious. Strong and muscular and deadly. Muscles that would take a lifetime to achieve. I couldn't believe he was mine. I ran my hands over his deliciously broad shoulders and his perfectly muscular arms. The light sprinkling of blonde chest hair tickled my fingertips and sent chills through my body. I followed the hair down his body where it tapered to his ripped abdomen and led to my prize, his huge cock that was very happy for the attention and as hard as a rock. I knew how he would feel inside of me and I wanted it. Now. He was my drug of choice.

His eyes smoldered with desire as he watched me like a predator watches prey. This was my game and he waited to see what I would do next. So I stepped back and marveled at his body. He kept his hands at his sides and waited. His muscles rippled under my fingertips and his body shuddered as I lightly ran my nails over his erection.

I wrapped my hands around him and sank to my knees. The hard heavy length of him jerked in my hands and his head dropped back to his shoulders. He was perfection, hard as steel, yet as smooth as satin. My eyes blazed green and my fangs descended. They stayed locked on his as I flicked my tongue out and circled the swollen head of his shaft. He groaned and twined his fingers into my hair, pushing my hot, wet mouth further down the hard length of him. I scraped him with my fangs as he forced himself as deep as I would take him.

I worried for a brief moment that my inexperience might turn him off, but the sounds coming from deep within his body allayed my fears. The feel of him in my mouth was electrifying. His taste, his scent and moans made me dizzy with power. He was intoxicating. Having him completely in my control was as much of a turn on as having him deep inside of me. I gripped his hips and relaxed my throat, taking more of him into me.

No longer concerned if I was doing it right, I followed my instincts and the movements of his body. Going down on him was hotter than I ever could have imagined. He made the sexiest sounds I'd ever heard and a hot warmth shot to my core. He tangled his hands roughly in my hair spurring me to move faster up and down the length of him.

"Angel, stop," he hissed. It made a popping sound as he pulled himself from my mouth. I could still taste him on my tongue and lips as he dragged me up his body, shredding my camisole and sexy black pants in his frenzy.

"I need to come inside you," he growled and moved to my breasts. His teeth, his lips and his tongue on my nipples were making me see Jesus. He was relentless, scraping my breasts with his fangs and driving me to a whimpering mess.

I cried out as he pierced my left breast. My back arched, my body jerked, and I screamed as I raked my nails down his back. A fiery orgasm shot violently through me as I kept screaming. As he drank from me, mini orgasms wracked my body. I shook like I was naked in a snowstorm, but the opposite was true. My skin and my insides blazed with a heat I'd never felt. This man could kill me with sex without even fucking me.

He moved down my body, leaving my swollen and sensitive breasts. His tongue made tight circles along my stomach and he moved lower. I was unable to move or speak. I felt limp and weak and fragile after the mind-blowing orgasm I'd just had, but he was nowhere near done. He laughed at my moans of protest and went after what he wanted.

Which was to own me completely.

His tongue manipulated me with expertise and deadly precision. My hips rocked. I lifted my body closer to his mouth, begging for more. I gasped and moaned as he licked and nipped. Tears streamed from my eyes as he took my sex into his mouth and bit down.

The roaring in my ears was deafening. I jerked and convulsed as he held my body open to his hunger. I couldn't take much more.

He rode out my orgasm with his head buried between my legs and his fingers teasing me mercilessly, taking every bit of me into his mouth. Claiming me like no one ever had or ever would.

"I love you, Angel," he said, studying my face.

"I love you too," I whispered, still shaking with aftershocks.

"I need to hear you scream again, Angel," he said with an evil, sexy smile. "I'm going to fuck you now until we accomplish that."

Oh. My. God. My limp rag of a body woke up immediately. The way he spoke to me was obscene and I loved it. He placed my hands on the evidence of his desire and positioned himself to reach his goal. He slowly entered me, making me feel complete. I closed my eyes and let myself feel.

"Watch me when I fuck you," Ethan demanded.

So I did. Riding a roller coaster of emotions, I watched his face while he entered my body. I didn't think anything could be more intimate than our bodies joining. I couldn't have been more incorrect. I felt open, vulnerable and near tears. His eyes blazed with need as he impaled my body with his. It was perfect.

With a forceful thrust he buried himself completely inside of me. My body tightened around his and I gasped. The sheer girth of him stretched me to my limits. He rocked into me slow and steady, but my writhing beneath him invited a much rougher pace. He accepted my invitation and pounded into me with a force and speed that would have killed a mortal woman. I wasn't mortal and I met every thrust with joyful abandon.

He growled his approval and I felt my world start to unravel. The spiral of my orgasm swallowed me like a volcano. I gripped him with my body and bit into his neck at the same time he pierced mine. As our essences mixed, shockwaves raced through my body and shudders rocked his.

I could feel my Magic and his power intertwining to become something entirely and uniquely its own. At the most basic level, intimacy with Ethan was changing who I was. This man made me better, stronger, sexier, happier. Our joining wasn't just sex—it was life changing and something I could no longer live without. He was necessary. He was right. I was his.

I rode the crest of multiple orgasms as we continued make love to each other with inhuman speed.

"Mine," he ground out.

"Yes, yours," I gasped. I gripped his shoulders as I felt him grow larger inside of me.

"Again," he growled.

"I'm yours."

My world detonated around me in breathtaking color. His body tensed and he roared as he came.

He was right. I was his, and he was mine.

Forever.

Chapter 37

"You've ruined me," I giggled, lightly running my fingertips along his collarbone.

"Back at ya, Angel," Ethan chuckled, pulling my exhausted, happy, naked body closer to his. He smoothed my hair from my face and looked deeply into my eyes. "I need you to understand something." He was very serious.

"Yes," I said slowly, gearing up to get pissed off.

"There's a bounty on your head," he said in a flat disgusted voice.

Oookay, not even close to what I expected him to say. I was expecting some kind of 'I'm the man and you're the woman. You have to stay put when I say so' garbage, not 'Somebody put up some money so a whole bunch of people will want to kill you.'

I tried to sit up, but he pulled me closer and held me still.

"The Rogues have put a bounty on you. They want retribution for you killing a large number of them in the caves. They want you alive, but as long as they physically have your head, they could bring you back as a full Demon."

"How much?"

"Ten million."

I was stunned. At least I wasn't cheap. "That is the most fucked up thing I have ever heard. You can make a Demon from someone's head?" My queasiness was back full throttle.

"Not just anyone's head," Ethan said, gently rubbing my back, "the head of someone who has Demon blood."

"That's just fantastic," I muttered, pressing on the bridge of my nose. The migraine that had been toying with me for two weeks was about to make good on its threat.

Ethan put his big hand under my chin and raised my face so our eyes met. God, he was pretty. "That is why I was so upset you left without telling anyone. I've almost lost you entirely too many times this week." He ran his hands through his hair and pressed his lips to my forehead. "I don't want you leaving the compound until we get to the bottom of who placed the bounty."

"Oh my God." I sat up. "My mother's memorial is tomorrow night. I have to be there." My hands were now in my hair. "What if I take Guards and...wear my shield and...blow any Rogues I see into pieces..." My brain was racing. "My big blonde klepto Vampyre sister will be there and I want you to meet her. I have no idea how to get hold of her and you have to thank her for turning me into a Vampyre. I promise I'll just kill anybody who causes problems."

"Angel," Ethan laughed and shook his head, "that would make you very conspicuous in front of the mortals." He closed his eyes for a moment. "This would require an extraordinary amount of trancing on our part if anything were to go wrong. Not to mention you could end up headless." He shook his head. "Can we postpone it?" he asked.

"Again?" I shrieked. "Nothing will go wrong. Please, I need to get this done. I want it over. I need to be there. Please."

As Ethan thought, he absentmindedly ran his thumbs over my knuckles. "Is the memorial in a contained building?" he asked. I nodded. "I suppose if we surround the place. I'll send a number of us in as guests and the Elite Guard will stand watch outside." I hugged him hard. "But Astrid, that's it. You have to promise me that apart from the memorial, you will stay on the compound until we have this under control."

"I promise." I curled into him, loving the way his skin felt against mine. "Ethan?"

"Yes?" he was wary.

"About Pam..." I started.

"No," he cut me off and tried to get out of the bed.

I quickly straddled him and pinned his arms over his head. He could get away if he wanted, but he was very happy with this position. Quite honestly, I was too.

"What if I guess?" I asked, pushing my breasts to his lips.

"Have you ever heard of fighting fair?" he laughed, freeing himself from my grip and cupping my bottom with both hands.

"Nope," I grinned. "Can I guess? I love guessing. Will you tell me if I'm right?"

I wiggled my bottom and he squeezed me tighter.

"Try," he challenged.

Alrighty then, how did Ethan know Pam? I knew it wasn't sexual, but she did say she loved him. Was she a former girlfriend? No...that didn't feel right. She threatened to beat his butt raw. That was just weird and rude, even for Pam. She swore at him the way she would with someone she cared a great deal about. She was thrown the first time she saw the pink diamond on my finger.

Holy hell...no way. The King had been wandering around the palace like a zombie looking for someone. He sensed her presence. Nana was the only other Angel I knew and she was connected to the Vampyres in a former life. Did that mean my Angel, Pam was connected to the Vampyres in a former life also? I believe it did.

"She's the Queen," I told him. I saw surprise flash across his face and he started to grin. I grew more confident. I knew it, I was right! "She's Queen Paloma, the woman who raised you. The woman your father has been waiting on for centuries." Damn, my entire life was one big jigsaw puzzle. Everyone was somehow connected to everyone. "Do you think she's come back to stay?"

"I don't know," Ethan sighed. "That's why I'm avoiding my father. I don't think I have the strength to keep this from him, but he knows she was here and it's killing him. He's just not functioning well and everyone is confused and worried."

I laid my head on his chest. "Do you want me to tell him the truth?"

"No, Pam made me promise," he reminded me, clearly frustrated.

"Yes," I agreed, "but she didn't make *me* promise..."

Ethan's body tensed. He rolled me over onto my back and loomed over me. His grin grew wide. "She didn't, did she?"

***

It was good to tell him. He had a right to know and I had a strong feeling Pam approved. I just wish I knew where the hell she and The Kev and Gemma were.

"Thank you," the King whispered, his beautiful eyes glittered with tears. "I knew she was here."

"Your Majesty."

"Father," he corrected me.

"Father," I said shyly. "I don't know if she's staying."

"Oh my child." He was so serene. "She is back. She'll come to me when she is able." He held my hands and glowed with joy. "Her work is not done, but it will be soon."

"How do you know?"

"I feel it here." He touched his heart and smiled. "She is the love of my life and you, my child, my Chosen One, have brought her back to me. You have saved me."

Oh my God, maybe that was it. Maybe my purpose was to reunite the King with his Queen. Was that how I was to save him? It seemed too simple. I was positive I'd have to take out a few Vamps and Demons. This would certainly have been a hell of a lot easier. Having a bounty on my head was not my idea of a good time, but if all I had to do to save the King was go find Pam's sorry ass, things were looking up.

Being alone with the King was lovely. His suite was beautiful. Very colorful, eclectic and comfortable, just like him. Ethan didn't want to be anywhere near this conversation. That way his promise to Pam would remain unbroken.

"Astrid, I will be with you at the memorial tomorrow night. Venus, Paris, Cathy, Sir James, Samuel and I will be your guests and twenty of the Elite Guard, including Ethan will be outside surrounding the building."

"Are you sure you'll be safe?"

"Yes, my child," the King chuckled. "I'm probably safer with you than I am with anyone else."

I was shocked. "Sire...um, I mean...Father, I fear you give me too much credit."

"You really have no idea how powerful you are, do you?" He began to pace the room. "Astrid, you are the Chosen One. Your Magic and skills far outweigh the most gifted Vampyre and the most evil Demon." He stopped and I could swear he peered into my soul. "You may not have control of it yet, but it's all there. I can feel it."

Shit, he was serious. I certainly hoped whoever was in charge knew what they were doing when they saddled me with this Chosen One crap, because I would have chosen someone else. Anyone else.

"Ah, Sir James," the King acknowledged his dear friend, "come in and join us." I looked at my de facto father and grandfather and giggled. They looked like they could be my brothers. My mate was older than my grandpa. I had entered a whole new world of strange.

"Astrid," Sir James smiled and led me to a lovely chocolate brown velvet couch, "there are several things I think you should know." He looked pointedly at the King. The King nodded gravely and took a seat next to me.

Sir James took my hand. "Astrid, the Chosen One has been blessed with many gifts, physically and magically."

He paused. I waited.

"There is one gift we cannot comprehend." He just stared at me.

"Well, if you guys don't understand it, I'm sure I'd have no clue," I laughed uncomfortably.

"How have you been feeling, child?" the King asked. I noticed a book in his hands.

"Okay, I suppose. I've been a bit headachy and nauseous."

The two men exchanged a smile.

"That makes you happy?" I was confused.

"Oh yes, Vampyres never get sick." The King clasped his hands together like a child. "Yes, so very happy."

"This is wonderful," Sir James muttered, paging quickly through the book that the King had been holding.

I held these men in high esteem and had grown to love them in a very short period of time, but I was starting to question their sanity. Their glee over my headaches and nausea was a bit upsetting. The King was practically doing a jig and Sir James was becoming frantic as he paged through his book.

"Got it," Sir James yelled. He slammed the page against his chest, hiding it from my view while the King knelt at my feet.

I knew their excitement should alarm me, but they were behaving like two little boys on Christmas morning. I started laughing. "What is going on?" The King was bouncing and Sir James was biting his nails. I'd never seen Vampyres act so human.

"What we are going to show you mustn't leave this room," Sir James whispered.

"You can't tell Ethan yet, though you will want to," the King said, trying to contain himself. "If you tell him, he will lock you in a room and throw away the key." Sir James nodded in agreement. "You must put what we are about to tell you into your mind and then shield it completely, so even Ethan can't see it. Not yet."

"What are you talking about?"

"Most of the information we have on the Chosen One is through pictures, not text," Sir James explained. "Some of it was drawn before written language existed."

"How long have Vampyres been around?" This was all news to me.

"Since the dawn of time," he said. "There is a picture we want to show you." His eyes were twinkling. "Not many of our kind have seen this. It's been held back so we would be able to very accurately recognize the true Chosen One."

"It may scare you," the King chimed in, still bouncing, "but we do think you'll be happy."

"Well, you guys certainly seem to be," I muttered, beginning to get nervous.

"Many things that seem impossible are not," Sir James said. "Until recently you had no knowledge of Vampyres or Demons or Angels or Fairies. Correct?"

"Correct," I answered.

"You, my child, are the Light in our Darkness. Your Vampyre and Demon heritage is your Darkness and your blood and compatibility with Angels and Fairies is your Light. You are very different from us. You embody impossibility becoming reality." He seemed about to burst. I felt a bizarre wave of dizziness come over me.

"Sir James, Your Majesty," I said.

"Call me Father."

"Call me Grandpa." They spoke simultaneously.

"Oookay, Father and Grandpa." I did like the way that sounded. "No disrespect, but could you please get to your point? You're freaking me out and I'm feeling dizzy and nauseous."

"That's fantastic," the King shouted, jumping to his feet and hugging Sir James.

I gave him the eyeball and he quickly reigned himself in. Good God, you'd think they were about to reveal the Second Coming.

"Wait," I stopped them. They looked at me expectantly. "I don't want to keep anything from Ethan. It's wrong."

"If you want to attend the memorial, then wait until afterward to tell him," Sir James said.

Finally I nodded.

Slowly Sir James turned the book around and showed me a picture. A beautiful picture. A picture that would change my life. Forever. I gasped and my eyes filled with tears. I looked at both of these men who watched me with adoring eyes.

"Is that true?" I whispered.

"Yes, my darling child, it's very true," the King said.

It was too much. The room began to spin and I grabbed the hands of my father and grandfather. They both held me lovingly as my world faded to black.

Chapter 38

"If you're going to strap daggers to your thigh, I would recommend a dress with a full skirt." Venus dropped the pile of clothes she was carrying onto my bed.

"But if I need to fight, pants would make more sense," I countered.

"True...but where would you put your knives?"

I considered my options. "If I wear ankle boots, I could carry two there, and if I wear some kind of jacket, I can strap a smaller sword and a gun to my back."

That could work. "I could also carry some throwing stars in my pocket."

"Just don't hug anyone," Venus laughed.

"Or go through a metal detector," Gemma added, appearing from out of nowhere in a gust of Fairy Glitter.

"Gemma," I shouted, tackling her in a hug. "Where have you been?"

"I've been close by," she grinned and hugged me hard.

Did she just run her hands over my stomach?

I quickly glanced at her to see if she knew, but she was busy hugging Venus.

"Is Pam or The Kev with you?" I asked, grabbing her hand and pulling her down on the bed.

"No, I haven't seen Pam in several days. The Kev and I have been to the Fairy Royal Court. I've been presented," she giggled.

"Like a Deb?" I laughed. "Did you wear a white dress and go to a ball?"

"No, actually I got sent back here to break the fourth Mortal

String, whatever the hell that turns out to be," she sighed.

"No one would tell you?" Venus asked.

"No one knows," she replied. "Although from everyone's attitude, and let me just tell you some of those Fairies have 'tudes, it seems like it will be freakin' awful." Gemma absentmindedly hummed *'Wanna be Startin' Somethin'* as she played with my hair.

"God, I've missed you. So much has happened while you were gone," I said, wondering how much she might know.

I watched her closely. She didn't appear to be in on my secret.

Damn, I wanted to talk to someone about it, but I gave my word to the King and Sir James.

I had hoped that as a Fairy, Gemma would sense it.

I really thought she knew when she touched my stomach.

"I want to be with you tonight at the memorial." She squeezed my hand. "Venus, do you think anyone would mind if I stayed here at the Cressida House for a few days?"

"Hell no," Venus plopped down on the bed with us. "There are guest suites or you can have a slumber party in my room. Of course it won't be quite as fancy as the Prince's quarters that Little Miss Astrid now occupies," she laughed.

"Speaking of the Prince, where is Ethan?" Gemma asked.

"He left before I got up to scout out the memorial site," I told her, examining the pile of clothes. "I've been thinking..."

"Oh, Lord help us," Venus groaned and Gemma laughed.

I punched her in the arm and continued. "I've been thinking that I'd like to give Paris my Nana's house and give my house to Old Charlie and Niecey from my art class. Paris told me they're getting married and need a bigger place."

"Paris Hilton?" Gemma asked.

"Yep, I think she'd be happy there."

"So you'll live...?" Venus teased.

"Where ever Ethan does." I stuck my tongue out at her and she snorted.

"So you've given in...finally." Venus giggled.

She jumped off the bed with Vampyre speed to avoid my right hook headed her way.

"I think it's beautiful. He loves you completely." Gemma hugged me again and started humming *'Ben'*.

"I love him too. For better or worse, I love him. Completely."

"Oooo, Astrid's got it bad," Venus sang as she pulled different outfits out of bags for me to try on.

"Nope," I grinned, "Astrid's got it good! Now help me pick

out something to wear to the god-awful shindig we have to go to."

***

"You are exquisite." Ethan gave me an irresistible grin, taking in my fitted black Prada pants, the tailored white low-cut blouse made from a beautiful soft Egyptian cotton and the stunning jade green Armani raw silk jacket. I was determined to expand the Vampyres' Prada wearing obsession. He took both of my hands in his. "I want to be very clear with you Astrid, I'm not happy about you leaving the compound. You will be careful."

Why did I find his primitive he-man stuff so sexy? What was wrong with me?

"If there is even a hint of trouble, you will transport back to the Cressida House. We'll have the place surrounded, but we don't know how much Magic the Rogues are capable of."

"It will be fine," I assured him, touching his chest. I was unable to keep my hands off of him. I wanted to remind him I had crazy mad powers being the Chosen One and all, but was afraid he wouldn't let me go. God, if he knew my secret. The King was right. He would lock me in a room. Of course, locking me in a room wouldn't hinder my going anywhere. "Anyway, I want you to meet my big, sticky-fingered, evil sister-sire tonight at some point."

"Fine," he said. "See if she will join you back here afterward."

"I want to meet her, too." Gemma hopped up off of our bed and placed her hands over Ethan's and mine.

She closed her eyes and muttered words in a language that sounded Swedish. A buzz of electricity shot into my hands and arms. Ethan jerked back and laughed. It didn't hurt, it tickled.

"Ooo," I squealed dancing around. "What was that?"

Gemma grinned, "I sped up something that will happen soon anyway."

"What?' Ethan and I asked simultaneously.

"Talk to him with your mind," she told me.

"My mind?"

"Yes, you know, that tiny thing that's housed inside your head," Gemma said.

"Dude, that was harsh," I moaned.

"Dude, just do it," she laughed.

Hi Ethan, you have a lovely ass, I thought at him.

Ethan's eyebrows shot up and he chuckled. Oh my God, it worked.

Thank you, my love. I happen to find your ass riveting, especially in those pants.

Really? I love the way yours dents in on the sides. It makes my knees weak and my mouth water.

That's good to know. His eyes turned emerald green and he gave me that lopsided sexy smirk. *Unfortunately you're waking up parts of my body that will demand satisfaction if you don't stop.*

Why's that unfortunate? Do we have time? I grinned at him, aching for his touch and then some.

You're killing me, he moaned.

"Okay, friends," Gemma cut into our mental foreplay. "I'm fairly sure I know what you're doing." She rolled her eyes. "But the reason I sped this up is so you can communicate if Astrid is in trouble. Not to have mind sex."

"Whoops," I said.

Ethan grabbed me and kissed me until my toes curled. God, I loved him.

"You won't see me, but I'll be there," he whispered. "And later tonight I'd like to thoroughly evaluate your ass...and I'm feeling the need to have you handle mine."

"Just your ass?' I giggled.

"Definitely not just my ass," he shot back. "Or yours."

"Your Majesty," Venus bowed her head, entering our room with an arsenal of weapons in her arms. "Astrid," she smirked, clearly having heard our banter.

"Sorry," I muttered.

"Your Highness, the rest of the Elite Guard is waiting for you in the foyer. The King, Sir James, Cathy, Paris and Samuel are on their way up here to get armed and then we'll go," Venus relayed as she loaded a semi-automatic.

"Would you ladies give us a moment?" Ethan asked my friends.

"Certainly," Gemma said, then took Venus by the hand and left.

"Ethan, I don't think we have time to...you know."

"I do know," he smiled suggestively, "but that's not why I asked them to leave."

"Oh." I tried unsuccessfully to hide my inner slut's disappointment.

"Come here." He put his arms out and I fell willingly into them. His lips covered mine. His kiss was surprisingly gentle but full of promise. "Astrid, I love you. I never thought I would find my mate, but the Heavens and Angels decided to smile on me. Nothing can happen to you. I need you to be alert and wary of everyone. Despite your mother's indifference to you, I understand your need to do this. Your heart is huge and it's one of the things I love most about you. But there can be no secrets...not anymore, not ever." He pressed his lips to my neck and a shiver of longing and desire coursed through me.

Damn. I was hiding a whopper of a secret from him.

"What are you thinking?" Ethan tilted his head and searched my face.

"About how much I love you," I sighed, tracing his lips with my fingertips. "I want to tell you all my secrets tonight when this is all over."

"Good secrets?"

"Good secrets," I giggled. It felt wrong and lonely not to share this miracle with him.

"Until tonight then." He held me close to his body, kissed me thoroughly and left.

I dropped down on the leather couch, amazed at how much my life had changed in just a little over a month. I was crazy in love with a Prince and my friends were Vampyres, Fairy Queens and Angels. I had custody of four adorably violent little Demons and I was going to do the impossible.

I, a Vampyre, was going to have a baby with the love of my life.

Every silver lining must have a small tear and mine was no exception. My mother had died violently while I watched. My father was a disgusting Demon King. And I was dead, but the good far outweighed the bad. I gently laid my hands on my stomach and wondered if the little miracle in there could possibly love me as much as I already loved him or her.

Chapter 39

It was ninety-eight degrees.

About one hundred and fifty sweaty townsfolk stood outside the Town Center Hall in their redneck Sunday best to pay their respects to a woman they didn't really know or like. Brad and Angelina must have advertised, because I knew these people were not friends with my mother.

She didn't have friends. She barely had acquaintances.

I supposed they were here out of respect for Nana—or maybe me. I knew some were here just to be nosy, but I was truly moved by the turnout.

Martha and Jane were dressed up. They'd traded their sweatpants for tight polyester leggings paired with house slippers and some kind of shiny stretchy tops. It was hard to look away, kind of like a train wreck. The house slippers were hurtin' me bad.

Niecey and Charlie and several others from my senior center art class held gaily-wrapped boxes. I would bet on my non-life they contained phallic gifts for me. I grinned and continued to glance around.

I smiled and waved at Hattie, who was able to attend because we weren't at the funeral home. Then my gut dropped. The frighteningly-clad old biddies were marching toward me. I tried to run, but they were damn fast for old ladies.

"Sorry about your mother," Martha snapped.

"She was a whore, bless her heart," Jane added.

"Yes...well, aren't we all." I patted her on the head like a dog. This confused her and amused me.

"We like that Paris Hilton." Martha got up in my face.

I backed up a few steps to get away from her hot rancid breath.

"Paris likes you too." Damn, sometimes a highly developed sense of smell was not a gift.

"She doesn't own any hotels," Jane informed me, touching my arm and coming dangerously close to my breast.

Why did they feel the need to get so close to me? Were they hitting on me? Please God, no. Their invasion of my personal space was unsettling and alarming. Why were they being so nice, relatively speaking? "Well..." I backed further away. "We all have our crosses to bear."

"Yes, like all homophobics actually wanting to suck dick," Martha said, grimacing.

"Exactly," I said, "just like that." I grinned and waited to see what was going to come out of Jane's mouth.

"All Republicans are hookers," Jane choked out and turned an awesome shade of purple.

"Wow," I laughed and quickly made my getaway as they slapped each other silly. Sweet Baby Jesus, I needed to get Paris to teach me how she'd done that.

My Vampyre entourage was blending into the crowd. How was that possible? They must be cloaked. They were far too pretty not to be noticed. Ethan was right, I didn't see him or any of the Elite Guard, but I could detect his scent and it made me smile.

I spotted Gemma trapped by Brad Pitt and Angelina Jinkers-Pitt. Time to save my girl. I knew she would do the same for me.

"Astrid, please accept our condolences. You are looking lovely on this fine evening," Brad droned.

"Get a load of that shit," Angelina hooted, slapping Brad on the back. "He's turned into a pussy! If I tell him to lick my shoe, he will! Watch!"

I watched. He licked.

Oh my God, what had I done? I felt sorry for him. Angelina was horrid and mean. Brad had never been mean. Stupid and chauvinistic and foul, but not mean. I looked at Gemma. She was as shocked and dismayed as I was. I had two choices...Green Eye Angelina and turn her into a lady or Green Eye Brad and return him to his former disgusting self.

"Brad, could I talk to you privately for a moment?" I took his arm and led him around to the side of the building.

"Hey," Angelina yelled, "tell him to dance like a monkey. It's hilarious."

An expressionless Brad on autopilot began to spastically

undulate and make monkey sounds. I was so stunned, I stopped and watched. It was revolting.

My eyes flashed green and I slammed poor Brad Pitt up against the wall of the building, effectively ending the monkey dance. "Look at me," I hissed. "You no longer have to obey your wife. You have not been yourself for about three weeks. That's over. You are now the same disgusting, good ol' boy pervert you've always been, bless your heart. Do you understand me?"

"Yes." He was dazed.

"Good," I snapped. "Now why in the hell is everyone waiting outside the building, Brad?"

He stared at me, confused and lost. Oh God no, was it non-reversible? My stomach roiled with baby nausea and guilt. Had I sentenced him to a lifetime of servitude, including shoe-licking and monkey dancing?

"Well, now darlin'," he started slowly, but his leer warmed up. "There's some hot-as-shit big blonde in there that I wouldn't mind gettin' down on, if you know what I mean," he snorted and grabbed his crotch. "She's a-sayin' no one's allowed in 'til you get your sweet, tight ass cheeks here."

Alrighty then. "Did she actually say 'sweet, tight ass cheeks'?" I asked.

He thought for a moment. "Naw, that was just me complimenting your fiiine as wiiine butt." He went to grab his package again and I stopped him with a glare that brought him close to peeing himself.

"Since my cheeks are here, we may as well let everyone in and get this over with." I sighed, disgusted with him, but somehow more disgusted with myself for having tried to change him.

"We tore up that big photograph and built that there monument you wanted, sweet potato," he proudly informed me.

"What monument?"

Brad slapped his jiggly thigh and burped, "I just love how you pretend to forget stuff, Sugarbuns. You are one hundred percent on the right track to gettin' into my pants. A man sure loves him a dumb woman with nice tits. So you just keep that shit up and you'll get a piece of me in no time."

"Pardon me while I vomit, Brad." God, he was a wart. "But what the fuck are you talking about?"

He cocked his greasy, bald, combed-over head, grabbed his package and grinned, "Why dontcha just come on in and see, schnookie-bottom?"

"I'm not referring to your pencil dick, Brad. I'm referring to the monument."

He stood there and looked confused. Whether it was about his dick or the monument, I didn't know, but I didn't have time for this shit. I left him there to go in and get to the bottom of this.

Good God, what had Brad Pitt built? And who told him to build it? It had to have been Julie. Where in the hell was she, anyway? I quickly went in. On the far end of the meeting hall was a very large something covered in white sheets. It stood about ten feet high and about fifteen feet wide.

I tried to make my way towards the tower of sheets, but the room was jam packed with people. How did they get in here so fast? I picked up on snippets of conversations as I pushed my way through the crowd. Chats about my mother, my Nana, how much better female blood was than male blood, Brad Pitt's monkey dance...

I whipped around. *Who in the hell was debating the benefits of male versus female blood?*

I scanned the people in my vicinity. All mortals. Had I misunderstood?

"Julie," I called out to my sister, spotting her on the other side of the room. That sister thing was going to take some getting used to. She was surrounded by a group of well-dressed people wearing hats. They looked like they were going to the Kentucky Derby. How odd, they definitely weren't locals. She was talking to them with great animation.

"Hey Julie," I tried again. She glanced my way and smile-grimaced. Lovely.

Who were those people? I could only see their backs from this angle. There were about thirty of them and they were all riveted by my big, blonde bitchy sister. Maybe she was more fun than I'd given her credit for. Maybe I shouldn't be so mean. Maybe she was tight on funds due to the extravagant shindig she was throwing for our mother and that was why she clipped my fingernail polish and God knows what else. Maybe she was desperate.

A waiter passed with a tray of hors d'oeuvres in one hand and flutes filled with champagne on a tray in the other. *What the fu...?* We catered the memorial? No wonder everybody and their brother showed up. Free booze in a dry county!

"Are you okay?" a small voice asked.

I turned expecting to find Paris standing there, but it was a man. A small, slightly built, delicious little man who was definitely not human stood in front of me.

"I'm...um...fine, and you?" I was so taken with this creature.

He smiled at me and I felt a wash of tingly Magic rain over me. "I'm fine too," he giggled and took my hand, putting gentle pressure on it. A warm and floaty feeling danced through my body making me sigh with pleasure.

"Who are you?" I asked, refusing to let him go.

"I'm a friend of Lucinda, your Nana. I have a message for you."

God, he was such a lovely little thing. I wanted to squeeze him. I knew my jaw had clenched and my lips had pooched out. It was the face I got when I saw a crazy cute baby or puppy. I was itching to pick this little man up and take him home with me and feed him and play with him and dress him up and...

"I'm sorry, but what are you?" I didn't want to be rude, but I was this close to grabbing him, cuddling him to my bosom and showering him with kisses.

He tilted his head which made him even more adorable. "I'm a Sprite and I only have about thirty seconds left in this dimension."

"Oookay," I pinched my leg to make sure I was awake.

"Remember," the edible little Sprite said. "Beyonce is a genius."

"Beyonce is a genius?" What the hell was he talking about? "Do you mean Beyonce the singer or my Beyonce—the Demon?" What kind of cryptic bullshit message was that?

He pursed his precious little lips and shrugged his delightfully tiny shoulders and disappeared in a shimmering mist. I looked around to see if anyone noticed. Nope, they were too busy with the free booze and pigs-in-a-blanket.

"What did that little bastard want?" Samuel whispered in my ear, startling me. "Those damn Sprites can be rude and disgusting. Did he grab your ass?"

"No." I tried unsuccessfully to suppress my laughter at the thought. "He was a total gentleman and gave me a message from my Nana, but it was bizarre and I don't get it."

"What did he say?"

"He said, 'Beyonce is a genius'." I shook my head.

"To the left, to the left, 'Single Ladies', 'Crazy in Love' with Jay Z, Beyonce?" Samuel asked without a hint of irony.

His knowledge of popular music delighted me. Who knew Samuel was a Beyonce fan? "No," I replied, "I think he meant my little Demon baby, but it's still useless. Samuel, I had the worst urge to squeeze that little man. What the hell was that?"

"It's the Sprite charm. Those little shits look all cuddly and sweet, but they bite. Never, ever put your fingers near their mouth," he warned.

"You're joking."

"Nope."

"He seemed to like me."

"Goddamn." Samuel shook his head in amazement. "Sprites hate Vampyres. They're not fond of other groups who bite. You are most definitely the Chosen One. I don't think there's a species yet that hasn't been attracted to you." He began to blend back into the crowd, but not before he saluted me with his middle finger. "Keep your eye on the King," he said wiggling his finger. I didn't even try to hide my laughter as I gave him the finger back.

I had kept my eye on the King since we arrived. I knew where he stood at every moment. I had not let him out of my line of vision once. Even when I reversed Brad Pitt, I could still see the King.

"Don't forget, I'm quite the killing machine myself." The man in question grinned at me and discreetly placed his hand on my stomach.

"I know." I grinned back, covering his hand with my own. "Can the humans see you guys?"

"Yes, but we've dulled our appearances. We've also cloaked our scent so the Rogues would not recognize that there are other Vampyres here."

"Could the Rogues be cloaking themselves too?" I asked, unnerved by the thought.

"No," The King assured me, "they would need guidance from a Vampyre at least five hundred years old or older. It's possible, but highly unlikely."

I felt my tension subside. That was a relief. "Well, so far, so good," I smiled.

He squeezed my hand. "I'll be near the front entrance with Cathy. The only other way in or out is behind that...What is that?" the King asked, indicating the sheet covered lump on the other side of the room.

"I'm not sure. I think my sister Julie had a monument built."

"Dear God," the King muttered and I laughed.

"My sentiments exactly. Look, we'll stay for another hour or so and then we can leave."

"Whatever makes you happy, child." He touched my face and glided towards the front door.

I shook a bunch of hands and hugged a lot of people as I tried to get closer to Julie and the sheet covered monstrosity that everyone kept inquiring about. I saw Paris and Venus watch the crowd on my left. Sir James and Gemma watched on my right. Samuel had the back door covered and the King and Cathy were at the front entrance.

Ethan, can you hear me?

Are you all right? He sounded tense. I felt bad for worrying him, but I needed to be here. I needed to pay tribute to a woman I loved despite the fact she didn't return it.

I'm fine and so is the King. Anything unusual outside?

No. He sounded relieved.

I met a Sprite, I told him.

Did he grab your ass?

No. Samuel asked me the same thing, I laughed.

Those guys are pricks, very sneaky. They use that cute thing to take advantage of women and get into their pants.

Ewww, I groaned, *that's foul.*

Yes, he agreed. *Now focus and pay attention in there. I love you.*

I love you too. I smiled and scanned the room. My eyes were drawn to Julie who looked shaken and pale, even for a Vampyre. She was staring in the direction of the entrance. I quickly looked at the front door. Only Cathy and the King. Did she know them? She caught my eye, pointed at me and mouthed *Don't fuck up,* and then made her way to the back exit. God, she was definitely more my mother's daughter than I was.

I tried to get over there to see if she was all right, but the crowd was against me. *Ethan, my sister just left the building through the back exit. See if you can stop her and introduce yourself. She looked upset.*

Holy Mother of God, Ethan gasped. *What does your sister look like?*

Tall, blonde, beautiful, Russian-looking...She's wearing a red dress, I told him.

Oh fuck no, he ground out. *She's my...*

What? What was he saying? *She's supposed to be dead, for five hundred years.* He sounded furious.

My stomach dropped and I started to shake. What was he talking about? My sister was supposed to be dead? No, wait...His sister was supposed to be dead. Is Julie his sister? No, of course not. His sister's name was Juliet. Oh shit, was his sister my sister? Did I mate with my brother?

Ethan! I was panicked. I was trying to put this together, but my brain was shutting down to protect me from something big and ugly.

I'm going after her. His voice conveyed his fury.

That was the last thing I heard from him before all hell broke loose.

Chapter 40

The Rogues did have someone over five hundred years old to help cloak their scent. They had Julie, or rather Juliet. They also had hats to disguise the fact that they all resembled me.

It happened in slow motion, like a bad, bloody horror movie. Juliet left the building. The hat-wearing Rogues let out inhuman screams, the doors magically bolted themselves shut and people started dying.

Glass shattered and rained down from above as Heathcliff and the rest of the Elite Guard stormed the building. Unable to get through the doors and unwilling to give up, they pulled a Paris Hilton and came blasting through the windows. We were outnumbered, but not by much.

A dagger ripped into my thigh before I had the wherewithal to activate my shield. It hurt like hell and destroyed yet another piece of my Prada wardrobe. Do not mess with my friends, myself or my Prada. I quickly touched my chest and a burst of Glitter Magic engulfed me. Without a thought, I grabbed the dagger from the offending Rogue, plunged it into her heart and twisted, killing her instantly. One down...a lot to go.

Shit, where was the King? My eyes frantically searched the room. Oh thank God, he was surrounded by five Elite Guards. He was safe.

I watched in abject horror as two Rogues ripped the arms off of the Police Chief and ate him.

Niecey was crying hysterically and crouched down in the middle of the room with Charlie, frozen in fear. I grabbed them and tossed them to Venus, who flew to the windows with my friends and outside to safety. Thus the routine began.

Try to mortally wound a Rogue or toss a mortal out of the window.

The people from my town ran around like bumper cars, not knowing who to trust. They were fighting the good Vampyres who were trying to shield them from death. It was a total clusterfuck.

One would think the Rogues would be gunning for me, with a ten million dollar bounty on my head, but they weren't. I wasn't safe from harm, but they were trying to kill everything, not just me. They were destroying anything they could get their hands on or their teeth into.

At least the humans were starting to understand the windows were the key to staying alive. They began to willingly go to the Elite Guard who were closest to the walls.

Four Rogues were feasting on a pile of still living mortals they'd trapped in a corner. The screams and moans were brutal to hear. Chills shot through me as I spotted Martha and Jane trying to fight their way out of that corner. Martha's face was covered in blood and Jane was dragging her by her hair trying to get her to safety.

Goddamn it, I hated those women, but nobody was going to kill them while I stood there and watched. Rage boiled in my veins. I pressed hard on my Angel Wing tattoo and hurtled myself towards the corner at a speed that rendered me invisible to the human eye.

With my bare hands, I ripped the head off of the Rogue who was trying to choke Jane. He dropped to the ground with a thud. I quickly unsheathed my katana and beheaded two others while the fourth tried to run. I pivoted and shot silver bullets from my fingertips completely shredding the top half of that Rogue Vamp.

"Holy Jesus Christ," Jane shrieked. "What in the hell are you?"

Martha lay practically dead on the floor. Jane approached me fearlessly and examined my fangs and blazing green eyes. I stood silently.

"Well, I'll be damned," she wheezed, "you're a Vampyre." She shook her head and grabbed me for support, "A fake boob-ed, slutty creature of the night. Bless your hea..." She collapsed at my feet.

I realized her entire back had been ripped open and she was bleeding out. Son of a bitch, I had always envisioned killing them, but it was just a fantasy, not something I actually wanted to happen. I looked at the two old bags dying on the floor in front of me and a hot flash of grief gripped me.

"Paris," I yelled. "Get over here."

We stared at the gals for a moment. I could feel my nausea bouncing around. I had a sour feeling in the pit of my stomach. I wasn't sure if it was my baby or the decision I had just made.

"They're dying," Paris whispered

"Change them," I said through gritted teeth.

"What?"

"Change them," I barked. "You care about them, right?"

"Right." Her eyes lit up with joy.

"You'll be in charge of them, not me," I bit out and pressed hard on the bridge of my nose wondering where in the hell my self-preservation instincts had gone.

Paris grinned. "Yes."

I rolled my eyes and an uncontrollable smile split my face. "Fine. Do it." I turned away and threw myself back into the fight before I changed my mind. I had certainly already lost it. I had just sentenced myself to an eternity of being called an irresponsible slut. I should be filled with dread. I wasn't. I felt proud. Therapy...I definitely needed therapy.

Oh God, no...Angelina Jinkers-Pitt lay scattered in pieces all over the floor. Brad ran around picking up her body parts and trying to put them back together. His tear-drenched eyes met mine.

"Help me," he moaned. "If we find it all, they can sew it back on." He held her arm up to her hand to make his point. His voice was rough with shock. "I need some ice so she doesn't turn black. Do you have any ice on you, darlin'? I need ice for my baby..." He began to shake violently, then began to vomit. He tried to pick up the pieces of his wife that he had dropped, but he slipped in her blood and landed on the pile that used to be Angelina.

This shit had to stop. Who the fuck did these Rogues think they were? They were destroying my people. The backward-ass rednecks that I loved. They had to die.

Amidst the raging battle, I gently picked Brad up off of what was left of Angelina and made eye contact with Heathcliff. He was beneath one of the windows, just having completely torn apart three rogues with his bare hands. He nodded. I threw Brad across the room and Heathcliff flew him to safety. I looked at poor Angelina. She was mean, but she didn't deserve this. I swallowed the bile that had risen in my throat and dove back in with a vengeance.

I heard a scream and my body went cold. Gemma. She wasn't equipped to fight these bastards. Why in the hell did I let her come tonight? She could die because of me. My eyes flashed and my fists clenched. Damn it, I could hear her...why couldn't I see her?

"Over there," Venus shouted, and pointed to the far left side of the building.

There she was. Three Rogues had her. One held a dagger to her neck, while the other two pinned her to the wall.

"Come and get her," a male Rogue hissed at me.

Shit, shit, shit. I tried to enter their minds so I could make them explode, but they were closed to me. Why were they closed to me?

I approached slowly, dropping my katana and dagger as I went. How was I going to kill them without hurting Gemma? I held my hands up. "Let her go," I ground out. "If you do, you can leave free and clear."

"You will join us, Astrid," the female spat. Her eyes were wild and unfocused.

"Yes," I said. "I will go with you."

"No," Gemma gasped. "Baby."

She did know. She knew I had my baby inside of me. I felt a tingling in my stomach. It wasn't the nausea I'd been experiencing. It was magical. It was a beautiful little spark of life. I smiled reassuringly at Gemma with a strength and purpose I never knew I possessed. I had a better chance of getting away from the Rogues than she did. She had no chance at all. I loved her so much. There was no way in hell she was going to die today, and neither was I. We had far too much to live for.

Gemma's eyes began to turn an icy silver blue. She was furious. The Rogues were so fixated on me they didn't seem to notice that the beautiful little Fairy they had trapped was morphing into a god-awful looking monster.

She was magnificent. She glowed an iridescent silver and became the size of a large SUV. She was covered in silver and golden scales and her fangs made my fangs look like baby teeth. Her claws were obscene and as sharp as knives. I was astonished. I clapped my hands together in delight for my beautifully grotesque best friend.

She ripped into the Rogues with a viciousness I'd never seen. I'd heard Fairies were incredible warriors, but this was crazy. She cut one Rogue completely in half, starting at the head and ending at the crotch. The other two screamed and tried to run, but she pierced them with her claws. She swung them around violently before she popped them into her mouth and ate them.

Alrighty then...didn't see that one coming.

"Well, I do believe that was the fourth Mortal String,"

Gemma's sweet voice said, coming out of the bloody-fanged mouth of her alter ego. "Can you believe I ate them?" she giggled.

"Um...no," I said, retrieving my katana and dagger. "That was pretty fucking gross," I told her.

"Yep," she agreed, "but they were tasty." She paused. "I don't really know how to change back."

The Rogues had frozen when Gemma shifted and the Elite Guard had captured them, tying them up with barbed silver chains, silver handcuffs and leg shackles. Only ten out of the thirty had survived.

I scanned the room and took inventory of my people. I knew Ethan had taken Luke, Princess Raquel and Princess Lelia to go after Juliet. I had so many questions for that bitch. Most of the Elite guard was accounted for. The King and Sir James were with Heathcliff, Cathy and Venus. I knew Paris had left with the old ladies, so everyone was here and okay.

Samuel.

"Where is Samuel?" I demanded.

Venus looked down. Heathcliff stepped forward and took my hands, "He didn't make it."

"Where is he?" My voice broke and my eyes filled.

Heathcliff led me to Samuel's body. He'd been decapitated. I felt raw and jagged inside. He was my friend and I loved him. I sat down on the floor and took his broken body into my arms and I cried. I tried to push his head back onto his shoulders. It rolled off and nestled close to my thigh. I felt a kinship with Brad Pitt in that moment. I wanted to put some ice on Samuel and sew him back together. I could still hear his voice, giving me shit and encouragement at the same time. He and The Kev had made me the fighter that I had become. He made me feel good about being a Vampyre. He was my friend when everyone else treated me like a pariah. I was going to miss him terribly. How in the hell could the Chosen One not save one of her chosen ones?

I felt something pounding deep within my body. If I'd had a working heart, that's what it would have sounded like as it broke...but I didn't. It was grief—mind-numbing, angry grief. Samuel turned to dust in my arms. Oh my God...my wish. I still had my wish. My mood shifted from despair to pure joy. Magic flowed through me, everyone within ten feet of me getting doused with Fairy Glitter.

"Hear Me, O Fairies," I sang out in a strong voice. I clutched handfuls of Samuel's dust. "Please give my friend Samuel back his life...that is my wish."

I closed my eyes and the building began to shake. My body

was suffused with heat and Samuel's ashes were on fire. Literally. I dropped his dust and scooted away. And then...nothing.

I turned to Gemma. My desperation was palpable. "My wish...can't I use my wish?"

"It's too late," she whispered, her huge gleaming body pressing against mine.

"What do you mean?" I shouted, scattering what remained of Samuel everywhere.

"In order to bring someone back, they must still have a body."

I hated her answer and I tried to hurt her. I slammed my body into hers as my tears blinded me. "Why don't you help me...why? You're the fucking Fairy Queen," I screamed.

"It's not my place to determine fate, Astrid," she said, her own sparkling tears flowing. "I'm not God."

I looked at Samuel's ashes, feeling shame that I hadn't saved him. I slowly turned to Gemma and additional shame washed over me. She tentatively held her arms out to me and I collapsed into her hulking embrace.

"I'm sorry," I whispered to her. "I'm so sorry."

"Me too," she said. "I'm sorry too."

Chapter 41

Sixteen mortals and twenty Rogue Vampyres died. Eight of the Elite Guard had died, including my Samuel.

"How do we explain this?" I asked Heathcliff. The death toll was high and the damage was massive.

"Fire," he said.

"What fire?" I looked around to make sure we weren't on the verge of getting crispy.

"The fire we will start when we're done in here."

"What about the humans that escaped?" I asked. The horrific image of my townsfolk all battered and bloody as we flew them to safety was stuck in my head, but that paled in comparison to Brad Pitt sobbing over Angelina lying dead and mutilated on the ground. I pushed the images away.

To pay my respects to Samuel, I would stay strong. He always told me to cry hard and then get over it. After that, laugh heartily and go out and kill something. Ahhh, the logic of a very old Vampyre...I wasn't sure I could do it, but I'd try. I had already cried. Now it was time to move on, laugh and kick some ass.

"The humans have been tranced. They believe a fire broke out during the memorial and people got trapped," Heathcliff said, briskly assessing the damage in the room.

"What about bones and DNA and things left in the ash that could cause questions and lead to problems far bigger than what we're dealing with here?" I had a hard time comprehending problems bigger than what I was looking at, but I knew they existed.

"Don't worry," Heathcliff assured me. "There will be

nothing left after this fire." He glanced quickly at Gemma. "Are you stuck like that?"

"Not sure." She shrugged her massive shoulders.

"Gem, where is The Kev?" I asked, still awed by her transformation.

"He's forbidden to come to me until I have completed the fourth Mortal String. I'm gonna go out on a limb and say I need to shift back before I'm done. I wish to God I knew how. I'm feeling a little self-conscious like this," she giggled.

It was beyond surreal to hear a huge, scaly monster giggle, but leave it to Gemma to make the stuff of nightmares appealing.

"Okay then." Heathcliff considered the options. "We could probably cover Gemma with those sheets draped over that...what is that?" he asked, referring to the mound on the far side of the room.

"It's a monument." I shook my head. "I'd like to make it clear that I had nothing to do with it. My sister...or rather..." I looked to the King. "Your dau..."

"We'll discuss that later," Heathcliff cut me off. "When we are sure."

He raised an eyebrow and I nodded. It would be cruel to say something to the King, if Julie wasn't Juliet. Although the chances of that were slim to none.

"Hey, I know," Gemma volunteered. "I'm the size of a truck," she laughed. "Just cover me and put me behind one of your vehicles and pretend to tow me back to the Cressida House."

"Good God almighty." Venus threw her head back and let out a huge peal of laughter. "That I've gotta see."

"You had best not be laughing at me," Gemma warned Venus, her silver-blue eyes twinkling. "I eat people."

Venus squealed and darted away from Gemma's massive body. "I'll go get your outfit," she laughed as she ran to the other side of the room to retrieve the sheets.

I tentatively let my lips curve into a smile. The moment I did, I felt Samuel's spirit pass through me. It tickled and a small laugh escaped from my sad body. A warmth folded around me for a heartbeat and then floated away. I felt sure that Samuel would be hanging out with my Nana in Heaven. I knew I was going to be okay. Samuel would expect me to be okay.

There was an audible gasp as Venus revealed the monument. It was the tomb. The tomb from my dreams. How was that possible?

"My God." The King was awestruck. "It looks like a crypt for a Queen. A Queen from when I was human."

I knew they were discussing the tomb, but I couldn't hear them. All I could make out was static. A compulsion, stronger than any I'd ever known controlled me. I walked slowly toward the tomb, my hands outstretched. I could feel the tingling in my fingertips. It quickly spread down my arms, through my chest and into my legs. I knew my heart lay dormant in my body, but I would swear I felt it pounding in my chest. My stomach twisted and although I didn't breathe I felt like I was suffocating. A gust of wind burst through the Town Hall and blew my hair wildly around my head. The sense of deja vu was chilling.

"Push, Astrid," she gasped. Oh my God, the lady was in the tomb.

I placed both of my hands on the tomb and began to push. The tomb started to crumble under my fingers. The stone turned to cold hard diamonds—beautiful sparkling sharp ice that sliced into my hands. My hands bled, but I didn't stop. I was so close. The blood ran from my hands, down my arms and seeped into the soft white cotton of my shirt. The stunning diamonds were awash in my blood...I knew if I pushed a little more...I could...The pain was becoming intolerable. Every nerve ending in my body was on high alert, screaming for me to stop.

If I could just push harder...I felt silk, soft slippery silk between my fingers. Her dress...I was touching her dress. I was so close to her. I knew I could save her. I needed to pull her out. I looked down and watched my blood turn her beautiful sheer, green silk dress to crimson. She was laughing with joy. She was so proud of me. I had waited my whole life to hear her tell me she loved...

A brilliant flash of light exploded as the tomb continued to crumble. I backed away as the light bounced around the room, momentarily blinding me. Streaks of red lightening zipped down from the ceiling, bathing the rubble in an angry pink glow. Where in the hell was the tomb lady?

"Hello, Astrid," a hollow voice rasped.

"Mother?" I gasped. She was breathtaking, but there was something wild and untamed about her now. Unhinged might be a better term. Her pale green dress, stained with my blood, billowed around her. It was definitely my mother, but she appeared to be transparent.

"In the flesh." She flashed her teeth at me and gave a brittle laugh. "Well, almost."

"Are you a ghost?"

"No, darling, I'm in between worlds...for the moment."

"Can I touch you?" I needed to touch her. I had always needed to touch her and I had prayed my entire life that one of these times she would want to touch me back.

"With those filthy hands? I think not." She gave me a withering stare. "Besides, as you can see, I'm not quite corporeal."

She leaned toward me with a real and gentle smile on her face. She was so pretty. My body tingled to be the recipient of that look. I reached for her. She reached for me and released a blast of red lightening from her hand. It grazed my shoulder, sending shock waves of excruciating pain through my body and bitch-slapped me back to the reality of the abusive relationship I'd always had with my mother. I refused to make a sound. How did that lightening get through my shield?

"Whoops, sweetie." She made a sad face. "Did that hurt?"

I couldn't speak. I wanted to scream in agony, but I refused to cry in front of her. I stood silently and watched her.

"You see, Astrid," she said, her voice clipped and business-like, "I have three hours to find someone. Someone very important to me." She smiled and reached out to me. I flinched away. Her smile disappeared and her eyes turned cold and hard. "I need to borrow your body."

"What? No!" I was shocked. Fear and anger knotted up inside of me. She was not taking my body, whatever that meant. I was not the only one inhabiting my body right now and I sure as hell didn't want her to know that.

"You don't have to be a bitch about it," she hissed.

Then from behind me, a pathetic chorus of voices began calling out.

"Take mine."

"I'll die for you, sweet mother."

"Take me, mommy."

"I am yours, mother."

"I love you."

The Rogues began wailing and moaning and crying. They were calling her Mother.

Holy shit, she was their mother? They were the brothers and sisters Julie told me about?

This was fucking fantastic. Those killing machines that ate people were my siblings? I'd bet a lot of money that we shared the same Demon King daddy. I felt ill.

Her eyes whipped to the corner of the room where the Rogues, her children, were chained. She gasped and quickly masked her astonishment and rage at their presence. She was such a good mother. Her tone was venomous. "You're worthless," she screamed at them. "Look at you chained like a common human."

Their wailing was pitiful. They were begging her to use them, to love them. I thought I had nothing in common with them, but I was wrong. We all wanted that monstrosity's love.

Her voice was low and calm. Truly terrifying. "None of you have accomplished what your sister has." She pointed at me. They spat and bared their fangs. "I had such high hopes for all of you, but you failed me. For five hundred years I've been giving birth to you hideous creatures and I hate all of you." She smiled at them. The wails increased to deafening volumes.

"Shut up," she screamed. She floated toward her children and they cowered in fear. "There, there..." She gave them a hostile glare. "Don't be frightened. All I ever wanted was for one of you to release me between my wretched mortal lives, but you were too stupid and useless to do it."

She shot lightening at two of them, severing their heads off. "God, that felt good!"

Joy bubbled in her laugh and her eyes shone bright.

"The stupidest and most worthless one of all accomplished what none of you could. Bow to her," she shrieked, killing three of my brothers who dared to defy her. "Bow to the bitch. She has released me."

They bowed. I'd pretty much had all of her compliments that I could take. She was batshit crazy and I had to get rid of her. Except I had no idea how.

"Are you a Demon?" I asked her.

She pivoted mid-decapitation and gave me a lovely smile. "No, my sweet," she cooed, "your daddy is a Demon. He's Abbadon, King of the Demons.

I glanced back. The Elite Guard had surrounded the King. They looked dull and colorless to me. They were cloaked. She couldn't see them.

"What about Julie, Mother?" The puzzle that was piecing itself together did not look good. "Is she really my sister? We look nothing alike."

"I know." She eyed me with disdain. "Juliet is beautiful...hard to believe you're sisters."

Why did her hatred still hurt? "We must have different fathers." I tried to goad her into completing the picture.

"Yes," she sighed and looked wistful and lost. "She's quite old." My mother's voice dripped with jealousy. "She's immortal, just like you, Astrid."

"How old is she?" I asked. Please say a hundred or two hundred or even four hundred. Do not say five hundred or so. Do not let her be Ethan's sister. Do not let my mother be the...

"She's five hundred and nineteen, isn't she, Petra?" The

King stepped out from behind the Elite Guard and shed his cloaking. He confronted the horrific creature that had given birth to me.

"Brilliant," Petra screamed in delight. "I don't need your body after all," she told me. "Astrid, Astrid...God, if I'd known you'd be so useful, I would have treated you better. You brought me what I wanted. You're such a good girl!"

Her eyes were wild and she shivered in anticipation.

The puzzle came together in my mind with a sickening click. My mother was Petra, the banished wife of the King. Juliet was her daughter. Juliet was my sister. Juliet was Ethan's sister. Which means I mated with my brother. Wait. Think...They have different mothers and we have different fathers so...I'm so confused, but I'm pretty sure that Ethan and I weren't committing incest. His father was the Vampyre King and mine was the Demon King. His mother died in childbirth and mine was the psychotic bitch flying around the room trying to kill everybody and take over the world. We were safe. Thank you, Jesus. As relieved as I was that I hadn't mated with a relative, I was also terrified that my lovely mother was getting ready to do some bad mamba jamba.

"What do you want, Petra?" I asked, stepping between her and the King.

"Isn't it obvious, dear?" she replied sharply. "I want to live forever. I'm so sick and tired of dying and starting over, time after time," she moaned. She was coming unhinged. I watched in fascination as her eyes turned black with fury. "What I'm really sick of is fucking your Demon father. I hate fucking Demons and producing worthless shit," she screamed.

Her eyes blazed with insanity. She flew on a gust of wind back to the Rogues who, despite her hatred of them, reached lovingly for her. "You are scum," she spat as they sobbed. She laughed maniacally and blasted them with red lightening, killing all of them instantly.

She wants to live forever. She wants the King. She wants...*Oh shit, no.*

I unsheathed my katana and waited. She flew around me. I kept the King behind me the entire time. Heathcliff, Cathy, and Venus sprinted in and we had the King sandwiched between us. Gemma moved forward with Sir James and the rest of the Elite Guard drew their weapons.

"Do you think you can kill me with your little toys?" She was positively gleeful. "I'm a spirit, you imbeciles. Watch," she yelled. She ran her body through Sir James' outstretched sword. Nothing happened. She was becoming more transparent with each passing moment.

"Shit," Cathy muttered.

"Agreed," Heathcliff whispered. "How in the hell do we kill her?"

"Astrid, I think this is where you being the Chosen One comes in," Venus said. My panic escalated.

"Don't forget," the King added, "I know her quite well and I'm not helpless. I'm completely armed."

"With all due respect my Liege, not against a transparent flying psycho witch shooting red lightening out of her hands," I said and I started to laugh. I tried to suppress it, but I couldn't. The utter insanity of what was happening was too much. It was either laugh or freak out.

We were Vampyres trying to kill what basically amounted to a ghost, who happened to be my mother and the former wife of the King. She wanted to drink the King's blood, rip his heart out and eat him. Then she planned to take over the world with my Demon daddy, which besides being disgusting, was so not going to happen today.

I had apparently been created for this exact moment and I had absolutely no idea what in the hell to do. I didn't know how to kill her and therefore I couldn't keep the King safe. I let my spirit leave my body and tried to enter her, but there was nothing to enter. My spirit floated through her as if she wasn't there. If she was non-corporeal, how was she causing such damage?

"I don't have much time, Astrid," she said through clenched teeth. "Move away from my husband, or I'll kill everyone in the room."

"Can't do that, Mom." I decided on a new tactic. "Does my father know you don't like to fuck him? God, I wouldn't want to have sex with something that disgusting either. I don't know how you did it for five hundred years."

She began to hiss and turn more transparent.

"I don't think he likes you much either, because after he beat the hell out of you, he stood there and watched while all of his friends ate you...and he laughed the whole time."

"Shut up," she hissed. Her face hardened with rage and her flying became erratic.

"It must suck to get knocked up century after century by someone who hates you. If memory serves, I believe he called you a bitch. Now that's just not nice."

"I've had enough of this," she shrieked. "Abaddon loves me."

She raised her hands in the air and red lightening rained

down striking everywhere. I threw my body over the King. Heathcliff, Venus, and Cathy piled on top. Petra let out a piercing wail and wave after wave of dark Magic surged through the room. I couldn't see or hear. The evil juju she was causing felt like icy pinpricks all over my skin. I knew I was screaming. I could feel the vibrations in my body. I had just lost the ability to hear it.

Then it stopped. It was over. We all stood up and realized Petra was gone. So was the King.

"Oh dear God, where is he?" Sir James began to frantically search the room for the King.

Cathy and Venus dug through the rubble while Heathcliff looked through the pile of dead Rogues.

"Astrid," Gemma said. "Where did she take him?"

"I don't know." I dropped to the ground and hugged my knees to my chest.

"Where are they?" Gemma asked again.

"I told you I don't know," I ground out, my jaw clenched tight.

"Yes, you do," she said calmly. "Focus."

I closed my eyes tight, fighting against my desire to attack her. Why did she think I knew? They were all wrong. I was not the Chosen One. I was nothing.

I tried to focus. On what? I didn't know. I pushed everything out and let my spirit float freely inside of my own body. I had never done this before. The minute I relaxed, images raced through my mind like a crack addict channel surfing. Ethan's smile, Nana's eyes, Angelina Pitt's scattered remains, Samuel's middle finger, Ross' Velcro hair, Abaddon's claws, undulating Demons, Petra and the King surrounded by the gorgeous rocks at Diamond Caverns.

"The caves," I gasped. "She took him to Diamond Caverns, near the Portal to Hell."

"It will take at least thirty minutes flying at full speed," Heathcliff said, tucking his dagger into his belt and readying himself.

"He'll be dead," Sir James said.

"It will take me thirty seconds and he will not be dead. It's not his day to die," I told them. I flung my arms out scattering Fairy Glitter everywhere and disappeared.

***

Ethan burst through the doors of the Town Hall, followed by Luke, Princess Raquel and Princess Lelia. "We lost Juliet, but it's definitely her." He scanned the room quickly. "Where's

Astrid? Where's my father?"

"Queen Petra took your father to Diamond Caverns and Astrid transported after them," Sir James told him.

"Goddamn it." Ethan turned to leave.

"Ethan!" The serious tone of Sir James' voice stopped him. "She's pregnant."

Ethan blanched and everyone except Gemma gasped. "How? That's not possible," he whispered.

"She's the Chosen One. It's ordained," Sir James smiled.

Ethan's fists clenched as tears of disbelief and joy threatened to fall. This was something he had never even imagined, something no Vampyre had the right to even dream of. This was the secret she was going to share tonight. He gathered himself, turned to his people and roared, "Fly. Now."

As they hit the air, Cathy flicked her fingers at the Town Hall. It exploded and burst into a raging fire equal only to the white hot fury burning through Ethan's body at the thought of harm coming to the two...no, the three people he loved most in the world.

Chapter 42

It was too quiet. Was I wrong about where they had gone? Was I too late?

I pressed my body against the wall of the cave and quickly made my way through the corridor, looking for the Portal to Hell. I knew I was close. I could smell the sulfur and burning flesh. I squatted down and laid my palms on the limestone floor, absorbing as much Magic as my body would take in. I had depleted myself by transporting and I needed no weaknesses right now, real or perceived.

"Are you okay, Mommy?"

What the fu...? My pockets were talking. Four little grinning heads popped out. I slapped my hand over my mouth to keep from screaming.

"Oh my God, you scared me to death," I chastised Ross, Honest Abe, Rachel and Beyonce. "How did you get into my pocket?" I whispered.

"We be here the whole time, Mommy," Honest Abe giggled softly, "and you already dead." Ross high-fived him for the death joke. I rolled my eyes.

"Your Mommy worse than my Mommy." Beyonce shook her head in disgust. "She bad."

"Yep," I agreed. "You guys need to stay in my pocket. It's going to get ugly and I want you safe. Do you understand me?"

I tried to be stern, but I was so happy to see them I almost cried. I was scared. Scared I would screw up, and there was simply no room for error.

"We hear you, Mommy," Rachel said sweetly. The others nodded.

If I'd had time, I'd examine that answer a little deeper. It sounded as if they were acknowledging what I said without agreeing to abide by it. I had their number. I pulled that crap all the time with Nana growing up. I heard moaning and laughing. We all froze. I pushed them back into my pocket and moved toward the voices.

I got down on my stomach and shimmied to the archway of a magnificent room, with crystals cascading like diamond curtains from the ceiling to the floor. The King was bound with silver chains and my mother floated around him. She was agitated and angry.

"I despised you for not changing me." Her lips were thin and her eyes were slits of fury. "Then I found out how noble you were, knowing how it would have killed me." Her laugh was reminiscent of nails on a chalkboard. "I just hated you more, you stupid, stupid man."

"What are you waiting for, Petra?" The King goaded her. Why was he doing that? Did he want to get his heart ripped out?

"I haven't finished my story yet," she snapped furiously at his challenging words. She was beginning to flicker and become more transparent. The angrier she got the more she faded. My King was a smart man.

"I have spent the last five hundred years building an army of Rogues," she shrieked. She stilled suddenly and composed herself. "Our daughter helped me," she smiled at him with intense pleasure. Her moods shifted on a dime, like a schizophrenic.

"How did you convince her?" he asked. I could tell Juliet was a painful subject for him. So could my mother.

"It didn't take much," she giggled. "I gave her all the affection she craved and then I withheld it until she begged," she informed him icily. God, somebody should have tied her tubes hundreds of years ago. She was the sorriest excuse for a mother I'd ever seen.

"So you begat half Demons, Juliet turned them into Vampyres, and you turned them into monsters," he said with disgust.

"Correct," she cooed. She raised her hand and shot a bolt of lightning at his chest. He grunted in pain, but he did not cry out. God, he was tough. I had been ready to lose it after a graze on the shoulder, but he stayed quiet even when the equivalent of a jagged burning spear got shoved into his chest.

I could see blood seeping through his shirt and I watched in horror as she flew to him and lapped at it. She raised her head, her face was covered in his blood and she smiled.

"I did love you," she whispered seductively. "You're so pretty, but you loved that bitch Paloma more than you loved me," she growled and went back to licking and sucking at his chest.

How was she doing that? She was a spirit. It had to be the caves. The level of Magic in this particular room was high. I could feel it wash over me. She was becoming less transparent the more blood she drank. Shit, this was bad. No, wait...it might be good. As long as she didn't drain him completely, the more human she became, the better chance I had of killing her. It was difficult, but I waited.

"Get your skanky, skinny-ass, fucked up, demon-slut hands off of my man," Pam bellowed and the room shook.

"You!" Unintelligible curses spewed from Petra's mouth as she tried to clutch the King to her, but she wasn't solid enough to accomplish it. Her face was a mask of rage. "You're too late, whore," she screamed. "He's dead."

Time for a change of plans.

"Of course he's dead, he's a Vampyre," I yelled as if I was in a vaudeville show and I had the punch line of the joke. I placed myself directly in front of my mother, blocking her view of Pam.

Petra screeched like a harpy and buzzed around the room like the Tasmanian Devil, shooting lightning at the King with every pass. His body jerked and convulsed on the floor. He was bleeding heavily. Both Pam and I tried to make our way to him, but the lightning was too much. Every time we tried we were flung back into the walls.

Petra was insane. Her eyes blazed and she couldn't seem to focus on any one thing. The King was almost dead. I wasn't sure what she had done, but it wasn't good. I needed to get him away from her before she ripped his heart out.

I flicked my fingers at Petra and knocked her across the room. Thank God. She was solid enough that some of my Magic would work.

"Pam, get the King," I yelled to her. She didn't need to be told twice. She transported across the room and covered his body with hers.

"I have been waiting five hundred years to get back in your pants," she threatened him. "Don't you dare die on me now." Pam removed the silver, shook him and forced him to feed from her.

"I'm going to kill you," my mother shrieked and flew at me like a freight train.

I ducked and shot a spray of silver bullets from my

fingertips as she crossed over me, but they went right through her. Magic, yes. Conventional weapons, no.

I focused and yanked my spirit from my body and tried to enter her. Again, nothing. There was not enough of her to enter. How in the hell was I supposed to kill her?

Petra, not being one to give up, came back at me screaming like a banshee and shooting lightning from her hands.

I felt a piercing hot knife of lightning slice into my stomach. Oh God, no. No, no, no. I dropped to the floor and clutched my stomach. My hands were covered in blood. Rage boiled through me. I will kill her over and over again for the rest of my life if she harmed my baby. I tried to get up, but I couldn't, not yet.

The tingling I'd felt earlier was gone. My little spark of life disappeared. My baby had died. I knew it, and the grief that ripped through my body was debilitating. I was consumed with a white hot fury. That woman had tried to destroy me, but I never let her. I was so much stronger than I had ever given myself credit for. I'd be goddamned if she was going to destroy my baby.

"Hear me, O Fairies," I gasped through my pain. "Let my baby live...that is my wish." I was glad I was on the floor as a wave of dizziness consumed me. My body convulsed and curled into a tight ball. My hands still clutched my stomach, so I was very aware that the bleeding had stopped.

A chilly blast of Magic engulfed me and it came back...the little spark of life came back. I could feel it smiling inside of me. My tears of joy made little pools of red on the limestone floor. I closed my eyes and I saw him. A beautiful little boy who looked just like his daddy. He tilted his little head to the side and blew me a wet baby kiss. I opened my eyes and the image disappeared, but his presence inside me remained strong.

I slowly lifted my head to gauge where the bitch would come from next, but she was gone. Where in the hell was she? I scanned the room. She was nowhere to be found.

I crawled across the floor toward Pam and the King. If we could get out before she returned, there was a chance we would all live.

Something wasn't right. Pam wasn't feeding the King. She was feeding from the King. His body was limp in her arms and her face was dripping with his blood.

"What in the hell are you doing?" I dragged myself to my feet.

She grinned at me. Oh thank God, she was doing some weird Angel thing with the King to save him. Immortals had the strangest habits. "Pam, we have to get out of here."

She nodded, and then she tore the King's hand off and ate it.

What the fu...? I staggered back in shock and disgust. I gagged as I watched her chew and swallow his hand.

"Pam." I moved toward her. "Stop."

She looked up. For a moment she was terrified and confused, then it was gone. She stared back at me with an expression of supreme satisfaction in her eyes, but they weren't her eyes. They were Petra's eyes.

Son of a bitch, Petra had gone into Pam's body and was going to fulfill her destiny through Pam. Her smile broadened and she winked at me.

I saw red. Since I'd become a Vampyre I'd been living one cliché' after another. I had been rooted to the ground, felt thick silence, heard a pin drop, but none could compare to seeing red. A heat suffused my body and I trembled with an anger so deep it was boundless.

Pam was immortal...if I killed her she'd come back. Right? I needed to get her off the King before it was too late. I reached into my pocket to retrieve a throwing star. I would behead Pam and then when my mother left Pam's body, I'd kill Petra with every bit of Magic I had left in me. Even if Pam didn't come back, I knew she'd never be able to live with the fact she'd cannibalized and killed the love of her life. I would want the same done for me.

My pockets began to shriek as I went for my throwing stars. I looked down and Beyonce began to recite.

"Between this world and the next,
There's only one way to kill.
A magic secret blown in the ear
Do not cave into yourself
Be strong like a rock and save us."

Oh my God, Beyonce *was* a genius! That little ass-grabbing Sprite was telling the truth. It was in the poem all along. That was why Nana sent me the message. "Cave into yourself" says it's in the caves. "Between this world and the next" is exactly where Petra was.

To kill her I'd have to blow a magic secret into her ear. Secret, something not meant to be known by others. Magic...something wonderful.

I finally knew how to kill my mother, and damn, I was looking forward to it.

I watched in horror as Pam began to ingest the King's arm. Dinnertime was so over. I flew across the room at over two hundred miles an hour and plowed into Pam, throwing her into the wall so hard I was sure I broke every bone in her body. The impact was so severe it knocked Petra right out of her.

Petra's screams were inhuman. "No, I'm not done," she wailed.

"Oh yes, you are," I muttered, trapping her mostly solid body in the corner. She growled and snapped like an animal. I needed to calm her down. "Mother," I hissed, "stop it. I knocked you out of her body so you can enter mine. I want to be the one who saves you, not her."

It took her a few minutes to focus on me and comprehend what I had said. "Yes, yes darling," she grunted, "that's wonderful." She smiled and her eyes rolled back in her head, "Hurry, I'm still hungry."

Oh hell no...that was disgusting. "Mother, I want one thing from you." I moved closer to her.

"What do you want, my sweet?" She was shaking with excitement. Her tongue was foamy and hanging out of her mouth like a rabid dog.

"No, Astrid," Pam moaned. "Don't."

"Shut up," Petra growled at her. "Can we kill her?" she whined like a spoiled child begging for a toy.

"Of course," I told her lovingly. "Right after you grant my wish, I'll kill her. I want to hug you and I want you to hug me back."

She looked taken aback. "Why?"

Even when I was about to get her everything she ever wanted, she still couldn't hide her disdain for me.

"Because you've never hugged me and that's what I want," I said.

She considered for a mere heartbeat. My mother lifted her arms to me, the very same way I had always dreamt her doing it. "Come hug Mommy, sweetheart."

I leaned into her and she hugged me. My chest clenched and tears flooded my eyes. This was what I had wanted my whole life. She held me tight and it felt so good. I lay still in her arms for a moment, memorizing the feeling. I loved her as much as I hated her, but it was way too little...way too late.

"Mother?' I whispered in her ear.

"Yes?" she answered. She trembled with excitement.

"I'm pregnant."

It was definitely a secret and God knew it was Magic. I blew in her ear and she died in my arms.

I stared at her beautiful dead body for what felt like an eternity. Why did I love this horrible woman?

Was it simply because she was my mother and daughters

were supposed to love their mothers?

I realized in that moment that I didn't love her, not in the true sense of the word. I loved the idea of loving her. I didn't hate her either. I felt nothing. She was nothing to me. When you die, the only things you leave behind are memories in the minds of those who loved you. That was how you lived on. My mother would not live on...at least not through me. I put her down on the cold floor and I walked away from her. Forever.

Pam limped over to me, a mess of broken bones and bruises. "Well, Asscrack, you scared the fuck out of me for a second there, but you did good." She reached up and stroked my face lovingly. I knew what unconditional love was. I didn't get it from my own mother, but I was lucky enough to have some amazing people in my life who adored me.

I moved to the King. He opened his eyes and smiled. "You are beautiful, child." He was clearly in pain, but his arm and hand were already growing back. Incredible.

I lifted him and carried him to Pam. They cradled each other lovingly. I collapsed on the ground next to them. All I could think about was how much I loved Ethan and our baby boy...and how much I wanted a long hot bath. I had no idea how he would react to the news of our son, but I had a feeling he'd be over the moon. I couldn't wait to tell him...God, I had so many questions for Sir James.

The clapping started slowly and gained speed until the wind from the motion was blowing my hair around my head. I looked up and there stood my Demon daddy. Could this day get any worse?

"Hello, daughter," he said, his voice still ragged as if shards of glass were caught in his throat. "I see you've killed your mother."

"Yes Sir, I did." I almost laughed. The ridiculousness of my life never failed to amuse me at the most inappropriate times.

"Leave her alone, Demon." The King tried to sit up.

"This has nothing to do with you, old man," the Demon King barked. Old man? Wasn't that the pot calling the kettle black?

"What do you want?" I interrupted. I was sick of cryptic bullshit. I wanted to get right to the point.

"You," he said.

"Not gonna happen," I shot back. It was starting to look like my day could get worse.

"Do you dare defy me?" he roared. The room shook with his fury. His huge teeth clicked and his burnt bloody body trembled with rage.

Right about the time I knew I was a goner, my pocket started dancing.

Oh. My. God.

I quickly looked down because my grin almost split my face.

I turned to the King. "If anything happens to me, tell Ethan everything. Everything." He nodded, but his eyes were troubled.

I said a quick prayer and knelt down before the Demon King.

"I'm so sorry Daddy," I cowered. "I will never defy you again. I'd like to give you a gift."

I heard Pam gasp, but I ignored her.

My father's smug satisfaction was delightful to me. He nodded his head.

I reached into my pocket and presented my father with my baby Demons.

"Snack time," I yelled as I tossed them at the Demon King.

They shrieked with joy and they ate him. Every disgusting, smelly, foul inch of him.

"You will pay for this," he screamed in agony. Terror shot through me.

My mother had done a shitload of damage after being eaten by Demons. I sincerely hoped my daddy couldn't do the same.

Of course, my mother was a reincarnated mortal and had been eaten after she was already dead. My daddy was a live meal.

Wrapping my mind around all this was too much. I'd figure it out later. At best, he was gone for good. At worst, it bought me a little time.

The grunts and shrieks and cracking of bones as my babies ate about did me in, but it was him or me.

I had no plans to visit Hell any time soon. I wanted to go home. I needed to tell Ethan he was going to be a daddy and he was going to have to marry me human-style. I was not going to walk around town knocked up and single.

My little Demons finished their meal in no time flat, let out some rather disgusting belches and jumped back into my pocket. It still amazed me that something three inches high could eat something the size of my daddy. The mechanics of that were mind-boggling.

I had looked away while they dined. The image of my babies chowing down on my daddy was not one I wanted to remember. It was bad enough that I could hear it.

I was so lost in my own little dream world planning my wedding and ignoring the feeding frenzy, I neglected to realize that the room had suddenly filled with Bad Demons.

I should have known nothing good could come from killing both of your parents in one day.

***

The Vampyres entered the Cavern fully armed and ready to fight. Princess Lelia ran to her mother Pam, and held her as she cried. The King was attended to immediately.

"Where is she?" Ethan demanded.

"They took her," Pam whispered. The shock of what had happened and seeing her daughter had almost rendered her speechless.

"Who took her?" Ethan's voice was clipped. He was panicked.

"The Demons," the King said raggedly. "Astrid killed Petra and Abaddon, and then the Demons came through the Portal. They called her their Queen and forced her down to Hell."

Ethan was furious. He went deathly still. Power and anger rolled off of him, filling the room. It rumbled through the floor and shook the walls. No one moved.

"She killed over twenty Demon-Vampyres today alone, including their King. How did common, run of the mill Demons force her to do anything?" he roared.

"They threatened her," Pam choked out.

"With what?" Ethan demanded.

"Son, Astrid is pregnant..."

"I know," Ethan said, perilously close to destroying something.

"They told her they would slip inside her and kill the baby." Pam's voice was flat and sounded dead.

Without pause, he turned to Heathcliff and Raquel. "If I'm not back in three days, come for me. If I'm gone, find her and bring her home."

They nodded.

"What are you doing?" the King gasped.

"What does it look like I'm doing?" His voice was controlled—barely. "I'm going to Hell to get my child and my mate."

"You can't," the King gasped trying to rise. "A Vampyre won't last more than a week in hell."

"Then I suppose I'll have to work fast."

"That's a death wish," the King muttered, taking an amulet from his pocket and tossing it to his son.

"Without her, I have nothing to live for. What is this?" he asked, examining the clear stone.

"It will kill one. Only one. The one meant to rule. Use it wisely."

"Post guards at this entrance and kill any demon that comes through," Ethan said, checking his arsenal.

"But this is neutral territory," Heathcliff said.

"And your point is?" Ethan inquired coldly.

"It shall be done, my Liege." Heathcliff bowed his head.

Ethan nodded curtly, stepped through the Portal and disappeared.

THE END (for now)

Note From the Author

If you enjoyed this book, please consider leaving a positive review or rating on the site where you purchased it. Reader reviews help my books continue to be valued by distributors/resellers and help new readers make decisions about reading them. I value each and every reader who takes the time to do this and invite you all to join me on my website, blog, Facebook, Twitter, or Goodreads.com for more discussions and fun.

You are the reason I write these stories and I sincerely appreciate you!

Many thanks for your support,
~ Robyn Peterman

Read an excerpt from:

Fashionably Dead Down Under

Coming Spring 2014!

Chapter 1

Pain—then ice—then intolerable heat. A second took years, yet time stood still.

The claws of those that trapped me were razor sharp. They tore through my flesh as the ones who owned them grunted and screamed with delight.

I struggled for balance, but realized I was standing on air. Violet and silver dust engulfed me as I choked on the odor of burning flesh and anger.

How was this happening? I was supposed to be planning my wedding to my hotter-than-Satan's-underpants Vampyre Prince, not taking a ride to Hell with smelly and disgusting Demons.

Shitshitdamnitshit.

***

Journey? The soundtrack in Hell was Journey? I would have thought Nine Inch Nails or AC DC, but certainly not Journey...Don't get me wrong, I loved Journey, but *Don't Stop Believing* just didn't seem like an appropriate anthem for the Underworld. Was I even in Hell? Maybe this was Purgatory or some other random plane of existence? Although I would expect Barry Manilow, John Tesh or Kenny G if I was stuck in Purgatory.

"Where in God's name am I?" I muttered as I gingerly pried my dry eyes open.

One thing I was absolutely sure of—I definitely wasn't on Earth. The ride to wherever the hell I was with the stinky Demons had sucked the big one. It was violent, smelly and it hurt like a son of a bitch.

Easing my body to a sitting position was difficult but doable. Now, to figure out where I was...

"You've got to be kidding me," I moaned, both from the pain shooting through my limbs and the simple fact that *Faithfully* was blasting from invisible speakers hidden somewhere in my cell.

Wait. Was this a cell? A trap? A bedroom?

A bedroom? I was in a bedroom?

This couldn't be Hell. It had to be some kind of holding area. The Underworld was supposed to smell like sulfur and look like post-Armageddon. This place looked more like some douchenoggle with big bucks and debatable taste had shopped at all the most expensive home stores on Fifth Avenue...while they were drunk.

My body ached like I'd been beaten and I checked myself for wounds. Surprisingly I was fine. Maybe all that flesh tearing had been an illusion. Being a Vampyre I healed quickly, but the trip to Hell, or where ever I was, had been rather turbulent. Turning my head took effort, but I needed to figure out my location and how to get out.

Interesting. I was on a large bed draped in cheesy and predictably slippery black silk. The walls of what I decided to assume was a massive bedroom were all done in burnished gold leafing. Thick and ornate crown molding framed the walls. The shades of the molding were more muted and depicted horrific scenes of mutilation and decapitations of some kind of animal looking thing. Okay, this was more like the Hell I expected. The artwork added to the ambience— frescos of orgies and graphic depictions of group sex and death graced what had to be twenty-foot high walls. The floor was so highly waxed it literally sparkled—the uninviting cold black marble stretched from one end of the huge room to the other.

Trying to block out Steven Perry singing *Lovin', Touchin', Squeezin'* was almost impossible. I had a bizarre urge to sing along...

Wait a fucking minute...were the walls breathing?

Stop. Pull yourself together—walls didn't breath. I needed to deal with the situation at hand. I would not let Steven Perry or walls with a heartbeat derail me from getting the hell out of Hell.

First things first, I needed to get up. I wasn't chained to the bed. I was able to move as freely as my battered body would allow. I suppose the most unnerving part was that no one was around...or were they? I hadn't seen anyone or anything since my forced arrival. Could Demons cloak themselves like I could?

"Astrid," a disembodied voice hissed from out of nowhere.

"Holy Hell," I screamed and dove under the bed, slamming the side of my head on the metal frame and bending back all the fingers on my left hand. "Who's here?" I shouted, nursing my painfully throbbing fingers and head not to mention the rest of my body.

"Al Pachino."

"Al Pachino lives in Hell? I didn't even know he died." Plus he seemed more like a Purgatory guy to me. "Bullshit," I muttered, cautiously peeking out from under the bed. There was no one in the room but me. Maybe the walls *were* alive. "You are not Al Pachino. You don't even sound like Al Pachino. Who in the hell are you?"

"I'm part of you," the wall whispered.

"I'm a fucking wall?"

The wall laughed heartily. So heartily it pissed me off. "So, did you enjoy your trip, Astrid?"

"Are you kidding me? It sucked," I snapped and scanned the room for a hidden Demon. There had to be someone in here. Walls did not talk.

"What on earth did you expect my dear? You'd just killed their leader who happened to be your Father," the voice informed me. "Not to mention you offed your psychotic bitch of a somewhat human mother not even ten minutes before your father arrived."

"My father was no prize either. He was a gross, stinky, disgusting and evil Demon and wasn't even upset that I snuffed out my mother," I shot back. Fine. I'd lost it. I was talking to a wall…

"Darling girl, if you were able to kill both your parents why didn't you stop the Demons from taking you to Hell?"

"Well, Wall, you seem to know quite a bit already. I'm sure you know exactly why I couldn't stop the Demons."

"Couldn't or didn't?" the wall inquired politely.

I'd had enough of the wall. "What does it matter? I was a bit tired from offing my parents and I had, um…other reasons." Damnit, this was impossible. Was I really talking to a wall? Yes. Yes, I was.

"Ah, yes," the wall said lovingly. "Your unborn child. That child will also be part of me."

"Look, no offense, but you're a freakin' talking wall. I don't really see the connection between you, me and my baby."

"If you're not going to be pleasant, I'll leave," the wall huffed and the heartbeat disappeared. WTF?

Fucking. Awesome. The wall was gone because I pissed it off. Not only had I made myself an orphan earlier and earned a lovely unplanned trip to the Land of Damnation, but I'd made a talking wall in Hell angry with me. What did a girl have to do to catch a freakin' break? I'd done everything that was expected of me and still I got the shaft...I'd fulfilled the crazy Vampyre Prophecy. I'd saved the Vampyre King and proved I was indeed their Chosen One. Although I might have reconsidered the job had I known ending up in Abyss of Darkness was part of the description.

"Are you screwing with me?" I shouted at the wall as *Open Arms* surrounded me on all sides. The incredible urge to sway and sing along was almost debilitating. There had to be something subliminal going on here...Was Journey part of some evil plan? Was it laced with hidden references to Hell and debauchery? Was Steven Perry a succubus? Either someone downunder was obsessed with 80's pop music or I wasn't in Hell at all.

"Oh my god," I gasped as crawled out from under the bed. I very slowly stretched out my cramped legs and arms. "I clearly fucked someone over in a former life to have to deal with this."

"Why would you think that?" the disembodied wall voice hissed.

"Mother fucker," I screeched, grabbing a pillow off the bed and hurling it at the wall. "Do not scare me like that. I've had enough surprises today."

The wall chuckled in reply.

The Demons had unceremoniously dragged my ass through the portal to Hell insisting I was their new queen—*like that was ever going to happen.* If they hadn't arrived in such large numbers, I might not be sitting in Hell right now talking to a wall and trying to make my body work, but I was...and I was furious.

However, as unhappy as I was about my new address, I would hazard a guess that my beautiful mate, Ethan, had gone ballistic. He would have arrived at the caves by now where my deadly family reunion had taken place and would know that I'd been abducted. My gut clenched at the thought of what he would do. His father, the King of the Vampyres, would have clued him in to the somewhat unbelievable story of my pregnancy and Ethan would...Shit, I didn't know what he'd do, but I needed to get out of here quickly before he attempted to come to Hell and rescue me.

I'd lost enough. I would not lose the man who was my world and I flat out refused lose my baby. Unease skittered up my spine like little mice and I shivered involuntarily as Steven Perry began to belt out *Wheel in the Sky*. OMG.

Could the talking wall keep me from leaving? Time to find

out.

On the far left side of the room was a bay window. I wondered how high up I was and if I could jump. What was I thinking? I could fly for fuck's sake. I grimaced and stood. I just needed to find a way out of the garish bedroom and make my way to a portal that would take me back to Earth.

Of course since I had no idea what that portal might look like or where to find one, that might prove to be a clusterfuck in the making. Awesome. I needed to figure out where I was.

Walking hurt so I decided to fly to the window and check out the landscape. After two pathetic attempts that resulted in my ass hitting the floor—hard, I realized my powers weren't the same in Hell as they were on Earth. Not. Fucking. Good.

"Looks like you lost some power, my dear," the wall said.

"Ya think?" I snapped. Why was I even talking to the wall? It was a *wall*. I would ignore it and if it got mad—so be it.

My eyesight, hearing and sense of smell were still bionic, but my ability to cloak myself was gone along with my ability to fly. I needed to get the hell out of the room.

Staying low and away from the walls just in case they had hands too, I slipped out of the bedroom and made my way down a massive hall. Ironically—or maybe not—Steven Perry belted out *Separate Ways.*

Who in the hell knew Journey had so many hits?

Something was off besides the fact that the walls talked. Why was I able to breath and why in the hell did Hell smell so good? Was I even a Vampyre anymore? If descending to I-have-a-shit-ton-of-money-and-no-taste-and-Journey-is-the-best-band-ever Land meant that I had turned into a full Demon someone was going to pay.

Not wanting to show fear, but filled with dread that made my heart beat like the drum section of a percussion happy high school band, I stood in the center of the dimly lit hallway. If the Demons had wanted me dead they would have already killed me. I was creeped out that I'd been talking to a wall and had seen no one. It felt like I'd plopped down in the middle of a game with no rules...

This world was filled with dark magic and Steven Perry...and strangely, I found that combination appealing. Very appealing. It was unlike the foul magic of my Mother or my Father and his minions. This was smarter and a whole hell of a lot more dangerous.

Thankfully my body was becoming my own again. The pain was receding although I was still without my undead powers.

Voices. I heard voices…and they didn't belong to Steven Perry or anyone from Journey as far as I could tell. A man and a girl.

Oh, I wanted to go home. Where were my ruby slippers or at the very least a Fairy Godmother? This was bad…very, very bad.

Moving quietly toward the sound with as much outward calm as I could muster my stomach roiled. Why, why, why did shit like this seem to happen to me on a daily basis? My karma couldn't be that bad…I'd just defeated massive evil. I killed my vicious Father and my bat-shit crazy Mother in the space of twenty minutes. Not something I was proud of or wanted to brag about, but it was me or them and clearly I had more to live for…I was a kick butt half-Vampyre half-Demon who was pregnant. I was a virtual impossibility. I could do this. I'd talk my way out and go home. Or I'd whack a bunch more Demons and go home. Done. No fucking problem.

However, when I reached the source of the voices my courage disappeared. The sheer amount of magic in the room was like nothing I'd ever felt. The darkness wound around me like a perfectly cut cashmere wrap and the magnetic pull was intoxicating. There was no turning back. It felt right to be where I was in this very moment. I was positive this was where I would get some answers. Luckily I slipped into the room unnoticed. In the spirit of self-preservation and utter terror, I quickly hid behind a massive black brocade curtain as Steven Perry appropriately busted into *Who's Crying Now.*

***

"Dixie, this behavior is unacceptable!" the man bellowed.

He was magnificent and frightening. His magic was stronger than any I'd ever witnessed. I sipped farther into the shadows so I wouldn't be seen. Fuckity fuck fuck. Every instinct in my body screamed at me to run away, but that was impossible…my chances of sneaking by them a second time were nil. This was a mistake—possibly a deadly one. But, I'd been drawn here by an unmistakable pull. As much as I wanted to disappear, I wanted to stay even more.

The beautiful man stood at least six feet six inches tall and had long raven black hair—identical to the girl named Dixie he was displeased with. She was stunning, yet her demeanor was meek. Their eyes were golden like mine, although his turned ruby red as his anger mounted. Was the girl related to the man? Who in the hell were they?

Their skin color differed. His was more of a pale mocha and

hers was a peaches and cream. They were both long and lanky and reeked of magic. The girl, Dixie, appeared to be about nineteen or twenty and the man? Who knew...

"I'm sorry," she muttered staring at her fingernails. She picked nervously at the chipped black polish.

"Would you like to explain these grades?" The air crackled with his anger and energy. He threw the paper to the ground at her feet.

Grades? WTF? This was Hell...people got report cards in Hell?

"Um...I studied?" she whispered, ducking her head to avoid a blow.

"No child of mine receives straight A's." His voice was soft and menacing.

I was so fucking confused I almost stepped out from my hiding place, but sanity prevailed and I stayed put.

"I said I was sorry, Dad. I'll try harder to fail next time."

One question answered...

"Where did I go wrong?" he lamented. I watched him pace. His presence filled the room completely, leaving little space for anyone or anything else. His very expensive black leather pants and black silk shirt matched his hair perfectly. It was clear the girl loved him and was upset with his displeasure.

He threw his hands up in disgust, "I've given you everything, and this is how you repay me?"

"Didn't realize there was a price," she muttered quietly.

"Everything has a price," he hissed.

Damn, he had really good hearing.

Dixie shrunk down low and waited. I held my breath wishing I hadn't chosen this particular room to explore.

"You will drop the goody-goody act. You will be rude, promiscuous and scandalous. You will not be compassionate unless I am concerned and I expect you to flunk out of The Demon College just like all of your sisters did. Do you understand me?" he demanded.

"I'm really sorry, Dad," she sounded like a broken record—this was clearly a familiar conversation for them.

"I am Satan," he bellowed and the room vibrated. "I have a reputation to uphold. You are a Demon Princess, you have a Porsche, your own bungalow in the most exclusive zip code in Hell and certainly more money than anyone your age should have access to and yet you throw all this in my face? Why Dixie, why?" He wearily dropped down on the couch next to the girl and she put her arms around him.

"I love you," she whispered.

The ghost of a smile touch his lips. "And I you."

He wrapped his arms around her and looked into her eyes. "Is it true that you donated one million dollars of my money to feed hungry humans on Earth?"

"Yes," she buried her face against his chest. "I did."

He heaved an enormous sigh, "I have to punish you, you know."

"I know."

He put his finger under her chin, forcing her to meet his eyes. "If I don't punish you, all hell will break loose down here. No pun intended," he grinned.

"Daddy, that pun was totally intended," she giggled.

"That it was." He stood up and ran his big hands through his hair and turned and mesmerizing gaze on her. "You are so like your mother."

"And that's a bad thing?" she challenged.

"It's an *interesting* thing," he conceded. His voice was melodic and hypnotizing.

"Dad?"

"Yes, Dixie?"

"What's my punishment?"

He gave her a terribly evil and intoxicating smile. "I'll have to think about it." He turned and walked toward my hiding spot. Shit. Why did I have to be so freakin' tall? Please walk by me. Please. He stopped a foot from where I hid. I held my new-found breath and prayed to everything and anything I could think of...including him.

"Come out, Astrid. I've been expecting you."

Sweet baby Satan, this day couldn't get any worse. Actually it probably could...

CHAPTER TWO

Shitfire, hell and damnation. This was bad. Satan was expecting me? How was that even possible? And how did he know I was hiding behind curtain number two? Although he *was* Satan or Lucifer or Beelzebub or the Prince of Darkness or...

"I prefer Satan. Lucifer is fine on Tuesdays and the Prince of Darkness will do in a pinch," he said smoothly in his dark, rich voice.

Son of a—I quickly slammed my brain doors shut and hoped I still had at least that ability. Test it, my filterless and quick to come up with horrific ideas brain told me. Fine...*Satan is a douchebag who wears ladies underpants and picks his nose*...Nothing. No reaction. Thank you Jesus and Buddah and Moses and Judas and whoever else was kind enough to be helping me out at the moment. Wait. I take back the Judas thing. Don't want to pray to a dude who gets people crucified. Dumb, dumb, dumb. I idly wondered for a moment if Judas lived down here. Focus. Satan was on the other side of the curtain I was hiding behind and he'd requested the pleasure of my company. Fuck.

I was southern and I had manners. If I could teach art to genital-obsessed seniors, I could converse with Satan. Right? Right. If he was expecting me, he was probably aware of my recent patricide and matricide...Would he be impressed or pissed? After all, my Father had been in charge of Hell. Wait. How was my stanky Father in charge down here if Satan existed? This made no sense. Were the Vampyres wrong? Was my Father a big fat hairy liar? Who in the hell did I kill an hour ago? Was he even my Father?

"I'm waiting," Satan informed me in a tone that got my feet moving quickly.

"Hi," I said as I burst from the curtains and shoved my hand out to shake his, acting like it was the most natural thing in the world to be eavesdropping on the King of Debauchery's conversation from behind black brocade. "I'm Astrid and there was clearly some major fuc...mistake. I don't live down here and I'm not dead. Well, actually I am dead, but not dead-dead. I'm undead and my undead, um...husband is going to be pissed. I'm a newlywed of sorts in a Vampyre undead way and I need to go home, your Honor of Darkness. Now." I expelled a loud and long breath as I hadn't inhaled through my insane diatribe.

"Interesting," he purred and watched me. He hadn't taken my hand and I let it drop limply to my side. "So you're the Chosen One."

"Apparently," I snapped, annoyed that he didn't have the decency to shake my hand. "And you're the bad guy."

"Occasionally," Satan laughed and all the air left my lungs. God, he was beautiful...and scary.

"Cigarette?" he offered holding a pack of my favorite brand out to me.

I was soooo tempted. I could breathe for God's sake. Would one measly cigarette hurt me? Um, yes. Yes, it would. In my struggle with temptation, I'd all but forgotten I was pregnant. Would I have taken it if I didn't have my little miracle inside of me? I'd like to think no, but I wasn't too sure. Hell was going to be hell.

"No, I quit," I said looking away from my former vice.

"Such a shame," he replied watching me intently.

It was if he could read me without diving into my mind. Shit. Time for a change of subject..."I thought my Dad was in charge down here."

"You do realize *down* is a misnomer," he informed me. He was in my space and I itched to take a step back, but knew in my gut if I moved away I would lose a few points in whatever fucked up game we were playing.

"I'm not following," I said politely, very aware he avoided my statement.

"My dear beautiful creature," Satan said moving even closer. "It's a misconception is that Hell is below and Heaven is above. What does that even mean? Nothing is up or down, that's just mundane human mythology. Most likely the poor mortal fools made the mistake because Hell is occasionally called the Underworld. So very literal, those humans...Hell and Heaven are simply on different planes, accessible through Portals. Earth was modeled after a combination of the seasons, climates and terrains of Heaven and Hell. We all share the same moon, sun and stars."

"Interesting. So about my father..." I said, ungracefully changing the subject. Again. Although what he said was fascinating and I did want to know more I was in a bit of a time crunch. The faster I could get out of here the better. I was certain Satan already knew if he was going to kill me, so I had very little to lose. I wanted answers not a history lesson.

"Yes," he replied silkily. "Tragic ending."

"Who was he?" God, the Devil was more cryptic than the Vamps. "I thought he was in charge down here."

That stopped the Devil in his tracks. "Did he tell you that?" he demanded in a voice that made my stomach drop to my toes.

"Um, no...not exactly. I guess I just assumed or maybe my mom told me." Under no circumstance would I tell him the Vampyres believed my dead pappy, Abaddon, was the leader of the Underworld.

"How rich," he laughed, going from deadly back to blindingly beautiful in the matter of a moment. "Your father," he spat derisively, "was definitely not in charge here. He was my minion and managed a certain—how shall I put it—area of Hell...but he was weak and stupid—unfit to rule."

I stayed silent. The way he stared at me made my skin heat. He was breathtaking, but I wasn't pulled to him in a sexual way. It was a power thing...I think.

"Daddy, you should tell her more," Dixie said quietly from across the room. I'd forgotten she was still here. Her Father's presence was so large and overwhelming everything around him disappeared.

"She's on a need to know basis," he informed his daughter. "Welcome to Hell, Astrid. Say hello to your cousin, Dixie."

"My cousin?" WTF? If she was my cousin then he was my...

"Uncle," Satan supplied as I quickly re-shut the faulty doors in my mind. *Damnit to hell*. I was one walking defect...nothing worked.

"That's just awesome," I gushed inching my way to the door, "but I have to go. It's been kind of lovely meeting you and I seriously hope we don't have too many get-togethers and..."

"Halt," my Uncle, the Fucking Devil hissed.

I did.

"Don't you think it only fair that you learn about your other part of your heritage?" he half asked-half insisted turning his back on me.

"Um, no that's okay. I've seen enough in the last couple of hours to last a life time…a long one—like mine."

"Unacceptable," he replied so quietly I wasn't sure I heard him, but the if look on Dixie's face was anything to go by, things were about to get hinky. Shit. "You will stay here until I deem it reasonable for you to leave. You will immerse yourself in the Demon culture and you will get to know your family."

"There's more than just the two of you?" I asked hoping there wasn't.

"Oh yes, my lovely niece. Many more."

"There will be people looking for me," I said racking my brain for any excuse to leave.

"That should be fun," Satan grinned and I almost fainted. His charm was addictive.

"The longer I'm here the better the chance that there will be problems for you."

"Trust me my dear, there are already problems…Plus time runs differently here than it does on your chosen plane," he said and turned to leave.

"What the hell does that mean?" I demanded. I had no clue if he knew I was pregnant, but if time was screwed down here what did that mean for my baby?

"It means," my uncle replied slowly while staring me down, "that I determine how much time you miss on Earth. A week here could equate with a minute in your world…or it could equate to a year or ten. That my dear will be up to you."

"To me?"

"Yes, good behavior will be in you favor. Remember that."

With that he disappeared in a blast of black glitter and smoke.

Son of a bitch, this day just kept getting worse…

"Come with me," my cousin Dixie said. "You'll stay at my place during your visit."

I rolled my eyes at the use of the term visit, but didn't correct her. There was something fragile and trusting about Dixie. Honestly, I kind of liked her, but more than that I was hoping I could use her to get the hell out of…well…Hell.

311

CHAPTER THREE

Dixie's bungalow was really freakin' nice. Gorgeous and graceful—very much like her.

Actually all of Hell was lovely. It reminded me of Kentucky in the spring...but on crack. Blooming tress and roses and climbing blossoms everywhere. Literally.

The scented air calmed me with its familiarity and I wondered how in the hell my Father fit in here.

Dixie drove us from the Devil's estate back to her place in her Porsche. That's right a Porsche.

"Um, Dixie, did you know my dad?"

She paused and considered her answer. Her body language was stiff and childlike. "Well, I'd met him, but he lived in another area."

"Another area? Like a different state?"

"Kind of," she hedged. It was clear she had no clue what she could tell me and what she couldn't. This could work to my advantage...use the naive cousin. Find out what I need to know and get the hell out of dodge.

"Look, I won't tell anyone what you tell me. I thought I was supposed to learn about my, um...heritage. How exactly am I supposed to do that if no one answers my questions?"

"Good point," she agreed. "Listen, I have my therapy group coming over for a session. How about we talk afterwards."

"Fine." I caved.

Maybe if I was agreeable I could make her like me and she would slip up and tell me how to find a portal.

"Can I sit in on your session?"

She giggled and shook her beautiful head. "Yep, but stay

over on the side of the room. It gets somewhat violent at times."

"Noted." Hell was weird.

***

There were three in Dixie's group besides her and the therapist, who was sporting a full body cast. WTF? They were as curious about me as I was about them. We all chatted a bit then Dixie simply introduced me as her cousin. Nothing more. Nothing less. That was fine with me. I eyed the strange Demons and wondered if any of them would accept a bribe to get me to a portal.

Carl, Myrtle and Janet...I dubbed them the strong man, the bizarre little one and the bearded lady. Literally. Janet had a beard...

Then there was the very angry therapist, who if she had a name, I was not made aware of it. Again, fine by me. She was creepy and she smelled strange.

I sat back in my corner and watched Hell's version of the Jerry Springer show unfold.

The tension in the room was palpable. I scanned Dixie's living room for exits just in case this wonky little party of weird got out of hand.

Carl, the Strong Man, rubbed his bald head the same way I rubbed my calf when it fell asleep. He rubbed so hard and fast, I was sure the skin was going to come off and his brain would fall out. I waited in anticipation and fear to hear what he had to say. I hadn't heard him speak yet. He did a few bizarre dance moves when I'd asked him a question earlier. I'd bit down hard on the inside of my cheek, so I didn't laugh at him and I backed off. Janet, his bearded girlfriend, interpreted for him, but no more. The therapist, sporting a bad attitude and a thin reedy voice, was very clear. Carl had to speak for himself.

I wondered if this wrinkle would cause a violent episode. I kind of hoped it would. A small zap of something warm shot through my body at my destructive little thought. I dismissed it and continued to watch the scene play out. Janet squeezed Carl's hand and smiled.

"I enjoy uthing my metal detector at family functionth. Preferably not my family. I made forty-nine dollarth and theventy-two thenth in jutht under nine hourth at a family reunion latht Auguhst." Carl smiled. He actually had beautiful teeth and cute dimples, but the lisp...Hoo baby, now I knew why he preferred to communicate through interpretive dance. On Earth he could have had speech therapy, but in Hell I'm sure he got the crap beat out of him.

313

"All right then Carl," the therapist snapped, "have you ever considered just stealing the money from the purses and wallets of the party guests? Or perhaps holding them at gunpoint and demanding their money and jewelry?"

"Um...no," Carl muttered, "I can't thay that hath ever occurred to me." He scratched his bald head in confusion.

As far I could sense, Carl didn't have magic or power. Hmmm.

I watched the therapist jot down notes and make disapproving tsking sounds. She avoided looking at me at all. Acted as if I didn't exist. Interesting. She clearly didn't want me here. Maybe she was the one to bribe...

"Janet," the therapist smiled nastily through her bandages, "you have a waxing and electrolysis appointment after this session."

"But I like my hair," Janet stammered, her stubby little fingers instinctively went to her face to protect her beard and 'stache. Was she going to cry?

"Yes, but you've had over three hundred years to become evil and you have not succeeded. Your *hair*," the smelly, bitchy counselor sneered in disgust, "seems to be your most prized possession, so it will be taken from you." She smiled. She really was a bitch.

"Forever?" Janet whispered. Her little body trembled and

"Forever," the therapist wasped.

"I am so glad I busted on your ass with the coffee table," Myrtle muttered under her breath.

"What was that, Myrtle?" the therapist hissed.

"Nothing." Myrtle smiled and gave me a covert thumbs up. Again I had to chomp down on my cheek to keep from laughing.

I found myself happy that Myrtle had nailed the therapist with a coffee table, of all things. Myrtle was my kind of girl. My guess was that it had been quite an entertaining show. A burst of magic rushed through my body as the violent thought manifested itself in my brain.

Glancing down at my fingers I noticed a black glitter coating them. WTF? Was this Demon voodoo magic? I quickly rubbed it off and tried to focus on the meeting. Satan had sent me with Dixie for a reason. There must be something in all this strangeness I was supposed to learn...

"Soooo Janet," the nasty shrink challenged, "do you have any hobbies you'd like to share?"

Janet took a deep breath, regained control of her shaky little body and got back up in the saddle. "I too enjoy taking other peoples money, but I really enjoy working in television. I spend all of my free time, plus some of the time I'm supposed to be stoking the Hell Fires, following news trucks around and appearing in the background of live news reports!"

"She's been on TV at least forty-two times in the last three months alone," Myrtle gushed, giving Janet a high five.

Did Hell have it's own TV stations?

Janet, gaining confidence from the high five, proudly shouted, "All of the local stations have taken restraining orders out on me!"

"Interesting," the mean ho-bag therapist droned. "Have you ever attacked a reporter or shouted obscenities on live television?"

Janet was crushed. "No. I haven't."

"I thought not," Miss Meanie replied writing in her notebook. "I'd like to point out that Muffy the Contortionist is no longer part of our group. She has graduated. She blew up a Dairy Queen on Earth last night. Apparently she felt she had been over charged."

"Lucifer's Bouncing Balls, I hadn't even noticed her absence! Was anyone hurt?" Janet gasped and pulled on her beard in distress.

"Unfortunately, no," the icky therapist said, "but we hope she makes better choices next time." She took a pause, giving each of the group the Evil Eye through her bandages while still ignoring me as if I didn't exist. "Myrtle, you're next."

Myrtle fidgeted in her chair. I figured she had to be a couple of hundred years old like Janet, but she looked like she was about fifteen. Most Demons, like Vampyres, stopped aging somewhere between twenty and thirty, so it was difficult to determine true age. I wasn't sure why Myrtle looked so young.

"Um…well, I enjoy going to Earth and playing dead in public places. When I'm surrounded by humans I take perverse pleasure in jumping up and scaring the fucking shit out of them as they wail in anguish over my perceived death."

WTF? These Demons were nuts.

"Have you caused any heart attacks or strokes doing this?" Miss Bitchy Shrink grilled Myrtle.

"No, I can't say I have. A couple of them have wet themselves," she offered meekly.

"Anything else?"

"Ummm, sure." I watched Myrtle rack her brain. "I do enjoy kidnapping people's dogs and cats. I groom them and dye their fur so they resemble wild animals. I then return them to their rightful owners in the dead of the night. I derive huge amounts of satisfaction watching our citizens walk their tigers, skunks and panda bears around town."

Everyone was speechless. That had to be one of the weirdest things I'd ever heard.

"Do you ever eat any of the animals you kidnap?" the therapist asked.

"No, I'm a vegetarian," Myrtle informed the group.

"A vegetarian Demon?" the bitch from hell shrieked, her eyes turning blood red.

Myrtle cowered behind the chair she'd formerly been sitting in. Janet started crying and braiding her beard, Carl looked mighty uncomfortable and Dixie looked like she wanted to do some damage. I suppose a veggie-Demon was an anomaly, but this shrink was a hag.

"I've heard of that," Dixie piped up, ignoring the look of hatred from the therapist. She tried not to fidget, but I could tell she was lying from a mile away. I was actually enjoying myself. These people were fucking crazy. "Those Demons get their protein from soybeans." Dixie had a captive audience so clearly she decided to elaborate. "I've heard of Veggie-Demons destroying thousands of acres of soybean fields on Earth just for an appetizer." She had to have yanked that whopper right out of her rear end.

Myrtle glanced over at Dixie gratefully. The lovely therapist looked as if she wanted to nail my cousin's ass to the wall, but she didn't dare. Dixie may have issues, but she was the head honcho's daughter. No one was stupid enough to fuck with that...or were they?

"Sooo, Your Highness," the bandaged skank began, "let's go over your list of problems...or should I say virtues. Shall we?" She laughed wickedly. "You're a straight A student, you remember birthdays, you clean your room, people describe you as kind, you pioneered the first Meals on Wheels in Hell, you donated a million dollars to feed *humans* on Earth, and you're a virgin," she sneered. "What do you have to say for yourself?"

How on Satan's Red Earth did she know Dixie was a virgin? Was Dixie a virgin? Wait. That was none of that bitches business...and why did I even care? I barely knew my cousin, but I was pissed.

I glanced around the little bungalow for something to throw at that woman's already injured head and I felt a dark power and magic run through me. Different from my Vampyre magic. *Stop. This was not good.*

Did Satan send me here so I'd get pissed and turn fully into a Demon? If I pulled on the dark magic and destroyed the therapist would I be permanently stuck in Hell?

I took a deep breath and said nothing. Thankfully I didn't have to. Myrtle stepped in.

"I don't know about you guys," Myrtle grunted, "but I'm feeling the need to bust on Dixie's coffee table and beat the living hell out of our therapist again."

Carl, Janet and Dixie grinned from ear to ear and I couldn't suppress the giggle that escaped my lips. Miss Bitchy Pants stood up and backed her way towards the front door.

"All of you, including *the Vampyre* have to report to the Dark Palace," she haughtily informed us.

"Now?" Janet asked hopefully. I assumed she hoped to avoid the enforced hair removal she was about to endure.

"No!" Meanie snapped, "this evening. After you get de-haired, you repulsive..."

"Enough," Carl shouted advancing on the horrid woman. She turned and ran from the house. Like a coward...foul, disgusting, bandage covered cowardice hag.

We stood quietly and looked at one another, the Princess, the Strong Man, the soon to be hairless Bearded Lady, Myrtle...and me.

Myrtle broke the silence. "So you're a Vampyre?"

"Apparently," I answered hoping she didn't attack. I kind of liked her and really didn't want to kill her.

"Cool," she muttered and the rest of the freak show nodded their approval.

"She's part Demon too," Dixie added, giving me a shy smile.

"Very small part," I explained. "And I need to get home. Soon."

"I'm sure Daddy will send you home. I think he just wants to know you better."

"That's just awesome," I replied in a voice laced with sarcasm.

"He's really not that bad when you get to know him," Dixie said.

"He's worse," Myrtle mouthed to me out of Dixie's line of vision.

Fucking great. This was going to be a good time.

Coming in Spring 2014

Visit www.robynpeterman.com.

317

Connect with Robyn Peterman

WEBSITE

http://www.robynpeterman.com

EMAIL

robyn@robynpeterman.com

TWITTER

https://twitter.com/robynpeterman

FACEBOOK

http://www.facebook.com/pages/Robyn-Peterman

CONTEMPORARY BOOK BLOG

http://robynpeterman.blogspot.com

PINTEREST

http://pinterest.com/robynpeterman/boards/

GOODREADS

http://www.goodreads.com/author/show/6545317.Robyn_Peterman

About the Author

Robyn Peterman writes because the people inside her head won't leave her alone until she gives them life on paper.

Her addictions include laughing really hard with friends, shoes (the expensive kind), Target, Coke Zero Cherry with extra ice in a styrofoam cup, bejeweled reading glasses, her kids, her super-hot hubby and collecting stray animals.

A former professional actress, with Broadway, film and T.V. credits, she now lives in the south with her family and too many animals to count.

Writing gives her peace and makes her whole, plus having a job where you can work in your underpants works really well for her. You can leave Robyn a message via the Contact Page and she'll get back to you as soon as her bizarre life permits! She loves to hear from her fans!